Winner's English

# 英语大赢家

## 最新流行美语全情景话题 320

上册

本书主审 中央人民广播电台　王丽君
本书主编 北京外国语大学　江　涛
本书审订 [美]Alex G. Liu
　　　　　[美]Devon Williams

石油工业出版社

# 《江涛英语》系列丛书编委会

顾　问　[美]彭铁城　[美]Eve Bower

主　编　江　涛

副主编　孟　飞　陈　超　梁　妍　王　宏　李秀丽

# 《英语大赢家》丛书编委会

主　审　中央人民广播电台　王丽君

主　编　江　涛

审　订　[美]Alex G. Liu　[美]Devon Williams

副主编　孟　飞　陈　超　王　宏　瞿斯亮　瞿　莉　郑　妍
　　　　王园林　李秀丽

编　委：（按姓氏笔画排列）

马　辉　马　磊　王　洁　王　晶　王　榆　王世君
王宁宁　东　刚　叶适宜　刘　静　刘凤先　刘尚杰
刘　莹　刘晓雯　孙　洁　朱芳英　许　悦　张　菁
张晓青　李　莉　李　杨　李　婷　李庆煜　李春庆
李晓鹏　杨　颖　杨　雪　杨少芳　杨春霞　汪全芳
陈红玲　单　勇　周　丽　周雅娴　招敏仪　郑小倩
郑雪玲　金　玲　姚　岚　胡　嫚　胡　莲　胡凤霞
赵籽君　赵艳丽　赵顺丹　徐　佳　徐上标　徐向群
桂　风　秦　彤　谈　伟　谈　媛　高端娟　曹　娟
曹　菲　盛　洪　黄　星　黄　胜　黄　晶　龚雪琼
彭　珺　彭　静　彭雪静　斯虎子　董　军　韩　怡
褚振飞　褚小雯　雷伟燕　詹　洁　虞源源　路　潞
廖正芳　廖海辰

[美] Eve Bower　　　　　[英] Charlie Black
[美] Steven Hasinger　　[美] Caroline Catts
[澳] Chris Green　　　　[加] Wesley Brown

# 丛书序

　　我在美国待了23年，最大的感触，就是美国国力的强大。可以说，其国力的强大源于整个国家和民族对于教育的重视和理智，这使得美国无论在科技上，还是经济上，都有着源源不断的智力支持。

　　这23年来，无论是在大学任教，还是从1998年我受聘微软总部研究院，从事自然语言处理，包括中文法检错、机器翻译等工作，我和我的美国同事们相处得非常愉快，他们乐观、积极、幽默。无论是课堂讨论还是brainstorm（头脑风暴），多数美国人的交流方式或是教学方式是启发式的，不矫揉、不造作，也不让人难为情。

　　我非常支持祖国当前的号召——建设学习型的国家。中国是应该学习国外的先进科学技术、先进管理理念，并借鉴西方的教育模式和方法，而所有的这一切，皆始于学习英语。

　　我反对把英语学习妖魔化，大多数中国人把英语当作一门知识来学，而英语恰恰如同Dos或是Windows视窗一样，只是一种工具。学习知识，要不厌其精，挖掘越深才越有所得；而掌握一种工具，只有不厌其烦，才能越来越熟练。用钻研的态度去研究一种工具，便平添了很大的心理压力，效果自然不佳。

　　江涛是我回国后所接触的一批年轻人中有朝气、有理想、有激情，敢于实践自己梦想的一个。他们有着开阔的视野，充沛的精力，极强的学习能力、团队合作能力和执行能力，最为重要的是，在我看来，他们还有很珍贵的一点——责任。

　　很突兀的有一天，江涛寄来稿子，请我作序。我一般不愿替人写序了，但看了书稿后，不禁感叹，有志不在年高。看杂技我们都知道，把一个盘子转起来不难，难的是把所有盘子都转起来，整套书稿虽然是口语教材，题材较为容易，可是在语音、语法、语素、话题、场景、功能的融合上可见编者们的煞费苦心和独具匠心，没有相当的功底和耐性，配方不会这么容易研究出来的。

　　尤为一提的是，这套书语言生动时尚，既非街头俚语，又非陈旧方言，所有的语言都融入到了一个家庭中，幽默地演绎出来。整本稿子，乍一看，像是流行美国的哪部家庭喜剧的脚本。快乐地学习语言，不知不觉地熟练应用。这真是一套不可多得的适合中国人练习英语的口语教材。

2008年祖国举办奥运会，是每一个炎黄子孙的骄傲，得知该书被选为中央人民广播电台的"迎奥运"的空中英语教材时，不仅替江涛高兴，也为全国的英语爱好者学习者们高兴。

乘风破浪会有时，直挂云帆济沧海。是欣然为序。

**彭铁城**

（美籍华人，前微软总部研究院计算语言学家，

现美国高科技教育集团公司总裁。

纽约大学语言博士，美国资深英语教学专家。）

2007年6月

非常感谢大家选择这套《英语大赢家》系列丛书，这是我们对 2008 年祖国奥运的献礼！

丛书以发音为切入点，以口语为核心突破点，辅以语法与各类知识点，并将趣味和生动贯穿始终。本套丛书分为《上册》和《下册》，基本覆盖了各个水平段和年龄段的学员的需求。其中：《上册》主要针对曾经学过英语，但长期不用，需要掌握日常生活及简单沟通的英语，或有英语学习热情的社会人群，以及欲参加各类英语口语等级考试（PETS，GESE）初级段的社会考生或青少年。《下册》主要针对在工作和生活中有与英语国家人士交流需求的白领，欲成为 2008 年奥运志愿者的大学生，欲参加各类英语口语等级考试（PETS，GESE）中级段的社会考生或大中学考生。

以下是众多中外专家凝结在该套丛书中的若干智慧结晶：

**真正的"洋为中用"**

该套丛书是英语专家在分析调研了数万份不同水平段的调查问卷后，结合中国人讲英语的实际需求，考虑了中国人学习英语的实际软肋，吸收了美国专家的建议而编写的，力求"止国人之渴"；经由中外老师联合办公，不间断交流，充分借鉴吸收各类媒体素材，共同编写，力求"引正本之源"；再由美国若干普通家庭现场朗读后，提出修改意见，力求"显大众之本色"；随后由中国老师为主，根据中国学生的认知特点设计编写练习，力求"投学生所好"；最后由中外专家互相审定而成，力求"归学术之路"。

**真正的"实用主义教材"**

该套丛书包括 7 大场景，80 个口语地点，320 个基本话题，基本涵盖人们日常讲英语的所有场景地点和话题。

　　同时该套丛书囊括英语交流中必需的 40 种功能句型，80 个口语常用的语法点，40 个语音突破口。

　　在《上册》中创新性地加入了经典语境背诵，把在正文对话中的经典语法及剧情重编成一段朗朗上口的独白，用于初学者背诵，以加强培养语感和语境。

　　在《下册》中加入了语素和经典篇章。语素部分主要用于向中国学生介绍与正文"看听学"相关的背景知识，用于解决中国学生由于缺乏外国文化或是风俗常识而导致无法进行地道交流的尴尬局面。经典篇章部分主要用于面向外国友人介绍目前中国积极健康、和谐发展的现状和中国的文化习俗，以供中国学生向国外介绍中华文化之需。

### 真正的"高能高分"

　　该套丛书覆盖了全国公共英语等级口语考试（PETS），英国伦敦三一学院英语口语等级考试（GESE）的场景和话题，按照难易程度融入到本套口语教材的课程中，并在插页难度表中标明了每一课对应的口语考试级别，供学习者参考。力求通过本套口语教材的学习，达到对话自如，并轻松拿下各类口语考试的目的。

### 真正的"寓教于乐"

　　"懂得幽默，才识其文化"。该套丛书参考美国流行家庭、社区情景喜剧，融众家之所长，本身也是一套具有国内自有知识产权的家庭喜剧剧本。所有的场景、情节故事都发生在一个和谐的家庭中，既有鬼马精灵的小弟弟 Daniel 和他的跟班 Pig Tom，也有好学勤奋好为人师的姐姐 May 和她那火辣时尚的同班姐妹 Cucci；既有呆头呆脑爱看 *American idol* 的爸爸 Benjamin，更有超级精明无比爱心购物成狂的妈妈 Shirley。在幽默、生动、俏皮的剧情演绎中，潜移默化地纠正我们的发音，流利我们的口语，展现我们的英语风采。学习英语，将一路轻歌快语，过程不再枯燥！

　　"智者千虑，必有一失"，望各界同行、莘莘学子不吝赐教。

2007 年 6 月

# 目录
CONTENTS

## Act 1　日常生活场景 Daily Life

**Scene 1　家 Home** ·········· 2

Topic 1　看电视 Watching TV ······· 2

Topic 2　奥运梦 Olympic Dreams ········ 4

Topic 3　客人来访 Visitors ·········· 6

Topic 4　激励 Encouragement ······ 8


**Scene 2　社区 Community** ········ 10

Topic 1　社区布告栏 Bulletin ········· 10

Topic 2　天气 Weather ··········· 12

Topic 3　宠物 Pets ··········· 14

Topic 4　体育活动 Sports Activities ··· 16


**Scene 3　菜市场 Food Market** ··· 18

Topic 1　逛菜市场 Food Market ······· 18

Topic 2　买卖 Buying and Selling ······ 20

Topic 3　识别颜色 Colors ·········· 22

Topic 4　营养 Nutrition ·········· 24


**Scene 4　厨房 Kitchen** ·········· 26

Topic 1　洗菜 Washing Vegetables ······ 26

Topic 2　烹饪 Cooking ·········· 28

Topic 3　厨具 Cookers ·········· 30

Topic 4　餐具 The Dishes ········· 32


**Scene 5　车站 Station** ·········· 34

Topic 1　交通规则

　　　　Traffic Regulations ········· 34

Topic 2　交通工具 Vehicles ·········· 36

Topic 3　打的 Taxi ············ 38

Topic 4　路牌广告 Advertisements ····· 40


**Scene 6　公交车 Bus** ·········· 42

Topic 1　公交车路线 Bus Route ···· 42

Topic 2　人口 Population ········· 44

Topic 3　IC 卡和售票

　　　　IC Cards and Tickets ······· 46

Topic 4　下错站

　　　　Get off at the Wrong Stop ······ 48


**Scene 7　逛街 Street** ············ 50

Topic 1　公共环境

　　　　Public Environment ········· 50

Topic 2　寻物 Lost and Found ······· 52

Topic 3　问路 Ask for Directions ········· 54

Topic 4　偶遇

　　　　Meeting with Someone ········ 56


**Scene 8　加油站 Gas Station** ······ 58

Topic 1　出行 Departure ········· 58

Topic 2　加油 Gas Station ········ 60

Topic 3　行程 Travel Route ·········· 62

Topic 4　汽车快餐 Fast Food ········· 64

# Act 2　娱乐休闲场景 Entertainment and Fun

## Scene 9　公园 Park ·················· 67

Topic 1　奥运公园 Olympic Park ······ 67

Topic 2　周末安排 Weekend Plans ······ 69

Topic 3　野餐 Picnics ··············· 71

Topic 4　拍照 Taking Pictures ··········· 73

## Scene 10　动物园 Zoo ··········· 75

Topic 1　动物表演
Animal Performance ··· 75

Topic 2　动物和国家
Animals and Countries ········ 77

Topic 3　领养动物 Pet Adoption ··· 79

Topic 4　野生动物园
Wildlife Sanctuary ·········· 81

## Scene 11　电影院 Cinema ··· 83

Topic 1　大牌明星 Superstars ·········· 83

Topic 2　电影分类 Different Movies ··· 85

Topic 3　经典影片 Classic Movies ··· 87

Topic 4　爱情 Love ··············· 89

## Scene 12　名胜古迹
Places of Interests ··· 92

Topic 1　旅游计划 Travel Plans ··· 92

Topic 2　文化遗址 Cultural Relics ··· 94

Topic 3　自然风光 Natural Scenery ··· 96

Topic 4　出游国外 Travelling Abroad ··· 98

## Scene 13　爬山
Mountain Climbing ··· 100

Topic 1　爬山 Mountain Climbing ······ 100

Topic 2　登山用品
Outdoor Supplies ··············· 102

Topic 3　索道 Cable car ············· 104

Topic 4　景致 Scenery ············· 106

## Scene 14　海和海滨
Sea and Seashore ··· 108

Topic 1　四季和天气
Seasons and Weather ········· 108

Topic 2　海滩运动 Beach Sports ······ 110

Topic 3　恋爱故事 Love Stories ··· 112

Topic 4　结婚照 Wedding Photos ··· 114

## Scene 15　游乐园
Amusement Park ······ 116

Topic 1　童话世界 Fairytale World ··· 116

Topic 2　摩天轮 Ferris Wheels ········· 118

Topic 3　注意事项 Notices ··········· 120

Topic 4　广播寻人 Broadcasting ······ 122

# 目录
## CONTENTS

## Act 3　学校场景 School

### Scene 16　小学 Elementary School ·············· 125

Topic 1　外星人 UFO and E. T. ······ 125

Topic 2　学校课程 School Courses ·············· 127

Topic 3　参加培训班 Training Courses ·············· 129

Topic 4　劳动卫生 Cleaning ······ 131

### Scene 17　初中 Junior High School ·············· 133

Topic 1　运动会 Sports Meetings ······ 133

Topic 2　学校设施 School Facilities ·············· 135

Topic 3　喜欢的老师 Favorite Teachers ·············· 137

Topic 4　住校生活 Campus Life ····· 139

### Scene 18　图书馆 Library ········· 141

Topic 1　借书 Borrowing Books ······ 141

Topic 2　问询处 Information ············ 143

Topic 3　好书推荐 Recommended Books ·············· 145

Topic 4　还书 Returning Books ······ 147

## Act 4　餐饮和零售业场景 Catering Industry and Retail Trade

### Scene 19　餐厅 Restaurant ······ 150

Topic 1　点菜 Order ·············· 150

Topic 2　用餐 Dining ·············· 152

Topic 3　健康饮食 Healthy Diet ····· 154

Topic 4　买单 Payment ·············· 156

### Scene 20　旅馆 Hotel ········· 158

Topic 1　预定 Reservation ·············· 158

Topic 2　入住 Check-in ·············· 160

Topic 3　换房 Changing Rooms ·············· 162

Topic 4　退房 Check-out ·············· 164

### Scene 21　停车场 Parking Lot ·············· 166

Topic 1　停错车位 Wrong Parking ······ 166

Topic 2　停车与收费 Parking Fee ······ 168

Topic 3　事故 Accidents ·············· 170

Topic 4　交通问题 Traffic ·············· 172

### Scene 22　冰吧 Ice Bar ······ 174

Topic 1　酷暑 The Heat ·············· 174

Topic 2　巧克力火锅 Chocolate Hot Pot ·············· 176

Topic 3　自助餐饮 Buffet ·············· 178

Topic 4　情人节 Valentine's Day ······ 180

### Scene 23　服装市场 Clothing Market ········· 182

Topic 1　选择服饰 Choosing Clothes ·············· 182

Topic 2 试穿 Try-on ·············· 184

Topic 3 折扣 Discount ·············· 186

Topic 4 售后服务

　　　　After-Sale Services ·········· 188

## Scene 24 家电超市 Household Appliances Supermarket ··· 190

Topic 1 电器促销 Household

　　　　Appliances on Sale ·········· 190

Topic 2 买电器 Purchasing

Household Appliances ········ 192

Topic 3 家电维修 Maintenance ····· 194

Topic 4 信用卡 Credit Cards ········ 196

## Scene 25 超市 Supermarket ··· 198

Topic 1 寄存 Depositing ·············· 198

Topic 2 购物 Shopping ·············· 200

Topic 3 预防偷盗

　　　　Preventing Shoplifting ········· 202

Topic 4 城市变迁 Changes ············ 204

## Act 5　运动场景 Sports

## Scene 26 操场 Playground ······ 207

Topic 1 比赛 Competitions ·········· 207

Topic 2 体育明星 Sports Stars ········ 209

Topic 3 拉拉队队长 Cheerleader ····· 211

Topic 4 后勤服务 Rear Services ······ 213

## Scene 27 慢跑 Jogging ·········· 215

Topic 1 白领运动 Sports for

　　　　White-collar Workers ········· 215

Topic 2 慢跑 Jogging ·············· 217

Topic 3 运动交友

　　　　Workout Buddies ·············· 219

Topic 4 运动受伤 Sports Injuries ······ 221

## Scene 28 健身房 Gymnasium ··· 223

Topic 1 办理健身卡

　　　　Membership Cards ·············· 223

Topic 2 健身器械

　　　　Fitness Equipment ·············· 225

Topic 3 健康与节食

　　　　Health and Diet ·············· 227

Topic 4 瑜伽 Yoga ·············· 229

## Scene 29 奥运体育馆 Olympic Stadium ······ 231

Topic 1 奥运场馆

　　　　Olympic Stadium ·············· 231

Topic 2 奥运项目

　　　　Olympic Sports ·············· 233

Topic 3 指引外宾

　　　　Guiding Foreigners ·············· 235

Topic 4 奥运文化

　　　　Olympic Culture ·············· 237

# 目录
## CONTENTS

## Act 6  公共服务场所 Public Service

**Scene 30  居委会 Neighborhood Committee** ············ 240

Topic 1  遛鸟 Pet Bird ············ 240

Topic 2  扭秧歌 Yangge Dance ············ 242

Topic 3  照顾老人 Caring for the Old ············ 244

Topic 4  二手房 Second-hand Houses ············ 246

**Scene 31  医院 Hospital** ············ 248

Topic 1  咨询 Consultation ············ 248

Topic 2  挂号 Registration ············ 250

Topic 3  就诊 Seeing a Doctor ············ 252

Topic 4  探望 Paying a Visit ············ 254

**Scene 32  药店 Pharmacy** ············ 256

Topic 1  家庭药箱 Medicine-kit ············ 256

Topic 2  买药 Buying Medicine ············ 258

Topic 3  中药 Chinese Medicine ············ 260

Topic 4  处方 Prescriptions ············ 262

**Scene 33  派出所 Police Station** ············ 264

Topic 1  110 报案 Reporting a Case ············ 264

Topic 2  民警出警 On the Case ············ 266

Topic 3  社区安全 Community Security ············ 268

Topic 4  办理身份证 Applying for I. D. Card ············ 270

**Scene 34  理发店 Barbershop** ············ 272

Topic 1  洗发 Washing Hair ············ 272

Topic 2  理发 Haircut ············ 274

Topic 3  美发 Hairdressing ············ 276

Topic 4  形象设计 Designing ············ 278

**Scene 35  旅行社 Travel Agency** ············ 280

Topic 1  假期安排 Holiday Plans ············ 280

Topic 2  导游 Tour Guiding ············ 282

Topic 3  民俗旅游 Folk – custom Tourism ············ 284

Topic 4  背包客 Back-packers ············ 286

**Scene 36  邮局 Post Office** ············ 288

Topic 1  寄包裹 Send a Parcel ············ 288

Topic 2  订阅 Subscribing ············ 290

Topic 3  集邮 Stamp Collection ············ 292

Topic 4  汇款 Remittance ············ 294

**Scene 37  银行 Bank** ············ 296

Topic 1  存款 Depositing ············ 296

Topic 2  换钱 Changing Money ············ 298

Topic 3  兑现 Cashing a Check ············ 300

Topic 4  理财 Financing ············ 302

英语大赢家
**Winner's English**

**Scene 38　电信 Telecom** ············ 304

　Topic 1　互联网 The Internet ········· 304

　Topic 2　买手机

　　　　　Purchasing a Cellphone ······ 306

　Topic 3　手机充值卡

　　　　　Pre-paid Phone Cards ········ 308

　Topic 4　网络安全 Internet Security ··· 310


**Scene 39　博物馆 Museum** ······ 312

　Topic 1　电影 Movies ··············· 312

　Topic 2　历史博物馆

　　　　　Museum of History ······ 314

　Topic 3　文物保护 Conservation

　　　　　of Cultural Relics ············· 316

　Topic 4　四大发明 The Four Great

　　　　　Inventions ··············· 318

**Scene 40　报亭/公共电话 News-
　　　　　stand/Call Box** ······ 320

　Topic 1　卖报 Selling Newspaper ······ 320

　Topic 2　报亭轶事 Anecdotes of

　　　　　the Newsstand ················· 322

　Topic 3　免费赠品 Free Gifts ······ 324

　Topic 4　买地图 Buying a Map ········· 326


**附录一：常用中英亲属称谓**

　　　　**对应表** ················ 328

**附录二：常用中英量词一览表** ······ 330

**附录三：常用英美发音一览表** ····· 332

**附录四：中央人民广播电台"经济**

　　　　**之声"全国各地收听频率**

　　　　**表（FM、AM）** ················ 333

## 上册人物关系表　Characters

| 人物英文名字 | 人物中文名字 | 人物介绍 |
|---|---|---|
| Benjami（Ben） | 本杰明（本） | 爸爸 清华大学生化研究所研究员 |
| Shirley | 雪莉 | 妈妈 会计 |
| May | 阿美 | 姐姐 高中学生 |
| Daniel（Danny） | 丹尼尔（丹丹） | 弟弟 小学生 |
| Lisa | 利萨 | 远亲，北大一年级学生 |
| Tom | 汤姆 | 丹尼尔同班同学兼好友 绰号（Pig Tom：汤姆猪） |
| Barbie | 芭比 | 丹尼尔家的宠物狗，雌性 |
| Wendy | 温迪 | 阿美的小学同学 |
| Gucci | 古奇 | 阿美最好的朋友 拉拉队队长 |
| Jane | 简 | 妈妈的好朋友 |
| Adam | 亚当 | 简的儿子，初一 |
| Todd | 托德 | 美国教授，本杰明的朋友，科学家 |
| Lenna | 蕾娜 | Todd 的妻子 |
| Terry | 泰瑞 | 本杰明的朋友 外国人 |
| Clive | 克莱夫 | 古奇的男朋友，阿美的同学，篮球队长 |
| Jenny & Susan | 珍妮和苏珊 | 阿美的同学，是篮球队后勤人员 |
| Trainer | 健身教练 | 雪莉的私人教练 |
| Klas | 克劳斯 | 社区的老人 喜欢养鸟、下棋 |
| Leif | 雪弗 | 本杰明和雪莉的侄子；大学四年级，即将毕业。 |

# 英语大赢家 *Winner's English*

## Act 1

# 日常生活场景
## Daily Life

# 家 Home

## Goals

在这个场景中，我们将学到：

1. 前元音 /iː/、/i/ 和 /e/、/æ/ 2 组发音
2. 表达感情的单词
3. 问候句型
4. 时间的表达方法

 看电视
## Watching TV

 玩转语音

及格时间：10 秒
你的纪录：——秒
及格时间：5 秒
你的纪录：——秒

1. Silly Billy! Silly Billy!    Why is Billy silly?
   Silly Billy hid a shilling.    Isn't Billy Silly?
2. There is a red hat on his black bed.

    看电视是好是坏？每个家庭都会讨论一番。可这次爸爸不许丹尼尔看动画片，却为自己开了绿灯，怪不得丹尼尔大喊不公平呢！

**Dad**：Daniel, have you finished your home-work?

**Daniel**：Not yet, Dad. I am watching *Ultra-man* instead.

(*Father gets angry and turns off the TV.*)

**Daniel**：No, no, Dad. Please. This program is on only once a week.

**Dad**：Daniel, as a matter of fact, TV is bad for your health.

**Daniel**：What makes you think that?

**Dad**：It's full of violence and you are so young.

**Daniel**：But there are cartoons on TV. Bees, big trees, seas, and a lot of other interesting things.

爸爸：丹尼尔，你完成作业了吗？

丹尼尔：还没呢，爸爸。我正在看《奥特曼》。

(父亲生气了，把电视关了。)

丹尼尔：不，爸爸，求求您了。这个节目一个星期才放一次的。

爸爸：丹尼尔，事实上，电视不利于你的健康。

丹尼尔：您怎么会这样想呢？

爸爸：电视上充满着暴力行为，而你太小了。

丹尼尔：但是电视上还有卡通片啊。蜜蜂，大树，大海，还有其他很多有趣的东西。

Dad：Wait. What's the time, honey?

Daniel：About 6:00.

Dad：It's homework time now. Go and do your homework and then go to bed.

(*Father turns on the TV*)

Dad：(*murmur*) *American Idol*, there you go.

Daniel：Dad, it's not fair. I am so disappointed with you!

爸爸：等等。现在几点了,亲爱的?

丹尼尔：大概6:00了。

爸爸：现在是家庭作业时间。去做作业,然后上床睡觉。

(爸爸打开了电视)

爸爸：(自言自语)《美国偶像》来了!

丹尼尔：爸爸,不公平。我对你太失望了!

## 生词小结

**program**   *n.*节目
**as a matter of fact**   事实上
**health**   *n.* 健康
**cartoon**   *n.* 动画片,漫画
**honey**   *n.* 蜜,宝贝儿
**fair**   *adj.* 公平的
**disappointed**   *adj.* 失望的

## 注释

**Ultraman**   奥特曼   日本著名动画片
**American Idol**   美国偶像   美国著名选秀类电视节目

## 语音小结
## Pronunciation —— 前元音 /iː/ √/i/ 和 /e/ √/æ/ 2组发音

1. /iː/   **TV bee tree sea**
   发音小贴士:舌尖抵下齿,舌前部向硬腭尽量抬起,嘴唇向两边伸开,成扁平形,像微笑一样。

2. /i/   **finished think pictures study**
   发音小贴士:舌尖抵下齿,舌前部向硬腭抬起,比/iː/低,唇形扁平,开口比/iː/大,大约可容纳一个小指尖。

   对比练习   /iː/和/i/ seat and sit   leave and live   feet and fit   deep and dip

3. /e/   **yet beg American then**
   发音小贴士:舌尖抵下齿,舌前部稍抬起,开口比/i/大,大约可以容纳一个食指尖,双唇稍扁。

4. /æ/   **have Dad angry Saturday**
   发音小贴士:舌尖抵下齿,舌前部稍抬起,比/e/低,开口比/e/大些,开口可容纳食指与中指,双唇成扁平形。

   对比练习   /e/和/æ/ fed and fat   pet and pat   bed and bad   beg and bag

**Recitation**
经典背诵

Daniel：Hi, my name's Daniel. I like watching TV. There are a lot of interesting cartoons on it. I always watch the *Ultraman* after I finish my homework. Dad says TV is bad for my health. But he watches it everyday at 6:00. He likes watching the *American Idol*. It's not fair. I'm young.

# Topic 2 奥运梦
## Olympic Dreams

奥运就要来了,大家都在关注,阿美和丹尼尔正在讨论奥运梦想,可是这对姐弟好像从来也谈不到一块儿。

May: Hi, Daniel.

Daniel: Hi, May. Is dinner ready?

May: What's up?

Daniel: I'm so hungry I could eat a horse.

May: Soon, Dad is watching TV.

Daniel: What's on? American Idol again?

May: No, a show about 2008 Beijing Olympic Games.

Daniel: Oh, yes, they are coming soon.

May: You know, the Bird Nest is just not far from here.

Daniel: Really? Can you imagine? We can see Beckham in 2008 right here! I am so excited.

May: Daniel, you are so boyish. Beckham is old at that time.

Daniel: You are a girl. Of course you are not boyish. What do you expect of the Olympics, sister?

May: I want to be a volunteer in 2008. And I will give the foreign friends a big hand.

Daniel: How big are your hands? Even bigger than father's?

May: Wow, that's harsh, Danny.

阿美:嗨,丹尼尔。

丹尼尔:嗨,阿美。晚饭准备好了吗?

阿美:怎么了?

丹尼尔:我饿了,我能吃下一匹马。

阿美:快了,爸爸在看电视呢。

丹尼尔:什么节目?又是"美国偶像"?

阿美:不,是关于2008年北京奥运会的。

丹尼尔:噢,是啊,马上就要开办了。

阿美:知道吗,鸟巢就离这里不远。

丹尼尔:是吗?你能想象吗?2008年我们就能在这儿看见贝克汉姆啦!我很兴奋!

阿美:丹尼尔,你太幼稚了。贝克汉姆那个时候就老啦。

丹尼尔:你是个女孩儿,你当然不幼稚啦。那你对奥运会有什么期待,姐姐?

阿美:2008年我想成为一名志愿者,我要帮那些外国朋友们大忙。

丹尼尔:你的手有多大?比爸爸的手还大吗?

阿美:哎呀,真让我伤心,丹尼尔。

---

**生词小结**

**What's up** 怎么了?
**hungry** *adj.* 饥饿的

**注释**

**Bird Nest** 鸟巢 2008年北京奥运会标志性体育场馆

**Olympic** *adj.* 奥林匹亚的(奥林匹克)
**imagine** *vt.* 想象
**excited** *adj.* 兴奋的
**boyish** *adj.* 孩子气的,幼稚的
**volunteer** *n.* 志愿者
**give...a big hand** 给……很大帮助
**stranger** *n.* 陌生人

**Beckham** 贝克汉姆 原英格兰队队长,国际足球巨星

**You are a girl. Of course you are not boyish.**
在这里,boy 是男孩的意思 boyish 是孩子气的意思,但丹尼尔说他姐姐是女孩(不是男孩),当然不 boyish,这是一种幽默的自嘲方式。

**How big are your hands?** 丹尼尔不知道上文的意思,完全断章取义,直接问姐姐的手有多大?

## 单词扩展 Vocabulary Builder

| 表达感情的单词 | |
| --- | --- |
| 基础词汇 | 提高词汇 |
| happy 高兴的 | glad 开心的 |
| afraid 害怕 | frightened 受惊的 |
| sorry 难过的 | sad 悲伤的 |
| angry 愤怒的 | mad 疯狂的 |
| moved 被感动的 | touched 被感动的 |
| surprised 吃惊的 | amazed 惊讶的 |
| disappointed 失望的 | depressed 沮丧的 |

## D 家庭总动员
## o it together

两人一组,一方随机大声读出上面词汇的英文和中文,另一方用该词汇填入下面的句子,大声朗读并表演出来,并用中文给出一个理由。

**I am so**（　　　　　　　　　）.

【例】家长读 happy 高兴的
孩子读 I am so happy. 因为我考试得了 100 分!

**R**ecitation 经典背诵

May：Hi, My name's May. I'm Daniel's elder sister. The 2008 Beijing Olympic Games is coming soon. We are very excited about it. Our home is not far from the Bird Nest. I want to be a volunteer in 2008. And I will give the foreign friends a "big" hand. I am so excited.

# Topic 3 客人来访
## Visitors

听 学 读 看

利萨是丹尼尔家的远房亲戚，彼此有三年时间没见过面了。她现在是北京大学一年级的学生，利用课余时间去拜访丹尼尔一家。

**Benjamin**：Lisa, I'm so glad to see you. How are you doing?

**Lisa**：Fine. I miss you so much, uncle Benjamin.

**Benjamin**：Me too. We haven't seen each other for years.

**Lisa**：It's been 3 years now.

**Benjamin**：How time flies! Now you are a college student out of a little girl.

**Lisa**：How is aunty Shirley?

**Benjamin**：Couldn't be better.

**Lisa**：How has May been?

**Benjamin**：She's been good. She is in grade one in Joy Chain high school. And she dreams to be a volunteer in 2008.

**Lisa**：That's great. How about little Daniel then?

**Benjamin**：He started to elementary school last year. He is counting the days to the Olympic Games. How are your parents doing?

**Lisa**：Not bad. They plan to visit you next year.

**Benjamin**：Really, I'll be so excited to see them. Make yourself at home, Let me make some tea for you.

**Lisa**：OK, thank you, uncle Benjamin.

本杰明：利萨，见到你真是太高兴了。你好吗？

利萨：很好啊。我非常想念您，本杰明叔叔。

本杰明：我也是啊。我们有好几年没见了，是吧？

利萨：是啊，我们有3年没见了。

本杰明：时间过得多快啊！你现在都是个大学生了，不再是个小女孩了。

利萨：雪莉阿姨还好吗？

本杰明：好得不能再好了。

利萨：阿美现在怎么样？

本杰明：阿美很好。她在卓成高中读一年级。她现在做梦都想当2008奥运会的志愿者。

利萨：那太好了。那么丹尼尔怎么样呢？

本杰明：他去年上了小学，他现在天天盼着奥运会。你父母好吗？

利萨：还行。他们打算明年来看您。

本杰明：是吗？真是盼望与他们见面。你先坐，我去给你沏茶。

利萨：好啊，谢谢您，本杰明叔叔。

## 生词小结

**uncle**   n. 叔叔
**each other**   彼此，互相
**college**   n. 大学
**aunty**   n. 阿姨

## 注释

**He is counting the days.**   他在数日子。意思是焦急地盼望。

dream　*vt.* 做梦
**elementary school**　小学
**make tea**　沏茶

# F功能性句型扩展
## unctional structure —— 问候句型

**请朗读以下句型，家长和孩子交替进行。**

1. 打招呼（非正式）

　　Hello. 你好。（回答）Hello. 你好。

　　Hi. 你好。（回答）Hi. 你好。

　　How're things going? 你怎么样

　　What's up? 怎么了?

　　How's everything? 怎么样了?

　　How's it going? 怎么样了?

2. 打招呼（正式）

　　Good morning. 早上好。（回答）Good morning. 早上好。

　　Good afternoon. 下午好。（回答）Good afternoon. 下午好。

　　Good evening. 晚上好。（回答）Good evening. 晚上好。

　　Good night. 晚安。（回答）Good night. 晚安。

　　How are you? 你好吗?

　　How're you doing? 你好吗?

　　Nice to meet you. 很高兴见到你。（回答）Nice to meet you. 很高兴见到你。

　　How do you do? 你好。（回答）How do you do? 很高兴见到你。

3. 回答

　　Fine, thanks, and you? 很好，谢谢，你呢?

　　Good. Thanks, how about you? 很好，谢谢，你怎么样?

　　Not bad, you? 不赖，你呢?

　　Couldn't be better. 好得不能再好了。

　　Great. 好极了。

　　Just so so. 一般化。

　　Nothing new. 没什么新鲜事。

　　Same old, same old. 老样子。

　　Awful. 糟透了。

**Benjamin：**Hello, I'm Benjamin, Daniel is my son. He started elementary school last year. And May is my daughter. She is a high school student. Shirley is my wife. Lisa is my brother's daughter. Lisa visits us sometimes. She is a college student now. We are so happy together.

## 激励
### Encouragement

利萨离开之后,阿美和妈妈聊起了利萨,利萨取得了英语口语竞赛的一等奖,而阿美却想哭,为什么呢?

**May:** Lisa wins the first prize in the English speech contest of her college.

**阿美:** 利萨在她大学里的英语口语竞赛中得了第一名。

**Mom:** Really? That's really wonderful. I'm so happy for her.

**妈妈:** 是吗? 那真是太棒了。我真为她感到高兴。

**May:** But I always feel disappointed. I have many problems with English learning.

**阿美:** 可是我总是感觉很失落。我学英语时遇到很多问题。

**Mom:** Honey, cheer up.

**妈妈:** 亲爱的,振作一点。

**May:** I feel confused about the grammars.

**阿美:** 很多语法我都搞不清。

**Mom:** I'm sure you'll do fine if you try your best.

**妈妈:** 我确信只要你努力,你一定会做好。

**May:** And my writing is not good. I feel so frustrated.

**阿美:** 而且我作文写得不好。我很失落。

**Mom:** Be confident, and never give up.

**妈妈:** 自信一些,别放弃。

**May:** I know that, mom. But sometimes I'm just sad.

**阿美:** 我知道的,妈妈。可是有的时候,我就是难过。

**Mom:** Keep your chin up. Remember? Nothing is impossible to a willing heart.

**妈妈:** 昂首挺胸。记得吗? 有志者,事竟成。

**May:** Yes, mom. You are right. Nothing is impossible to a willing heart. I will keep going.

**阿美:** 是,妈妈。您说得对。有志者,事竟成。我会继续努力的。

---

**生词小结**

the first prize　一等奖
speech contest　演讲比赛
wonderful　*adj.* 极好的,棒的
problem　*n.* 问题
cheer up　振作起来
confused　*adj.* 困惑的,迷惑的
grammar　*n.* 语法
confident　*adj.* 自信的

**注释**

**Keep your chin up.** 这句话直译是"抬起你的下巴",意译为"振作起来"。

**Nothing is impossible to a willing heart.** 这句话直译是"对于一颗有毅力的恒心来说,没有什么不可能"意译为"有志者,事竟成"。

## G语法小结
rammer ——— 时间的表达方法

1. 美式读法,直接读数字

9:00 读作 *nine* 或 *nine o'clock*

8:01 读作 *eight o one*

9:15 读作 *nine fifteen*

9:32 读作 *nine thirty two*

2. 英式读法,用 past 和 to 来辅助计算读数字

(1) 当分钟数小于或等于 30 分钟时

表达法是"几点过几分",先说表示分钟的数字,然后说 past,最后说表示小时的数字。如:

9:01 读作:*one past nine*

9:15 读作:*fifteen past nine* 或 *a quarter past nine*

10:30 读作:*thirty past ten* 或 *half past ten*

(2) 当分钟数大于 30 分钟时

表达法变成"差几分几点"。先说表示差几分的数字,然后说 to,最后说表示小时的数字,如:

8:32 读作:*twenty eight to nine*

9:45 读作:*fifteen to ten* 或 *a quarter to ten*

## D家庭总动员
o it together

两人一组,一方任意在图上标注时间,并问"What's the time?"另一方则用美式读法回答。

**Recitation**
经典背诵

**Shirley:** Hello, I'm Shirley, Daniel and May's mother. Benjamin is my husband. May is not happy today. She is upset. She has some problems in learning English. And her writing is not so good. She feels disappointed. Hey, honey, cheer up. Be confident and never give up. Remember! Nothing is impossible to a willing heart.

# Act 1

日常生活场景 · Daily Life

**SCENE ②**

# 社区 Community

## Goals

在这个场景中,我们将学到:

1. 中元音 1 组,后元音 1 组
2. 表达天气的单词
3. 问候句型练习
4. 频率的表达方法

## Topic 1 社区布告栏 Bulletin

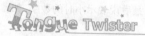 玩转语音

1. Elizabeth's birthday is on the third Thursday of this month.
2. All I want is a proper cup of coffee made in a proper copper coffee pot, believe it or not, I just want a cup of coffee in a proper copper coffee pot.

及格时间: 10 秒
你的纪录:——秒
及格时间: 25 秒
你的纪录:——秒

阿美和丹尼尔放学回家,在布告栏处看见了停电通知。停电了,丹尼尔就看不了他最爱的动画片《奥特曼》了,同时爸爸也看不了《美国偶像》了。于是两人决定带着家里的小狗芭比去玩。

Daniel : Oh, come on, *Ultraman*!

May : What's up, Bro? What's in the bulletin?

Daniel : It says that there will be a blackout from 5 p. m. to 7 p. m. in our neighborhood today.

May : Blackout? Even the TV has the limit.

Daniel : ( *staring at May angrily* ) Don't you know you will look like a monster in the blackout?

May : Oops, no, Daddy can't watch *American Idol*, either!

Daniel : That's not the point. Come on, can you imagine that there will be no electricity on such a hot day?

May : Oh, my god! No air-conditioner!

丹尼尔:噢,天哪,《奥特曼》!

阿美:怎么啦? 弟弟。布告栏上面说的是什么?

丹尼尔:布告上说社区今天晚上5点到7点要停电。

阿美:停电? 就连电视也不能看了。

丹尼尔:(怒视着阿美)难道你不知道你现在看起来就像黑暗中的魔鬼吗?

阿美:啊,爸爸也看不了他的《美国偶像》了!

丹尼尔:那根本就不是重点。拜托,你能够想象在那么热的天没有电的情况吗?

阿美:噢,天哪,空调也用不了了!

**Daniel:** OK, since you are the smart one, can you come up with a better plan? So that we won't be baked like cookies here.

**May:** How about playing Barbie out there in the neighborhood?

**Daniel:** Barbie? You know, I might be seven, but I'm not a girl.

**May:** Do you have a better plan?

**Daniel:** All right, all right.

**丹尼尔:** 既然你很聪明,你能想出一个更好的计划吗?这样的话我们就不会像被烘烤的饼干一样了。

**阿美:** 那么带小狗芭比一块儿去社区玩怎么样?

**丹尼尔:** 芭比? 虽然我只有七岁,但是我又不是女孩子。

**阿美:** 那么你有更好的计划吗?

**丹尼尔:** 算了,随便。

---

**生词小结**

| | | | |
|---|---|---|---|
| limit | *n.* 限度,限制 | air-conditioner | *n.* 空调 |
| monster | *n.* 怪物 | smart | *adj.* 聪明的,漂亮的 |
| blackout | *n.* 停电 | bake | *vt.* 烘,烤 |
| electricity | *n.* 电 | bulletin | *n.* 公告 |

**注释**

bro. = brother

**You know I'm seven, but I'm not a girl.** 在这一句中,丹尼尔认为只有女生才会和小狗一起出去玩。

---

**P**ronunciation 语音小结 —— 中元音1组,后元音1组

**中元音:**

1. /əː/ girl birth bird further
   发音小贴士:舌身平放,舌中部抬起至中间位置,牙床开得较窄,嘴唇展开程度似/iː/。

2. /ə/ conditioner neighborhood better about
   发音小贴士:舌中部稍抬起,比/əː/低,牙床半开,双唇扁平,该音俗称懒音,一张口就可以发出。

   对比练习 /əː/和/ə/ birth and teacher   word and doctor   sir and driver   work and today

**后元音:**

3. /ɔ/ monster watch not hot god
   发音小贴士:舌尖不触下齿,舌身尽量降低、后缩,开口大,双唇稍稍收圆。

4. /ɔː/ all horse bore lord
   发音小贴士:舌尖不触下齿,舌后部抬得比/ɔ/高,双唇收得比/ɔ/圆而小,且向前突出。

   对比练习 /ɔ/和/ɔː/ box and thought   doctor and daughter   hot and sworn   lot and sauce

---

**R**ecitation 经典背诵

**May:** When blackout happened in our community my little brother Daniel couldn't watch his favorite cartoon *Ultraman*, and my Dad couldn't watch *American Idol* either. So they would say blackout is a disaster. But for me it's fine. I'd just play out with our dog Barbie. And that is really fun.

# 日常生活场景 · Daily Life

外面天气比较凉爽,阿美和丹尼尔一块儿带着他们家的狗芭比来到了社区的院子里玩耍。两人聊起了各自喜欢的天气,他们都会喜欢什么样的天气呢?

**May:** Hurry up, Daniel, it's Barbie time.

**Daniel:** All right, Sis!

**May:** Come on, it's cool outside.

**Daniel:** I really wish Mom and Dad were here with us.

**May:** Hey, Daniel, what's your favorite weather? Snowy or sunny?

**Daniel:** Me? Er, I like hot weather, just like today.

**May:** What? Are you crazy?

**Daniel:** I like to watch Barbie sticking her tongue out.

**May:** Ew, Danny, gross!

**Daniel:** By the way, what's your favorite weather?

**May:** I love snowy, because it is very very romantic.

**Daniel:** Look, is that Tom?

**阿美:** 快点,丹尼尔,现在是芭比时间。

**丹尼尔:** 知道了,姐姐。

**阿美:** 哎呀,外面真凉爽。

**丹尼尔:** 真希望爸爸妈妈也和我们一块出来。

**阿美:** 对了,丹丹,你最喜欢什么天气呢?下雪天还是晴天?

**丹尼尔:** 我?嗯,我喜欢热天,就像今天一样。

**阿美:** 什么?你疯了吗?

**丹尼尔:** 我就喜欢看芭比吐她的舌头。

**阿美:** 丹丹,你真是恶心!

**丹尼尔:** 那么,你最喜欢什么样的天气呢?

**阿美:** 我最喜欢下雪天,因为非常浪漫。

**丹尼尔:** 看,那是汤姆吗?

---

**生词小结**

| | | | | |
|---|---|---|---|---|
| **cool** | *adj.* 凉的,凉快的 | | **stick** | *vi.* 伸出,刺 |
| **favorite** | *adj.* 最喜爱的 | | **tongue** | *n.* 舌头 |
| **weather** | *n.* 天气 | | **gross** | *adj.* 令人厌恶的 |

## 单词扩展 Vocabulary Builder

### 表达天气的单词

| 基础词汇 | 提高词汇 |
| --- | --- |
| fine 晴朗的 | foggy 有雾的 |
| hot 热的 | breezy 有微风的 |
| cold 冷的 | muggy 闷热的 |
| rainy 下雨的 | humid 湿润的 |
| windy 有风的 | chilly 寒冷的 |
| snowy 下雪的 | freezing 严寒的 |
| cloudy 多云的 | downpour 倾盆大雨 |
| sunny 阳光充足的 | drizzly 下毛毛雨的 |

## **D**o it together 家庭总动员

两人一组，一方随机大声读出基础词汇的英文和中文，另一方用该词汇填入下面的句子，大声朗读并表演出来，并用中文给出一个理由。

I like (                  ) weather.

【例】家长读 breezy 微风

孩子读 I like breezy weather. 因为很凉快。

**R**ecitation
经典背诵

**Daniel**：My sister May and I play with Barbie out in our neighborhood every day in summer. The weather outside would be cool. Mom and Dad would sometimes go out with us too. But actually, I like hot weather very much. Because I enjoy it when Barbie is sticking her tongue out.

## 日常生活场景·Daily Life

# Topic 3 宠物
## Pets

听 学 看 丹尼尔在社区遇见了他的同班同学汤姆并告诉了阿美有关汤姆的绰号。那他们之间又发生了什么好玩的事呢?

| | |
|---|---|
| **Daniel**:Pig Tom is over there. | **丹尼尔**:汤姆猪在那边。 |
| **May**:Pig Tom? | **阿美**:汤姆猪? |
| **Daniel**:That's Tom's nickname. | **丹尼尔**:汤姆的绰号。 |
| **May**:You are always a naughty boy. | **阿美**:你总是很调皮。 |
| **Daniel**:It's just me. | **丹尼尔**:没错,这就是我。 |
| (*Tom is coming.*) | (汤姆来了。) |
| **Daniel**:Hey, Tommy, What a coincidence! | **丹尼尔**:汤米,真是巧啊! |
| **Tom**:Hi, Daniel, May. Is this your dog, Daniel? | **汤姆**:你好,丹尼尔,阿美。丹丹,这是你的狗吗? |
| **Daniel**:It's Barbie, you know that. Hey, Barbie, say hello to Pig Tom. | **丹尼尔**:你知道的,这是芭比。喂,芭比,快和汤姆猪打招呼。 |
| **May**:Daniel! | **阿美**:丹尼尔! |
| **Daniel**:Come on, it's just a joke. By the way, do you have a dog,Tommy? | **丹尼尔**:开玩笑而已。对了,你养狗吗?汤米。 |
| **Tom**:I have a little white cat. | **汤姆**:我有一只小白猫。 |
| **Daniel**:Oh, a cat? Come on. | **丹尼尔**:噢,猫? |
| **Tom**:Come on, cats are gentle. | **汤姆**:猫是非常温顺的。 |

**生词小结**

**nickname**　*n.* 绰号,昵称
**luck**　*n.* 运气
**joke**　*n.* 笑话,玩笑
**gentle**　*adj.* 温和的,文雅的
**know**　*vt.* 知道

**注释**

**Pig Tom**:这是 Daniel 给他的同学 Tom 取的绰号。
**What luck!** 真巧。
**Tommy** 是 Tom 的昵称。

# 情景练习
## Scene practice —— 问候句型练习

**仔细阅读下面五个场景, 两人一组, 使用问候句型(见7页), 用一用, 练一练。**

1. Tom says "Good Morning!" to Daniel. How should Daniel reply?

2. May meets Mr. Jiang in front of the school gate. It's three o'clock in the afternoon. How should she greet him?

3. If Shirley says to Tom "How are you?", how should he reply?

4. May's classmate says to her "Hello, how are you today?", but May doesn't feel very well. What should she say?

5. It's Monday morning. May is sitting in the classroom. Her friend comes in. How should May greet her and ask about her weekend?

## Recitation
### 经典背诵

**Daniel:** Pig Tom is Tom's nickname. He is my good friend, actually, but I like messing with him from time to time. He is dull sometimes, but he is a good friend. He has a cat, he thinks cats are very gentle and he loves them very much. But I don't really like cats.

日常生活场景 · Daily Life

体育运动
Sports Activities

在了解到汤姆喜欢猫之后,丹尼尔就问汤姆最喜欢的体育运动。结果,汤姆的回答却很令丹尼尔吃惊。那么汤姆的回答到底是什么呢?

Daniel：Do you often do exercise?

Tom：Certainly.

Daniel：OK, and what kind of sports do you usually play?

Tom：I often play badminton with my parents.

Daniel：You? Play badminton? That's unbelieveable! You are shorter than a racket.

Tom：Hey, I'm good at playing it.

Daniel：Says who?

Tom：My parents.

Daniel：Oh, I see.

Tom：How about you, Daniel?

Daniel：I'm a real man, and I like football.

Tom：Well, who is your favorite football player?

Daniel：I like Ronaldo the most.

丹尼尔:你经常做运动吗?

汤姆:当然了。

丹尼尔:那你经常都做些什么样的运动呢?

汤姆:我经常跟我的父母打羽毛球。

丹尼尔:你? 打羽毛球? 这太让人难以置信了! 你还没有羽毛球拍大呢。

汤姆:喂,我打得还很不错呢。

丹尼尔:谁说的啊?

汤姆:我父母亲啊。

丹尼尔:我明白了。

汤姆:那你呢,丹丹?

丹尼尔:我是真正的男子汉,我喜欢足球。

汤姆:那么你最喜欢的足球明星是谁呢?

丹尼尔:我最喜欢罗纳尔多。

| 生词小结 |

**exercise**　*n.* 运动,练习
**sport**　*n.* 体育运动
**badminton**　*n.* 羽毛球
**parent**　*n.* 父(母)亲
**racket**　*n.* 羽毛球拍
**football**　*n.* 足球

| 注释 |

**I got it.** 表示的意思是"我懂了,我明白了",而在此处丹尼尔的意思是说他明白为什么会有人说汤姆擅长于打羽毛球。

**Says who?** 意为"谁说的?" 通常用于质疑对方的说法,表示不相信。

**Ronaldo** 即罗纳尔多,为巴西著名足球运动员,是全世界许多青少年的偶像。

## G语法小结 rammer —— 频率的表达方法

—*How often does May do revision?*
—*She does revision once a week.*

how often 意为"多久一次",指动作发生的频率,回答时一般是用表示频率的副词,如:once(一次),twice(两次),three times(三次),sometimes(有时),usual(通常),often(常常),never(从来不)等。如:

➤ "*How often do you watch TV?*" "你多长时间看一次电视?"
"*Three times a week.*" "一星期三次。"

➤ "*How often do you visit your friends?*" "你多长时间拜访你朋友一次?"
"*Once a week is OK.*" "一周一次就行了。"

➤ "*How often do they have a party?*" "他们多长时间举办一次聚会?"
"*Usually, once every month.*" "通常每月举办一次。"

➤ "*How often does May write in her diary?*" "阿美多长时间写一次日记?"
"*Sometimes once a week.*" "有时候一个星期一次。"

## D家庭总动员 o it together

两人一组,一方朗读下面的中文句子,另一方挑选出合适的翻译。

1. 爸爸,你多久对妈妈说一次"我爱你"?
   每天一次。

2. 亲爱的,你多久哭一次?
   从来不。

3. 妈妈,你多久做一次饭?
   每天做两次。

4. 你多长时间去做一次体育运动?
   一周一次。

5. 你多长时间打一次羽毛球?
   一天一次。

1. How often do you do the exercise?
   Once a week.

2. How often do you play badminton?
   Once a day.

3. Mom, how often do you cook?
   Twice a day.

4. Dad, how often do you say "I love you" to Mom?
   Once a day.

5. Darling, how often do you cry?
   Never.

**Tom**：My name is Tom, I'm Daniel's classmate and good friend. He likes playing football very much, but I like playing badminton. I usually play it with my parents. My parents think that I am good at badminton. I'm proud of it so I'm willing to practise it hard in my spare time.

# 菜市场 Food Market

## Goals

**在这个场景中,我们将学到:**

1. 后元音2组
2. 表示蔬果和肉类的单词
3. 表达爱好与厌恶的句型
4. 人称代词

## Topic 1 逛菜市场 Food Market

 **玩转语音**

1. How many cookies could a good cook cook if a good cook could cook cookies? A good cook could cook as much cookies as a good cook who could cook cookies.

2. One smart fellow, he felt smart. Two smart fellows, they felt smart. Three smart fellows, they all felt smart.

及格时间:25秒
你的纪录:——秒
及格时间:15秒
你的纪录:——秒

丹尼尔刚在学校学会了一些蔬果和肉类的表达,但很多蔬果他以前并没有见过。恰好妈妈要去菜市场,他央求妈妈带他一起去买菜,这下倒可以看看他学得怎么样了。

**Daniel:** Mom, where are you going?

**Mom:** I am going to buy some food to cook for supper.

**Daniel:** Good. I wanna come with you.

**Mom:** How strange! Our little emperor now asks to help out with shopping.

**Daniel:** We learnt about vegetables and meat at school. But I never see the real thing.

**Mom:** Wow, that's something new. Let's go!

*(Daniel and mother enter the food market.)*

*(Mom points to the spinage and asks.)*

**Mom:** What's this, honey?

**丹尼尔:**妈妈,你要去哪里?

**妈妈:**我正要去买菜做晚饭。

**丹尼尔:**太好了,我想和你一起去。

**妈妈:**真奇怪! 我们家的小皇帝主动要求去买菜。

**丹尼尔:**我们在学校里学了很多有关蔬菜和肉的知识,但是很多我从没见过。

**妈妈:**哦,真新鲜。那我们出发吧!

(丹尼尔和妈妈一起走进了菜市场。)

(妈妈指着菠菜问。)

**妈妈:**知道这是什么吗,宝贝?

(*Daniel thinks over for a while.*)

Daniel：Er, is it cabbage?

Mom：Cabbage? Is that what they teach at school now? OK, honey, it's spinage.

Daniel：Yeah, I know, this is Popeye's favorite food.

Mom：There we go.

Daniel：Mom, come here. I know this, it is carrot, am I right?

Mom：Bingo! It's dark outside, let's hurry up.

（丹尼尔想了一会儿。）

丹尼尔：呃，是卷心菜吗？

妈妈：卷心菜？这就是现在学校教的东西吗？好了，孩子，这是菠菜。

丹尼尔：哦，我知道了，原来这就是大力水手最喜欢的食物呀！

妈妈：我们走吧。

丹尼尔：妈妈，来这边。我认识这个，是胡萝卜，对吗？

妈妈：答对了！外面天已经黑了，我们快点吧。

**生词小结**

emperor    *n.* 皇帝
help out with    帮助解决难题
vegetable    *n.* 蔬菜
spinage    *n.* 菠菜
cabbage    *n.* 卷心菜
carrot    *n.* 胡萝卜

**注释**

**Wow, that's something new.** 哦，真新鲜。在上一句中，Daniel 说很多蔬菜不认识，妈妈用了一种调侃的语气来和 Daniel 开玩笑。言外之意就是：真新鲜，原来你也有不认识的东西啊。

**Popeye** 大力水手，美国的一部著名动画片。

**Bingo!** 表示肯定的说话，意思为"你答对了"。

**语音小结**
Pronunciation —— 后元音 2 组

1. /ʌ/ **Mom some but supper**
   发音小贴士：舌尖和舌端两侧轻触下齿，舌后部靠前部稍抬起，双唇向两边平伸，开口较大。

2. /ɑ:/ **market are dark park**
   发音小贴士：舌尖离开下齿，舌身平放后缩，舌后部稍抬起，口张开，开口最大。
   对比练习　/ʌ/ 和/ɑ:/　study and park　money and party　honey and star　subject and dark

3. /u/ **could cook good cookies**
   发音小贴士：舌尖离开下齿，但不与上齿接触，舌身后缩，舌后部向软腭抬起，双唇收圆稍向前突起。

4. /u:/ **you food school to**
   发音小贴士：舌尖离开下齿，舌后部向软腭抬起，抬得比/u/ 更高，双唇收得比/u/ 更圆、更小且向前突出，口腔肌肉始终保持紧张状态。
   对比练习　/u/ 和/u:/　book and fool　hook and noon　wood and pool　good and soon

**Recitation**
经典背诵

Daniel：My Mom and I sometimes go to the Food Market together. I've learnt something about vegetables in school but when it comes to the real thing, it's not so easy for me to tell their exact names. Mom would help me with them. She'd make a great teacher I think.

# Act 1

日常生活场景 · Daily Life

## Topic 2 买卖
### Buying and Selling

听 学 读 看

　　妈妈准备买几样蔬菜和肉回家做晚饭,选好以后和店员讨价还价。妈妈的砍价技术如何,我们来看看吧。

**Mom**：Excuse me, how much is the spinage?

**Vendor**：3 yuan per kilogram.

**Mom**：That's too expensive. What about the carrots?

**Vendor**：The same.

**Mom**：How about 2.5 yuan a kilogram? I come here all the time.

**Vendor**：Come on. I'm out on a limb here. How much do you want?

**Mom**：Two kilograms of carrots and one kilogram of spinage.

**Vendor**：All right, all right. Sold. Goes for 7.5 yuan.

(*Mother gives 10 yuan to the vendor.*)

**Vendor**：Here is your change.

**Mom**：Daniel, would you like some beef for supper?

**Daniel**：Cool! I like beef. And I try to be stronger than Popeye.

**Mom**：Sure, honey. But you are going to buy it by yourself.

**Daniel**：Excuse me. How much is the beef?

**Vendor**：Sorry kid, it's pork. We sold out all the beef.

**Daniel**：That's a shame, thanks anyway.

妈妈：请问,菠菜怎么卖?

小贩：每公斤三块钱。

妈妈：太贵了。胡萝卜怎么卖?

小贩：一样的价钱。

妈妈：两块五一斤怎么样啊? 我总是来你这里买菜呢。

小贩：别呀! 您总不能让我亏本吧。您想买多少呢?

妈妈：两公斤的胡萝卜和一公斤菠菜。

小贩：好吧,卖您了。一共七块五。

(妈妈拿出十元钱给售货员。)

小贩：找您零钱。

妈妈：丹尼尔,你晚饭想吃牛肉吗?

丹尼尔：太好了。我喜欢牛肉。我要变得比大力水手更强壮。

妈妈：当然可以了,孩子。但是你要自己去买牛肉。

丹尼尔：请问,这个牛肉怎么卖?

小贩：小朋友,这是猪肉。牛肉已经全部卖完了。

丹尼尔：太可惜了,但还是谢谢您。

---

**生词小结**

expensive　*adj.* 贵的
percent　*n.* 百分之……

**注释**

anyway　不管怎样
Come on. 这是比较随意的口头禅,就像在

be twenty percent off　打八折

be next to nothing　极便宜,几乎免费

kilogram　n. 千克,公斤

limb　n. 树枝,肢

beef　n. 牛肉

pork　n. 猪肉

sell out　卖完

shame　n. 遗憾的事

说:来吧,让我们做什么事情,或者不做什么之类,也可以表达"加油"的意思。

**I'm out on a limb here.** 这句话多用来形容自己已经到了无可退让的地步。

**Here is your change.** 找您零钱。

**That's a shame.** 这是美式英语中表达遗憾的一种说法。在英式英语中,一般用 It's a pity.

## 单词扩展 Vocabulary Builder

### 表示蔬果和肉类的单词

| 基础词汇 | 提高词汇 |
| --- | --- |
| meat 肉 | mutton 羊肉 |
| beef 牛肉 | pork 猪肉 |
| fish 鱼 | chicken 鸡肉 |
| tomato 西红柿 | sausage 香肠 |
| potato 土豆 | cucumber 黄瓜 |
| onion 洋葱 | leek 韭葱 |
| apple 苹果 | watermelon 西瓜 |
| pear 梨 | mushroom 蘑菇 |
| orange 橘子 | peach 桃子 |
| banana 香蕉 | |

## Do it together 家庭总动员

两人一组,一方随机大声读出上面词汇的英文和中文,另一方将该词汇填入下面的句子,大声朗读并表演出来。

**How much is the (　　　　　　　　)?**

【例】家长读 beef 牛肉

孩子读 How much is the beef?

*Recitation* 经典背诵

**Vendor**：Hi, I am a vendor. Welcome to the Food Market. Many people come to my stand for the food. I always give them my best price. All the vegetables are twenty percent off after 5:00 p. m. Although the job keeps me busy all the time, I find it quite fun.

## Topic 3 识别颜色
### Colors

买完菜后,妈妈和丹尼尔走出菜场,妈妈边走边随手指着蔬菜,教丹尼尔辨识颜色,丹尼尔好像不愿听这个哦,来看看是为什么吧!

**Mom**：Honey, do you know what color the carrot is?

**Daniel**：Mom, it's orange?

**Mom**：Wow, my son is so clever.

(*Daniel frowns and speaks seriously*)

**Daniel**：Mom, that's a stupid question.

**Mom**：Really?

**Daniel**：I am not a child at all. I know more.

**Mom**：Oh, my son looks like a grown-up.

**Daniel**：Sure. Mom, I can take care of you.

**Mom**：No kidding. So tell me what's your favorite color?

**Daniel**：I like blue. You see, that's the color of the sky. I wanna be a superman.

**Mom**：Why?

**Daniel**：I hope I can fly to any place like superman. So I can touch the sky.

(*Daniel simulates flying.*)

**Mom**：OK, superman. Put on your cape, we are going to fly home.

妈妈：孩子,你知道胡萝卜是什么颜色吗?

丹尼尔：妈妈,是桔黄色的吧。

妈妈：哇,我儿子好聪明呀。

(丹尼尔皱了下眉,很认真地说)

丹尼尔：妈妈,这是一个很傻的问题。

妈妈：哦?

丹尼尔：我已经不再是个小孩子了。我知道得更多。

妈妈：哦,我的儿子看上去像个小大人。

丹尼尔：当然了,妈妈。我可以照顾您呢。

妈妈：不是开玩笑吧,那告诉我你最喜欢什么颜色?

丹尼尔：我喜欢蓝色。你看,这是天空的颜色。我想成为超人。

妈妈：为什么呢?

丹尼尔：我希望可以像超人那样飞来飞去。这样我就可以触摸到天空。

(丹尼尔模仿飞的样子。)

妈妈：好的,超人,穿上你的斗篷,我们准备飞回家了。

---

**生词小结**

**frown** *vi.* 皱眉头
**seriously** *adv.* 严肃地,认真地
**stupid** *adj.* 愚蠢的,傻的
**question** *n.* 问题
**grown-up** *n.* 大人
**take care of** 照顾

**注释**

**to tell you the truth** 说实话
**No kidding.** 别开玩笑啊。这是妈妈调侃丹尼尔的一种说法。
**Superman** 超人。美国系列电影《超人》中的主人公。

**touch** *vt.* 接触
**simulate** *vt.* 模仿
**cape** *n.* 斗篷

# 功能性句型扩展 —— 表达爱好与厌恶的句型
**F**unctional structure

**请朗读以下句型,家长和孩子交替进行。**

1. 问句

What's your favorite color? 你最喜欢什么颜色?

Do you like travelling? 你喜欢旅行吗?

What kind of tea do you like? 你喜欢哪种茶?

Would you like meat or vegetable? 你喜欢肉还是蔬菜?

Which do you prefer, singing or dancing? 你喜欢唱歌还是跳舞?

2. 回答(喜欢)

I like/love vegetable. 我喜欢蔬菜。

I like/ love/ enjoy/ prefer doing something. 我喜欢做某事。

I like/ love/ enjoy/ prefer something. 我喜欢某事/某物。

I prefer to swim rather than play football. 相比踢足球,我更喜欢游泳。

I am interested in doing something. 我对做某事很感兴趣。

I am interested in something. 我对某事/某物很感兴趣。

3. 回答(不喜欢/厌恶)

I don't like/ prefer apple. 我不喜欢苹果。

I dislike orange. 我不喜欢橘子。

4. 与某人喜好一致

So do/am I.

Oh yes, I am/do too.

Yes, me too.

5. 与某人喜好不一致

Oh, are/do you?

I'm not really.

I don't really.

Oh, do you? / really? /are you? / I must say it's not something I know very much about.

**Recitation**
经典背诵

Daniel: Sometimes my Mom asks me some questions about the color of things. I think it's a stupid question. I am not a child any more. I am a grown-up. To tell you the truth, my favorite color is blue. That's the color of the sky. I wanna be a superman. So I can fly and touch the sky.

# Topic 4 营养
## Nutrition

回家后,妈妈用刚买的菜做了一顿丰盛的晚餐。可是丹尼尔想吃姐姐买回来的巧克力蛋糕,故意挑剔胡萝卜难吃。那阿美有没有识破他的鬼把戏呢?

**Daniel**：Yuck. The carrots taste awful and salty. Hi sis, how do you like them?

**May**：I like them very much. They are delicious.

**Daniel**：Well, you can have all my carrots.

**May**：Daniel, hold on for a minute. What are you trying to pull there?

**Daniel**：Nothing. Just that I don't care for these carrots.

*(Pause briefly)*

**Daniel**：Hi, sis., I saw you buy some chocolate cakes. I am done with the main course. It's about time for some dessert.

**May**：Oh, you want my chocolate cakes, so to speak!

**Daniel**：No, no, I'm just thinking of some dessert. And I have had enough carrots.

**May**：Daniel, carrots contain much Vitamin C. It is good for you.

**Daniel**：I know, but chocolate cake is even better.

**May**：Oh, stop it! You know you need vegetables. You will end up fat if you don't watch your diet, now.

**Daniel**：Well, actually, I don't mind eating carrots, but chocolate cakes are much better. You know I was born with a sweet tooth.

**丹尼尔**：妈呀。这些胡萝卜又难吃又咸。姐姐,你觉得怎样?

**阿美**：我很喜欢。它们很好吃。

**丹尼尔**：那好,你可以把我的胡萝卜全吃了。

**阿美**：等一下,丹尼尔。你又有什么鬼点子啊?

**丹尼尔**：没有。只是不喜欢这些胡萝卜嘛。

（停了一会）

**丹尼尔**：嗨,姐姐。我看到你买了一些巧克力蛋糕。我已经吃完主食了,现在是甜点时间。

**阿美**：哦,也就是说,你想要我的巧克力蛋糕。

**丹尼尔**：不,不。我只是想要些甜点。我已经吃厌胡萝卜了。

**阿美**：丹尼尔,胡萝卜含有丰富的维生素C。对你有好处。

**丹尼尔**：我知道,但是巧克力蛋糕更好。

**阿美**：不行! 你要知道,你需要多吃蔬菜。如果你现在不注意自己的饮食,你会变胖的。

**丹尼尔**：好吧,事实上,我不介意吃胡萝卜,但是巧克力蛋糕更好些。你知道我天生爱吃甜食。

---

**生词小结**

**Yuck** *interj.* 讨厌
**awful** *adj.* 糟糕的
**delicious** *adj.* 美味的,可口的
**hold on for a minute** 等一下
**chocolate** *n.* 巧克力
**course** *n.* 一道(菜),课程
**dessert** *n.* 甜点
**Vitamin** *n.* 维生素

**注释**

**What are you trying to pull there?** 这句话直译是"你想要扯出什么",意译为"你又想到了什么鬼把戏"。

**so to speak** 也就是说

**I have enough with the carrots.** 这句话直译是"我已经吃了足够的胡萝卜",言下之意是说吃胡萝卜吃烦了,吃厌了。

**You will end up fat if you don't watch your**

diet　*n.* 饮食
stomach　*n.* 胃

**diet, now.** 这句话直译是"如果你不注意你的饮食,你将会以肥胖结束",意译为"如果你不注意你的饮食,你会变胖的"。

**You know I was born a sweat tooth.** 这句话直译是"你知道的,我天生有个甜牙",言下之意是说自己特别爱吃甜食。

## G rammer 语法小结 —— 人称代词

| 数 | 单　数 | | | 复　数 | | |
|---|---|---|---|---|---|---|
| 人称/格 | 第一人称 | 第二人称 | 第三人称 | 第一人称 | 第二人称 | 第三人称 |
| 主格 | I | you | he, she, it | we | you | they |
| 宾格 | me | you | him, her, it | us | you | them |

人称代词在句子中的成分

1. 主语
   *I am Daniel.* 我是丹尼尔。
   *We are students.* 我们是学生。
   *She is married.* 她结婚了。
   *They are married.* 他们结婚了。
   *You are very beautiful.* 你(你们)很漂亮。

2. 宾语
   *I love you.* 我爱你。
   　　在这个熟知的句子里,有两个人称代词 I 和 you,其中 I 是做主语,而 you 在这个句子中就做 love 的宾语。例如:
   *Thank you!* 谢谢!
   连这个简单的句子里也有人称代词做宾语的用法,可知人称代词做宾语还是很常见的,又如:
   *Put it on the table.* 放到桌子上。
   *Tell him to call back.* 告诉他等会儿打过来。

3. 表语
   *It's me.* 是我。
   *It was her.* 是她。
   　　第三人称代词 she 除了可以表示"她"之外,还可以表示国家,带有很亲切的感情,例如大家在表达热爱自己的祖国或某个国家时可以说:
   *I love China. She is a great country.* 我爱中国,她是个很伟大的国家。

## D o it together 家庭总动员

两人一组,一方朗诵下面的中文句子,另一方挑选出合适的翻译。

1. 他是丹尼尔。
2. 他们去菜市场。
3. 谢谢你们了。
4. 我爱中国。她很美。
5. 他们是一家人。

1. I love China. She is beautiful.
2. They are a family.
3. Thank you!
4. He is Daniel.
5. They go to the Food Market.

**Recitation** 经典背诵

**May:** Mom cooks carrots for us very often. I like them very much and they contain much Vitamin C which is really good for my health. So I enjoy eating them from time to time. But Daniel just doesn't like them at all. Instead, he loves chocolate cakes. I've always told him he will end up fat if he doesn't watch his diet. It's a shame that he would never listen to me!

# Act 1

日常生活场景·Daily Life

## 厨房 Kitchen

### Goals

**在这个场景中，我们将学到：**

1. 双元音 2 组
2. 表示调味品的单词
3. 爱好与厌恶句型练习
4. 物主代词

# Topic 1 洗菜
## Washing Vegetables

 **玩转语音**

1. The great Greek grape growers grow great Greek grapes.

2. If you notice this notice, you will notice that this notice is not worth noticing.

3. Row, row, row your boat,
   Row, row, row your boat,
   Gently down the stream,
   Merrily, merrily, merrily, merrily
   Life is but a dream.

| 及格时间：5 秒 |
| 你的纪录：——秒 |
| 及格时间：10 秒 |
| 你的纪录：——秒 |
| 及格时间：14 秒 |
| 你的纪录：——秒 |

今天是 3 月 8 日妇女节，现在是晚饭时间。平时总是妈妈一个人做饭，但是今天会有什么不同吗？

**May：** Mom! How can I help with the washing up?

**Mom：** You peel the onions and wash them, then chop them.

**May：** OK! Then what can I do after I finish it?

**Mom：** Let me see. Wash the cabbage over there.

**May：** OK, got it.

**Mom：** What is your father doing now?

**May：** Reading newspaper on the couch.

**阿美：** 妈妈，我来帮忙洗点东西？

**妈妈：** 你把洋葱削一下，然后洗洗，再切碎。

**阿美：** 好的。那么做完了之后我做什么呢？

**妈妈：** 让我想想。把那棵卷心菜洗了吧。

**阿美：** 好的，明白了。

**妈妈：** 你爸爸现在干什么呢？

**阿美：** 坐在沙发上看报纸呢。

**Mom**：How about Daniel?

**May**：Staying with *Ultraman*, of course. You know he likes it very much.

**Mom**：Be careful of the peeler. Don't cut your fingers.

**May**：I will.

**Mom**：OK, we've finished. Can you get your father and brother?

**May**：OK!

妈妈:丹丹呢?

阿美:他当然是在看《奥特曼》啊。你知道他非常喜欢《奥特曼》的。

妈妈:当心,别切到你的手了。

阿美:恩。

妈妈:好了,我们的工作做完了,去叫你爸爸和弟弟吧!

阿美:好。

## 生词小结

| | | | |
|---|---|---|---|
| **peel** | *vt.* 削……皮,剥落 | **couch** | *n.* 长椅,睡椅,长沙发 |
| **onion** | *n.* 洋葱 | **peeler** | *n.* 削皮器 |
| **chop** | *vt.* 剁碎,砍 | **cut** | *vt.* 切,砍 |
| **finish** | *vt.* 完成 | | |

## 语音小结
**P**ronunciation —— 双元音 2 组

1. /ei/ newspaper staying say lay
   发音小贴士:口型由/e/向/i/滑动。发音过程中,下颚向上合拢,舌位也随之稍稍抬高。

2. /ai/ I likes eye sight
   发音小贴士:口型从/a/的部位向/i:/滑动。开始的/a/是前元音,舌位介于/æ/与/ɑ:/之间,发音时舌尖抵住下齿。发音过程中,下颚迅速向下移动,开口逐渐缩小。

   对比练习 /ei/和/ai/ may and fly   day and cry   fake and right   lake and night

3. /əu/ OK know soap open
   发音小贴士:口型由/ə/向/u/滑动。发音过程中下颚稍抬高,双唇由扁平收圆。

4. /au/ how now couch about
   发音小贴士:口型由/a/向/u/滑动,开始部分的/a/与/ai/中的/a/相同,由/a/向/u/滑动,双唇逐渐收成圆形,并把舌后部稍稍抬起。

   对比练习 /əu/和/au/ home and how   boat and cow   goat and mouse   poem and now

**R**ecitation 经典背诵

**Mom**：On Women's Day, I'd have a break from my housework. My husband Ben would cook for the family. But I would wash and chop the vegetables beforehand by myself. You know it's not really wise for you to trust the guys with cooking, though I'd appreciate it that he is willing to have a try.

烹饪
Cooking

妈妈和阿美洗完菜,该轮到爸爸和丹尼尔上场了,那么很少做饭的爸爸和丹尼尔会闹出什么样的笑话呢?

**Dad:** You stay beside me; I'll fry the meat in the oil first.

**爸爸:** 我先把肉炸一下,你站在我旁边。

**Daniel:** Daddy, what seasonings are you going to cook the meat with?

**丹尼尔:** 爸爸,你准备用什么样的调味品呢?

**Dad:** Er, I am gonna go with salt and sauce!

**爸爸:** 恩,用盐和酱汁就可以了。

**Daniel:** What? Are you kidding?

**丹尼尔:** 什么? 你没有开玩笑吧?

**Dad:** Is there anything wrong?

**爸爸:** 有什么不对吗?

**Daniel:** I remember Mom going with a lot of pepper for the meat.

**丹尼尔:** 我记得妈妈在炒肉的时候都会放很多的辣椒。

**Dad:** Really?

**爸爸:** 真的吗?

**Daniel:** (*nod*) Of course, sure!

**丹尼尔:** (点头)当然啦!

**Dad:** All right, pass me some pepper.

**爸爸:** 好,那就给我一些辣椒吧!

**Daniel:** Oh, Dad, you are burning the meat.

**丹尼尔:** 噢,爸爸,肉糊了。

**Dad:** Oh my god!

**爸爸:** 噢,我的天哪!

**Daniel:** Haha!

**丹尼尔:** 哈哈!

---

**生词小结**

**fry** *vt.* 油煎,油炸

**seasoning** *n.* 调料

**sauce** *n.* 调味汁,酱汁

**pepper** *n.* 辣椒

**nod** *vi.* 点头

**burn** *vt.* 燃烧,烧着

**meat** *n.* 肉

## 单词扩展 Vocabulary Builder

### 表示调味品的单词

| 基础词汇 | 提高词汇 |
|---|---|
| salt 盐 | curry 咖喱 |
| soy sauce 酱油 | lard 猪油 |
| wild pepper 花椒 | peanut oil 花生油 |
| gourmet powder 味精 | tomato ketchup 番茄酱 |
| green pepper 青椒 | star anise 八角,茴香 |
| sugar 糖 | wasabi(注:mustard 是芥末的学名,在美国 |
| vinegar 醋 | 日常口语中只用 wasabi)芥末 |
| chilli 干辣椒 | salad oil 色拉油 |

## 家庭总动员
Do it together

请家长随机大声读出词汇的英文,孩子说出该词的中文意思并用该词汇填入下面的句子,大声朗读,并将该句子翻译成中文。

**I am gonna go with(**       **) and (**      **)!**

【例】家长读 sugar and salt 糖和盐

孩子读 I am gonna go with sugar and salt! 我将用糖和盐!

### Recitation
经典背诵

Daniel：My Dad is not good at cooking. Everytime he tries to cook something he'd need me to be around for help. Most of the time, I can be really helpful since I've seen Mom cook so many times. So my father trusts me very much. But sometimes I'm not really sure about everything. That's why we two may cook something that tastes really strange.

 厨具
Cookers

忙活了半天,爸爸的菜终于要做好了,但是丹尼尔却找不到盛汤的碗了,后来找到了,那么他是在哪里找到的呢? 他找的碗是否是用来盛汤的呢?

**Daniel**：Dad, when will you finish your cooking?

**Dad**：Several minutes.

**Daniel**：So what should I do now?

**Dad**：Then, pass me a bowl for the soup.

**Daniel**：Where's the bowl gone?

**Dad**：Look for it yourself, please! Kinda busy here, Daniel!

**Daniel**：Dad?

**Dad**：Check the drawer.

**Daniel**：OK, got it, but its shape is so strange. I don't like it.

**Dad**：Can it hold soup?

**Daniel**：Maybe.

**Dad**：It smells sweet. Mom and May are gonna love it. Get them for dinner, Daniel!

**Daniel**：Mommy, dinner, please!

**丹尼尔**：爸爸,你什么时候才能做完饭啊?

**爸爸**：几分钟。

**丹尼尔**：那我现在该干什么呢?

**爸爸**：递给我一个盛汤的碗。

**丹尼尔**：碗在哪儿啊?

**爸爸**：自己去找找啊。我这儿现在非常忙,丹尼尔。

**丹尼尔**：老爸?

**爸爸**：看看那个抽屉里有没有。

**丹尼尔**：好了,找到了,但是它的形状好奇怪啊,我不喜欢这个碗。

**爸爸**：那它能盛汤吗?

**丹尼尔**：可能吧。

**爸爸**：闻起来可真是香啊。妈妈和阿美绝对会喜欢的。丹尼尔,叫妈妈和姐姐过来吃饭。

**丹尼尔**：妈咪,吃饭了。

---

**生词小结**

| | |
|---|---|
| **bowl** *n.* 碗 | **shape** *n.* 形状 |
| **soup** *n.* 汤 | **sweet** *adj.* 甜的,可爱的 |
| **drawer** *n.* 抽屉 | **dinner** *n.* 主餐,晚餐 |

## S情景练习
### cene practice ——— 爱好与厌恶句型练习

仔细阅读下面五个场景,两人一组,使用爱好与厌恶的句型(见 23 页),用一用,练一练。

1. Mom asks Daniel what sort of food he likes. What would Daniel say?

2. Tom wants to know if there is any sport Daniel doesn't like. What would Daniel say?

3. May tells Daniel that she doesn't like cooking. What would Daniel say if he agrees with her?

4. Daniel tells May that he doesn't like cheese very much. What would May say if she disagrees with him?

5. If you were Shirley, ask May if she prefers dancing or singing. What would you say?

*Recitation*
经典背诵

**Dad**:When I cook I always ask Daniel to help me. Sometimes I can't even find a bowl for soup. Then he would find it for me. The problem is that he'd always get the wrong one. But you know, I have no choice but use it. Anyway it works out so that's enough for my family to enjoy the dinner.

餐具

**The Dishes**

全家人正准备吃饭,丹丹却找不到他自己的勺子了。他经常乱丢东西,所以妈妈为了惩罚就让他自己找,那么最后丹丹是在哪里找到他的勺子的呢?

**Daniel**：Mom, help me with the bowls, please! I can't hold them.

**Mom**：Be careful, honey.

**Daniel**：Have you seen my spoon, Mom!

**Mom**：Look in the fridge, honey!

**Daniel**：No, not there.

**Mom**：You've put it there by yourself, and you are always absent-minded.

**Daniel**：Sorry, Mom, I don't like it either, but it's just me.

(*Barbie comes into the dinning room.*)

**May**：Everybody, I have found it. Look, it's in Barbie's mouth.

**Mom**：Come on, Barbie.

(*All the family members are at the table.*)

**Mom**：Oops!

**Dad**：What's up, honey?

**Mom**：Who added pepper to the meat? It's too spicy.

(*Daniel is laughing secretly.*)

丹尼尔:妈妈,拜托帮我拿一下碗,我抓不住了。

妈妈:宝贝,小心点。

丹尼尔:妈妈,看见我的勺子了吗?

妈妈:在冰箱里找找,宝贝!

丹尼尔:不,不在那儿。

妈妈:是你自己放的,你总是很健忘。

丹尼尔:对不起,妈妈,我也不想那样啊,但那就是我啊。

(芭比走进了餐厅。)

阿美:我找到了,看,勺子在芭比的嘴巴里叼着呢。

妈妈:快过来,芭比。

(全家人坐到了桌子旁准备吃饭。)

妈妈:天啊!

爸爸:怎么啦? 亲爱的!

妈妈:谁在肉里面加了辣椒? 太辣了。

(丹丹偷偷地笑了。)

---

**生词小结**

| | | |
|---|---|---|
| **spoon** *n.* 匙,勺子 | **member** *n.* 成员 |
| **fridge** *n.* 电冰箱 | **add** *vt.* 增加 |
| **absent-minded** *adj.* 健忘的 | **table** *n.* 桌子 |

# G 语法小结 —— 物主代词
rammer

## 一、物主代词表解

| 类型/词义 | 我的 | 你的 | 他/她/它的 | 我们的 | 你们的 | 他们的 |
|---|---|---|---|---|---|---|
| 形容词性物主代词 | my | your | his her its | our | your | their |
| 名词性物主代词 | mine | yours | his hers its | ours | yours | theirs |

## 二、物主代词的用法

1. 形容词性物主代词在句子中的成分

常做定语,相当于一个限定词,在词组或句子中,形容词性物主代词不能单独使用,后面必须加名词才能构成一个完整的意思。

*Is this your girlfriend?* 这是你的女朋友吗?

*This is her sister.* 这是她的姐姐。

*May I have your name?* 我能知道你的名字吗?

*They all put on their hats.* 他们都戴上了帽子。

2. 名词性物主代词在句子中的成分

(1) 作表语

*Is the book yours or mine?* 这是你的书还是我的书?

*This book is mine.* 这是我的书。

(2) 作主语

*That is not my car; mine is red.* 那不是我的车,我的车是红色的。

*Yours is on the table.* 你的在桌子上。

(3) 作宾语

*I don't like his works; I like yours.* 我不喜欢他的作品,我喜欢你的。

# D 家庭总动员
o it together

两人一组,一方朗诵下面的中文句子,另一方挑选出合适的翻译。

1. 你的碗这么奇怪,我喜欢我的。
2. 我的小狗叫芭比。
3. 我的勺子在这里。
4. 我的书放在桌上,你的放在哪?
5. 这书是阿美的还是她弟弟的呢?

1. My spoon is here.
2. My book is on the desk. Where is yours?
3. Your bowl is so strange. I like mine.
4. My puppy's name is Barbie.
5. Is this book May's or her brother's?

**Recitation**
经典背诵

**Shirley**：My son Danny is really naughty. For example, he keeps on putting his spoons everywhere. So many times when we are ready for our dinner, Daniel can't find his spoons. Moreover, he plays many tricks everyday. I should give him a lesson sometime, just for his own good.

# 车站 Station

## Goals

**在这个场景中，我们将学到：**

1. 双元音 2 组
2. 表示交通工具的词汇
3. 事物简单比较的句型
4. 反身代词

# Topic 1 交通规则 Traffic Regulations

 **玩转语音**

1. There those thousand thinkers were thinking where did those other three thieves go through.
2. How much oil boil can a gum boil boil if a gum boil can boil oil?

及格时间：10 秒
你的纪录：——秒

及格时间：7 秒
你的纪录：——秒

听 学 看

周一的早晨，妈妈送丹尼尔去上学。在走去公交车站的路上，丹尼尔模仿超人到处乱跑。妈妈随即教育丹尼尔要遵守交通规则。

(*Daniel opens his arms and runs here and there.*)

**Daniel：**Mom, am I like a superman? All I need is a cape.

**Mom：**No, just a super-boy.

**Daniel：**Mom, you always think of me as a child.

**Mom：**Yes, because a real man doesn't need Mom to worry about him so much. He can do things by himself.

**Daniel：**Sure!

**Mom：**Oh, my poor Danny, sure, you are a man. But you know, running like this in street is very dangerous.

**Daniel：**Superman is not afraid of any danger.

**Mom：**Do you remember the rules of road safety?

（丹尼尔张开双臂，到处跑来跑去。）

**丹尼尔：**妈妈，我像超人吗？我只需要个斗篷。

**妈妈：**不，只是个超级男孩。

**丹尼尔：**妈妈，你总是把我当成小孩子。

**妈妈：**当然了，因为一个真正的男人不需要妈妈为他担心那么多。并且他可以自己做许多事。

**丹尼尔：**我也可以啊！

**妈妈：**哦，我的小丹尼尔。你当然是个男人。但是你要知道，在街上这样乱跑是很危险的。

**丹尼尔：**超人不惧怕任何危险。

**妈妈：**你还记得交通规则吗？

Daniel：What?

Mom：Walk the sidewalk and please right-hand side.

Daniel：Don't play on the street or make any noise.

Mom：Yes, so you still remember, ah.

Daniel：Dear Mom, please permit of superman's naughty.

丹尼尔：什么?

妈妈：走人行道并且靠右走。

丹尼尔：不要在路上打闹,也不要大声喧哗。

妈妈：哈,你还记得啊。

丹尼尔：亲爱的妈妈,请允许超人淘气。

### 生词小结

worry about  担心
dangerous  *adj.* 危险的
remember  *vt.* 记得
safety  *n.* 安全
rule  *n.* 规则

sidewalk  *n.* 人行道
permit of  允许
naughty  *adj.* 淘气的
think of ... as  把……当作
be afraid of  害怕

## P语音小结 —— 双元音 2 组
Pronunciation

1. /ɔi/ superboy noise oil boil
   发音小贴士：/ɔi/口型开始部位在/ɔ/与/ɔ:/之间,由上述部位向/i/滑动,同时唇行由圆唇变为扁唇。下颚活动没有/ai/显著。
2. /iə/ here dear real clear
   发音小贴士：/iə/口型由/i/很快滑向/ə/,注意发/i/时用扁平唇,发音过程中,双唇稍稍张开。
   对比练习  /ɔi/ 和/iə/ boy and deer  toy and dear  enjoy and beer  employ and here
3. /ɛə/ there where wear repair
   发音小贴士：/ɛə/口型很快由/ɛ/滑向/ə/,/ɛ/是前元音,发/ɛ/时,开口和舌位高度在/e/与/æ/之间,舌位触下齿龈。
4. /uə/ poor sure pure tour
   发音小贴士：/uə/口型由/u/很快滑向/ə/,注意发/u/时不要把舌抬得过高,以免读成/u:/,发音过程中由稍圆展开。
   对比练习  /ɛə/ 和/uə/ hair and poor  repair and pure  area and sure  there and cure

**Recitation**
经典背诵

Mom：Daniel always thinks of himself as a real man. He knows about the rules of road safety but when it comes to real life, he doesn't really obey them. He always runs around in the street which is very dangerous. I can't stop worrying about him.

# 交通工具
## Vehicles

不一会,妈妈和丹尼尔就走到了车站,他们边等车边谈论起了交通工具。好像丹尼尔还有不少"高见"呢,那么他的"高见"会是什么呢?

**Daniel**：Mom, I've got something to tell you.

**Mom**：So, please!

**Daniel**：Aunt Jane buys a new bike for Tom. He is putting on grand airs.

**Mom**：I bought you a new one last year. Isn't it handsome?

**Daniel**：It is great. But Tom's bike is so much better than mine.

**Mom**：Frankly, he is more well-behaved than you.

( *Daniel murmurs.* )

**Daniel**：Nothing of that sort!

( *Mom feels a little anxious.* )

**Mom**：Why hasn't the bus come yet? Every morning we have to wait for so long.

( *Daniel behaves like an adult.* )

**Daniel**：Mom, it's OK. I will buy a big car one day. It is faster than the bus.

**Mom**：Really? I am looking forward to that. What about the traffic?

**Daniel**：Let me see.

( *Daniel thinks for a while.* )

**Daniel**：Yes. I will buy a plane for you. There is no traffic up there.

丹尼尔：妈妈,我有事情要对你说。

妈妈：说吧!

丹尼尔：简阿姨给汤姆买了一辆新的自行车。他现在可神气呢。

妈妈：我不是去年给你买了一辆吗? 难道它不好吗?

丹尼尔：是很好。但是汤姆的自行车比我的好。

妈妈：说实话,他也比你表现得好啊。

(丹尼尔小声嘀咕。)

丹尼尔：哪有这回事!

(妈妈感到有些着急。)

妈妈：为什么公交车还没有来啊? 每天早晨我们都要等这么久!

(丹尼尔表现得像个大人。)

丹尼尔：妈妈,没关系的。总有一天我会买一辆汽车的。它比公交车可快多了。

妈妈：真的? 我可盼着呢。那交通问题怎么解决呢?

丹尼尔：让我想想。

(丹尼尔考虑了片刻。)

丹尼尔：知道了。我给你买一辆飞机好了。在天上就不会出现交通堵塞了。

## 生词小结

grand     *adj.* 宏伟的, 壮丽的
handsome     *adj.* 英俊的, 漂亮的
frankly     *adv.* 坦白地
well-behaved     *adj.* 很乖的
murmur     *vi.* 嘀咕
anxious     *adj.* 焦急的
behave     *vi.* 行为
adult     *n.* 成年人
look forward to     期待
traffic     *n.* 交通

## 注释

**He is putting on grand airs.** 他神气十足。
**Nothing of the sort!** 哪有这回事! 该句用来表达否定或者不服气的意思。
**Let me see.** 让我想想。在想要表达"让我看看"时, 也可以用这句话。

## 单词扩展 Vocabulary Builder

### 表示交通工具的词汇

| 基础词汇 | 提高词汇 |
| --- | --- |
| taxi 出租车 | sports car 跑车 |
| jeep 吉普车 | truck 卡车 |
| ship 船 | fire engine 消防车 |
| boat 小船 | ambulance 救护车 |
| plane 飞机 | canoe 独木舟 |
| train 火车 | jet plane 喷气式飞机 |
| bus 公交车 | helicopter 直升机 |
| bike 自行车 | ferry 渡船 |

## 家庭总动员
### Do it together

两人一组, 一方随机大声读出上面词汇的英文和中文, 另一方将该词汇填入下面的句子, 大声朗读出来, 并用中文给出一个理由。

I want to own a (             ).

【例】家长读 bike 自行车
宝贝读 I want to own a bike. 我骑上去很神气!

### Recitation 经典背诵

Daniel: I like bikes. I've got one but I want a new one because my friend Tom's bike is so much better than mine. The traffic here is bad so it's really convenient to go around on a bike rather than wasting time stuck in traffic. Maybe I should get a car or even a plane for my Mom in the future. I don't want her to wait for the bus anymore.

打的
Taxi

公交车迟迟没有来,眼看时间一分一秒地过去,妈妈最终决定乘坐出租车。在出租车上,妈妈和司机聊了些什么呢?

**Mom**：Joy Chain elementary school, please.

**Taxi driver**：Will do.

**Mom**：How frustrating! The bus is still not coming.

**Taxi driver**：Ma'am, take your kid to school?

**Mom**：Yes. I am in a hurry. Please take a shortcut.

**Taxi driver**：No problem. Don't worry, the taxi is faster than the bus.

**Mom**：The traffic is terrible on Monday morning. It takes us almost 1 hour to get to school.

**Taxi driver**：My son is the same. But he always makes an early start in the morning, and enjoys listening to the English programme "Let's talk in English" on the way.

**Mom**：That's wonderful. He is killing two birds with one stone.

**Mom**：Sir, please turn right at the next corner. And stop at the taxi stand.

**Taxi driver**：OK!

**Mom**：What is the fare?

**Taxi driver**：It's 14. 5 yuan.

(*Mother gives 15 yuan to the taxi driver.*)

**Mom**：Keep the change!

**Taxi driver**：Thanks, Ma'am.

**妈妈**：麻烦去卓成小学。

**出租车司机**：好的。

**妈妈**：真让人烦躁! 公交车到现在都还没到。

**出租车司机**：女士,您是送孩子上学吧?

**妈妈**：是啊,我赶时间。请走近路吧。

**出租车司机**：没问题,别担心,出租车可比公交车快多了。

**妈妈**：周一早晨,交通总是很糟糕。到学校要花近一个小时的时间呢。

**出租车司机**：我儿子也是这样的。但他早晨总会早些出发,在路上他喜欢听"让我们一起来学英语"这个英语节目。

**妈妈**：这太好了。他还真是一箭双雕啊。

**妈妈**：师傅,请在下一个路口右转。停在出租车站牌那边好了。

**出租车司机**：好的!

**妈妈**：多少钱?

**出租车司机**：十四块五。

(妈妈给师傅十五块钱。)

**妈妈**：不用找了!

**出租车司机**：那谢谢您了。

## 生词小结

frustrating  *adj.* 令人沮丧的

kid  *n.* 孩子

be in a hurry  赶时间

shortcut  *n.* 近路，捷径

terrible  *adj.* 严重的

programme  *n.* 节目

fare  *n.* 费用

change  *n.* 零钱

## 注释

**He is killing two birds with one stone.** "一箭双雕。"或者也可以翻译为"一石二鸟"。多用来形容用更少的力气，一次完成两件或多件事情。

**Keep the change!** "不用找零了。"

# **F**unctional structure 功能性句型扩展 —— 事物简单比较的句型

请朗读以下句型，家长和孩子交替进行。

1. 同级比较

（1）as...as 句型（和……一样）

*She is still as busy as a bee.* 她仍十分忙碌。（和蜜蜂一样忙）

*He is as greedy as a wolf.* 他贪得无厌。（和狼一样贪婪）

*Our life is as sweet as honey.* 我们的生活像蜜一样甜。

（2）not as ...as 或者 not so...as 句型（不同于……）

*The food isn't as good as yesterday.* 今天的饭菜没有昨天的好。

*It isn't so cold as yesterday.* 今天没有昨天冷。

2. 比较级句型

（1）more than 句型

*Dancing is more interesting than singing.* 跳舞比唱歌要有趣。

（2）the more...the more 句型

*The more you learn, the more you know.* 学得越多，知道得也就越多。

3. 最高级句型

*Yellow is the most beautiful color.* 黄色是最漂亮的颜色。

*Father is the tallest in our family.* 爸爸是我们家最高的人。

*Where is the nearest bus-stop?* 最近的公共汽车站在哪？

**Recitation** 经典背诵

**Taxi driver**：Hello, I am a taxi driver. I enjoy talking with my passengers. Every morning I take my son to school. And he enjoys listening to the English programme on the way. One of my passengers once said my son is very clever to kill two birds with one stone.

# Topic4 路牌广告
## Advertisements

在出租车停靠的站点处，妈妈发现广告牌上贴着一张钢琴辅导班的广告宣传，随即抄下了相关内容。丹尼尔在一旁露出了不悦的神情，这是为什么呢？

( *Daniel speaks to himself.* )

**Daniel**：That's great! We made 20 minutes earlier.

**Mom**：Good thing, we took a taxi.

**Daniel**：Mom, you are the best!

**Mom**：Hey, look there. It is an advertisement of the piano training class on the billboard. The place is not far from our home.

**Daniel**：Mom, come on. What are you thinking about?

**Mom**：Your sister is in high school now; no one plays the piano at home.

**Daniel**：Don't tell me you want me to do that?

**Mom**：Why? Why not! The piano is right there.

**Daniel**：But I don't like playing the piano. And the homework keeps me busy enough.

**Mom**：Anyway, I will have a look at the piano class after work by myself.

**Daniel**：How depressed!

（丹尼尔自言自语。）

**丹尼尔**：太好了！我们早到了20分钟。

**妈妈**：是啊，幸好我们搭了出租车。

**丹尼尔**：妈妈，你最棒了！

**妈妈**：喂，看那里。广告牌上有个钢琴培训班的广告。那个地方离我们家不远。

**丹尼尔**：妈妈，求你了。你又在想什么呢？

**妈妈**：你姐姐现在读高中了，家里的钢琴没人弹了。

**丹尼尔**：不要告诉我你想让我弹。

**妈妈**：为什么不呢？钢琴就摆在那里呢。

**丹尼尔**：但是我不喜欢弹钢琴。并且家庭作业已经够我忙了。

**妈妈**：不管怎样，下班后，我会自己先去看一下那个钢琴培训班。

**丹尼尔**：真郁闷。

---

### 生词小结

| | |
|---|---|
| **speak to oneself** 自言自语 | **be far from** 远离 |
| **advertisement** *n.* 广告 | **think about** 考虑 |
| **piano** *n.* 钢琴 | **play the piano** 弹钢琴 |
| **training** *n.* 训练 | **busy** *adj.* 忙碌的 |
| **billboard** *n.* 广告牌 | **depressed** *adj.* 沮丧的 |

---

## G语法小结 —— 反身代词
rammer

| 单数 | myself<br>我自己 | yourself<br>你自己 | himself / herself / itself<br>他/她/它自己 |
| --- | --- | --- | --- |
| 复数 | ourselves<br>我们自己 | yourselves<br>你们自己 | themselves<br>他们自己 |

另外 oneself 也是反身代词,它表示某人自己。

1. 反身代词在句子中主要作宾语

*Enjoy yourselves!* 玩得开心!

*Let me introduce myself.* 让我来自我介绍一下。

*She speaks to herself.* 她自言自语。

*They teach themselves.* 他们自学。

2. 反身代词还可以用在一些固定短语中

(1) by oneself 独自一人,自己(没别人帮助)

*I can do it by myself.* 我能自己做。

*He lives by himself.* 他一个人住。

(2) for oneself 替自己,为自己

*She cooks for herself.* 她自己做饭。

*I can buy food for myself.* 我能为自己买食物。

*You can decide for yourself.* 你可以自己做决定。

## D家庭总动员
o it together

两人一组,一方朗诵下面的中文句子,另一方挑选出合适的翻译。

1. 他只考虑他自己。
2. 我过去总把自己当作一个大人。
3. 丹尼尔自言自语。
4. 请注意你自己的行为!
5. 丹尼尔可以自己弹钢琴吗?

1. Please behave yourself!
2. Can Daniel play the piano by himself?
3. Daniel speaks to himself.
4. He only thinks about himself.
5. I always thought of myself as an adult.

R*ecitation*
经典诵

Daniel:Mom always wants me to take different training classes. These days she says I should learn to play the piano. That's really a disaster for me. The homework already keeps me busy enough. My poor little spare time! I am just a little boy!

## Act 1

日常生活场景·Daily Life

# 公交车 Bus

## Goals

**在这个场景中,我们将学到:**

1. 半元音 1 组
2. 大城市名称的单词
3. 比较句型练习
4. 指示代词

## Topic 1 公交车路线
### Bus Route

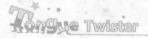 **玩转语音**

1. I wish to wish the wish you wish to wish, but if you wish the wish the witch wishes, I won't wish the wish you wish to wish.

2. Jenny and Jimmy went to Jamaica and Germany in January, but Joan and John went to Jordan and Japan in June and July.

及格时间: 13 秒
你的纪录: —— 秒

及格时间: 13 秒
你的纪录: —— 秒

今天是周末,爸爸带着丹尼尔去西单图书大厦购买图书,但是走到了公交车站牌处却忘记了具体的路线,那么最后他是怎么解决这个问题的呢?

**Daniel**: Dad, do you know which bus we should take?

**Benjamin**: Of course, er, let me check the bus schedule first.

**Daniel**: Be quick, please!

**Benjamin**: Why can't I find the bus your mother told me yesterday?

**Daniel**: Mom has told you about the direction 3 times yesterday.

**Dad**: But I was watching *American Idol* at that time.

**Daniel**: We need to ask someone.

**丹尼尔**: 你知道我们坐哪路车吗?

**本杰明**: 当然啊,恩,让我先看一下公车牌。

**丹尼尔**: 快点吧!

**本杰明**: 为什么我没有看见你妈妈昨天跟我说的那路公车呢?

**丹尼尔**: 妈妈昨天跟你说了三次公交路线。

**爸爸**: 但是那个时候我在看《美国偶像》啊。

**丹尼尔**: 我们要问问其他的人。

(*There comes Bus* 29)

**B**enjamin：Excuse me? Does this bus go to Xi-dan Book Building?

**C**onductor：No, it doesn't. You need to take Bus 52.

**B**enjamin：Do I have to change to some other bus on the way?

**C**onductor：No.

**B**enjamin：I see, thanks. Oops! The Bus 52 is coming. Daniel, come on. Let's go.

（来了一辆29路车）

**本杰明**：你好,请问一下这车到西单图书大厦吗?

**售票员**：不到。你应该乘52路。

**本杰明**：那我还需要转车吗?

**售票员**：不需要。

**本杰明**：我知道了,谢谢。啊,52路来了,丹尼尔,快,我们走。

---

生词小结

| take | *vt.* 拿,取 | ask | *vt.* 问,要求 |
| schedule | *n.* 时间表,一览表 | excuse | *vt.* 原谅 |
| quick | *adj.* 快的,迅速的 | change | *vt.* 改变 |

---

## **P**ronunciation 语音小结 —— 半元音 I 组

**1.** /w/ which we why when

发音小贴士:舌后部向软腭抬起,双唇收得圆而小,并向前突出,音一经发出就立即向后面的元音滑动,声带振动。

**2.** /j/ yesterday yet yes yellow

发音小贴士:舌前部尽量向硬腭抬起,双唇向两边伸展成扁平形。该音一经发出立刻向后面元音滑动,声带振动。

**特别提示**:在美音辅音系统中比英音多了个清辅音/hw/,和浊辅音/w/相对,有不少美国人把 wh 开头的单词念成/hw/,如 what/hwat/,why/hwai/

对比练习　/w/和/j/ west and your　wet and you　wise and young　water and yard

---

Dad：I have no sense of directions at all. So many times when I go out to some place by bus I would have to ask the conductor how to get there. Thanks to them that they are always so helpful. But I don't know how they can remember so many places?

日常生活场景·Daily Life

 人口
**Population**

听 学
读 看

爸爸和丹尼尔上了车,丹尼尔听见旁边的两位乘客在谈论着公交公司的事情,他们具体在谈论些什么呢? 一起来看看吧。

| | |
|---|---|
| **Man**: Hey, do you know the bus company network system crashed? | **男**:嗨,你知道公交公司网络瘫痪这件事吗? |
| **Woman**: I heard about it several days ago! | **女**:我几天前就听说了。 |
| **Man**: That is unbelievable! | **男**:那太让人难以置信了! |
| **Daniel**: Daddy, can you tell me what they are talking about? | **丹尼尔**:爸爸,你能告诉我他们在谈论的是什么吗? |
| **Benjamin**: They are talking about the network of the bus company. | **本杰明**:他们在说公交公司网络的问题。 |
| **Daniel**: Why is their network not working? | **丹尼尔**:那为什么他们的网络不能够正常运行呢? |
| **Benjamin**: Because of the IC cards. | **本杰明**:因为 IC 卡的问题。 |
| **Daniel**: The IC card? | **丹尼尔**:IC 卡吗? |
| **Benjamin**: Yes, Beijing is a big city and there are about 7,000,000 people using IC cards on buses. | **本杰明**:对啊,北京是个大城市,总共有7,000,000 人用公交 IC 卡。 |
| **Daniel**: And? | **丹尼尔**:然后呢? |
| **Benjamin**: All the people were checking the balance of their cards on the Internet at the same time, that's why the system crashed. | **本杰明**:所有的人都去网上查看他们卡里的余额,所以就产生了网络问题。 |
| **Daniel**: Oh, that is horrible! | **丹尼尔**:噢,那太可怕了! |

**生词小结**

**crash**  *n.* 崩溃
**network**  *n.* 网络
**system**  *n.* 系统,体系
**unbelievable**  *adj.* 令人难以置信的

**check**  *vt.* 查询
**balance**  *n.* 余额
**horrible**  *adj.* 可怕的

## 单词扩展 Vocabulary Builder

### 大城市名称的单词

| 基础词汇 | 提高词汇 |
| --- | --- |
| New York 纽约 | Moscow 莫斯科 |
| Sydney 悉尼 | London 伦敦 |
| Toronto 多伦多 | Venice 威尼斯 |
| Rome 罗马 | Detroit 底特律 |
| Washington 华盛顿 | Seoul 首尔 |
| Tokyo 东京 | Athens 雅典 |
| Paris 巴黎 | Los Angeles 洛杉矶 |
| Cairo 开罗 | Berlin 柏林 |

## D家庭总动员
o it together

两人一组，一方随机大声读出上面词汇的英文和中文，另一方用该词汇填入下面的句子，大声朗读并用中文说出该词汇所代表的城市的标志性建筑或者是事物。

( ) is a big city.

【例】家长读 New York 纽约

孩子读 New York is a big city. 纽约的标志性事物是自由女神像。

### Recitation 经典背诵

Daniel: People talk about the network system of the bus company a lot these days. I had no idea why until my father told me that there are lots of people using IC cards on buses, and when they get back home they would check their balance at the same time, then the system crashed, which is a big problem.

# Topic3 IC 卡和售票
## IC Cards and Tickets

听 学 读 看

售票员走过来卖票，本杰明和丹尼尔用的是现金而不是公交 IC 卡，所以要贵几毛钱。这下他们会有什么新的想法呢？一起来看看吧！

**Benjamin:** Am I in the right direction to the Xidan Book Building?

**Conductor:** Yes, you are right.

**Benjamin:** How much is the fare?

**Conductor:** 2 yuan.

**Daniel:** Excuse me, How about IC card? What's the difference?

**Conductor:** Pay by IC card is cheaper than cash.

**Daniel:** How much cheaper?

**Conductor:** 6 or 8 jiao, that depends.

**Daniel:** Can I apply for an IC card?

**Conductor:** Of course, you can ask your parents to apply for a student IC card for you.

**Daniel:** OK, thanks. Daddy, why don't we just get an IC card, it saves much money.

**Benjamin:** Tell your Mom if you want.

**本杰明：**这是去西单图书大厦的车吗？

**售票员：**对，是的。

**本杰明：**多少钱一张票？

**售票员：**2 元。

**丹尼尔：**请问，用 IC 卡是多少钱呢？有什么区别吗？

**售票员：**用 IC 卡比现金便宜些。

**丹尼尔：**便宜多少呢？

**售票员：**便宜6到8角，视情况而定。

**丹尼尔：**那么我能办一张 IC 卡吗？

**售票员：**当然可以啦，你可以叫你的父母给你办一张学生公交 IC 卡。

**丹尼尔：**我知道了，谢谢！爸爸，为什么我们不办一张 IC 卡呢，很省钱的。

**本杰明：**你想要的话就去告诉你妈妈。

### 生词小结

**right** *adj.* 正确的
**direction** *n.* 方向，指示
**fare** *n.* 费用
**card** *n.* 卡
**difference** *n.* 差异，不同

**cheap** *adj.* 便宜的
**cash** *n.* 现金
**depend** *vt.* 依靠
**save** *vt.* 节省，节约

# Scene **6**

公交车 · Bus

## S情景练习 Scene practice —— 比较句型练习

仔细阅读下面五个场景,两人一组,使用比较句型(见39页),用一用,练一练。

1. If you were May, you prefer dancing to singing, what would you say?
2. If you were Shirley, your favorite color is yellow, what would you say?
3. If you were Daniel, father and mother, who do you like better?
4. If you were Daniel, you think your father is the tallest in your family, what would you say?
5. Benjamin wants to express he is very very busy, if you were Benjamin, what would you say?

**Conductor:** I am a conductor of bus 52. The IC card is getting more and more popular these days. I think that's not only because it's convenient to use but also it's cheap. That's an advantage the modern life offers.

## Topic4 下错站
### Get off at the Wrong Stop

丹尼尔和爸爸下车了,但是他们却没有看见图书大厦,仔细一看标志,原来是下错了站,那他们最后是怎么去的图书大厦的呢?

**Daniel**：Dad, where is the Book Building?

**Dad**：I'm looking. Can you still remember what the conductor said?

**Daniel**：She said that when we get off at the bus, the Book Building is right by the bus stop.

**Dad**：But I don't see it.

**Daniel**：Oh, Dad, look at the sign, please!

**Dad**：Oh, my god! We get off at the wrong stop. I'm so sorry, honey.

**Daniel**：OK, Dad, it happens.

**Ben**：It's my fault. So what can we do now? Walk?

**Daniel**：Come on, I'm too tired!

**Dad**：OK, you promise don't tell your mother about it, we'll take a taxi.

**Daniel**：Sure, I promise.

**Dad**：If you keep your promise, I will also let you watch *Ultraman* this evening.

**丹尼尔**：爸爸,图书大厦在哪里呢?

**爸爸**：我在找啊。你还记得售票员是怎么说的吗?

**丹尼尔**：她说我们下车之后,图书大厦就在车站旁边啊。

**爸爸**：但是我没有看见啊。

**丹尼尔**：噢,爸爸,看那个标志。

**爸爸**：噢,天哪,我们下错站了。对不起,宝贝。

**丹尼尔**：算了,爸爸,常有的事。

**爸爸**：都是我的错。那我们现在怎么办呢? 走过去吗?

**丹尼尔**：啊,我好累啊!

**爸爸**：好,如果你答应我不将这件事告诉你妈妈,我们就坐的士过去。

**丹尼尔**：当然,我向你保证。

**爸爸**：你要是遵守你的诺言,今天晚上我就让你看《奥特曼》。

**生词小结**

| | | | |
|---|---|---|---|
| conductor | *n.* 售票员 | happen | *vi.* 发生 |
| get off | 下车 | fault | *n.* 错误,过失 |
| sign | *n.* 记号,标志 | promise | *vi.* 承诺,许诺 |
| wrong | *adj.* 错误的 | | |

## G 语法小结
### rammer —— 指示代词

指示代词包括 this 这个,that 那个,these 这些,those 那些。其中 this,these 分别表示这个、这些,指近处的人或物。that 和 those 分别表示那个、那些,指离说话人较远处的人或物。

1. 指示代词在句中的成分

(1) 作主语

*Tommy, this is my sister May.*　汤姆,这是我的姐姐阿美。

*That is my little dog, Barbie.*　那是我的小狗,芭比。

*Those are my parents.*　那是我父母。

*What are these?*　这些是什么?

*Who is this?*　(电话用语)你是哪位?

*This is May.*　我是阿美。

(2) 作宾语

*Could you give me that?*　能给我那个吗?

*Do not you know this?*　你不知道这个吗?

(3) 作定语

*This house is very beautiful.*　这个房子非常漂亮。

*That dog is mine.*　那只狗是我的。

*Are you going out this evening?*　你今天晚上出去吗?

2. 指示代词 that 在口语中常用短语

(1) that is( to say)　这/那就是说

*That's to say, you love me?*　那就是说,你爱我?

(2) that's all　只是,就这样

*Please don't do it again, that's all.*　以后别再这么做了,就这些。

*That's all.*　就这么多。/ 就这样。

## D 家庭总动员
### o it together

**两人一组,一方朗诵下面的中文句子,另一方挑选出合适的翻译。**

1. 那是 52 路车。
2. 那不是西单图书大厦。
3. 那是的士。
4. 那是 IC 卡。
5. 那是公交公司的问题。

1. That is the taxi.
2. That is IC card.
3. That is the problem of the Bus Company.
4. That is not Xidan Book Building.
5. That is Bus 52.

### Recitation
经典背诵

Daniel：My father is really careless. Sometimes he can't even get off the bus at the right stop. But when that happens, he would always asks me to keep a secret from Mom then take a taxi, instead. So I don't think my Mom knows what kind of person she is married to.

SCENE ⑦

# 逛街 Street

## Goals

**在这个场景中,我们将学到:**

1. 爆破辅音 3 组
2. 表示日用品的单词
3. 表达问路和指路的句型
4. 不定冠词和定冠词

 公共环境
**Public Environment**

### Tongue Twister 玩转语音

1. A skunk sat on a stump. The skunk thought the stump stunk, and the stump thought the skunk stunk.
2. Picky people pick Peter Pan Peanut Butter. Peter Pan Peanut is the peanut picky people pick.

及格时间:15 秒
你的纪录:——秒

及格时间:13 秒
你的纪录:——秒

听 学 看

天气很好,妈妈让阿美带着丹尼尔去街上走走,缓解学习压力。走在路上的时候,丹尼尔随口吐口香糖,这引起了阿美的强烈不满,随即教育弟弟要维护公共卫生。

(*Daniel casually spits the gum. May feels angry.*)

**May:** Daniel, you can't spit the gum everywhere.

**Daniel:** Come on, just a little piece.

**May:** Do you know how many people chew gum everyday?

**Daniel:** I have no idea.

**May:** Just in Beijing, people consume 300,000 pieces of gum every day.

**Daniel:** That's amazing.

**May:** If all the people spit out the gum like you, the whole world would become a big trash can.

**Daniel:** Come on, you are making too big deal out of this.

(丹尼尔随地乱吐口香糖。阿美感到很生气。)

**阿美:** 丹尼尔,你不可以随处乱吐口香糖。

**丹尼尔:** 哎呀,只是一小块。

**阿美:** 你知道每天有多少人嚼口香糖吗?

**丹尼尔:** 不知道。

**阿美:** 仅仅是在北京,每天人们要吃掉300,000 块口香糖。

**丹尼尔:** 真令人吃惊!

**阿美:** 如果所有人都像你一样随地乱吐口香糖,整个世界将变成一个大垃圾箱。

**丹尼尔:** 你说得也太夸大其辞了吧。

May：I just want to remind you to behave yourself.

Daniel：OK, dear sister, I see. This kind of thing will not happen again.

May：In order to meet the Olympics, we should pay attention to the protection of public environment.

Daniel：OK, Mom!

May：Hey, don't call me that.

阿美:我只是想提醒你要规矩些。

丹尼尔:好的,亲爱的姐姐,我知道了。再也不会发生这种事了。

阿美:为了迎接奥运会,我们都应该注意维护公共环境。

丹尼尔:好的,老太婆!

阿美:嘿,不准这么叫我。

## 生词小结

**casually**   *adv.* 随意地
**spit**   *vt.* 吐
**chew**   *vt.* 咀嚼
**consume**   *vt.* 消耗
**amazing**   *adj.* 令人吃惊的
**trash**   *n.* 垃圾
**remind**   *vt.* 提醒
**happen**   *vi.* 发生
**protection**   *n.* 保护
**public**   *adj.* 公共的
**environment**   *n.* 环境

## 注释

**You are making too big deal out of this.** 你也太夸大其辞了。这个句子直译为"你从这里制造了太大的事情出来",言下之意是你说得也太夸张了,一点小事也被你夸大了。
**OK, Mom!** 在这里 Mom 并不是妈妈的意思。一般美国人在感叹一个人啰嗦的时候,会说 OK, Mom!
**behave yourself** 行为规矩些
**pay attention to** 注意

## P 语音小结 Pronunciation —— 爆破辅音 3 组

1. /p/和/b/ piece people become big

   **发音小贴士:**双唇紧闭,然后突然张开,使气流冲出口腔发出爆破音

   /p/是清辅音,要送气,声带不振动

   /b/是浊辅音,发音时不送气,但声带振动

   对比练习  /p/和/b/ pea and bee   pack and back   path and bath   pig and big

2. /t/和/d/ spit little remaind every day

   **发音小贴士:**舌尖紧贴上齿龈,形成阻碍,然后突然下降,气流冲出口腔发音

   /t/是清辅音,要送气,声带不振动

   /d/是浊辅音,不送气,声带要振动

   对比练习  /t/和/d/ tip and dip   time and dime   bright and bride   seat and seed

3. /k/和/g/ can speak gum again

   **发音小贴士:**舌后部隆起,紧贴软腭形成阻碍,然后突然离开,气流冲出口腔发音

   /k/是清辅音,要送气,但声带不振动

   /g/是浊辅音,不送气,但是声带振动

   对比练习  /k/和/g/ back and bag   pick and pig   lack and lag   leak and league

## Recitation 经典背诵

May：Daniel casually spits the gum around which makes me angry. Only in Beijing, people consume 300,000 pieces of gum every day. If all the people spit out the gum like Daniel does, the city would become a big trash can. The 2008 Beijing Olympics is coming soon, we should pay more attention to the protection of public environment.

# Topic 2 寻物
## Lost and Found

姐弟二人碰见一个人在四处找他丢失的钥匙串,他们对这个陌生人伸出了援助之手,并帮助他找到了钥匙串。

**Stranger**: Excuse me, did you see a set of keys?

**May**: What kind of keys?

**Stranger**: Five keys and a small FooWa ornament.

**May**: What a shame! I didn't see them.

**Stranger**: Well, can you help me look for it? That's my first time here.

**May**: Sure. It's my pleasure. I'd like to help you look for the missing keys.

**Stranger**: It's very kind of you.

**May**: It's not a big deal.

*(After a few minutes, May finds the lost keys.)*

**May**: Hey, I found them.

**Stranger**: Oh, thank God! I don't know how to thank you, guys.

**May**: You're welcome.

**Stranger**: Can I leave my number? I'd like to keep you in touch.

**May**: Sure.

**Stranger**: 15644332211. Frank, and I'm a physician. Nice to meet you.

**May**: Well, My name is May. From Joy Chain High School. Nice to meet you, too!

**Stranger**: I really like to see you again. But only out of work.

陌生人:你好,你看到一串钥匙了吗?

阿美:什么样的钥匙?

陌生人:五个钥匙和一个福娃的饰物。

阿美:真可惜! 我没有看见。

陌生人:好的,你能帮我找找吗? 我第一次来这里。

阿美:好的,我很乐意帮你找丢失的钥匙。

陌生人:你人真好。

阿美:没什么。

(几分钟后,阿美找到了丢失的钥匙。)

阿美:嗨,我找到了。

陌生人:谢天谢地! 我都不知该怎么谢你才好。

阿美:不客气。

陌生人:我能给你留个号码吗? 我希望能和你保持联系。

阿美:可以啊。

陌生人:15644332211。弗兰克,我是名医生。很高兴认识你。

阿美:你好,我叫阿美。是卓成高中的学生。我也很高兴认识你!

陌生人:我真的期待再次见到你。不过希望不是在医院哦。

## 生词小结

set    *n.* 串
key    *n.* 钥匙
ornament    *n.* 装饰物
look for    寻找
missing    *adj.* 不见的, 缺少的
keep in touch with    保持联系
physician    *n.* 医师
out of work    工作之外

## 注释

**That's my first time here** 从这个句子的字面看是"这是我第一次来这里", 言下之意是"我对这里不熟。"

**It's not a big deal.** "没有什么大不了。"big deal 是指"大事, 重要的事", 这句话可以用来表达不客气。如"Thank you for all the trouble", 就可以用 It's not a big deal 回答。

**But only out of work.** 这句话是弗兰克和阿美开的一个小小的玩笑。Frank 希望还有机会和阿美再次见面, 可身为一名医生, 他希望不要在工作场所和阿美见面, 那很可能意味着阿美生病了。

# 单词扩展 Vocabulary Builder

### 表示日用品的单词

| 基础词汇 | 提高词汇 |
| --- | --- |
| key 钥匙 | tooth brush 牙刷 |
| comb 梳子 | tooth paste 牙膏 |
| soap 肥皂 | razor 剃须刀 |
| towel 毛巾 | slipper 拖鞋 |
| purse 钱包 | handbag 手提包 |
| hammer 锤子 | umbrella 雨伞 |
| raincoat 雨衣 | rain cape 雨披 |
| toilet paper 卫生纸 | shampoo 洗发水 |

# 家庭总动员
## Do it together

两人一组, 一方随机大声读出上面词汇的英文和中文, 另一方用该词汇填入下面的句子, 大声朗读出来, 并用中文给出一个理由。

**Did you see my (　　　　　　　　　　)?**

【例】家长读 key 钥匙
宝贝读 Did you see my key? 我要用钥匙开门。

**Recitation** 经典背诵

**Stranger**：Hi, my name is Frank. I am a physician. This is my first time in Beijing. I lost a set of keys. There are five keys and a small FooWa ornament on it. A girl, May, helped me find them. It's very kind of her. I gave my number to her because I hoped to see her again.

# Topic 3 问路
## Ask for Directions

听 学 看

在帮弗兰克找到钥匙串后,姐弟俩又碰见了一个迷路的外国人。他想去逛琉璃厂,姐姐热情地给他指路。

**Foreigner:** Excuse me, I'm lost. Can you show me where I am in this map?

( *He holds a map in his hand.* )

**May:** Er, let me see. Oh, look, you're right here. Pretty close to the Olympic Park.

**Foreigner:** That's great! It's not my day. I just have very bad sense of direction.

**May:** Is this your first time here? Where are you going?

**Foreigner:** I am supposed to go to Liu lichang.

**May:** Oh, there are many Chinese antique stores. They get paintings, too. Do you get interested in them?

**Foreigner:** Yes. Yes. Can you tell me how to get there?

**May:** Wow, it is quite far away from here. I'm afraid you're gonna have to take Bus No. 713.

**Foreigner:** Where is the nearest bus-stop?

**May:** Go straight ahead and turn right on the second intersection. You can't miss it.

**Foreigner:** Thanks a lot.

**May:** You are welcome.

**外国人:** 你好,我迷路了。你能告诉我我现在处于地图上的哪个位置吗?

(他手里拿着一张地图。)

**阿美:** 呃,让我看看。哦,看,你就在这里。离奥运公园很近。

**外国人:** 真是糟糕!今天真不顺。我的方向感的确很差。

**阿美:** 这是你第一次到这里吧?你想去哪里?

**外国人:** 我想去琉璃厂。

**阿美:** 哦,那里有很多中国古董店,也有中国画。你对那些感兴趣吗?

**外国人:** 是的,是的。你能告诉我怎么去那里吗?

**阿美:** 哇,那离这里很远呢。恐怕你得乘公交713路才能到。

**外国人:** 最近的公共汽车站在哪?

**阿美:** 直走,在第二个路口处右转。你不会错过的。

**外国人:** 非常感谢。

**阿美:** 不客气。

### 生词小结

**lost** *adj.* 迷失的
**close to** 离……很近
**sense** *n.* 感觉
**suppose to** 想做

### 注释

**That's great!** 这是句反语。表面上看是说"太好了",实际则是在表达对今天坏运气的一种抱怨和不满。

**It's not my day.** 这句话直译为"这不是我

antique　*n.* 古董
get interested in　对……感兴趣
far away from　离……很远
straight　*adj.* 直的　*adv.* 一直，笔直地
intersection　*n.* 十字路口

的日子"，言下之意今天诸事不顺，一连串的坏事情发生在自己身上，喝口凉水都塞牙，真是郁闷的一天。

gonna　等同于 going to

## F功能性句型扩展 —— 表达问路和指路的句型

**请朗读以下句型，家长和孩子交替进行。**

### 1. 问路句型

Can you tell me the way to Liu Lichang, please? 能告诉我去琉璃厂怎么走吗？

Excuse me, could you tell me how to get to the Olympic park? 请问，去奥林匹克公园怎么走？

How do I get to the station? 去车站怎么走？

Excuse me, where is the nearest bus stop? 请问，最近的公共汽车站在哪儿？

Excuse me, where can I find the library? 请问，怎么去图书馆？

Do you know where the food market is, please? 你知道菜场在哪吗？

### 2. 指路句型

Go straight ahead and turn right at the second traffic lights. 一直往前走，在第二个红绿灯处右转。

Take the first turning on the left. 在第一个拐弯处左转。

Take the second turning right. 在第二个拐弯处右转。

Turn right at the crossroads. 在十字路口右转。

Keep straight on until you get to the bus stop. 一直走，走到公汽站。

I am sorry I can't. I'm a stranger here myself. 对不起，我也不知道如何走。我对这里不熟。

**Recitation** 经典背诵

Foreigner: Hi, I am a foreigner. I've always had a bad sense of direction especially when I travel in a foreign country. One time I planned to go to Liu Lichang where there are many Chinese antique stores. But I got lost and just went to some other place in the middle of nowhere instead. Luckily, with a girl's help I got to the right place later. What a wonderful girl!

Topic 4 偶遇
Meeting with Someone

阿美突然在街上遇见了自己多年没有见面的小学同学,两个人随即在路边寒暄了几句。

**May:** Oh, my God, Wendy, is that you?

**Wendy:** Oh, hi, May. Long time no see.

**May:** Yes, we haven't seen each other since elementary school. I miss you so much.

**Wendy:** Yeah. So what's new?

**May:** Nothing much except I've got in a very exciting school.

**Wendy:** Really? What school is that?

**May:** Joy Chain High School. How about you?

**Wendy:** Oh, me? I am at the Affiliated High School of Peking University.

**May:** Wow, you are always so great!

**Wendy:** Say, what time is it?

**May:** 4:00 p. m. Why?

**Wendy:** Oh, God! I've got to run. I've got an appointment with my foreign teacher at 4:30. She helps me with my oral English.

**May:** That's great. So where are you going?

**Wendy:** The Olympic Park. You can go with me if you like. Where is the nearest stop for Bus No. 713?

**May:** Listen honey. Turn left at the first intersection and go straight to the end of the road.

阿美:哦,天哪,温迪,是你吗?

温迪:哦,嗨,阿美。好久不见。

阿美:是啊,小学毕业后我们就一直没有再见面。我很想念你。

温迪:我也是。你最近怎样?

阿美:也没什么,不过我进了所不错的学校。

温迪:真的吗? 是什么学校?

阿美:卓成高中。你呢?

温迪:哦,我吗? 我现在在北大附中读书。

阿美:哇,你总是这么棒!

温迪:对了,现在几点了?

阿美:四点了。怎么了?

温迪:天哪! 我得走了。我约了外教四点半见面。她帮我练英语口语。

阿美:太好了。那么你要去哪里?

温迪:奥林匹克公园。如果你愿意,可以和我一起去。最近的有公共汽车713 的公交站在哪?

阿美:听着。在第一个路口往左拐,一直走到路的尽头就是了。

---

**生词小结**

**elementary** *adj.* 初步的,基本的
**study** *vt.* 学习
**affiliated** *adj.* 附属的
**university** *n.* 大学
**appointment** *n.* 约定
**foreign** *adj.* 外国的,外国人的
**help with** 帮助
**oral** *adj.* 口头的

**注释**

**Long time no see.** 好久不见。

**So what's new?** 这句话多用于两个朋友见面互相询问彼此近况。最近有什么新情况,或者最近过得怎么样之类的。

**Nothing much except I've got in a very exciting school.** Nothing much 是指 Nothing much new,没有什么新的动向。

# G语法小结
## rammer —— 不定冠词和定冠词

### 1. 不定冠词 a 和 an

不定冠词 a 和 an 表示"一(个,只,支,本……)",放于可数名词单数前表示"泛指",也可表示某人或某物属于某一种类。

a 限用于读音为辅音开头的单数可数名词之前。如:a book(一本书),a bike(一辆自行车)等。an 限用于元音读音(a, o, e, i, u)开头的单数可数名词之前。如:an apple(一个苹果),an orange(一个橘子),an egg(一个鸡蛋)。如果该名词前有个修饰语,则以该修饰语的第一个字母读音是辅音还是元音而定。如:

a desk 一张课桌——an old desk 一张旧课桌——a big desk 一张大课桌

an apple 一个苹果——a nice apple 一个好吃的苹果——a green apple 一个青苹果

a car 一辆车——a Chinese car 一辆中国造的车——an English car 一辆英国造的车

### 2. 定冠词 the

(1) 定冠词 the 是特指,表示"这个,那个"

*I have two pens. The red one is more expensive than the blue one.*

我有两支钢笔。红色的那支比蓝色的那支贵。

(2) 定冠词的用法

① 乐器前加 the。

*play the piano* 弹钢琴   *play the violin* 拉小提琴

② 宇宙独一无二的东西前加 the。

*The earth moves around the sun.* 地球绕着太阳转。

③ 表示"方向"时加 the。

*the north* 北方   *the south* 南方   *the east* 东方   *the west* 西方

④ 在固定短语中加 the。

*in the morning / afternoon / evening* 在上午/下午/晚上

⑤ 再次提到上文提到过的人或物,加定冠词 the。

*May has an apple, the apple is big and red.* 阿美有个苹果,苹果又大又红。

⑥ 指谈话双方都知道的人或物。

*Let's go and give it to the teacher.* 咱们去把它交给老师吧。

⑦ 用在表示"姓"的复数名词前,表示一家人或夫妇二人。

*the Whites* 怀特一家/怀特夫妇二人

(3) 零冠词

零冠词就是不用冠词,以下两种情况不用冠词:

① 在星期、月份等名词前。

*on Monday* 周一   *in March* 三月

② 在球类运动、一日三餐和语言的名词前。

*play basketball* 打篮球   *have supper* 吃晚餐   *in English* 用英语

# D家庭总动员
## o it together

两人一组,一方朗读下面的中文句子,另一方挑选出合适的翻译。

1. 我家离奥运公园很近。
2. 请跟医生保持联系。
3. 妈妈爱弹钢琴。
4. 她有很多油画。
5. 我在北大附中读书。

1. She has many pieces of oil paintings.
2. Please keep in touch with the physician.
3. I am at the Affiliated High School of Peking University.
4. My house is close to the Olympic Park.
5. Mom likes playing the piano.

Recitation 经典背诵

Wendy:Hi, I am Wendy, May's classmate in elementary school. We haven't seen each other for a long time. May has entered a good school. And she is having a very exciting school experience. I entered another good school. That's why I'm having an English class with a foreign teacher to improve my oral English.

## SCENE 8

# 加油站 Gas Station

### Goals

**在这个场景中，我们将学到：**

1. 摩擦辅音 2 组
2. 表示金钱和数量的单词
3. 问路和指路句型练习
4. 名词复数

# Topic 1 出行 Departure

 **玩转语音**

1. Where she sits she shines, and where she shines she sits.
2. Sandy sniffed sweet smelling sunflower seeds while sitting beside a swift stream.
3. There was a fisherman named Fisher who fished for some fish in a fissure. Till a fish with a grin, pulled the fisherman in. now they're fishing the fissure for Fisher.

| | |
|---|---|
| 及格时间：6 秒 | |
| 你的纪录：—— 秒 | |
| 及格时间：7 秒 | |
| 你的纪录：—— 秒 | |
| 及格时间：15 秒 | |
| 你的纪录：—— 秒 | |

天气不错，全家人今天要出去郊游，但是去郊游之前，还需要做点什么呢？一起来看看吧。

**Dad：** Nice weather! Is everything all set, Honey?

**Mom：** Just a moment, please! Be quick, Daniel, May!

**Dad：** Everybody, hurry up! We should go to the gas station first.

**Daniel：** Why, Dad?

**Dad：** Fill the gas tank lest it run out of the gas on our way to the suburbs.

**Daniel：** I see.

**Dad：** Help me with the bag, please, Daniel!

**爸爸：** 天气不错！亲爱的，所有的东西都准备好了吗？

**妈妈：** 请等一下。丹尼尔，阿美，快点！

**爸爸：** 大家快点，我们首先还要去加油站。

**丹尼尔：** 为什么啊？爸爸。

**爸爸：** 要去加油站把油加足以免在去郊区的路上油不够了。

**丹尼尔：** 我明白了。

**爸爸：** 丹尼尔，帮我拿一下袋子。

Daniel：My pleasure！

Dad：Come on, you get in the back seat, and Mom gets in the front seat.

Daniel：Yes, sir.

Dad：Are you all ready, guys?

Daniel：We are ready. Let's roll！

**丹尼尔:**乐意效劳！

**爸爸:**你们两个坐后排,妈妈坐前面。

**丹尼尔:**遵命,长官。

**爸爸:**大家都准备好了吗?

**丹尼尔:**一切都准备好了,我们出发吧！

### 生词小结

**moment** *n.* 一会儿

**hurry** *vi.* 匆忙,赶快

**gas** *n.* 汽油

**fill** *vt.* 填充

**suburb** *n.* 郊区

**front** *adj.* 前面的

### 注释

**Let's roll!** roll 的意思为滚动,摇摆,但是在此处 Let's roll 并不是让我们滚动起来的意思,而是让我们行动起来的意思。

## 语音小结 —— 摩擦辅音 2 组
Pronunciation

1. /ʃ/和/ʒ/ should station show shout pleasure measure leisure television

   发音小贴士:舌尖和舌端抬起,靠近齿龈后部,整个舌身抬起靠近上颚,形成一条狭长的通道,气流由此通过摩擦发音,双唇稍向前突起,略成长方形

   /ʃ/ 是清辅音,发音要送气,但声带不振动

   /ʒ/ 是浊辅音,声带要振动

   对比练习　fish and treasure　ship and vision　wash and usual　dish and garage

2. /s/和/z/ set gas station first is please zero zoo

   发音小贴士:舌端靠近齿龈,但不要紧贴,气流由舌端和齿龈间流出,摩擦发音

   /s/是清辅音,声带不振动

   /z/是浊辅音,声带要振动

   对比练习　sister and zip　second and seize　sound and quiz　suit and dizzy

### Recitation 经典背诵

Dad：My family like going out for picnics a lot. The children always enjoy it. We would sometimes go to the suburbs which is really fun. But of course I should make sure that we have enough gas so the first place for the "big day" is always the gas station.

 加油
### Gas Station

听 学 读 看　来到了加油站,妈妈和孩子们坐在车里,爸爸下车加油,在加油的时候,爸爸和工作人员似乎聊上了,来看看他们聊了些什么吧!

Attendant：May I help you, sir?

Benjamin：Fill it up with regular, please.

Attendant：Should I take a look at your battery?

Benjamin：No, thanks. I'm in a hurry.

Attendant：Your car is ready.

Benjamin：Good! How much is it?

Attendant：250 yuan, please!

Benjamin：That is expensive.

Attendant：You should know about the oil crisis.

(*Ben comes back to the car.*)

Shirley：How much did the gas come up to?

Benjamin：250 Yuan.

Daniel：I don't think that is a reasonable price.

服务员:有什么可以为您效劳吗? 先生。

本杰明:请给我加 87 号油。

服务员:要我帮您看一下电池吗?

本杰明:不用了,谢谢。我很急。

服务员:油加好了。

本杰明:好的,多少钱?

服务员:250 元。

本杰明:太贵了。

服务员:你应该知道石油危机。

(本回到了车里。)

雪莉:多少钱啊?

本杰明:250。

丹尼尔:我认为这个价格不合理。

---

**生词小结**

**battery**　*n.* 电池

**ready**　*adj.* 准备好的

**expensive**　*adj.* 昂贵的,贵的

**crisis**　*n.* 危机

**reasonable**　*adj.* 合情合理的

---

**注释**

1. regular 此词的意思为"有规律的,有规则的",但是在此处 regular 表示87 号油。

2. 在中国加油的数量单位我们用公升来表示,但是在美国却使用的是加仑。加仑又有英制和美制之分,英制1 加仑等于4.546公升,美制1 加仑等于3.785 公升。

## 单词扩展 Vocabulary Builder

### 表示金钱和数量的单词

| 基础词汇 | 提高词汇 |
| --- | --- |
| $1 one dollar 1 美元 | $6.50 six dollars fifty cents 6 美元 50 美分 |
| $10 ten dollars 10 美元 | £6.55 six pounds and fifty five 6 英镑 55 便士 |
| 1C one cent 1 美分 | £3.75 three pounds and seventy five 3 英镑 75 便士 |
| 10C ten cents 10 美分 | $18.29 eighteen dollars twenty nine cents 18 美元 29 美分 |
| 1P one penny 1 便士 | $362 three hundred sixty two dollars 362 美元 |
| £5 five pounds 5 英镑 | $3.50 three dollars fifty cents 3 美元 50 美分 |
| £10 ten pounds 10 英镑 | $175 one hundred seventy five dollars 175 美元 |
| £20 twenty pounds 20 英镑 | £800 eight hundred pounds 800 英镑 |

## D 家庭总动员
o it together

　　两人一组，一方随机大声读出上面词汇的英文和中文，另一方用该词汇填入下面的句子，大声朗读并把该句子翻译成中文，然后将所听到的钱数写出来。

—**How much is it?**

—( 　　　　　　　 ), **please!**

【例】家长读 ten pounds 十英镑

　　　孩子读 —How much is it?

　　　　　　—ten pounds, please!

　　　　　　—这个多少钱啊?

　　　　　　—十英镑。(然后在纸上写出 £10)

## Recitation
经典背诵

　　　　　　Dad：Because of the oil crisis, the gas price goes up quickly. It would cost me 250 yuan to fill my gas tank now. That's really expensive. I wonder whether there will be one day when I can't afford to drive a car anymore.

行程
Travel Route

听 学 看

加完了油，爸爸开着车向郊区行去，但是健忘的爸爸却突然忘记了去海滩的具体路线，这下爸爸有麻烦了，来看看怎么回事吧！

Dad：Where are we heading, Shirley?

Mom：It's up to you.

Dad：En, I can't remember the exact direction.

Mom：What happened to your memory?

Daniel：If I had known that, I could have helped you, Dad!

Mom：All you think about is your *American Idol*!

Dad：I'm so sorry!

Daniel：Take it easy, Dad!

Mom：Go straight, then turn left at the first intersection, you will see the exact road signs.

Dad：Got it. Yahoo!

Mom：I hope this will teach you a lesson!

Dad：Yes, Madam!

爸爸：我们应该走哪边呢？雪莉。

妈妈：你决定吧。

爸爸：恩，我好像忘记了具体的方向。

妈妈：你的记忆力到底是怎么了？

丹尼尔：爸爸，如果我知道，我就帮助你了。

妈妈：不要只想着你的《美国偶像》。

爸爸：那是我的错！

丹尼尔：爸爸，看开点！

妈妈：一直往前开，然后在第一个街口向左转弯，然后你就可以看见具体的标志了。

爸爸：知道了，太棒了！

妈妈：我希望你记住这次教训！

爸爸：遵命，长官！

---

生词小结

| | | | |
|---|---|---|---|
| exact | *adj.* 具体的 | block | *n.* 街区 |
| memory | *n.* 记忆 | teach | *vt.* 教 |
| straight | *adj.* 直的，直接的 | | |

## 情景练习
### Scene practice —— 问路和指路句型练习

仔细阅读下面五个场景,两人一组,使用问路和指路的句型(见55页),用一用,练一练。

1. If you were Wendy, and you wanted to ask the way to the nearest stop for Bus No. 713. What would you say?

2. If you were May, how would you show the way to Wendy?

3. If you were Daniel, and you got lost and asked the policeman the way to the library, what would you say?

4. Wendy wants to know the way to Liu Lichang, if you were her, what would you say?

5. If you were Shirley, and you wanted to ask the way to the food market, what would you say?

**Recitation**
经典背诵

**Daniel**:On our way to the suburbs, Dad always gets confused with the directions. Interestingly, Mom would blame him at first and then give him the right directions. Dad promises Mom that he would not make the same mistake again. But you know that each time has its follower.

汽车快餐
Fast Food

车开在路上,丹尼尔看见了路边的麦当劳店,就想吃汉堡,但是爸爸妈妈会不会给他买呢?

Daniel：Dad, when will we get there?

**丹尼尔:** 爸爸,我们什么时候才能到啊?

Dad：Won't take much longer now.

**爸爸:** 用不了多久。

Daniel：Mommy, can I ask you something?

**丹尼尔:** 妈咪,我能问一个问题吗?

Mom：Yes, please!

**妈妈:** 好的,说吧!

Daniel：Do you think our food is enough?

**丹尼尔:** 你认为我们的食物够吗?

Mom：Yeah?

**妈妈:** 呃?

Daniel：I mean there is a McDonald's right over there.

**丹尼尔:** 我的意思是那边有个麦当劳。

Mom：Hold on, I know where this is going.

**妈妈:** 打住,我知道你的最终目的。

Daniel：Come on, just some cheeseburgers.

**丹尼尔:** 妈妈,就只买几个芝士汉堡而已。

(*Dad can't do anything but drive the car to the McDonald's sale window.*)

(爸爸没有办法,只有把车开到了麦当劳餐厅的外买窗口。)

Attendant：Can I help you?

**服务员:** 您要什么?

Dad：3 double cheeseburgers to go, please!

**爸爸:** 3 个双层芝士汉堡带走。

Attendant：All right. Would you care for a cup of coffee?

**服务员:** 好的,您还要一杯咖啡吗?

Dad：No, thanks. I've got what I want.

**爸爸:** 谢谢,不用了。我已经买了该买的。

---

**生词小结**

| | |
|---|---|
| **get** *vi.* 到达 | **cheeseburger** *n.* 芝士汉堡 |
| **enough** *adj.* 足够的 | **window** *n.* 窗户 |
| **mean** *vt.* 意味着 | **coffee** *n.* 咖啡 |

## **G**语法小结 **rammer** —— 名词复数

名词的复数可以分为规则名词复数和不规则名词复数。

1. 规则名词复数

（1）一般情况单词复数

| 种　类 | 规　则 | 例　词 |
|---|---|---|
| 普通情况 | 加 s | *sisters* 姐妹 *brothers* 兄弟 *schools* 学校 *books* 书本 |
| 以 s,x,ch,sh 结尾的词 | 加 es | *watches* 手表 *buses* 公共汽车 *dishes* 菜 |
| 以"辅音 + y"结尾的词 | 变 y 为 i 再加上 es | *lady* 女士 *ladies* *country* 国家 *countries* |

（2）以 o 结尾的词，多数加 es 构成复数

　　*hero* 英雄 *heroes*　　*potato* 马铃薯 *potatoes*　　*tomato* 西红柿 *tomatoes*

（3）以 oo 结尾或元音字母 + o 结尾的单词，加 s 构成复数

　　*radio* 收音机 *radios*　　*zoo* 动物园 *zoos*　　*bamboo* 竹子 *bamboos*

（4）以 f 或 fe 结尾的单词，通常变 f 为 v，再加上 es 或 s

　　*self* 自身 *selves*　　*wife* 妻子 *wives*　　*life* 生活 *lives*

2. 不规则名词复数

| 不规则名词 | 复　数 | 词　义 |
|---|---|---|
| man | men | 男人 |
| woman | women | 女人 |
| child | children | 孩子 |
| mouse | mice | 老鼠 |
| policeman | policemen | 警察 |
| policewoman | policewomen | 女警察 |
| gentleman | gentlemen | 绅士 |

## **D**家庭总动员 **o it together**

请一方读出以下单词，另一方用复数表达。

fireman glass block doctor cup woman teacher battery face zoo memory

firemen glasses blocks doctors cups women teachers batteries faces zoos memories

**R**ecitation　经典背诵　　　Dad：Daniel loves cheeseburgers. He would not miss any chance to get one. He would always keep on asking whether we have enough food when we stop near the McDonald's on our way to places. I know what he really wants. So I would just say yes. You know it's the only way!

英语大赢家 *Winner's English*

# Act 2

# 娱乐休闲场景
# Entertainment and Fun

# 公园 Park

## Goals

在这个场景中,我们将学到:

1. 摩擦辅音 2 组
2. 表示户外活动的单词
3. 表达拒绝的句型
4. 名词所有格

奥运公园
**Olympic Park**

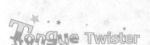 玩转语音

1. A flea and a fly flew up in a flue. Said the flea, "Let us fly!" Said the fly, "Let us flee!" So they flew through a flaw in the flue.

2. Hassock hassock, black spotted hassock. Black spot on a black back of a black spotted hassock.

及格时间: 20 秒
你的纪录: —— 秒
及格时间: 10 秒
你的纪录: —— 秒

全家决定周末出游,丹尼尔想去海洋馆,妈妈想去颐和园,爸爸又有其他的事情,大家意见不统一。最后他们的决定是什么呢?

**May:** Daddy, are you going to the park with us this weekend?

**Dad:** Honey, I have a lot of work to do.

**May:** So you can't go with us, right?

**Dad:** No.

**May:** Daddy, you always arrange your schedule so tight on weekdays. You should have a rest on weekends.

**Dad:** What park do you want to go to?

**May:** Daniel wants to go to the aquarium. While Mom wants to visit the Summer Palace.

**Dad:** Haven't we been these places already?

**May:** Yeah. I don't agree with them, but I don't have better choice.

**阿美:** 爸爸,你周末会和我们一起去公园吗?

**爸爸:** 孩子,我有许多工作要做的。

**阿美:** 所以你不能和我们一起去,对吗?

**爸爸:** 是的。

**阿美:** 爸爸,你平时总是把你日程安排的那么紧。你应该在周末休息一下的。

**爸爸:** 你们想去什么公园?

**阿美:** 丹尼尔想去海洋馆。但是妈妈想去颐和园。

**爸爸:** 我们不是已经去过这些地方了嘛!

**阿美:** 是啊。我不赞成去这些地方,但是我也没有更好的选择。

娱乐休闲场景 · Entertainment and Fun

Dad：What about the Olympic park?

May：Right, ah, It is so close to our home. How come we've never thought of that?

Dad：The Olympic Park has a small forest. It is fit for picnic.

May：Very well, Go ahead.

爸爸：去奥林匹克公园怎么样？

阿美：好啊。那离我们家很近的。我们怎么之前没有想到那里呢？

爸爸：奥林匹克公园里有一个小森林。很适合野餐。

阿美：太好了，就去那里了。

### 生词小结

arrange    *vt.* 安排
schedule   *n.* 日程安排
tight      *adj.* 紧的
have a rest   休息一下
aquarium   *n.* 海洋馆
agree with   赞同
choice     *n.* 选择
forest     *n.* 森林
be fit for   适合
picnic     *n.* 野餐

### 注释

**Summer Palace** 颐和园。是清代的皇家花园和行宫，为我国四大名园之一。

**How come we've never thought of that?** 我们怎么之前没有想到那里呢。How come 表示"怎么回事"，"怎么会呢"。

**Olympic park** 奥林匹克公园。奥林匹克公园是北京举办 2008 年奥运会的心脏，容纳了 44% 的奥运会比赛场馆和为奥运会服务的绝大多数设施。其中还有一个占地面积为 7.6 平方公里的森林公园。

**Go ahead** 用在口语中表示"可以"，"去吧"，"开始"等意思。

## 语音小结 Pronunciation —— 摩擦辅音 2 组

1. /f/ 和 /v/ **fit for visit very**

   发音小贴士：下唇轻触上齿，气流由唇齿间的缝隙中通过，摩擦成音

   /f/ 是清辅音，声带不振动

   /v/ 是浊辅音，发音时声带振动

   对比练习  /f/ 和 /v/  fast and vast  leaf and leave  safe and save  few and view

2. /h/ 和 /r/ **honey have rest right**

   发音小贴士：/h/ 口腔自然张开，气流不受阻碍自由冲出口腔，只在通过声门时产生摩擦发音。口型依后面元音变化，声带不振动。

   /r/ 舌尖向上卷起，停在口腔中央，舌身两侧收拢，双唇略突出，气流从舌面和硬腭间流出发音

   对比练习  /h/ 和 /r/  hill and rill  hat and rat  head and read  habit and rabbit

### Recitation 经典背诵

May：On weekends our family usually drive out for fun. That's really something great to do. But the problem is it's usually hard for us to find a place we all feel like going to. So before making the final decision we always have a "fight". The good thing is that we kids always win.

**周末安排**
Weekend Plans

听 学 看

最终全家决定去奥林匹克公园,爸爸和丹尼尔一起商量在公园进行什么活动。

Daniel：Daddy, I am so glad you come out with us.

Dad：Honey, I am sorry that I am too busy most of the time.

Daniel：It doesn't matter. But I really haven't gone for a picnic for a long time.

Dad：What did you do last weekend?

Daniel：It was boring. Just did my homework and practiced the piano.

Dad：Did you play football with other children?

Daniel：Ahh, I was not available last Sunday. I was too busy almost as much as you.

Dad：Cool, we can take the football, shuttlecock and badminton racket to the park.

Daniel：Hooray！I can play football with daddy. Mom and sister can play badminton.

Dad：After that, we will have a picnic.

Daniel：That's great. We can also take the dragon kite with us. After the picnic, we can fly it.

Dad：Okay, it sounds good.

丹尼尔：爸爸,您能和我们一起出去玩,我真是太高兴了。

爸爸：宝贝,我很抱歉,很多时候我总是太忙。

丹尼尔：没关系。不过我真的很久没有出去野餐了。

爸爸：你上周末做什么了?

丹尼尔：太无聊了。只是写家庭作业,练钢琴。

爸爸：和其他小孩子踢足球了吗?

丹尼尔：哈,我上周日没有时间。我几乎和您一样忙呢。

爸爸：好的,我们可以带着足球,羽毛球和羽毛球拍去公园。

丹尼尔：好耶! 我可以和爸爸一起踢足球。妈妈就和姐姐打羽毛球。

爸爸：之后,我们一起野餐。

丹尼尔：太棒了。我们也可以带着那只龙风筝。野餐后可以放风筝。

爸爸：好的,听起来不错哦。

**生词小结**

**boring** *adj.* 无聊的
**practice** *vt.* 练习
**available** *adj.* 可用的,可获得的
**shuttlecock** *n.* 羽毛球
**badminton racket** *n.* 羽毛球拍
**have a picnic** 野餐

**注释**

**I was too busy almost as much as you.** 我和您几乎一样忙呢。爸爸之前说自己总是很忙。在这里人小鬼大的丹尼尔模仿爸爸的语气说自己也很忙,上周日都没有时间和小朋友一起去踢足球呢。

## 娱乐休闲场景 · Entertainment and Fun

**dragon** *n.* 龙
**kite** *n.* 风筝
**fly** *vt.* 放(风筝)

**It sounds good.** 听上去不错。这句话在口语中表达赞同和认可的意思。

## 单词扩展 Vocabulary Builder

### 表示户外活动的单词

| 基础词汇 | 提高词汇 |
| --- | --- |
| fishing 钓鱼 | rowing 划船 |
| skating 滑冰 | skiing 滑雪 |
| football 足球 | volleyball 排球 |
| basketball 篮球 | baseball 棒球 |
| tennis 网球 | golf 高尔夫球 |
| swimming 游泳 | softball 垒球 |
| ping-pang 乒乓球 | badminton 羽毛球 |
| picnic 野餐 | flying a kite 放风筝 |

## 家庭总动员
Do it together

两人一组,一方随机大声读出上面词汇的英文和中文,另一方用该词汇填入下面的句子,大声朗读并表演出来,并用中文给出一个理由。

**I prefer (　　　　　　　　　　).**

【例】家长读 football 足球
孩子读 I prefer football. 我喜欢和爸爸一起踢足球。

**Recitation** 经典背诵

Daniel：My Dad is always busy with his work. But once he has some time he would go out with us for picnics or stuff like that. Then it would be really a big day for me. But before we can go I'd have to finish the homework first which can be a bit boring. But anyway, it's all worth it. Just think of the good time we're gonna have.

# Topic 3 野餐
## Picnics

姐姐帮妈妈一起准备周末野餐的食物和用具,让我们快去听听她们在聊些什么吧。

**Mom**：May, do you mind helping me prepare for the picnic?

**May**：Sure. Have you checked the weather report?

**Mom**：Yes. It says it will be sunny all day. No sign of rain at all.

(*Mom puts the sausage in the basket.*)

**Mom**：This is your father's favorite sausage.

(*Mom puts sandwiches in the basket.*)

**Mom**：Sandwiches for you and Daniel.

**May**：No, thanks Mom. I'd like some toast and chicken wings.

**Mom**：Okay. Please take some fruit salad and crackers for me.

**May**：Done. Oh, don't forget to take napkins, disposable plates, cups and picnic blanket.

**Mom**：All set. May, can you help me take all these things to the living room?

**May**：Yes, madam.

**Mom**：Ask Daniel to give you a hand?

**May**：No, mom, I can manage it by myself. His help just causes more trouble.

**妈妈**：阿美,介不介意帮我准备野餐的东西?

**阿美**：当然可以了。你有没有看天气预报?

**妈妈**：看了。它说明天一整天都是晴天。没有丝毫下雨的迹象。

(妈妈把香肠放在篮子里。)

**妈妈**：这是你爸爸最喜欢的香肠。

(妈妈把三明治放进篮子里。)

**妈妈**：这是给你和丹尼尔准备的三明治。

**阿美**：妈妈,谢谢,我不要了。我想要些吐司面包和鸡翅膀。

**妈妈**：好的。给我带些水果沙拉和饼干吧。

**阿美**：弄好了。哦,别忘了带餐巾纸,一次性的盘子和杯子,还有野餐布。

**妈妈**：带了。阿美,能帮我把东西拿到客厅去吗?

**阿美**：是,长官。

**妈妈**：让丹尼尔帮你一下吗?

**阿美**：不了,妈妈。我自己可以应付的。他只会帮倒忙。

---

**生词小结**

| | | | |
|---|---|---|---|
| **prepare** | *vt.* 准备 | **fruit** | *n.* 水果 |
| **sausage** | *n.* 香肠 | **salad** | *n.* 沙拉 |
| **sandwich** | *n.* 三明治 | **cracker** | *n.* 饼干 |
| **toast** | *n.* 吐司面包 | **napkin** | *n.* 餐巾纸 |
| **chicken wing** | *n.* 鸡翅膀 | **disposable** | *adj.* 一次性的 |

**注释**

**all set** 字面意思是"全部设置好了",在此是说阿美提醒妈妈带的东西妈妈都已经准备好了。

**give you a hand** 给你帮忙

## 娱乐休闲场景·Entertainment and Fun

## F功能性句型扩展 —— 表达拒绝的句型
unctional structure

请朗读以下句型，家长和孩子交替进行。

1. 委婉拒绝别人的帮助

No Mom, I can manage it by myself. 不用了，妈妈。我自己可以的。

No, thanks. 不用了，谢谢。

No, it's all right, thanks. 不用了，我可以的。谢谢。

That's very kind of you, but I think I can manage. 你人真好，不过我想我可以应付的。

Thank you very much for offering, but I think it'll be all right. 非常感谢你的帮助，但是我想我可以处理的。

Please don't bother. I think I can manage. Thanks all the same. 不用麻烦了。我想我自己可以应付的。仍然很感谢。

I'm afraid it won't be possible, but thank you very much anyway. 我想不需要了，不过仍然很谢谢你。

2. 委婉拒绝帮助别人或者做某事

I'd love to, but… 我很想，但是……

I'm afraid I can't do that. 我恐怕不能做那件事。

I'm sorry but I can't help you. 抱歉，我不能帮你。

I wish I could help you, but I can't. 我希望能帮你，但我不能。

I'm sorry, but I'm busy right now. 对不起，我现在很忙。

I'm not the right person to ask. 你不该问我。

Don't give me a hard time. 别让我为难。

You are asking too much. 你要求得太多了。

3. 直接拒绝帮助别人或者做某事

Please ask somebody else. 请问别人吧。

I don't want to do that. 我不想那么做。

Not a chance! 绝对不行！

There is no room for discussion. 没有商量的余地。

Cut it out! 别说了。

I said no and I mean it. 我说不行就不行。

Stop harping on it. 别啰嗦了。

**Recitation**
经典背诵

May：Mom and I are supposed to prepare for picnics every time. Sausages for Daddy, sandwiches for Daniel and some toast and chicken wings for myself. We'd also never forget to take napkins, disposable plates, cups and picnic blanket with us. With these we can definitely have a really good time.

# 拍照
## **Taking Pictures**

奥林匹克公园是个漂亮的地方,弟弟忍不住央求爸爸给他拍照。让我们去看看他们拍照时发生了怎样的故事吧。

**Daniel**：Look, Dad, many people are doing morning exercises here.

**Dad**：Yes. I used to come out here with my grandpa as a child.

**Daniel**：Really? You were so happy then.

**Dad**：Aren't you happy now? I hadn't seen the piano when I was a child.

**Daniel**：Daddy, don't mention it.

**Dad**：The park is so beautiful. It is a good thing I have taken the camera.

**Daniel**：Dad, I'd like to take a picture with the status.

**Dad**：All right. Give me a big smile. Are you ready? Cheese!

**Daniel**：Daddy, we can't have a photo of the whole family. We can take one here.

(*Father turns to the tourist for help.*)

**Dad**：Excuse me, sir. Could you take a photo for us? Just press this button.

**Tourist**：Okay. Everybody gets closer.
 Good. Keep the pose and cheese. OK, OK, one more, please. Alright.

**Dad**：Thanks a lot.

**Tourist**：My pleasure.

**丹尼尔**:看,爸爸,好多人在这里晨练呢。

**爸爸**:是啊,我还是小孩子的时候,也常常和我爷爷去公园晨练。

**丹尼尔**:真的吗? 那你那时候真是太幸福了。

**爸爸**:难道你现在不幸福吗? 我小时候还没有见过钢琴呢。

**丹尼尔**:爸爸,快别提了。

**爸爸**:这个公园真漂亮。幸好我带了相机。

**丹尼尔**:爸爸,我想在这个雕塑这儿拍张照。

**爸爸**:好的。笑一个。准备好了没? 茄子!

**丹尼尔**:爸爸,我们家都没有全家福呢。我们在这里照一张吧。

(爸爸请一个游客帮忙)

**爸爸**:你好,这位先生。能帮我们拍张照吗? 按一下这个键。

**游客**:好的。大家都挨紧点。
 好的。保持不动,笑一个。好嘞,再来一张。好了。

**爸爸**:太谢谢了。

**游客**:不客气。

---

**生词小结**

**used to**　过去常常
**mention**　*vt.* 提及

**注释**

**do some exercises** 做运动
**take a picture with** 和……拍照

## 娱乐休闲场景·Entertainment and Fun

| | |
|---|---|
| **beautiful** *adj.* 美丽的 | **turns to… for help** 向……求助 |
| **status** *n.* 雕塑 | **Cheese!** Cheese 是奶酪的意思,因为读这个单 |
| **keep** *vt.* 保持 | 词的时候嘴角张开,呈微笑的状态,所以在拍 |
| **pose** *n.* 姿势 | 照的时候,人们喜欢大声说出这个单词来做出 |
| **alright** *adv.* 好吧 | 一个微笑的姿态。 |

## Grammer —— 名词所有格

英语中很多名词可以加 's 来表示所有关系,这就是名词所有格。

1. 名词所有格主要用于表示人的名词,表示"(某人)的"

单数名词在词尾加 's,复数以 s 结尾的,只在结尾加 ',不以 s 结尾的,加 's。例如:

*my teacher's book* 我老师的书

*May's diary* 阿美的日记

*the boys' basketball* 那些男孩的篮球

2. 表示无生命的名词,一般用"of + 名词"的结构

*the gate of the amusement park* 游乐场的大门

3. 有些表示时间、距离等无生命和表示世界、国家、城镇等名词,除了用"of + 名词"的结构外也可以在词尾加 's 变成相应的所有格

*ten minutes' walk* 十分钟的路程

*today's newspaper* 今天的报纸

4. 用 and 连接的两个或两个以上的名词,如果一物为两人所共有,则只在后一个名词后加 's,如果不是共有的,则两个名词后都加 's

*May and Danny's room* 阿美和丹尼尔的房间（共有）

*May's and Danny's rooms* 阿美的房间和丹尼尔的房间(不共有)

5. 双重所有格

双重所有格由"of + 名词所有格"构成。如:

*a friend of my brother's = one of my brother's friends*

## Do it together 家庭总动员

两人一组,一方朗诵下面的中文句子,另一方挑选出合适的翻译。

1. 丹尼尔同意爸爸的选择。
2. 请保持你的姿势。
3. 阿美正在放丹尼尔的风筝。
4. 我能给你照张相吗?
5. 我能看看今天的日程安排吗?

1. Can I take a photo of you?
2. Can I have a look at the schedule of today?
3. May is flying Daniel's kite.
4. Daniel agreed with Dad's choice.
5. Please keep your pose!

**Recitation** 经典背诵

**Dad:** The park is a good place for many things. Some people like doing exercises here. My family always make it a place for picnics. And nowadays, it's popular to take photos in there. I think that's a really good idea. So we're planning to take some photos with the whole family there. Why not? Where else can you find such beautiful sceneries?

# 动物园 Zoo

## Goals

**在这个场景中,我们将学到:**

1. 摩擦辅音 1 组,破擦辅音 1 组
2. 动物名称的单词
3. 拒绝句型练习
4. 肯定句和否定句

动物表演
**Animal Performance**

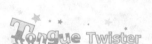
玩转语音

1. I thought a thought. But the thought I thought wasn't the thought I thought I thought.
2. If two witches would watch two watches, which witch would watch which watch?

及格时间: 8 秒
你的纪录:——秒
及格时间: 8 秒
你的纪录:——秒

全家人来到了动物园,爸爸和妈妈一组,姐姐和弟弟一组。妈妈看见有马戏团表演就想过去看,但是爸爸好像有点不乐意,怎么回事呢?

**Mom:** Hey, look, there is a circus show over there.

**Dad:** I'm not in the mood.

**Mom:** It's the circus.

**Dad:** I don't want to sit there and watch them torturing the animals.

**Mom:** Oh, come on, they give them treat too.

(*Shirley and Benjamin is in the crowd of the people watching the monkey's performance.*)

**Mom:** Oh, look, that little monkey is so cute.

**Dad:** Cute? Hope so.

**Mom:** Oh, it is coming to us, come on, Ben, get a banana to it.

**Dad:** Me? No way, keep him away from me, please.

**妈妈:** 哎,看,那边有马戏团表演。

**爸爸:** 我没有心情。

**妈妈:** 是马戏团啊。

**爸爸:** 我不想坐在那儿看他们折磨那些动物。

**妈妈:** 哦,不会,他们也会好好照顾动物的。

(雪莉和本杰明挤在看猴子的人群中。)

**妈妈:** 看,那个小猴子真是可爱。

**爸爸:** 可爱? 希望吧。

**妈妈:** 噢,天哪,它朝我们走过来了。本,给它根香蕉。

**爸爸:** 我? 没门,快让他离我远点。

Mom：Why are you acting so strange today?

Dad：I've said that I've got a problem with the circus. I'm not kidding.

Mom：That's weird!

妈妈：你今天真是奇怪。

爸爸：我说了我不是很喜欢马戏团。我没有开玩笑。

妈妈：真是奇怪！

---

**生词小结**

**circus**　　*n.* 马戏团

**mood**　　*n.* 心情

**torture**　　*vt.* 拷问，曲解

**crowd**　　*n.* 人群

**performance**　　*n.* 表演

**cute**　　*adj.* 可爱的

**strange**　　*adj.* 奇怪的

**weird**　　*adj.* 怪异的

**注释**

**I'm not in the mood.** 我没有心情。

---

## 语音小结 Pronunciation —— 摩擦辅音 1 组, 破擦辅音 1 组

**1.** /θ/ 和 /ð/ everything mouth three through there them they that

发音小贴士：舌尖在上下齿间，略微伸出，气流由舌齿间的窄缝流出，摩擦发音

/θ/ 是清辅音，声带不振动

/ð/ 是浊辅音，声带振动

对比练习　/θ/ 和 /ð/　thank and this　think and that　thing and their　through and brother

**2.** / tʃ /和/ dʒ/　watch lunch rich teach justice jasmine jazz age

发音小贴士：舌尖舌端抬起顶住上齿龈后部，形成阻碍，气流冲破阻碍摩擦发音，冲破阻碍后舌和齿龈间仍保持一个狭缝。

/tʃ/是清辅音，声带不振动

/dʒ/是浊辅音，声带振动

对比练习　/tʃ/和/dʒ/　cheap and jeep　much and bridge　cheese and job　check and joke

---

**Mom**：My husband is allergic to some animals especially monkeys. Everytime we go to the zoo he would refuse to go to see the circus performance with me, which is my favorite. That's really funny. He is such a grownup. But, how could he be allergic to monkeys? I just don't understand it.

# Topic 2 动物和国家
## Animals and Countries

丹尼尔看见不远处的笼子里有个动物，但是却分辨不出到底是什么，会是什么呢？该不会是什么恐怖的动物吧！

Daniel：May，look，what's that in the cage?

May：Don't you know that? It's panda.

Daniel：Of course I know. I just can't see it very well.

May：OK，then put on your glasses，and do you know what does the panda eat?

Daniel：Of course，Bamboo!

May：That's right.

Daniel：I also know they are given to other countries as gifts for friendship.

May：You sound quite knowledgeable.

Daniel：Not really，panda is my favorite animal.

May：Actually，it likes milk too.

Daniel：Any way，in a word，panda is our friend.

May：Do you know other famous animals in the world?

Daniel：Yeah，let me think，the kangaroo and koala bear from Australia are very famous.

May：That's right. OK，let's move on.

丹尼尔：阿美,快看,那个笼子里的是什么啊？

阿美：你不认识吗？是熊猫啊。

丹尼尔：我当然知道了,我只是看不清楚而已。

阿美：那就把你的眼镜带上,那你知道熊猫吃什么呢？

丹尼尔：当然知道了,吃竹子啊！

阿美：恩,对。

丹尼尔：我还知道他们被当作象征友好的礼物送给其他国家。

阿美：你还很博学啊。

丹尼尔：也不是啦,熊猫是我最喜欢的动物。

阿美：事实上,它也喜欢喝牛奶。

丹尼尔：不管怎么样,总的来说,熊猫是我们的朋友。

阿美：那你还知道世界上其他的一些有名的动物吗？

丹尼尔：让我想想啊,澳大利亚的袋鼠和考拉熊都很出名。

阿美：对啊,我们走吧。

---

### 生词小结

cage　n. 笼子

panda　n. 熊猫

bamboo　n. 竹子

country　n. 国家

friendship　n. 友谊

favorite　adj. 最喜欢的

knowledgable　adj. 知识渊博的

milk　n. 牛奶

kangaroo　n. 袋鼠

koala bear　n. 考拉熊

---

# Act 2

娱乐休闲场景·Entertainment and Fun

## 单词扩展 Vocabulary Builder

### 动物名称的单词

| 基础词汇 | 提高词汇 |
| --- | --- |
| dog 狗 | donkey 驴 |
| pig 猪 | elephant 大象 |
| duck 鸭子 | tiger 老虎 |
| cat 猫 | lion 狮子 |
| horse 马 | fox 狐狸 |
| rabbit 兔子 | wolf 狼 |
| sheep 绵羊 | bat 蝙蝠 |
| deer 鹿 | whale 鲸 |

## D 家庭总动员
### o it together

两人一组,一方随机大声读出上面词汇的英文和中文,另一方用该词汇填入下面的句子,大声朗读并表演出来,并用中文给出一个理由。

( ) is my favorite animal.

【例】家长读 elephant 大象

孩子读 Elephant is my favorite animal. 因为大象的鼻子很长。

**Recitation** 经典背诵

Daniel: The panda is my favorite animal. They like eating bamboos very much. They are often sent to other countries as gifts friendship. I am interested in animals. I also know the two famous animals in Australia, they are kangaroos and koala bears. May says that I am quite knowledgeable.

# Topic 3 领养动物
## Pet Adoption

爸爸被猴子吓着了，和妈妈坐在旁边休息。坐着没事，他们会聊些什么呢，一起来看看吧！

**Mom**：That's OK, Ben, just let it go. I thought you were just a little too much into it.

**Dad**：I wasn't kidding before, OK, I'm fine now.

**Mom**：Honey, have you ever heard that there are a lot of stray cats now.

**Dad**：Yes.

**Mom**：Now they are collected by some volunteers, and people can adopt them or make a donation for the shelters.

**Dad**：What are you saying? You are acting weird today.

**Mom**：I want to adopt a cat, and it can be Barbie's boyfriend too.

**Dad**：Haha, very funny, but it doesn't make any sense to me.

**Mom**：That's all right. At least I got myself left.

**Dad**：Seriously, if we will adopt any animals, we'd gotta to talk to Daniel.

**Mom**：I hope that he would grant me with that.

**Dad**：Hope so.

**妈妈**：好了,本,都过去了。
我还以为你只是有点奇怪。

**爸爸**：我刚才可没开玩笑,不过我现在已经好了。

**妈妈**：亲爱的,你听说了现在有很多流浪猫吗?

**爸爸**：恩。

**妈妈**：现在有一些志愿者们将猫们聚集起来,然后人们可以收养,或者是给它们捐款建住所。

**爸爸**：你想说什么? 你今天有点奇怪。

**妈妈**：我想领养一只小猫,然后他也可以成为芭比的男朋友。

**爸爸**：哈哈,太有趣了。但是对于我来说却没有任何意义。

**妈妈**：好的,至少我坚持我自己的意见。

**爸爸**：说真的,如果我们要领养任何动物的话,我们得先和丹尼尔谈谈。

**妈妈**：我希望他会答应。

**爸爸**：希望吧。

---

**生词小结**

**stray** *adj.* 迷途的,丢失的
**collect** *vt.* 收集
**donation** *n.* 捐赠

**注释**

**let it go** 顺其自然
**It doesn't make any sense to me.** 对于我来说却没有任何意义。

| | | |
|---|---|---|
| **shelter** | *n.* 庇护所 | |
| **adopt** | *n.* 收养 | |
| **funny** | *adj.* 有趣的 | |
| **grant** | *vt.* 同意 | |

**Get myself left.** 坚持自己的意见。

## S情景练习 — 拒绝句型练习
cene practice

仔细阅读下面五个场景，两人一组，使用拒绝句型（见72页），用一用，练一练。

1. Someone offers Benjamin a cigarette. If he wants to refuse politely, what would he say?

2. If you were Shirley, you have just bought a set of furniture. Someone offers to help you. You refuse politely. What do you say?

3. A friend offers to buy May some CDs, she refuses, what would she say?

4. If you were Daniel, a stranger offers you a drink. You refuse directly. What do you say?

5. A friend of Benjamin offers him a ticket for circus show, if you were Benjamin, you want to refuse it politely. What do you say?

### Recitation
经典背诵

**Dad:** Shirley says that there are a lot of stray cats in the street, and she wants to adopt one, thinking it may be our dog Barbie's boyfriend. It's kind of her to think of that, but it's surely weird to make a cat be a dog's boyfriend. Honestly speaking, our son Daniel would just get mad if he hears about his mother's idea.

# Topic4 野生动物园
# Wildlife Sanctuary

听 学 看

看完了熊猫,阿美和丹尼尔准备去看其他的动物,在去的路上,他们谈到了野生动物园,丹尼尔好像对此很感兴趣哦!

**May**：Daniel, have you ever heard about the wildlife sanctuary?

**Daniel**：Is that different from this kind of zoo?

**May**：Yes, of course.

**Daniel**：So tell me about it!

**May**：There are a lot of wild animals in that place, and also some special rules while visiting.

**Daniel**：Special rules?

**May**：There, you only have two ways for visiting.

**Daniel**：Details?

**May**：On their bus or in your own cars, and you won't be allowed to get off the bus until you reach the special region.

**Daniel**：Why not?

**May**：Because it is dangerous to get out of the car or bus. You can just imagine how fierce the wild animals can be.

**Daniel**：That makes sense. But that sounds interesting. Is there one in Beijing too?

**May**：Yes.

**Daniel**：I prefer to go there next time.

**May**：Yeah, sure, you won't be disappointed.

**阿美**：丹尼尔,你听说过野生动物园吗?

**丹尼尔**：那和这种动物园有什么区别吗?

**阿美**：当然有啊。

**丹尼尔**：那对我讲讲吧。

**阿美**：在那里啊,有很多野生动物,而且在你游览的时候,还有一些特殊的规定呢。

**丹尼尔**：特殊规定?

**阿美**：在那儿啊,你只有两种游览的方式。

**丹尼尔**：说详细点。

**阿美**：乘他们的车或者是自己开车,在你到达特殊区域之前,是不允许下车的。

**丹尼尔**：为什么呢?

**阿美**：因为下车太危险了。你可以想象一下野生动物是多么的凶猛。

**丹尼尔**：有道理。这听起来太有趣了。北京也有这样的动物园吗?

**阿美**：有啊。

**丹尼尔**：下次我选择去那里。

**阿美**：当然可以啦,你肯定不会失望的。

## 生词小结

| | | |
|---|---|---|
| **sanctuary** | *n.* 避难所 | |
| **allow** | *vt.* 允许 | |
| **region** | *n.* 地区 | |

| | |
|---|---|
| **fierce** | *adj.* 凶猛的 |
| **disappoint** | *vt.* 使失望 |

## Grammer 语法小结 —— 肯定句和否定句

肯定句,顾名思义是表示对事物作出肯定判断的句子,否定句表示对事物作出否定判断的句子,例如:

*I like the red rose.* (肯定句) 我喜欢那红玫瑰。

*I don't like the red rose.* (否定句) 我不喜欢那红玫瑰。

否定句有以下几个类型:

(1) 一般否定

*I don't know.* 我不知道。

*There is no person in the house.* 房里没人。

(2) 部分否定

*All the answers are not right.* 并非所有答案都对。

*Both of them are not right.* 并非两人都对。

(3) 全否定

*None of my families smokes.* 我的家人都不吸烟。

*There is nobody.* 一个人都没有。

*Neither of you is right.* 你们都不对。

(4) 半否定句

*We seldom/hardly/scarcely/barely hear such fine singing.*

我很少听到这么美妙的歌声。

*I know little English.* 我只懂一点儿英语。

*I saw few people.* 我看到几个人。

(5) 双重否定

*No gain without pains.* 没有付出就没有收获。

*He was not unable to do the job by himself.* 他不能自己做这个工作。

## Do it together 家庭总动员

两人一组,一方朗读下面的中文句子,另一方挑选出合适的翻译。

1. 爸爸不喜欢动物。
2. 妈妈想领养一只小猫。
3. 丹尼尔非常喜欢熊猫。
4. 丹尼尔没有去野生动物园。
5. 不是所有的动物园都有猴子。

1. Daniel likes the panda very much.
2. Not all zoos have monkeys.
3. Daniel didn't go to sanctuary before.
4. Dad doesn't like animals.
5. Mom wants to adopt a little cat.

### Recitation 经典背诵

Daniel：I'm so absorbed in the wildlife sanctuary that May has told me about. It is totally different from the ordinary zoo. The visitors can't get off the bus or their own cars unless permitted. And there are a lot of exotic animals too. That sounds fantastic. I hope I can go there next time with my family.

# 电影院 Cinema

## Goals

**在这个场景中,我们将学到:**

1. 破擦辅音 2 组
2. 各种电影种类
3. 总结句型
4. 用在时间和地点前的介词

# 大牌明星
## Superstars

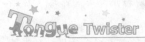  **玩转语音**

1. Extinct insects' instincts, extinct insects' instincts.
2. Never trouble about trouble until trouble troubles you!

及格时间: 5 秒
你的纪录:——秒
及格时间: 5 秒
你的纪录:——秒

星期六的晚上,阿美的好朋友古奇想约阿美一起去看电影。她们在报纸上看到了《幸福终点站》的预报,并对该片及该片的演员和导演展开了讨论。想听听她们说的是什么吗?

**Gucci**: Hey, May. How about getting together for a movie tonight?

**May**: Sure. What's playing?

**Gucci**: Well, Let me check the newspaper. What about *The Terminal*?

**May**: Wow, it stars Catherine Zeta-Jones, my favorite actress.

**Gucci**: Well, birds of a feather flock together. I like her too. She was in a lot of dramas.

**May**: She is so beautiful and elegant. And she is famous for her fine acting.

**Gucci**: What's more, she doesn't have scandals. And she likes to take part in the charitable activities.

**May**: Who is the director?

**Gucci**: Steven Spielberg. Another superstar.

古奇:嗨,阿美。今晚一起去看电影吧?

阿美:好啊。现在在上映什么电影?

古奇:呃,让我看看报纸。《幸福终点站》怎么样?

阿美:哦,这是我最喜欢的女演员凯瑟琳·泽塔·琼斯主演的。

古奇:呵呵,果然是物以类聚,人以群分啊。我也很喜欢她。她出演过许多文艺片。

阿美:她是如此的美丽优雅。并且她以其精湛的演技著称。

古奇:还有呢,她也没有绯闻。并且她喜欢参加慈善活动。

阿美:(这部电影的)导演是谁呢?

古奇:史蒂芬·斯皮尔伯格。另一位超级明星。

**May:** Yes, a legend, also. I still remember, his movies, *Jurassic Park* and *Schindler's List* got him nine Oscar awards in 1994.

**Gucci:** Can you introduce the story of *The Terminal* briefly?

**May:** It tells a romantic and humorous love story.

**Gucci:** This is a really exciting movie. Let's go to this one.

**May:** Oh, It's 5:45. It's on 6:30. We'd better go right away. Or there will be no seats for us.

**阿美:** 是啊,也是个传奇人物呢。我还记得,他的电影《侏罗纪公园》和《辛德勒的名单》在 1994 年为他赢得了 9 项奥斯卡奖。

**古奇:** 能简单给我讲讲《幸福终点站》这部电影是讲什么的吗?

**阿美:** 它讲述了一个浪漫而诙谐的爱情故事。

**古奇:** 真是部激动人心的电影。我们一起去看吧。

**阿美:** 哦,现在已经五点四十五了。电影六点半开演。我们最好马上走,否则就没有位子了。

---

### 生词小结

**drama** *n.* 戏剧
**elegant** *adj.* 高贵的,优雅的
**scandal** *n.* 绯闻
**charitable** *adj.* 慈善的
**activity** *n.* 活动
**director** *n.* 导演
**legend** *n.* 传奇,传奇人物
**romantic** *adj.* 浪漫的
**humorous** *adj.* 诙谐的,幽默的
**be famous for** 以……著称
**take part in** 参加

### 注释

**The Terminal**《幸福终点站》。美国爱情喜剧片,2005 年首映,由斯皮尔伯格导演,汤姆·汉克斯和凯瑟琳·泽塔·琼斯主演。

**It stars Catherine Zeta-Jones** 该片由凯瑟琳·泽塔·琼斯主演。请注意 star 有"以……为主演"之意。凯瑟琳·泽塔·琼斯是好莱坞著名女影星,其代表作有《佐罗的面具》、《鬼入屋》、《偷天陷阱》等。

**Birds of a feather flock together.** 物以类聚,人以群分。

**Steven Spielberg** 史蒂芬·斯皮尔伯格,美国著名导演,其代表作有《大白鲨》、《侏罗纪公园》、《辛德勒名单》、《失落的世界》、《拯救大兵瑞恩》、《幸福终点站》等。

**Jurassic Park**《侏罗纪公园》。由史蒂芬·斯皮尔伯格导演,本片获得了第 66 届奥斯卡最佳视觉效果等三项金奖。

**Schindler's List**《辛德勒名单》。由史蒂芬·斯皮尔伯格导演,该片获第 66 届奥斯卡最佳影片、最佳导演等六项大奖。

---

## Ｐ语音小结 Pronunciation —— 破擦辅音 2 组

**1.** /tr/和/dr/  trouble  actress  drop  drama

发音小贴士:/tr/先做好发/r/的姿势,然后舌尖上翘贴在上齿龈后部,发出短促的/t/后立即发/r/。

/tr/是清辅音,声带不振动。

/dr/是浊辅音,声带振动。

对比练习  /tr/和/dr/  train and drain  tree and dream  track and drunk  true and draw

**2.** /ts/和/dz/  seats  awards  birds  beds

发音小贴士:舌端先贴住齿龈,堵住气流,然后舌端略为下降,气流随之流出口腔而发音。

/ts/是清辅音,声带不振动。

/dz/是浊辅音,声带振动。

对比练习  /ts/和/dz/  seats and seeds  bats and beds  carts and cards  rates and raids

**Gucci:** Hi, I am Gucci, May's best friend. I like the actress in *The Terminal*. She is beautiful and elegant. What's more, she has no scandals. And she likes to take part in the charitable activities. The director of *The Terminal* is another superstar. It's a really exciting movie.

# Topic2 电影分类
## Different Movies

阿美和古奇在一起讨论各自喜欢的电影类型,古奇最喜欢的竟然是恐怖片,想知道阿美喜欢什么类型的电影吗?请往下看吧。

**Gucci**：I'v heard *The Hitchhiker* would be on next week. I want to see it.

**May**：Is it a horror movie?

**Gucci**：Yeah, I love horror movies the most. Would you like to go with me next weekend?

**May**：No way. I will be scared out of my wits.

**Gucci**：Well, What kind of movies do you like?

**May**：Er, let me see. Romance, comedy, documentary, action, science fiction, cartoon and so on.

**Gucci**：In a word, you like all the movies except for the horror movies.

**May**：Yeah, It seems like we don't talk the same language as far as movies are concerned.

**Gucci**：Not quite. I also like romance and comedy movies very much.

**May**：*The Terminal* is a movie of this type.

**Gucci**：So we can relax now.

**May**：Yeah, I could hardly wait to see it.

古奇：我听说《搭车人》将会在下周上映。我想去看。

阿美：这是部恐怖电影吗?

古奇：是啊,我最喜欢恐怖电影。你想周末和我一起去看吗?

阿美：决不。我会被吓得半死。

古奇：那你喜欢什么电影?

阿美：呃,让我想想。爱情片,喜剧片,纪录片,动作片,科幻片,卡通片,等等。

古奇：总而言之,除了恐怖片,其他你都喜欢。

阿美：是的。看起来在电影方面我们达不成共识。

古奇：也不是。我也很喜欢爱情片和喜剧片。

阿美：《幸福终点站》就是这类爱情喜剧片。

古奇：所以我们可以好好放松一下了。

阿美：是啊,我都等不及想看了。

---

**生词小结**

**horror**  *n.* 恐惧
**romance**  *n.* 浪漫
**comedy**  *n.* 喜剧
**documentary**  *n.* 纪录片

**注释**

**in a word** 总之
**as far as** 至于,就……而言
**go with** 和……一起
*The Hitchhiker*《搭车人》,好莱坞的恐怖片,

action    *n.* 动作
fiction    *n.* 小说
relax    *vt.* 放松

2007年1月上映。

**I will be scared out of my wits.** 我会被吓得半死。直译为"我把我的智慧都吓出来了"。言下之意是说自己被吓傻了。

**It seems like we don't talk the same language as far as movies are concerned.** 看起来在电影方面我们达不成共识。直译为"至于电影方面，我们看起来说的不是同一种语言"，言下之意是说我们没有共同话题，达不成共识。

## 单词扩展 Vocabulary Builder

### 各种电影种类

| 基础词汇 | 提高词汇 |
| --- | --- |
| cartoon movie 动画片 | romance movie 爱情片 |
| action movie 动作片 | disaster movie 灾难片 |
| horror movie 恐怖片 | documentary movie 纪录片 |
| comedy movie 喜剧片 | science fiction movie 科幻片 |
| musical movie 音乐剧 | crime movie 警匪片 |
| war movie 战争片 | drama movie 文艺片 |
| western movie 美国西部片 | thriller movie 惊悚片 |
| short movie 电影预告片 | adult movie 成人电影 |

## D 家庭总动员
Do it together

两人一组，一方随机大声读出上面词汇的英文和中文，另一方用该词汇填入下面的句子，大声朗读并表演出来，并用中文给出一个理由。

**What kind of movies do you like? I love (                    ) most.**

【例】家长读 cartoon movies

孩子读 I love cartoon movies most. 因为动画片里的人物很可爱。

**Recitation** 经典背诵

**May:** My friend, Gucci, loves horror movies the most. But I like almost all the movies except the horror movies. So sometimes it seems that we don't speak the same languages as far as movies are concerned. But Gucci also likes romance and comedy movies very much. So it's not that bad.

# 经典影片
## Classic Movies

在电影院门口,阿美和古奇看到了今晚回放《阿甘正传》的海报,这一次两个人找到了共同的话题,并最终决定改看这部电影。

**May**: Look, *Forest Gump* is on at 6:30.

**Gucci**: Really? It was on in 1994 for the first time. And it is really a classic.

**May**: Yeah, I am very impressed with Tom Hanks' performance in the movie.

**Gucci**: I am also impressed with the lines in the movie.

**May**: Life is like a box of chocolates, you never know what you're gonna ( going to ) to get.

**Gucci**: That's my favorite.

**May**: You know, it also won 6 Oscar awards in 1995. Unbelievable!

**Gucci**: It deserves. That film can give us a lot of inspiration.

**May**: Yes, the Forrest's experience can encourage the people in trouble.

**Gucci**: All in all, it will never lose its appeal.

**May**: Gucci, I have an idea. Do you want to see this movie together?

**Gucci**: Sure. Now you are talking.

**阿美**:快看,六点半将上映《阿甘正传》。

**古奇**:真的吗? 这部片子在 1994 年首映。它确实很经典。

**阿美**:是啊,我对电影中汤姆·汉克斯的表演印象深刻。

**古奇**:我对电影中的台词也印象颇深。

**阿美**:生命就像一盒巧克力,你永远都不知道你将会得到些什么。

**古奇**:那也是我的最爱。

**阿美**:你知道吗? 它在 1995 年获得了 6 项奥斯卡奖。真是难以置信!

**古奇**:这是它应得的。那部电影能给我们许多激励。

**阿美**:是啊,阿甘的经历可以鼓励处在困境中的人们。

**古奇**:总之,这部电影经久不衰。

**阿美**:古奇,我有个想法。你想和我一起看这部电影吗?

**古奇**:好的。你这次说到点子上了。

---

**生词小结**

**classic** *n.* 经典作品
**be impressed with** 对……印象深刻
**line** *n.* 台词
**deserve** *vi.* 值得
**inspiration** *n.* 鼓舞
**experience** *n.* 经历

---

**注释**

*Forrest Gump* 《阿甘正传》。该片是由罗伯特·泽梅基斯(Robert Zemeckis)导演,汤姆·汉克斯主演。在 1995 年的第 67 届奥斯卡金像奖最佳影片的角逐中,它一举获得了最佳影片、最佳男主角、最佳导演、最佳改编剧本、最佳剪辑和最佳视觉效果等六项大奖。

# Act 2

娱乐休闲场景·Entertainment and Fun

**encourage**  *vt.* 鼓励
**appeal**  *n.* 感染力

**Now you are talking.** 在 Topic 2 中阿美说她们之间在电影方面达不成共识。所以这次古奇就开玩笑说,这次终于达成共识,说到点子上了。她们都共同喜欢《阿甘正传》这部电影。

## F功能性句型扩展
unctional structure ——— 总结句型

请朗读以下短语和句型,家长和孩子交替进行。

All in all…  总之……
In short…  简言之……
To conclude…  总而言之……
In sum…  总之……
In brief…  简言之……

In a word…  简言之……
In other words…  换言之……
As far as I am concerned…  据我所知……
We can draw a conclusion that…  我们可以得出这样的结论……

Recitation
经典背诵

**May:** *Forest Gump* was on in 1994 for the first time. And it's never lost its appeal ever since. This movie gives us a lot of inspiration. But what I like most about it is Tom Hanks' performance which is really impressive. I just love it.

**Topic4** 爱情
Love

阿美在看完电影后，看到第二天放映《人鬼情未了》的海报，这是妈妈最喜欢的电影，因此她当即为爸爸妈妈买了两张电影票。那么爸爸妈妈到底有没有去看电影呢？

(*Dad and Mom walk to the cinema to see Ghost.*)

**Dad**：*Ghost* will be on at 6:30. It's already 6:15 now. Hurry up.

(*Mom feels a little angry.*)

**Mom**：You'd been hanging around before left home. Well, now, you are urging me for the movie. This has been fun!

**Dad**：Don't be upset. I am just afraid of missing the movie. It is your favorite.

**Mom**：In short, you become more and more impatient with me after wedding.

**Dad**：Why do you think so?

**Mom**：Every time I complain about the domestic chores with you, you just don't listen.

**Dad**：Nothing of the sort!

**Mom**：Don't interrupt me! In addition, every time I need your advice, you just say, "it's up to you."

**Dad**：Maybe I was busy with my work at that time, so I felt a little bored.

**Mom**：You mean, I am not busy with my work?

**Dad**：Honey, don't get me wrong. (Don't misunderstand me.) I don't know how to explain. But I really have eyes only for you and our children.

**Mom**：Do you still love me?

(爸爸和妈妈一起走着去电影院看《人鬼情未了》。)

**爸爸**：《人鬼情未了》将在六点半开演。现在已经六点十五了，快点啊。

(妈妈感到有点生气。)

**妈妈**：你在家磨磨蹭蹭的。现在又为了赶电影一直催我。真有意思！

**爸爸**：别着急。我只是怕错过电影嘛。这可是你最喜欢的电影。

**妈妈**：简而言之，结婚后你对我越来越不耐烦了。

**爸爸**：你为什么这样认为？

**妈妈**：每次我对你抱怨家务琐事时，你总是不听。

**爸爸**：哪有这回事！

**妈妈**：别打断我！另外，每次我需要你给些意见的时候，你只是说："你说了算。"

**爸爸**：可能是那个时候我忙于工作，感觉有些烦吧。

**妈妈**：你的意思是说，我工作不忙吗？

**爸爸**：亲爱的，不要误会我。我不知道该怎么解释。但是我真的非常在乎你和孩子们。

**妈妈**：那你还爱我吗？

**Dad**：Honey, maybe sometimes I seem careless, but I take great care to cooking breakfast every morning. That shows how much I love you.

(*Mom drops into silence.*)

**Mom**：Oh, honey, that's enough. Our love story is more touching than the *Ghost*.

**Dad**：Let's go to see the movie. It's time to begin.

**爸爸:**亲爱的,可能有时候我显得很粗心大意,但是每天早晨我都会很用心地做饭。这代表了我有多爱你。

(妈妈沉默了片刻。)

**妈妈:**哦,亲爱的,这足够了。我们的爱情故事比《人鬼情未了》还要动人。

**爸爸:**那我们就快去看电影吧。马上要开演了。

---

### 生词小结

**walk** *vi.* 走
**urge** *vt.* 催促
**upset** *adj.* 心烦意乱的
**impatient** *adj.* 不耐烦的
**interrupt** *vt.* 打断
**bored** *adj.* 烦躁的
**explain** *vt.* 解释
**careless** *adj.* 粗心的
**touching** *adj.* 感动的

### 注释

**Hurry up** 快点!
**hang around** 闲荡
**complain about** 抱怨……
**domestic chores** 家务琐事
**in addition** 另外,……
**be busy with** 忙于……
**cook breakfast** 做早餐
**take great care** 用心……
**drop into silence** 陷入沉思
**Nothing of the sort!** 没有这回事!
**It's up to you.** 由你决定!
**I really have eyes only for you and our children.**
我真的非常在乎你和孩子们。从字面上看,这句话是说我的眼睛放在你和孩子们的身上。言下之意是说非常在乎你和孩子们。

---

## G语法小结
### Grammer —— 用在时间和地点前的介词

1. 连接时间的介词

(1)at 表示时间概念的某一个点(在某时刻、时间、阶段等)

*at* 6:40 在六点四十

(2)on 表示具体日期

*They arrived in Beijing on February.* 他们二月份到达北京。

(3)in 作为连接时间的介词,有如下两重意思

①表示时段、时期。

*in* 1983 在 1983 年

②表示以说话时间为基点的"(若干时间)以后"。

*I will be back in* 10 *minutes.* 我十分钟后回来。

*The job will be finished in a week.* 这工作在一星期内完成。

(4) after 表示"在(某具体时间)以后"

*after supper* 晚饭后；*after the war* 战后

(5) for 表示"(动作延续)若干时间"

*I stayed in Beijing for two days.* 我在北京待了两天。

(6) since 表示"自(某具体时间)以来"，常用于完成时态

*He has worked here since 1965.* (指一段时间，强调时间段)自从1965年以来，他一直在这儿工作。

*He began to work here after 1965.* (指一点时间，强调时间点)从1965年以后，他开始在这儿工作。

2. 连接地点的介词

(1) in (表地点、场所、部位等)在……里，在……中

*in Class Two Grade Three* 在三年级二班

*in Beijing* 在北京

(2) on (表示接触)在……上

*on the wall* 在墙面上　*on the floor* 在地上

(3) under 在……正下方，在……下面，底下

*under the chair* 在椅子下　*under the tree* 在树下

(4) behind 在……后面

*behind the sofa* 在沙发后　*behind the tree* 在树后

## D 家庭总动员
### Do it together

**两人一组，一方朗诵下面的中文句子，另一方挑选出合适的翻译。**

1. 阿美把电影票放到桌子上。
2. 爸爸喜欢饭后散步。
3. 叔叔星期二将带丹尼尔去电影院。
4. 妈妈下班后忙于准备晚饭。
5. 电影五分钟后开演。

1. Mom is busy with supper after work.
2. Dad likes having a walk after supper.
3. The film will begin in five minutes.
4. May put the movie tickets on the desk.
5. Uncle will take Daniel to the cinema on Tuesday.

**Dad**: My wife often complains that I've become more and more impatient after the wedding. You know, I am always very busy and my carelessness just makes it worse. But I do care a lot about my family. I am a very responsible person to my family. So to make it up for her, I'd take her to movies from time to time. It works!

# 名胜古迹 Places of Interests

## Goals

**在这个场景中,我们将学到:**

1. 鼻辅音 1 组
2. 著名景点的词汇
3. 总结句型练习
4. 一般现在时

旅游计划
**Travel Plans**

 玩转语音

1. A monk's monkey mounted a monastery wall munching mashed melon and melted macaroni.
2. How many cans can a canner can if a canner can can cans? A canner can can as many cans as a canner can if a canner can can cans.
3. While we were walking, we were watching window washers wash Washington's windows with warm washing water.

及格时间:11 秒

你的纪录:—— 秒

及格时间:13 秒

你的纪录:—— 秒

及格时间:13 秒

你的纪录:—— 秒

听 学 读 看

五一黄金周要到了,阿美和丹尼尔回到家,妈妈在询问了两人的放假情况之后,决定在饭后商量五一的具体安排。不过妈妈好像提了要求哦,是什么呢?

| | |
|---|---|
| **Daniel:** Mom, Dad, we are back! | **丹尼尔:**爸爸,妈妈,我们回来了。 |
| **Mom:** Honey, how long is your vacation? | **妈妈:**亲爱的,你们放几天假? |
| **May:** 9 days, plus Saturday and Sunday. | **阿美:**加上星期六和星期天,九天假。 |
| **Mom:** How about you? Danny. | **妈妈:**你呢? 丹尼。 |
| **Daniel:** Me, too. | **丹尼尔:**我也一样。 |
| **Mom:** Is there any homework from your teacher? | **妈妈:**老师留了家庭作业吗? |
| **Daniel:** Sure, Mom, we can get it done in one single day. | **丹尼尔:**当然留了,妈妈。不过我们一天就能把它做完。 |
| **Mom:** You two promise? | **妈妈:**你们俩能保证吗? |
| **Daniel:** We promise. | **丹尼尔:**当然。 |
| **Mom:** You should get it done on time. | **妈妈:**你们一定要准时把作业做完。 |

Daniel：When are we gonna talk about our vacation plan?

Mom：After dinner.

Daniel：Are you gonna listen to our ideas?

Mom：Of course.

丹尼尔：那我们什么时候讨论我们的假
期计划呢？

妈妈：晚饭后。

丹尼尔：那你们会听我们的建议吗？

妈妈：当然会。

---

**生词小结**

| | | | |
|---|---|---|---|
| **vacation** | *n.* 假期 | **homework** | *n.* 家庭作业 |
| **Saturday** | *n.* 星期六 | **plan** | *n.* 计划 |
| **Sunday** | *n.* 星期天 | **listen** | *vi.* 听 |

---

# 语音小结 Pronunciation —— 鼻辅音 1 组

1. /m/ Mom me homework from

发音小贴士：双唇闭拢，堵住气流，软腭下垂，气流从鼻腔流出发音。

2. /n/ vacation Sunday done plan

发音小贴士：舌尖紧贴上齿龈，堵住气流，软腭下垂，气流从鼻腔流出发音，发音时口微张开。

对比练习 /m/ 和 /n/ mother and sun mouth and not meat and nose mine and know

3. /ŋ/ long single sing song

发音小贴士：舌位和/k/，/g/相同，软腭下垂，堵住口腔通道，气流从鼻腔流出发音，发音时口张开。

对比练习 /n/ 和 /ŋ/ note and wing nice and ring new and thing no and king

---

# Recitation 经典背诵

Daniel：On the Labor's Day, I'd always get 9-day holiday. Though the teachers would usually give us a lot of homework to do, we would just spend one day to get it done. Then I can have enough time just for family fun.

娱乐休闲场景·Entertainment and Fun

文化遗址

**Cultural Relics**

听 学 看 读

吃完饭，大家坐在一块儿讨论假期的安排。大家都想去哪个地方旅行呢？那么大家的意见又是否一致呢？

**Mom**：So, Ben, what do you think we should go for our vacation?

**Benjamin**：I prefer staying in Beijing.

**Daniel**：Why? Dad.

**Benjamin**：I think we should have a good rest during the vacation.

**Daniel**：But we have stayed here for a long time. We should go somewhere else.

**Benjamin**：Though we have stayed here for a long time, we still have some cultural relics to visit.

**Daniel**：We have visited so many, Dad. Can you tell me any we haven't been to yet?

**Benjamin**：Zhoukoudian is very famous.

**Daniel**：Come on, Dad, that isn't interesting.

**Benjamin**：But that is good for your study.

**Daniel**：And?

**Benjamin**：You two should know more about the cultural relics of our country.

**Daniel**：Come on.

妈妈：本，这个假期，你觉得我们该去哪儿？

本杰明：我觉得还是待在北京好。

丹尼尔：为什么啊？爸爸。

本杰明：我认为我们应该乘放假好好休息一下。

丹尼尔：但是我们已经在北京待了那么长的时间了啊。我们应该换一个地方。

本杰明：虽然我们在北京待了很长的时间，但是我们还有很多文化遗址还没有去参观呢。

丹尼尔：我们已经去过很多地方了，你能告诉我还有哪些地方没有去吗？

本杰明：周口店是最著名的。

丹尼尔：爸爸，那儿一点意思都没有。

本杰明：但是去那里对你们的学习有好处啊。

丹尼尔：还有呢？

本杰明：你们两个需要更多地了解一下我们祖国的文化遗址。

丹尼尔：拜托。

---

**生词小结**

| | | | |
|---|---|---|---|
| prefer | *vt.* 宁可 | cultural | *adj.* 文化的 |
| stay | *vi.* 待,停留 | relic | *n.* 纪念物,遗迹 |
| rest | *n.* 休息 | famous | *adj.* 著名的 |

## 单词扩展 Vocabulary Builder

### 著名景点的词汇

| 基础词汇 | 提高词汇 |
| --- | --- |
| Summer Palace 颐和园 | the Eiffel Tower 埃菲尔铁塔 |
| the Great Wall 长城 | the Statue of Liberty 自由女神像 |
| the Temple of Heaven 天坛 | Chinatown 唐人街 |
| the Forbidden City 紫禁城 | the Niagara Falls 尼亚加拉大瀑布 |
| Beihai Park 北海公园 | Sahara Desert 撒哈拉大沙漠 |
| Yellow Crane Tower 黄鹤楼 | Yellowstone National Park 美国黄石国家公园 |
| Potala Palace 布达拉宫 | Mount Fuji 富士山 |
| West Lake 西湖 | Pyramids 埃及金字塔 |

## Do it together 家庭总动员

　　两人一组，一方随机大声读出上面词汇的英文和中文，另一方用该词汇填入下面的句子，大声朗读并用中文给出景点所在地。

　　　　　　(                 ) is very famous.

【例】家长读 Summer Palace 颐和园
　　　孩子读 Summer Palace is very famous. 颐和园在北京。

### Recitation 经典背诵

**Dad：**For the vacation I suggest we stay in Beijing. We can have a good rest during the vacation. Though, we have been here for a long time, we can always find exciting places to go to. But I'm afraid my children won't agree with me. You know kids!

自然风光
Natural Scenery

爸爸的意见遭到了反驳,那么妈妈的意见是什么呢?大家会赞同妈妈的意见吗?

**May:** So, what do you think? Mom.

**Daniel:** Do you also want to stay in Beijing, visiting cultural relics?

**Mom:** Er, actually, no.

**Daniel:** So?

**Mom:** I would suggest we enjoy some natural scenery in Guilin. Though it would be a long journey there, we can always play cards on the train.

**Daniel:** Is there any interesting place for us to go?

**Mom:** Sure, we can go boating there and eat at the farm house.

**Daniel:** And?

**Mom:** In a word, we can enjoy things that are different from cities. What do you think?

**Daniel:** Compared Dad's opinion, I prefer mom's plan. But that's not perfect either.

**Mom:** All right, where do you want to go?

**Daniel:** If I tell you, you promise me that you won't laugh it off.

**Mom:** I won't, go ahead!

**阿美:** 妈妈,你认为呢?

**丹尼尔:** 你也想待在北京,去参观一些文化遗址吗?

**妈妈:** 事实上,我不是很同意这个观点。

**丹尼尔:** 所以呢?

**妈妈:** 我建议去桂林欣赏自然风光。虽然路途会远一些,但是我们可以在火车上打牌啊。

**丹尼尔:** 那个地方有什么好玩的吗?

**妈妈:** 当然有啦,我们可以划船,还可以吃到农家菜啊。

**丹尼尔:** 还有呢?

**妈妈:** 总之,我们能领略到与城市不一样的东西。你们觉得怎么样?

**丹尼尔:** 和爸爸的建议相比,我觉得妈妈的要好,但也不是最好的。

**妈妈:** 那好,你们俩想去哪里?

**丹尼尔:** 如果我告诉你,你答应我你们不会一笑置之。

**妈妈:** 不会的,说吧!

### 生词小结

| | | |
|---|---|---|
| **actually** | *adv.* | 事实上 |
| **natural** | *adj.* | 自然的 |
| **scenery** | *n.* | 风景 |
| **journey** | *n.* | 旅行 |
| **enjoy** | *vt.* | 享受 |
| **perfect** | *adj.* | 完美的 |
| **laugh** | *vi.* | 笑 |

### 注释

**laugh it off** 一笑而过

## 情景练习 —— 总结句型练习
**S**cene practice

仔细阅读下面五个场景,两人一组,使用总结句型(见88页),用一用,练一练。

1. At the end of the meeting, Benjamin has to conclude what he has said. If you were Benjamin, what would you say?

2. Shirley is asked to tell her experience briefly. If you were Shirley, what would you say?

3. May is the chairman of the union, she is required to conclude this year's work. If you were May, what would you say?

4. Daniel is very good at learning English, if you were Daniel, what would you say when asked to tell your way of learning English briefly?

5. If you were May, at the end of the speech, what would you say?

**R**ecitation
经典背诵

Mom:I don't like staying in Beijing during any vacations. I prefer to go to some new places like Guilin for the beautiful scenery. Though it would be a long trip, it would be more fun too. But I'm not sure whether other family members would want to do the same thing.

 出游国外
Travelling Abroad

爸爸妈妈的意见都遭到了孩子们的反对,尤其是丹尼尔,那么孩子们到底想要去哪里呢?

**Mom:** Can you guys be quick to tell me your decision?

**May:** Actually, Mom, Daniel and I want to go to Hawaii very much?

**Mom:** Hawaii? Are you out of your mind?

**May:** After reconsideration, we want to stick to our plan.

**Mom:** Can you tell me why?

**May:** Yes, because some of our classmates have been to Hawaii several times.

**Mom:** Is that all?

**May:** Of course not.

**Mom:** And?

**May:** We can also enjoy the different cultural customs.

**Daniel:** That is good for our study, too.

**May:** We can improve our English.

**Mom:** All right, Mom and Dad will consider that. Now you have to go to sleep.

妈妈:快说吧,你们的建议是什么呢?

阿美:事实上,我和丹尼尔都非常想去夏威夷。

妈妈:夏威夷? 你们两个真的是有点不正常。

阿美:经过我们的深思熟虑,我们决定坚持我们的计划。

妈妈:能告诉我原因吗?

阿美:因为我们班的好多同学都已经去过夏威夷好几次了。

妈妈:这就是所有的原因吗?

阿美:当然不是。

妈妈:还有什么呢?

阿美:我们还可以领略异国的风情。

丹尼尔:那对我们的学习也有好处。

阿美:我们能提高我们的英语。

妈妈:好吧,妈妈和爸爸会考虑你们的意见。现在你们该去睡觉了。

---

**生词小结**

decision　*n.* 决定
classmate　*n.* 同班同学
custom　*n.* 习惯
improve　*vt.* 提高
consider　*vt.* 考虑
sleep　*vi.* 睡觉

**注释**

**You are out of your mind.** *你疯了吧!*

# G语法小结
## rammer —— 一般现在时

一般现在时主要表示：

**1. 经常发生或反复发生的动作**

*Dad gets up at seven.* 爸爸七点起床。

*Mom works eight hours a day.* 妈妈一天工作八个小时。

*I go to school every day.* 我每天都去上学。

**2. 现在的情况或状态**

*They like eating.* 他们爱吃。

*Danny is a pupil.* 丹丹是小学生。

*Thank you, I don't need it.* 谢谢，我不需要。

**3. 永恒的真理**

*The sun rises in the east.* 太阳从东方升起。

*It snows in winter.* 冬天下雪。

但是在口语中，一般现在时也可以表示按计划、规定或时间表要发生的事,会有一个表示未来时间的状语。例如：

*The plane takes off at 9:00 a. m.* 飞机早上九点起飞。

*They arrive here tomorrow morning.* 他们明天早上到。

*When does the film begin?* 电影几点开始?

*My father is in his office from two to five this afternoon.* 我父亲今天下午两点到五点在他办公室。

在一般现在时中,如果主语是第三人称单数(he/she/it),谓语动词后需加 s 或者 es。如：

*He goes to school at seven every day.* 他每天七点钟上学。

*Mary likes English.* 玛丽喜欢英语。

# D家庭总动员
## o it together

描述一天的生活行程(用一般现在时)。

# Recitation 经典背诵

May: Daniel and I can never agree with our parents on vacation plans. What they want to do is just to stay in our own country. But Daniel and I both want to go to Hawaii very much where we think would be a fantastic place for a visit. I hope our dream will come true some day.

# Act 2

娱乐休闲场景 · Entertainment and Fun

# 爬山 Mountain Climbing

## Goals

在这个场景中,我们将学到:

1. 边辅音 1 组
2. 运动必需品词汇
3. 描写句型
4. 一般过去时

## Topic 1 爬山 Mountain Climbing

 玩转语音

1. Big black bugs bleed blue black blood but baby black bugs bleed blue blood.
2. A lusty lady loved a lawyer and longed to lure him from his laboratory.

及格时间: 10 秒
你的纪录:——秒
及格时间: 10 秒
你的纪录:——秒

丹尼尔一直都很想爬山,无奈爸爸总是太忙。明天恰逢爸爸休息,所以他决定说服爸爸带他去爬山,他能成功吗?

**Daniel**:Daddy, how are you going to spend your weekends?

**Dad**:I need to finish my research paper.

**Daniel**:Could you go with me to climb Xiang Shan?

**Dad**:Honey, I am sorry I have no time.

**Daniel**:Oh, Daddy, you should do more exercise. You are getting a little heavy.

**Dad**:I am afraid you are right. Recently, even going upstairs makes me out of breath.

**Daniel**:Then go climbing with me, Daddy. Mountain climbing can build your muscles like Popeyes.

**丹尼尔**:爸爸,你准备怎么过周末?

**爸爸**:我需要完成我的科研论文。

**丹尼尔**:能陪我去爬香山吗?

**爸爸**:宝贝,真抱歉,我没有时间。

**丹尼尔**:哦,爸爸,你应该多做做运动。你现在有些发胖了呢。

**爸爸**:我想你说得对。最近,爬楼都会让我上气不接下气的。

**丹尼尔**:爸爸,那就和我一起去爬山嘛。爬山会使你的肌肉像大力水手一样(强健)。

**Dad**: Terrific! It is also a good exercise to keep me fit.

**Daniel**: I give you my word, you must feel refreshed after mountain climbing.

**Dad**: OK, I'll go.

**Daniel**: That's a deal.

**Dad**: Sure.

**爸爸**:太棒了！爬山也是一种使我保持健康的运动。

**丹尼尔**:我向你保证,爬完山后,你一定会觉得神清气爽。

**爸爸**:好的,我和你一起去。

**丹尼尔**:一言为定。

**爸爸**:没问题。

---

**生词小结**

**research**   *n.* 研究
**paper**   *n.* 纸,论文
**go upstairs**   爬楼梯
**out of breath.**   上气不接下气
**muscle**   *n.* 肌肉
**keep fit**   保持健康
**refreshed**   *adj.* 神清气爽的

---

**注释**

**I give you my word.** 我向你保证。
**That's a deal.** 一言为定。

---

**P**ronunciation **语音小结** ——— 边辅音1组

1. 清晰音/l/ like  climb  little  black
   发音小贴士:出现在元音前。舌端紧贴上齿龈,舌前向硬腭抬起形成阻碍,气流冲破阻碍发音。/l/是浊辅音,发音声带振动。

2. 含糊音/l/ feel  health  build  deal
   发音小贴士:出现在辅音前后和词尾。舌端紧贴上齿龈,舌前下陷,舌后上台,舌面形成凹形,气流在此发出共鸣的声音。/l/也是浊辅音,声带振动。

   对比练习   meal and let   still and leave

**Daniel**: Daddy is a very busy man and most of the time he has little time for any physical exercises. Recently, even going upstairs makes him out of breath. So the other day I asked him to go climbing with me. Dad knew that mountain climbing was a good exercise to keep him fit. So he said "yes".

# Topic 2 登山用品
## Outdoor Supplies

爸爸终于妥协了,答应带丹尼尔去爬山。晚上的时候,爸爸和丹尼尔一起准备登山用品。来看看两人都准备了些什么吧。

**Daniel:** Daddy, do you mind helping me prepare the supplies for mountain climbing.

**Dad:** OK. I am coming.

**Daniel:** Is it gonna to rain tomorrow?

**Dad:** I have checked the weather report. It says it will be cloudy, but no rain.

**Daniel:** Just take my umbrella in case of rain.

**Dad:** Daniel, don't forget to take enough water and food.

**Daniel:** Definitely, or else, I will starve to death halfway up the mountain.

**Dad:** Me, too, haha.

**Daniel:** Daddy, may I take your compass? I feel so cool with it in my hand.

**Dad:** All right. Oh, I nearly forgotten, I left my sneakers at my office.

**Daniel:** It doesn't matter. I can go with you to the supermarket to pick up a new pair.

**Dad:** OK, after we finish our preparation, we'll go to the supermarket.

丹尼尔:爸爸,能帮我一起准备爬山的装备吗?

爸爸:好的,这就来。

丹尼尔:明天会下雨吗?

爸爸:我已经看过天气预报了。明天会是多云天气,但不会下雨。

丹尼尔:带上我的伞就行了,以防下雨。

爸爸:丹尼尔,别忘记带足够的水和食物。

丹尼尔:当然不会忘记。否则,我会在半山腰饿死的。

爸爸:我也是,哈哈。

丹尼尔:爸爸,我能拿上您的指南针吗?我感觉把它拿在手上很酷。

爸爸:好的。哦,我差点忘了,我把我的球鞋忘在办公室了。

丹尼尔:没关系。我可以现在陪你去超市买一双新的。

爸爸:好的,我们准备完一切,就去超市。

### 生词小结

| | | | |
|---|---|---|---|
| **supply** | *n.* 供给 | **or else** | 否则 |
| **cloudy** | *adj.* 多云的 | **halfway** | *adj./adv.* 中途的(地) |
| **umbrella** | *n.* 雨伞 | **sneaker** | *n.* 帆布胶底鞋 |
| **in case of** | 万一…… | **supermarket** | *n.* 超市 |
| **definitely** | *adv.* 确定地 | **pick up** | 买 |

## 单词扩展 Vocabulary Builder

### 运动必需品词汇

| 基础词汇 | 提高词汇 |
| --- | --- |
| tent 帐篷 | hiking boots 登山鞋 |
| compass 指南针 | hiking cap 登山帽 |
| map 地图 | sleeping bag 睡袋 |
| rope 绳子 | flashlight 手电筒 |
| camera 照相机 | backpack 背包 |
| blanket 毯子 | sneaker 帆布胶底鞋 |
| sport shoes 运动鞋 | sport shirt 运动鞋 |
| water 水 | food 食物 |

## D家庭总动员
o it together

两人一组，一方随机大声读出上面词汇的英文和中文，另一方用该词汇填入下面的句子，大声朗读出来，并用中文给出一个理由。

**Don't forget to take (　　　　　　　　).**

【例】家长读 water 水

宝贝读 Don't forget to take the water. 因为我们需要喝水。

## Recitation 经典背诵

Daniel：To prepare the supplies for mountain climbing, Daddy and I would take the umbrella in case of rain. And we also know the importance to take enough water and food with us. Though we spend a lot time on preparing, we still can't say that we get everything with us.

## 娱乐休闲场景·Entertainment and Fun

索道
**Cable car**

听 学 看

第二天清晨,丹尼尔兴高采烈地和爸爸一起去爬山。可是爬到半山腰的时候,爸爸实在是累得筋疲力尽,这可怎么办呢?

**Daniel:** What a beautiful day!

**Dad:** The weather is so crazy. It rained cats and dogs last night, but cleared up in the morning.

**Daniel:** I was worried about cancelling the climbing.

**Dad:** Honey, wait for me. I am too tired to move a step further.

**Daniel:** What about taking the cable car?

**Dad:** Attaboy, that's just what I am thinking.

**Daniel:** Wow, What a long queue this is!

**Dad:** Honey, be patient. It's better to wait than to climb with my legs broken.

(*After a few minutes, they get into the cable car.*)

**Daniel:** Daddy, look ahead in the distance, the mountains there. They roll all the way up to the sky.

**Dad:** Yeah, the scenery is beautiful. What's more, the air is fresh here.

**Daniel:** So you wanna stay here?

**Dad:** Of course not, I have to watch my *American Idol*.

丹尼尔:今天天气真好!

爸爸:天气真是变化无常。昨晚还下着瓢泼大雨,但是早晨就变晴了。

丹尼尔:我还担心要取消爬山呢。

爸爸:宝贝,等等我。我太累了,一步也挪不动了。

丹尼尔:乘坐索道怎么样?

爸爸:太好了,这正是我所想的。

丹尼尔:哇,排了好长的队啊!

爸爸:孩子,耐心点。等总比爬得筋疲力尽要好些。

(几分钟后,他们上了缆车。)

丹尼尔:爸爸,往远处看,那里有很多山。它们绵延起伏一直通向天边。

爸爸:是啊,这景色真美。而且,这里的空气也很新鲜。

丹尼尔:那么你想一直待在这儿吗?

爸爸:当然不想啊,我得回去看我的《美国偶像》。

---

**生词小结**

clear up　天放晴
be worried about　担心……
cancell　*vt.* 取消
cable car　缆车
queue　*n.* 长队

---

**注释**

**It rained cats and dogs last night.** 昨晚下起了瓢泼大雨。

**Attaboy.** 太好了。

**It's better to wait than to climb with my legs**

ahead    *adv.* 向前

in the distance    在远处

roll    *vt.* 滚

what's more    而且

broken. 等总比爬得筋疲力尽要好些。

# F功能性句型扩展 —— 描写句型
### unctional structure

请朗读以下短语，家长和孩子交替进行。

First/ Firstly/ First of all/ To start with/ In the beginning/ In the first place...    首先，第一

At first...    最初

Second/ Secondly...    其次……

For one thing..., for another...    首先……其次……

Besides...    此外

In addition...    除此之外

In particularly...    特别地

What's more...    而且，此外

Moreover/ Likewise/ Furthermore...    而且，此外……

Third/ Thirdly...    第三……

Last but not the least...    最后……

Finally...    最后……

**R**ecitation 经典背诵

**Dad**：When Daniel and I climb mountains, Daniel can run quickly but I always, soon, get too tired to move a step further. So I'd think about taking a cable car. The queue may be long. But it's better to wait than to climb, and also the scenery from the cable car is really fantastic.

# Topic 4 景致
## Scenery

到达山顶后,爸爸和丹尼尔边欣赏美景,边聊天。来听听他们都在聊些什么吧。

**Daniel:** Wow, the view from the peak is so grand!

**Dad:** Look, most of the maple leaves have turned red.

**Daniel:** Did you ever see this kind of beautiful scene?

**Dad:** Of course, my father used to take me to Xiang Shan or somewhere like that as a child.

**Daniel:** But my father did not. He didn't have much time.

**Dad:** Honey, I'm sorry. I promise you, this summer vacation, I will take you to Huang-shan Mountains. It is more beautiful and magnificent.

**Daniel:** Really? It's a deal. Have you ever been there?

**Dad:** Yes, I went there five years ago. You were still a baby at that time.

**Daniel:** It really gets me interested. Is it higher than Xiang Shan?

**Dad:** Surely. You can enjoy the beauty of numerous streams and waterfalls. The sea of clouds has a fairy tale beauty.

**Daniel:** Can I see the rainbow?

**Dad:** That depends. If you are lucky, you can see a vivid rainbow across over two peaks.

---

**丹尼尔:** 哇,从山顶往下看,景色真壮观!

**爸爸:** 看,大部分枫叶都变红了。

**丹尼尔:** 你曾经看到过这么美的景色吗?

**爸爸:** 当然,在我小的时候,我爸爸常带我去香山或者其他什么地方。

**丹尼尔:** 但是我的爸爸却不带我玩。他总是没有时间。

**爸爸:** 宝贝,真对不起。我向你保证,今年暑假,我一定带你去爬黄山。黄山更漂亮,也更壮观。

**丹尼尔:** 真的吗? 一言为定。你曾经去过吗?

**爸爸:** 是啊,我五年前去过那里。那个时候你还只是个小孩儿呢。

**丹尼尔:** 我对这个很感兴趣。它比香山高吗?

**爸爸:** 当然了。你可以欣赏数不胜数的溪流和瀑布。云海像童话一样美丽。

**丹尼尔:** 我能看到彩虹吗?

**爸爸:** 那不一定。如果你幸运的话,你可以看到跨越两座山峰的鲜艳的彩虹。

---

**生词小结**

| | | |
|---|---|---|
| **peak** | *n.* 山峰 | |
| **maple leaf** | 枫叶 | |
| **summer vacation** | 暑假 | |
| **magnificent** | *adj.* 重大的,壮观的 | |
| **numerous** | *adj.* 无数的 | |
| **stream** | *n.* 溪流 | |
| **waterfall** | *n.* 瀑布 | |
| **fairy tale** | *n.* 童话 | |
| **rainbow** | *n.* 彩虹 | |

**注释**

**That depends.** 视情况而定。

## G 语法小结
### rammer ——— 一般过去时

"My father used to take me to Xiang Shan or somewhere like that as a child" 中出现的语法现象为一般过去时。

1. 一般过去时主要表示

(1)在过去的时间里所发生的动作或存在的状态

时间状语有：yesterday, last week, an hour ago, the other day, in 1949 等

*I bought it yesterday.* 我昨天买的。

*Where did you go last night?* 你昨天晚上去哪里了？

(2)在过去一段时间内,经常或习惯性的动作

*When I was a child, I often played football in the street.* 我小的时候常在街道里踢足球。

(3)在常用口语句型 It is time sb. did sth.（早该……了）中用过去时

*It is time you went to bed.* 你早该睡觉了。

2. 一般过去时的构成

(1)规则动词过去式,一般在动词原形末尾直接加上-ed

look-looked    play- played

(2)以不发音的字母 e 结尾的动词,去掉末尾 e 再加-ed

live-lived love- loved

(3)末尾只有一个辅音字母的重读闭音节,先双写这个辅音字母,再加-ed

stop-stopped

(4)末尾是辅音字母 + y 结尾的动词,先变 y 为 i,然后再加-ed

study-studied

(5)不规则动词的过去式需特殊记忆

am( is)-was are-were go-went know- knew

get-got take-took have (has)-had eat- ate

## D 家庭总动员
### o it together

从右边的方框里找出与左边相对应的动词过去式,并填在横线上。

1. go _____
2. research _____
3. know _____
4. am _____
5. supply _____
6. cancel _____
7. keep _____

| |
|---|
| knew |
| was |
| kept |
| cancelled |
| researched |
| went |
| supplied |

1. went
2. researched
3. knew
4. was
5. supplied
6. cancelled
7. kept

**Daniel**：The view on the peak is really great. In different seasons you can see a lot of different sceneries, all of which are really amazing. So each time I go mountain climbing I would feel really happy. I think Nature is humanbeings' best friend.

# Act 2

娱乐休闲场景 · Entertainment and Fun

## 海和海滨 Sea and Seashore

### Goals

在这个场景中,我们将学到:

1. 辅音连缀(一)4 组 8 个组合音
2. 颜色词汇
3. 描写句型练习
4. 一般疑问句

 四季和天气
Seasons and Weather

 玩转语音

1. A pleasant place to place a plaice is a place where a plaice is pleased to be placed.

2. How can a clam cram in a clean cream can?

3. As one black bug, bled blue, black blood. The other black bug bled blue.

及格时间:9 秒
你的纪录:——秒
及格时间:7 秒
你的纪录:——秒
及格时间:8 秒
你的纪录:——秒

今天天气很好,爸爸妈妈商量着带丹尼尔和阿美去海滩玩。

Dad:Nice weather, honey!

Mom:The days are getting longer!

Dad:May and Daniel often like this kind of weather.

Mom:Yeah, they can enjoy themselves in the day time and it is not so hot.

Dad:Honey, how about taking them to the beach this weekend?

Mom:That's great!

Dad:Since last time we've climbed the mountain, we haven't gone out for a long time.

Mom:And this kind of weather is rare for

爸爸:亲爱的,今天的天气真好。

妈妈:白天也变长了。

爸爸:阿美和丹尼尔都喜欢这种天气。

妈妈:对啊,天气不是那么的热,他们可以尽情地玩耍。

爸爸:亲爱的,这个星期带他们去海边玩怎么样啊?

妈妈:好啊。

爸爸:自从上次我们一块去爬了山之后,我们已经很久没有出去玩了。

妈妈:而且在这个季节,这种好天气也非常

the season either.

Dad：Yes, I remember last year this time, the weather is so hot.

Mom：So we must seize this chance to go to the beach.

Dad：Daniel loves the beach very much!

Mom：He will enjoy himself this weekend.

爸爸：是的,我记得去年这个时候天气非常热。

妈妈：所以我们要抓住这次机会去海边玩。

爸爸：丹尼尔非常喜欢海滩!

妈妈：这个周末他一定会玩得很愉快。

---

## 生词小结

| | | | |
|---|---|---|---|
| hot | *adj.* 热的 | mountain | *n.* 山 |
| beach | *n.* 海滩,沙滩 | season | *n.* 季节 |
| climb | *vt.* 爬 | seize | *vt.* 抓住,掌握 |

---

## P语音小结 —— 辅音连缀(一)4 组 8 个组合音
### ronunciation

辅音音节组合发音:

/pr/与/br/　price　proud　bread　break

/pl/与/bl/　place　plate　block　blot

/kr/与/gr/　crucial　crack　great　glad

/kl/与/gl/　clean　clip　glass　glance

发音小贴士:(1)第一个辅音念得轻而短,很快过渡到第二个音上。

　　　　　(2)切忌在两个辅音之间加入元音。

对比练习　pride and bride　plant and blank　creat and grant　cling and glad

---

**Recitation**
经典背诵

Dad：I like summer because the days are longer. Though it may get a bit too hot sometimes, our family still love that season because it's the best time of year to go to the beach for fun on weekends. Then everything is really perfect when you come to the beach.

海滩运动
Beach Sports

一家人来到了海滩，玩起了沙滩排球，妈妈和丹尼尔一组，爸爸和阿美一组，那么最后谁胜谁负呢？

**Daniel**：That's unfair, Mom.

**Mom**：What's up? honey!

**Daniel**：Dad is bigger than you, but how come I'm smaller than May.

**Mom**：Honey, it doesn't matter. The key to play volleyball is to cooperate with each other.

**Daniel**：What should I do?

**Mom**：You go figure it out yourself.

**Daniel**：Got it, Mom.

**Mom**：OK, Ben and May, here we go. Be careful, Danny, the ball is coming. That is the green one.

**Daniel**：Mom, don't worry about me, I can do it.

**Mom**：Danny, back to your position. Move!

**Daniel**：OK. Bingo! We win. Give me five, Mom.

**Mom**：Yeah.

丹尼尔：妈妈，那不公平。

妈妈：怎么拉？宝贝！

丹尼尔：爸爸比你块头大，但是我又比阿美块头小？

妈妈：宝贝，没有关系。打排球的关键是互相合作。

丹尼尔：那我该怎么做呢？

妈妈：你慢慢就会懂的。

丹尼尔：知道了，妈妈。

妈妈：好了，本，阿美，开球吧。小心，丹丹，球过来了。就是绿色的那个。

丹尼尔：妈妈，别担心我，我能够应付的。

妈妈：丹丹，回到你的位置上去。快跑！

丹尼尔：好的。我们赢了。妈妈，来击掌。

妈妈：耶！

---

**生词小结**

| | | |
|---|---|---|
| **unfair** | *adj.* | 不公平的 |
| **volleyball** | *n.* | 排球 |
| **cooperate** | *vt.* | 相互合作 |
| **figure out** | | 领会到 |
| **position** | *n.* | 位置 |

**注释**

**how come** 为什么？

**finger sth. out** 将某事弄明白

**worry about** 担心

**Give me five.** 击掌

## 单词扩展 Vocabulary Builder

### 颜色词汇

| 基础词汇 | 提高词汇 |
| --- | --- |
| white 白色 | brown 棕色 |
| red 红色 | grey 灰色 |
| yellow 黄色 | rubine 宝石红 |
| blue 蓝色 | silver 银白色 |
| green 绿色 | beige 米白色 |
| black 黑色 | cream 雪白 |
| pink 粉红色 | khaki 卡其色 |
| purple 紫色 | palegreen 苍绿色 |

## 家庭总动员 Do it together

两人一组,一方随机大声读出上面词汇的英文和中文,另一方用该词汇填入下面的句子,大声朗读并说出自己是否喜欢该颜色,并用中文给出一个喜欢或者是不喜欢的理由。

**That is the (　　　　　　　) one.**

【例】家长读 white 白色

孩子读 That is the white one。我喜欢白色,因为白色的衣服夏天穿着凉快。

**Recitation** 经典背诵

Daniel：My family always have fun when we go to the beach. There，we can play volleyball together. Mom and I are on one team, Dad and May are on the other. I think this is unfair，because Dad's team is obviously stronger than mine. But Mom always says that the key to playing volleyball is cooperation. And she is right. We do win the game sometimes.

## Topic 3 恋爱故事
### Love Stories

听 学 读 看　　打完了排球，阿美和丹尼尔在海边玩耍。爸爸妈妈坐在不远处回忆着当年的种种往事。来听听他们都说了些什么吧！

**Mom：**How time flies!

**Dad：**May and Danny have already grown up.

**Mom：**I can still remember our first date.

**Dad：**Look at that big tree over there.

**Mom：**Yeah, oh my god! It's still there. We have our first date right on there.

**Dad：**Do you know that I fell in love with you at the first sight.

**Mom：**You were dull at that time.

**Dad：**But you agreed to go out with me at last.

**Mom：**(*smile*) I can't believe this for it's been 20 years since we got married.

**Dad：**So do you feel happy now?

**Mom：**I couldn't have been any happier!

**Dad：**Of course, we are the happiest family in the world.

**妈妈：**时间过得真快啊！

**爸爸：**阿美和丹丹都已经长大了。

**妈妈：**我仍然还记得我们的第一次约会。

**爸爸：**看那边的那棵大树。

**妈妈：**天啊！它还在那儿。我们第一次约会就是在那里。

**爸爸：**你知道吗，我对你是一见钟情。

**妈妈：**你那个时候真傻。

**爸爸：**但是你最后还是答应和我出去约会。

**妈妈：**(微笑)我们都结婚20年了，真是难以相信啊。

**爸爸：**那你现在觉得幸福吗？

**妈妈：**再幸福不过了！

**爸爸：**当然了，我们是世界上最幸福的家庭。

### 生词小结

| | | | |
|---|---|---|---|
| **date** | *n.* 约会 | **agree** | *vi.* 同意 |
| **first** | *adj.* 第一的 | **marry** | *vt.* 结婚 |
| **dull** | *adj.* 无趣的 | **happy** | *adj.* 幸福的 |

## S情景练习
### cene practice —— 描写句型练习

**仔细阅读下面五个场景,两人一组,使用描写句型(见105页),用一用,练一练。**

1. If you were Benjamin, you would meet someone you don't know in the railway station, how would you describe your own appearance to him or her?

2. If you were Daniel, and went to Guilin this summer vacation. If you are asked to describe the scenery there, what would you say?

3. If you were Shirley, you want to describe the skirt you like in the store to your colleague, what would you say?

4. If you were May, you are asked to describe your brother's appearance, what would you say?

5. If you were Shirley, you are asked to tell the procedure of making the cake, what would you say?

**Recitation** 经典背诵

**Mom:** Benjamin and I have been married for 20 years. He is a good husband and father though he may be a little bit dull at times. But I knew this when we were dating. He is an honest man which makes up his charm. That's why we have been a really happy family for all these years. So we are lucky to find each other, I suppose.

## Topic 4 结婚照
### Wedding Photos

爸爸妈妈聊天聊到了他们的结婚照,妈妈说那个时候的结婚照很土,爸爸就建议他们今天再照一次婚纱照。一起来看看吧!

**Dad:** Do you often recall our wedding?

**Mom:** Yeah, and our wedding photo always remind me of a lot of things.

**Dad:** Wedding photo?

**Mom:** We were all very old fashioned at that time. Now, the technology really gives the wedding pictures a new edge.

**Dad:** I think we can have some more photoes taken.

**Mom:** Can we? But there is no photographer.

**Dad:** That's not a problem. I heard there is a popular photo gallery on this beach.

**Mom:** Really? Let's get the children together.

(*All the family are on the beach.*)

**Daniel:** Mom, you are so beautiful today!

**Mom:** Am I? Today? What about all the other days?

**Dad:** You are always beautiful.

**Photographer:** Everybody, say cheese here.

(*All family members laugh into the camera.*)

爸爸:你现在经常会想起我们的婚礼吗?

妈妈:嗯,我们的结婚照总是会勾起我许多的回忆。

爸爸:结婚照?

妈妈:我们那个时候真是土。现在,科技真的将结婚照带上了一个新的舞台。

爸爸:我认为今天我们可以再照一次结婚照。

妈妈:可以吗?但是在这儿没有摄影师啊。

爸爸:没问题。我听说在这个海滩附近有一个很受欢迎的照相馆。

妈妈:真的吗?那叫孩子们一块儿吧。

(全家都在海滩上。)

丹尼尔:妈妈,你今天真是漂亮!

妈妈:是吗?就今天吗?那平时呢?

爸爸:一样漂亮。

摄影师:所有的人看这里,说"茄子"。

(全家都望着照相机笑了。)

---

**生词小结**

**wedding** *n.* 婚礼
**photo** *n.* 照片
**fashion** *n.* 时尚
**technology** *n.* 技术
**edge** *n.* 优势
**photographer** *n.* 摄影师
**popular** *adj.* 流行的
**photo gallery** 照相馆
**camera** *n.* 照相机

---

**注释**

**say cheese here** 在中国照相的时候我们习惯说"茄子",对应中国的"茄子",美国人说的是"cheese"。

## G 语法小结
### rammer —— 一般疑问句

一般疑问句可称为以 yes 或 no 回答的句子。一般疑问句的基本语序是:系动词 be/ 助动词/情态动词 + 主语 + 其他成分? 如:

*Are you from Japan? Yes, I am. / No, I'm not.*

*Is her sister doing her homework now? Yes, she is. / No, she isn't.*

*Does your mother work in a bank? Yes, she does. / No, she doesn't.*

*Do you live near your school? Yes, I do. / No, I don't.*

*Can you speak English? Yes, I can. / No, I can't.*

(1)句中有 be 动词(am/ is/ are …)、情态动词(can /may /must …)时,可直接将它们提到主语前。主语为第一人称,应将其改为第二人称

*I'm in Class 2 Grade 3. → Are you in Class 2 Grade 3?*

*We're watching TV. → Are you watching TV?*

*He can swim now. → Can he swim now?*

*My parents may come with us. → May your parents come with you?*

(2)陈述句中只有一个实义动词作谓语,且为一般现在时,变为一般疑问句时在句首加 do 或 does,主语后的实义动词用原形

*I love you. → Do you love me?*

*She wants to go to the movies. → Does she want to go to the movies?*

## D 家庭总动员
### o it together

**两人一组,一方朗诵下面的中文句子,另一方挑选出合适的翻译。**

1. 你喜欢打排球吗?
   是的,我非常喜欢。
2. 你觉得妈妈今天漂亮吗?
   是的,非常漂亮。
3. 你能帮帮我吗?
4. 你觉得现在幸福吗?
5. 丹尼尔会打排球吗?
   不,他不会打排球。

1. Do you feel happy now?
2. Can Daniel play volleyball?
   No, he can't.
3. Can you help me?
4. Do you like playing volleyball?
   Yes, I like it very much.
5. Do you think Mom is beautiful today?
   Yes, I think Mom is very beautiful today.

### Recitation
经典背诵

Dad:My wedding photoes always bring back lots of memories. My wife and I were very old fashioned at that time. Now the new technology has given wedding photos a new edge. So maybe someday we should more photoes taken, maybe have one taken on the beach with our children around. That would be a really good one.

# 游乐园 Amusement Park

## Goals

**在这个场景中，我们将学到：**

1. 辅音连缀(二)3 组 8 个组合音
2. 各种游乐项目词汇
3. 指示句型
4. 特殊疑问句

 童话世界
Fairytale World

 **玩转语音**

1. Yellow butter, purple jelly, red jam, black bread. Spread it thicker, say it quicker!
2. Fresh fried fish, Fish fresh fried, Fried fish fresh, Fish fried fresh.

及格时间：10 秒
你的纪录：——秒
及格时间：7 秒
你的纪录：——秒

丹尼尔和阿美在期中考试中都取得了好成绩，所以今天妈妈带他们俩来欢乐谷，他们玩得还挺开心的，一起来看看吧。

**May：** Do you know how happy I am? The Ant Kingdom is a perfect world with colorful fairy tales. It seems like the air is fresh here.

**Daniel：** Just kids like that.

**May：** Come on baby, stop trying to pretend like a man. If you go there, you are sure to like them.

**Daniel：** Hurry up! Hurry up! What lovely caterpillars are over there!

**May：** I said you are sure to like them. There is the Grand Parade Of Ants Carnival in a few minutes in the square. You will experience a dream of fantasy.

**Daniel：** What's that?

**阿美：**你知道我有多开心吗？蚂蚁王国是一个充满着多姿多彩童话的完美世界。连这里的空气都似乎新鲜了许多。

**丹尼尔：**只有小孩子才喜欢那种地方。

**阿美：**得了吧，小朋友，别老是装大人了。如果你到了那里，你一定会喜欢的。

**丹尼尔：**快点！快点！看那边的毛毛虫多可爱啊！

**阿美：**我就说你一定会喜欢它们吧。几分钟后在广场中会有蚂蚁狂欢大游行！你将会经历一个梦幻之旅。

**丹尼尔：**那是什么？

**May**：All kinds of insects dress themselves up. They drive straight their own Flower Cars along the Parade Avenue of Ants Kingdom.

**Daniel**：That's splendid. Can you take three pictures of me with them?

**May**：I thought you had grown out of such child practice.

**Daniel**：Cut it out. Look at my smile, and it seems like the flowers in the spring. Right?

**May**：Gross!

**Daniel**：Hurry up! The smile is frozen on my face.

**阿美**：所有"昆虫"都盛装打扮起来。他们将驾着自己的花车在蚂蚁王国的游行道径直地行进。

**丹尼尔**：太棒了！能帮我和它们拍三张照片吗？

**阿美**：我还以为你已经玩腻了这种小孩子的游戏了呢。

**丹尼尔**：打住。看我笑得就跟春天里的花朵一样。是不是呀？

**阿美**：恶心！

**丹尼尔**：快点！我的笑容都僵了。

## 生词小结

ant　*n.* 蚂蚁
kingdom　*n.* 王国
colorful　*adj.* 多姿多彩的
pretend　*vt.* 假装
caterpillar　*n.* 毛毛虫
parade　*n.* 游行
carnival　*n.* 嘉年华会,狂欢会
fantasy　*n.* 幻想
avenue　*n.* 大道
splendid　*adj.* 极好的

## 注释

**I thought you had grown out of such child practice.**
我还以为你已经玩腻了这种小孩子的游戏了呢。其中 grow out of 是指"因长大而不再做"。这是阿美反讽丹尼尔的一句话。Thought 用了过去式,表达的是"我过去以为你已经不再喜欢小孩子的游戏,可是现在却不这样认为了。"

**Cut it out.** 别提了,打住。

**dress up** 为打扮的意思。

## 语音小结 Pronunciation —— 辅音连缀（二）3 组 8 个组合音

发音小贴士：(1) 第一个字母发得很轻,很快过渡到下两个音节。
(2) 切忌在三个音节中加入元音。

**1.** /spr/与/skw/：**spring　spread　square　squash**
对比练习　/spr/与/skw/　spring and square　spread and squeeze　spray and squash

**2.** /str/、/skr/与/spl/：**straight　street　screen　splendid**
对比练习　/str/, /skr/与/spl/　straight and scream and split　street and screen and splendid　strong and script and split

**3.** /fl/、/fr/与/r/：**flower　fresh　three　throw**
对比练习　/fl/, /fr/与/r/　flee and free and three　fly and fry and thread　flog and frog and throw

**Recitation** 经典背诵

**May**：I like going to the Amusement Park very much. The Ant Kingdom is a perfect place with colorful fairy tales and I love it. But Daniel says only kids like that. But he is a kid himself too. Anyway each time we go there together we can experience a dream of fantasies.

# Topic 2 摩天轮
## Ferris Wheels

丹尼尔和阿美一起乘坐摩天轮,两个人俯瞰着下面的游乐设施,愉快地聊着彼此喜欢的项目。

**Daniel:** Wow, the ferris wheel over there is so big. I'd like to take a ride on it.

**May:** It is called Energy Collector.

**Daniel:** Look at your right-hand. Is it the zone of the Lost Maya Kingdom?

**May:** Maybe. Oh, I see the Jungle Flying Train. I once rode it. It was very exciting.

**Daniel:** I want to have a try later.

**May:** Me too. Daniel, look at your left side. Can you see the Air Force Ants.

**Daniel:** Wow, that's my favorite. It's like a superman shooting right up into the sky.

**May:** Good, you can make your dream come true here.

**Daniel:** Of course. After this, I want to show you to the Haunted House.

**May:** So you can prove you are a man.

**Daniel:** Bingo!

**May:** It's just you!

丹尼尔:哇,那边的摩天轮好大啊。我想去坐。

阿美:那叫聚能飞船。

丹尼尔:快看你的右手边。那是失落的玛雅主题区吗?

阿美:可能吧。哦,我看到丛林飞车了。我曾经坐过,太刺激了。

丹尼尔:我想一会去试一下。

阿美:我也是。丹尼尔,看你的左边。你能看到蚂蚁战队吗?

丹尼尔:哇,那是我的最爱。我坐在上面感觉像个超人,一直冲向蓝天。

阿美:好啊,你在这里可以梦想成真了。

丹尼尔:可以啊。在这之后,我想带你去鬼屋。

阿美:这样你就可以证明你是个男人。

丹尼尔:回答正确!

阿美:那就是你!

## 生词小结

| | |
|---|---|
| **ferris wheel** *n.* 摩天轮 | **force** *n.* 力量 |
| **energy** *n.* 能量 | **shoot** *vt.* 发射 |
| **collector** *n.* 收集者 | **come true** 实现 |
| **Maya** *n.* 玛雅,玛雅人 | **haunted** *adj.* 闹鬼的 |
| **jungle** *n.* 丛林 | |

## 单词扩展 Vocabulary Builder

### 各种游乐项目词汇

| 基础词汇 | 提高词汇 |
| --- | --- |
| roller coaster 过山车 | Rush hour 尖峰时刻 |
| magic theater 魔幻剧场 | Parade of insects carnival 虫虫狂欢大巡游 |
| Giant Derrick 大井架 | on-water performance 水上表演 |
| Dam gate 大水闸 | X-Games performance 极限运动表演 |
| Welcoming show 迎宾表演 | the chariot of sun 太阳神车 |
| Jungle Flying Train 丛林飞车 | haunted grove 异域魔窟 |
| sky wheel 摩天轮 | disco "O" Disk O |
| Mini shuttle 迷你穿梭 | Jungle climb 丛林攀爬 |

## 家庭总动员 Do it together

两人一组，一方随机大声读出上面词汇的英文和中文，另一方用该词汇填入下面的句子，大声朗读并表演出来，用中文给出一个理由。

**I'd like to take the (                    ).**

【例】家长读 sky wheel

孩子读 I'd like to take the sky wheel. 因为坐在摩天轮上很浪漫。

**Recitation 经典背诵**

May：In the Amusement Park, the Jungle Flying Train is the thing that I really have a passion for. And the Air Force Ants is Daniel's favorite. He says he would feel like a superman each time he is in it. To prove he is a man he would suggest we go to the Haunted House.

# Topic 3 注意事项
## Notices

在乘坐丛林飞车之前,欢乐谷相关工作人员事先播报游玩注意事项。

( *May and Daniel go together to ride the Jungle Flying Train.* )

Welcome to Happy Valley Beijing! And welcome to ride the Jungle Flying Train. For your safety, if you have the conditions of high blood pressure, heart disease, pregnancy, you are not allowed to aboard the Jungle Flying Train. It is also limit to the children under 1.4 meters in height.

The visitors should obey the seat ordinance and accept the inspection when it's necessary. Our big ride requests queue in. In the case of too many people, the queue time may take longer, please be patient for your ride.

Visitors should take care of your own belongings, keep your children with you. Don't leave anything behind you after taking the ride.

Come to enjoy an endless fun.

(阿美和丹尼尔一起去坐丛林飞车。)

欢迎来到北京欢乐谷!欢迎乘坐丛林飞车。为了您的安全,如果您有高血压,心脏病或者怀孕,请不要乘坐该游艺机。1.4 米以下的儿童也不得乘坐。

游客应遵守秩序,在必要的时候要接受检查。我们的游艺机要求排队进入。如果游客太多,队伍可能会很长,请耐心等待。

请游客保管好随身物品,带好自己的小孩。在乘坐完毕后请带走随身物品。

祝您玩得愉快!

## 生词小结

**condition** *n.* 条件
**pregnancy** *n.* 怀孕
**obey** *vt.* 遵守
**ordinance** *n.* 条例
**accept** *vt.* 接受
**inspect** *vt.* 检查
**necessary** *adj.* 必需的
**request** *vt.* 要求
**belonging** *n.* 所属物
**endless** *adj.* 无尽的

## 注释

**high blood pressure** 高血压
**heart disease** 心脏病

# F 功能性句型扩展
## unctional structure —— 指示句型

请朗读以下句型，家长和孩子交替进行。

### 1. 指示做某事

You do...　你要做……

You should do...　你应该做……

You have to do...　你必须做……

You must do...　你必须做……

As soon as..., you should do...　—……，你就要……

Remember to do...　记得要做……

Make sure you do...　你要确保做……

Take care to do...　当心做……

This is how you do it.　你要这样做。

### 2. 指示不得做某事

Do not do...　不得做……

Shouldn't do...　不应该做……

Don't have to do...　不需要做……

Mustn't do...　禁止做……

You are not allowed to...　你不准……

*Recitation* 经典背诵

May：To ride the Jungle Flying Train, there are some ordinance for us to obey. First, the children under 1.4 meters in height can't get on the ride. Second, We should accept the inspection whenever it's necessary. Third, we should take care of our own belongings. Anyway, safety comes first.

# Topic 4 广播寻人
## Broadcasting

听 学 看 　丹尼尔玩得非常高兴,他想要和妈妈姐姐玩捉迷藏的游戏。但是玩着玩着,好像又出事了,这次是怎么了呢?

**Shirley**：Excuse me. I seem to have lost my son.

**Announcer**：Take it easy, madam. And speak slowly. May I have your name first?

**Shirley**：Shirley.

**Announcer**：What's your son's name, please?

**Shirley**：Daniel.

**Announcer**：Can you describe his appearance to me?

**Shirley**：He is in a blue sportswear and a white sportsshoes. About 1.4 meters.

**Announcer**：OK, I see. Dear Daniel, please come to the broadcasting station when you've heard this, your mother is waiting for you. If other tourists see a boy in a blue sportswear and a pair of white sportss-hoes, 1.4 meters, please ask him to go to the broadcasting station. Thank you!

**雪莉:**你好。我好像和儿子走散了。

**播音员:**女士,请别急。慢慢说。请先告诉我您的名字好吗?

**雪莉:**雪莉。

**播音员:**请问您儿子叫什么?

**雪莉:**丹尼尔。

**播音员:**能跟我描述一下他的外貌吗?

**雪莉:**他穿着蓝色运动衣和白色的运动鞋。大约一米四高。

**播音员:**好的,我知道了。丹尼尔小朋友,听到广播后请速来广播站,你的妈妈在等你。如果有其他游客看到一个身穿蓝色运动衣和一双白色运动鞋,身高 1.4 米左右的小朋友,请让他速来广播站。谢谢!

---

**生词小结**

**broadcasting station** 广播站
**sportswear** *n.* 运动衣
**sportsshoes** *n.* 运动鞋
**appearance** *n.* 外貌
**describe** *vt.* 描述
**announcer** *n.* 广播员
**white** *adj.* 白色的
**meter** *n.* 米

---

**注释**

**Take it easy.** 别急,慢慢来。

## G 语法小结
### rammer —— 特殊疑问句

课文中的句子"What's your son's name, please?"是一个特殊疑问句。以疑问词开头,对句中某一成分提问的句子叫特殊疑问句。常用的疑问词有:what(询问事物),how much(询问价格),what time(询问时间),what kind of(询问种类),why(询问原因),who(询问人),where(询问地点),等等。

1. what 引导的特殊疑问句
   *What did Daniel do?* 丹尼尔干什么了?

2. Who 引导的特殊疑问句
   *Who is that boy?* 那个男孩是谁?

3. Which 引导的特殊疑问句
   *Which one do you like?* 你喜欢哪一个?

4. where 引导的特殊疑问句
   *Where's Daniel?* 丹尼尔在哪儿?

5. how 引导的特殊疑问句
   *How are you?* 你好吗?

6. why 引导的特殊疑问句
   *Why did May and her Mom look for Daniel?* 阿美和妈妈为什么要找丹尼尔?

## D 家庭总动员
### o it together

两人一组,一方朗诵下面的中文句子,另一方挑选出合适的翻译。

| | |
|---|---|
| 1. 你感觉嘉年华怎样? | 1. Which kind of ordinances should we obey? |
| 2. 你什么时候接受检查? | 2. When do you accept the inspection? |
| 3. 我们应该遵守怎样的条例? | 3. What do you think about the carnival? |
| 4. 谁给你买的运动衣? | 4. Which game do you like? |
| 5. 你喜欢哪个游戏? | 5. Who bought the sportswear for you? |

### Recitation
经典背诵

**Mom:** I don't like taking Daniel out. He is just too naughty and if you are not careful enough he would keep on making troubles. One time in the Amusement Park he got lost and we spent the whole day looking for him. He was such a trouble maker.

英语大赢家 **Winner's English**

# Act 3

# 学校场景
## School

# 小学 Elementary School

## Goals

**在这个场景中，我们将学到：**

1. 单音节重读与数字重读
2. 学校课程的单词
3. 指示句型练习
4. 一般将来时

## 外星人
### UFO and E. T.

**玩转语音**

1. Five frantic frogs fled from fifty fierce fishes.
2. Thirty-three thirsty, thundering thoroughbreds thumped Mr. Thurber on Thurber.
3. One-One was a racehorse. Two-Two was one, too. When One-One won one race, Two-Two won one, too.

| | |
|---|---|
| 及格时间：7 秒 | |
| 你的纪录：——秒 | |
| 及格时间：10 秒 | |
| 你的纪录：——秒 | |
| 及格时间：11 秒 | |
| 你的纪录：——秒 | |

汤姆和丹尼尔走在上学的路上，两人聊起了 UFO，丹尼尔说他见过 UFO，而且还和外星人说了话。这是真的吗？

Tom：Do you believe in UFOs?

Daniel：Of course, they are out there.

Tom：But I never saw them.

Daniel：Are you stupid? They are called UFOs, so not everybody can see them.

Tom：You mean that you can see them.

Daniel：That's right. I can see them in my dreams.

Tom：They come to the earth?

Daniel：No. Their task is to send the aliens here from the outer space.

Tom：Aliens from the outer space? Do you talk to them? What do they look like?

汤姆：你相信有不明飞行物吗？

丹尼尔：当然了，它们就在那儿呢。

汤姆：但是我从来就没有看见过啊。

丹尼尔：你笨吧你，它们叫做不明飞行物，所以不是每个人都能看得到的啊。

汤姆：那你的意思就是说你能看见。

丹尼尔：对啊，我在梦中看到他们。

汤姆：它们要到我们地球上来吗？

丹尼尔：不是。它们的任务是把外星人从太空送到地球上来。

汤姆：从外太空来的外星人吗？那你和他们说话了吗？他们都长什么样子啊？

Daniel: OK, OK, one by one, please!
They look like robots, but they can speak. Their mission is to make friends with human beings.

Tom: That means that you talk to them? In which language?

Daniel: Of course in English, they learn English on Mars too.

Tom: Wow. Sounds fantastic!

丹尼尔:好,好,打住,一个一个问好吗?
他们看起来就像是机器人,但是他们会说话,他们的使命就是和我们地球人做朋友。

汤姆: 那就是说你们对话了? 用哪种语言呢?

丹尼尔:当然是用英语,他们在火星上也学英语的。

汤姆:哇噻! 听起来太不可思议了。

### 生词小结

**believe** *vt.* 相信,信任
**stupid** *adj.* 笨的
**alien** *adj.* 外国的,相异的
**space** *n.* 空间
**mission** *n.* 使命
**Mars** *n.* 火星
**fantastic** *adj.* 难以相信的

### 注释

**UFO = unidentified flying object**　不明飞行物

## 语音小结 Pronunciation —— 单音节重读与数字重读

**音节概念**:音节可以是一个元音,或者是一个元音加上几个辅音。一般来说,元音可以构成音节,辅音不响亮,不能构成音节。(注:英语辅音字母中有 4 个辅音[m],[n],[ng],[l]是响音,它们和辅音音素结合,也可构成音节,但往往出现在词尾,一般是非重读音节)

英语单词含有一个音节叫做单音节,两个音节的叫做双音节,多个音节的叫做多音节。

**发音小贴士**:单音节词单独读时都读重音,都不必标重音符号。

**单音节重读**:you　are　saw　can

**发音小贴士**:整十倍数字读音时,重音在第一个音节上。

**数字重读**:thirty/ˈθəːti / 　thirteen/ˈθiːˈtiːn /
forty/ˈfɔːti / 　fourteen/ˈfɔːˈtiːn /
sixty/ˈsiksti / 　sixteen/ˈsiksˈtiːn /
fifteen/ˈfifˈtiːn / 　fifty/ˈfifti /

**比较**:twelve and twenty　eighty and eighteen　ninety and nineteen　seventy and seventeen

**对比练习**　my and atmosphere　say and computer　eye and banana　cup and telephone

## Recitation 经典背诵

Daniel: I believe in UFOs though I've never seen a real one. Sometimes they appear in my dreams which is really interesting. They told me their task is to send aliens from the outer space to the earth. Aliens look just like robots, and I talk with them in English. It's really funny.

# Topic 2 学校课程
## School Courses

听 学 看

学校又给丹尼尔他们年级加了几门课程,其中,丹尼尔最喜欢科学这门课,这使得汤姆非常的惊讶。看看究竟怎么回事吧!

**Daniel**：School has added several new courses to our grade this semester. I have more homework to do now.

**Tom**：What's your favorite course, Daniel?

**Daniel**：I like science most.

**Tom**：Science? That's a surprise.

**Daniel**：Surprise?

**Tom**：I thought you would like PE.

**Daniel**：I do like PE, but I am interested in science.

**Tom**：Are you interested in science? I can't believe it.

**Daniel**：Through this course, I can learn more about the world around us clearly.

**Tom**：Your parents would be happy if they knew that. Because you are always a naughty boy.

**Daniel**：Naughty? I'm naughty? I'm just clever. So I only do the things I am interested in.

**Tom**：Hope so.

**丹尼尔:**这个学期学校给我们年级又加了几门课。现在我有更多的家庭作业要做了。

**汤姆:**丹尼尔,你最喜欢的课程是哪门啊?

**丹尼尔:**我最喜欢科学。

**汤姆:**科学?太惊讶了。

**丹尼尔:**惊讶?

**汤姆:**我还以为你会最喜欢体育呢。

**丹尼尔:**我是喜欢体育啊,但是我对科学却非常感兴趣。

**汤姆:**你对科学感兴趣?我不太相信。

**丹尼尔:**通过这个课程,可以清楚地了解我们周围的世界。

**汤姆:**你的爸爸妈妈如果听见你这样说的话,绝对会很高兴的。因为你总是很顽皮。

**丹尼尔:**调皮?我很调皮吗?我只是聪明而已。我只做我感兴趣的事情。

**汤姆:**希望如此。

---

**生词小结**

grade  *n.* 年级
semester  *n.* 学期

science  *n.* 科学
surprise  *n.* 惊奇

## 单词扩展 Vocabulary Builder

### 学校课程的单词

| 基础词汇 | 提高词汇 |
| --- | --- |
| science 科学 | philosophy 哲学 |
| biology 生物学 | economics 经济学 |
| mathematics 数学 | ethics 伦理学 |
| law 法学 | sociology 社会学 |
| education 教育学 | psychology 心理学 |
| history 历史 | optics 光学 |
| Chinese 中文 | literature 文学 |
| geography 地理 | logic 逻辑学 |

## Do it together 家庭总动员

两人一组，一方随机大声读出上面基础词汇的英文和中文，另一方用该词汇填入下面的句子，大声朗读出来，并用中文给出一个理由。

I like (                    ) most.

【例】家长读 science 科学
孩子读 I like science most. 因为科学可以让我了解周围的世界。

### Recitation 经典背诵

Tom：We have many new courses this semester. Among them, Daniel told me his favorite course is science, which was a big surprise to me. He has always been very naughty and has no interest in studies. Now there would be no need for his parents to worry about their son's study any more.

# Topic 3 参加培训班
## Training Courses

听 学 看

汤姆的英语成绩不是很好,丹尼尔建议他去参加一个英语培训班,丹尼尔会推荐一个什么样的培训班呢? 看看就知道了。

Tom：Daniel, I can't catch up with the English teacher very well.

Daniel：What's the problem?

Tom：You are quite good at English, can you help me with it.

Daniel：That's OK. But you'd better take an additional course in some English schools.

Tom：English school? What is that?

Daniel：This kind of school is good at helping people to improve their English.

Tom：Is that different from our school's English course?

Daniel：Yes, before you start your training, they will test you on your English first.

Tom：Then?

Daniel：Then they will recommend you the class that suits you.

Tom：Really? How good can my English get there?

Daniel：You see how well I am doing. I studied there too.

Tom：All right. I'll tell my mother about it.

汤姆:丹尼尔,我跟不上英语老师的课。

丹尼尔:什么问题呢?

汤姆:你英语很好,你能帮我吗?

丹尼尔:可以啊,但是我建议你最好去一些英语学校学一些额外的课程。

汤姆:英语学校? 是什么学校啊?

丹尼尔:这种学校善于帮助大家提高英语水平。

汤姆:那和我们的英语课程有区别吗?

丹尼尔:当然有啊,在你进行培训之前,他们先会对你的英语进行测试。

汤姆:然后呢?

丹尼尔:然后,他们会推荐适合你的课程。

汤姆:真的吗? 那效果怎么样呢?

丹尼尔:你觉得我怎么样呢? 我也在那里学过。

汤姆:好的,我会告诉我妈妈的。

## 生词小结

**catch** *vt.* 抓住,领会
**additional** *adj.* 额外的

**train** *vt.* 训练,培训
**recommend** *vt.* 推荐

## S情景练习
### cene practice ——— 指示句型练习

仔细阅读下面五个场景,两人一组,使用指示句型(见 121 页),用一用,练一练。

(1) If you were Shirley, and you were telling your son Daniel what he should pay attention to in the Happy Valley, what would you say?

(2) If you were Benjamin, and you were telling May what she should pay attention to when using digital camera, what would you say?

(3) If you were Daniel's teacher, and you wanted to warn him not to talk in the class, what would you say?

(4) If you were Shirley, and you didn't approve of Daniel watching Ultraman, what would you say?

(5) If you were Daniel, and you were asking Tom not to forget to watch Ultraman, what would you say?

**R**ecitation 经典背诵

Tom: I can't catch up with our English teacher very well. Daniel is good at English. He suggests that I take an additional course in some English school. That school is said to be a really good one. So I hope it can help me with my English. I will tell my mother about it later.

# Topic4 劳动卫生
## Cleaning

听 学 看

今天轮到汤姆和丹尼尔值日,他们俩加快步伐来到了教室。汤姆负责擦黑板,而丹尼尔负责扫地。来看看他们做得怎么样吧。

**Daniel**：Don't talk too much, Tom. We are on duty today, we should hurry up.

**Tom**：OK.

(*Daniel and Tom reach the classroom.*)

**Daniel**：Tom, your task is to clean the blackboard.

**Tom**：How about yourself?

**Daniel**：I'm going to sweep the floor first.

**Tom**：Daniel, I am not tall enough to reach the top of the blackboard.

**Daniel**：Stand on the chair, Pig Tom. Use your brain.

**Tom**：OK, I've finished cleaning the blackboard.

**Daniel**：How about the podium?

**Tom**：Oh, I forgot about it. I'll get it.

**Daniel**：Be quick, please. Our teacher and classmates will come soon.

**Tom**：I will be done before they come.

**丹尼尔**：别废话了,汤姆。我们今天值日,我们得快点了。

**汤姆**：好的。

(丹尼尔和汤姆到了教室。)

**丹尼尔**：汤姆,你的任务是擦黑板。

**汤姆**：那你自己干什么?

**丹尼尔**：我先扫地啊。

**汤姆**：丹尼尔,我不够高,够不着上面的黑板。

**丹尼尔**：站在椅子上啊,汤姆猪。动脑子啊。

**汤姆**：好的。我的黑板擦完了。

**丹尼尔**：讲台呢?

**汤姆**：哦,忘记了。马上打扫完。

**丹尼尔**：快点,老师和同学们就快来了。

**汤姆**：他们来之前一定会做完。

## 生词小结

| | | | |
|---|---|---|---|
| **duty** | *n.* 职责,责任 | **floor** | *n.* 地板 |
| **reach** | *vt.* 够到 | **brain** | *n.* 大脑 |
| **clean** | *vt.* 打扫 | **podium** | *n.* 讲台 |
| **sweep** | *vt.* 打扫 | | |

## **G**rammer 语法小结 —— 一般将来时

一般将来时表示将要发生的事,可以用 shall/will + 动词原形、be going to + 动词原形来表示。

### 1. shall/will + 动词原形

will 可用于所有人称,shall 用于第一人称 I 和 we,例如:

*She will be back soon.* 她很快就会回来。

*I shall/will be free on Sunday.* 星期天我有空。

*It will rain tomorrow.* 明天要下雨。

### 2. be going to + 动词原形

(1) 说话人根据已有的迹象,判断将要或即将发生某种情况

*I feel bad. I think I'm going to die.* 我感觉很难受,我想我快不行了。

*Look at those black clouds! It's going to rain.* 看看那些乌云! 天快要下雨了。

(2) 表示主语打算在最近或将来进行某事

*He isn't going to see the film tomorrow.* 他明天不准备去看电影。

*I am going to be a teacher.* 我想当一名教师。

(3) 预测未来的事,可与 will 互换

*I think it is going to/will rain this afternoon.* 我觉得今天下午要下雨。

### 3. be + 不定式

be + 不定式表将来,按计划或正式安排将发生的事,例如

*We are to discuss the report next Saturday.* 我们计划下周六讨论报告。

### 4. be about to + 不定式

be about to + 不定式,表示马上做某事,但是不能与 tomorrow, next week 等表示明确将来时的时间状语连用。

*He is about to marry her.* 他马上就要娶她。

## **D**o it together 家庭总动员

两人一组,一方朗诵下面的中文句子,另一方挑选出合适的翻译。

1. 星期天我要扫地。
2. 她明天不打算跟我们一起去了。
3. 我们下周要去英语学校。
4. 我很快就回来。
5. 她马上就要结婚了。

1. We will go to the English school next week.
2. I'll be back soon.
3. I will sweep the floor on Sunday.
4. She won't go with us tomorrow.
5. She will get married soon.

## **R**ecitation 经典背诵

Daniel: Every time when Tom and I are on duty, I'd let him clean the blackboard, and I'd sweep the floor. He is really Pig Tom. He doesn't even know how to reach the top of the blackboard, so I have to help him solve the problem.

# 初中 Junior High School

## Goals

**在这个场景中,我们将学到:**

1. 双音节和多音节重读
2. 学校设施词汇
3. 表达感情的句型
4. 现在进行时

**Topic 1** 运动会
**Sports Meetings**

 **玩转语音**

1. Sandy sniffed sweet smelling sunflower seeds while sitting beside a swift stream.
2. Silly Sally swiftly shooed seven silly sheep. The seven silly sheep Silly Sally shooed shilly-shallied south.

及格时间: 10 秒
你的纪录: —— 秒
及格时间: 15 秒
你的纪录: —— 秒

亚当是丹尼尔从小一起长大的好朋友,住在同一个社区,现在读初中一年级。这天,亚当学校开运动会,他邀请丹尼尔一起去参加运动会。

**Adam**: Is it your first time to join the sports meeting of Junior High School?

**Daniel**: Yes, and it's great. What are the events at the sports meeting?

**Adam**: Long-distance race, dash, hurdle race, relay race, standing long jump, high jump, shotput and so on.

**Daniel**: Our neighbor, Bruce, will take part in the relay race. Let's go have a look.

**Adam**: OK, let's go.

**Daniel**: The competition will begin in 5 minutes, it's tense here.

(*On your mark. Set! Go!*)

**Adam**: Wonderful, Bruce is taking the lead.

**Daniel**: Other competitors have almost caught up with him. They are neck and neck.

**Adam**: Come on, Bruce. Come on, Bruce.

**亚当:**这是你第一次参加初中运动会吧?

**丹尼尔:**是的,太好了。运动会上都有哪些项目?

**亚当:**长跑,短跑,跨栏,接力赛,立定跳远,跳高,铅球,等等。

**丹尼尔:**我们的邻居布鲁斯将参加接力赛。我们过去看看吧。

**亚当:**好的,走吧。

**丹尼尔:**比赛将在五分钟后开始,气氛已经很紧张了。

(各就位。预备!跑!)

**亚当:**太好了,布鲁斯现在领先。

**丹尼尔:**其他对手快要赶上他了。他们并驾齐驱。

**亚当:**加油,布鲁斯。加油,布鲁斯。

Daniel：Wow, Bruce crossed the line first.

Adam：This is so exciting. Let's come to give him congratulations. Let's ask him out to dinner tonight.

Daniel：That's a good idea!

丹尼尔：哇，布鲁斯第一个冲到终点。

亚当：太激动人心了。我们一起去祝贺他吧。请他今晚和我们吃饭。

丹尼尔：那是个好主意！

生词小结

**join** *vt.* 参加
**dash** *n.* 短跑
**neighbor** *n.* 邻居
**go have a look** 看一看
**competition** *n.* 比赛
**tense** *adj.* 紧张的
**take the lead** 领先
**be neck and neck** 并驾齐驱
**congratulation** *n.* 祝贺

注释

**sports meeting** 运动会
**junior high school** 初中
**long-distance race** 长跑
**hurdle race** 跨栏
**relay race** 接力赛
**standing long jump** 立定跳远
**high jump** 跳高
**shotput** 铅球
**On your mark! Set! Go!** 各就位！预备！跑！这是田径比赛中裁判发令时喊的口令。
**Bruce hits the line first.** 布鲁斯第一个冲到终点。这句话直译为"布鲁斯第一个撞倒了线。"这里的线是指终点线，所以也就是第一个到终点。

## P语音小结 Pronunciation —— 双音节和多音节重读

**1. 双音节**

（1）event  shotput  dinner  daily

发音小贴士：双音节词的重音多数落在第一个音节上。

朗读练习：matter  better  happy  puppy  sever  clever  funny  rainy

（2）begin  after  tonight  miscall

发音小贴士：带 a, be, im, mis, pre, trans, to, un 等前缀的双音节词，重音落在第二个音节上。

朗读练习：allow  above  because  believe  interesting  imply  transport  transfer

**2. 多音节重读**

（1）wonderful  competitor  exciting  satisfy

发音小贴士：多音节词多数落在倒数第三个音节上。

朗读练习：colorful  glassful  elegant  electricity  interesting  immediately  manage  magazine

（2）competition  congratulation  influential  musician

发音小贴士：以 ic, ial, ian, ion 等后缀结尾的多音节词，重音落在倒数第二个音节上。

朗读练习：official  special  physician  musician  television  discussion  statistic  specific

**Recitation** 经典背诵

**Adam**：Hi, I am Adam, a student in Junior High School. Today I took Daniel to visit the sport events in my school. He was very happy. Our neighbur, Bruce, took part in the relay race. The competitors were neck and neck with him. But Bruce managed to cross the line first. We gave him our congratulations.

# 学校设施
## School Facilities

丹尼尔第一次参观初中学校,对这里的一切都充满了好奇。亚当热情地充当向导,给他一一介绍学校的设施。

**Daniel**：Adam, could you show me around the school?

**Adam**：No problem.

**Daniel**：What's the tallest building?

**Adam**：You mean the white building near the playground?

**Daniel**：Yes.

**Adam**：That is the library. And it has more than 1,000,000 books.

**Daniel**：What's the building to the south of the library?

**Adam**：You know, our school is divided into two parts：the junior high school and the senior high school. That is the new classroom building for our senior high school.

**Daniel**：Is there a swimming pool in your school?

**Adam**：Yes. There is a large swimming pool, but it is only available in summer.

**Daniel**：I do envy you. And I hope I can enter your school one day.

**Adam**：I believe that you can make your dream come true.

**丹尼尔**：亚当,能带我参观一下你们学校吗?

**亚当**：没问题。

**丹尼尔**：那栋最高的楼是什么?

**亚当**：你是说在操场旁边的那栋白楼吗?

**丹尼尔**：是的。

**亚当**：那是图书馆。里面有1,000,000本书。

**丹尼尔**：在图书馆南面的楼是什么?

**亚当**：你知道的,我们学校分为初中部和高中部。那是我们学校高中部的新教学楼。

**丹尼尔**：你们学校有游泳池吗?

**亚当**：有啊。有一个很大的游泳池,但是它只在夏天开放。

**丹尼尔**：我太羡慕你了。我真希望有天能进你们学校。

**亚当**：我相信你会梦想成真的。

---

**生词小结**

| | |
|---|---|
| **show around** 带……参观 | **senior high school** 高中 |
| **playground** *n.* 操场 | **swimming pool** 游泳池 |
| **library** *n.* 图书馆 | **envy** *vt.* 羡慕,嫉妒 |
| **divide** *vt.* 划分 | **enter** *vt.* 进入 |

学校场景 · School

## 单词扩展 Vocabulary Builder

### 学校设施词汇

| 基础词汇 | 提高词汇 |
| --- | --- |
| classroom 教室 | blackboard 黑板 |
| chair 椅子 | gym 体育馆 |
| desk 课桌 | auditoria 会堂 |
| chalk 粉笔 | dormitory 集体寝室 |
| hall 礼堂 | bathhouse 公共浴室 |
| library 图书馆 | office building 办公楼 |
| playground 操场 | canteen 学生食堂 |
| reading room 阅览室 | laboratory 实验室 |

## 家庭总动员 Do it together

两人一组，一方随机大声读出上面词汇的英文和中文，另一方用该词汇填入下面的句子，大声朗读出来，并用中文给出一个理由。

**That is the (           ).**

【例】家长读 library

孩子读 That is the library. 我们能在图书馆看书。

### Recitation 经典背诵

Daniel：Adam showed me around his school. His school is divided into two parts：the junior high school and the senior high school. The white building is their library. And it holds more than 1,000,000 books. And they also have a swimming pool. It is a nice school. I hope to go there in the future.

# Topic 3 喜欢的老师
## Favorite Teachers

丹尼尔一直对初中的学习生活充满好奇和憧憬，来看看我们的丹尼尔都对初中生活有些什么样的期待和疑惑吧。

Daniel：What courses are you taking?

Adam：Chinese, maths, English, chemistry, physics, biology and so on.

Daniel：What do you think about the teachers?

Adam：To be honest, I like most of them, except for my Chinese teacher. She is quite young, but her class is too boring!

Daniel：That's too bad. Do you have any foreign teachers?

Adam：Yes, my oral English teacher is an American. He is from a small town in California.

Daniel：What is he like?

Adam：He is great. He always tells us not to study for exams, and to pay more attention to communication rather than just memorizing.

Daniel：Are you able to follow him?

Adam：Not everything, but nearly. He speaks very clearly.

Daniel：Oh, that's good! He sounds like a good teacher.

Adam：Absolutely! If you come to our class, I am sure you will like him.

丹尼尔：你现在都有什么课程啊?

亚当：语文，数学，英语，化学，物理，生物，等等。

丹尼尔：你觉得你们的老师如何?

亚当：说实话，大部分老师我都喜欢，除了语文老师。她很年轻，但是她的课特别枯燥!

丹尼尔：这太糟糕了。你们有外教吗?

亚当：有啊，我的英语口语老师就是个美国人。他来自加利福尼亚的一个小镇。

丹尼尔：他人怎么样啊?

亚当：他很好。他总是告诉我们不要为了考试而学，要注意多交流，而非一味的死记硬背。

丹尼尔：你能听懂他说什么吗?

亚当：不是全部，但差不多。他说得很清晰。

丹尼尔：哦，那很好啊! 听上去他是个很不错的老师。

亚当：当然! 如果你去我们的课堂，我相信你也会喜欢他的。

### 生词小结

**Chinese** *n.* 语文
**maths** *n.* 数学
**English** *n.* 英语
**chemistry** *n.* 化学

### 注释

**California** 加利福尼亚。美国的一个州，位于美国西海岸。
**to be honest** 说实话，实话实说
**pay more attention** 注意……

physics  *n.* 物理

biology  *n.* 生物

communication  *n.* 交流,沟通

memorize  *vt.* 记忆

absolutely  *adv.* 绝对地

## **F**unctional structure —— 感情句型
### 功能性句型扩展

请朗读以下句型,家长和孩子交替进行。

1. 表达高兴的情绪(非正式表达)

   Oh, how nice /wonderful / marvellous! 哦,太好了/太棒了。

   Hey, that's fantastic/ terrific! 嘿,妙极了/太精彩了。

   I'm pleased about... 我很高兴……

   I'm excited about... 我很兴奋……

   It's a good/ splendid/ wonderful thing! 这是件好事!

2. 表达高兴的情绪(正式表达)

   I'm delighted to hear that. 听到这,我很高兴。

   It gives me great pleasure to hear... 我很高兴听到……

   It gives me great pleasure that... ……令我很高兴。

   I can't say how pleased I am to ... 说不出有多高兴。

3. 表达不高兴的情绪

   I am worried about... 我担心……

   I'm most upset about... 我非常生气……

Adam:I take many courses every semester. I like most of my teachers except my Chinese teacher. She is young but boring. And my favorite class is oral English. My oral English teacher is an American. He is from a small town in California. He is really cool and humorous so we all like his class very much.

# Topic 4 住校生活
## Campus Life

在校园里逛完后，亚当带丹尼尔去参观他的寝室。初中生的寝室会是什么样的呢？往下看就知道了。

Adam：Daniel, would you like to have a look at my dorm?

Daniel：Of course, I'd like to.

Adam：It is a small room, just for 4 people.

Daniel：What is in it?

Adam：It only has 4 beds and 4 writing desks, but it is spacious and bright.

Daniel：Do you get along with your roommates?

Adam：Of course. They are very friendly.

Daniel：Which floor are you on?

Adam：We are on the 5th floor, and there's a very nice view from the balcony.

Daniel：Oh, you can climb the stairs as a work-out.

Adam：Yes, that's a good idea.

Daniel：Wow, your roommates are cleaning the room.

Adam：Let's give them a hand.

亚当：丹尼尔，想不想去看看我的寝室？

丹尼尔：当然，我很想去。

亚当：那是个小房间，只住了四个人。

丹尼尔：里面有什么？

亚当：只有四张床和四张书桌，但是宽敞明亮。

丹尼尔：你和室友相处得好吗？

亚当：当然很好喽。他们都很友好的。

丹尼尔：你们住几楼？

亚当：我们住五楼，所以从阳台上可以看到美景。

丹尼尔：哦，你可以爬楼锻炼身体了。

亚当：是啊，这是个好主意。

丹尼尔：哇，你的室友正在打扫房间。

亚当：我们帮下忙吧。

## 生词小结

| | | | |
|---|---|---|---|
| **dorm** *n.* 寝室 | | **roommate** *n.* 室友 | |
| **spacious** *adj.* 宽敞的 | | **friendly** *adj.* 友好的 | |
| **bright** *adj.* 明亮的 | | **stair** *n.* 楼梯 | |
| **get along with** 和……相处 | | **work-out** *n.* 锻炼 | |

## G语法小结 —— 现在进行时
rammer

课文中的句子"Wow, your roommates are cleaning the room"中出现的语法现象是现在进行时。现在进行时由 be 的现在式(am / is / are) + 动词现在分词构成,表示动作正在进行,同时也表示动作的持续性。

(1)表示此刻正在进行或发生的动作

可以与时间状语 now, at the moment 等连用,也可不用时间状语,如:

*He is writing a love letter to his wife now.* 他正在给妻子写情书。

*The workers are building a new swimming pool.* 工人们正在建一个新的游泳池。

(2)表示按计划、安排和打算将要发生的动作

常有表示将来的时间状语,常见的能表示此意义的动词有:arrive, borrow, come, discuss, fly, give, go, join, leave, move, play, run, sail, set out, start, stay, stop, take off, wear, work 等。

*The athletes are arriving in Beijing tomorrow.* 运动员于明早到达北京。

*Aunt Shirley is returning this evening.* 雪莉阿姨今晚将回来。

(3)表示不断重复的动作

常和 always, forever, repeatedly 等频度副词连用。

*May is always helping others.* 阿美经常帮助别人。

*They are seeking after truth forever.* 他们永远追求真理。

## D家庭总动员
o it together

两人一组,一方朗诵下面的中文句子,另一方挑选出合适的翻译。

1. 他们正等着运动会的开幕式。
2. 丹尼尔正在宽敞的教室里读书。
3. 亚当正带丹尼尔参观他的宿舍。
4. 亚当的室友正在打扫教室。
5. 学校正在举行运动会。

1. Adam's roommates are cleaning the classroom.
2. Daniel is reading in the spacious classroom.
3. The school is holding a sports meet.
4. They are waiting for the opening ceremony of the sports meet.
5. Adam is showing Daniel around his dorm.

Adam: I live at school. I share a room with three other guys. Well, yes, it's a bit crowded but I don't complain about it because it's also more fun this way. We have almost everything in 4: 4 beds, 4 writing desks, etc. One thing I never forget to mention is the perfect view from our balcony. In a word, I enjoy my school life.

# 图书馆 Library

## Goals

**在这个场景中，我们将学到：**

1. 同词异义的不同重读
2. 图书种类词汇
3. 感情句型练习
4. 过去进行时

Topic 1 借书
Borrowing Books

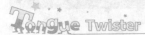 **玩转语音**

1. There are two minutes difference from four to two to two to two, from two to two to two, too.
2. After a minute examination, the president presents himself five minutes earlier.

及格时间：10 秒
你的纪录：——秒
及格时间：8 秒
你的纪录：——秒

爸爸和阿美一起去图书馆借书。阿美去找一些参考书、报纸和周刊，两人约好两小时后在借书处见面。阿美能如愿借到想要的书刊吗？

**May：** I go to look for some reference books, newspapers and periodicals. Can we meet at the counter in 2 hours?

**Dad：** OK, honey!

*(Counter)*

**Librarian：** Your admission card, please.

**May：** Here you are.

**Librarian：** Sorry, newspapers and periodicals are not for circulation.

**May：** OK, if I want to read them, what should I do?

**Librarian：** You can read them only in one of our reading rooms.

**May：** All right.

**Librarian：** Are those books yours?

**May：** Yes, these are my father's books.

**阿美：** 我去找一些参考书、报纸和周刊。我们两个小时后在借书处见可以吗？

**爸爸：** 好的，亲爱的。

（借书处）

**图书员：** 请给我你的借书卡。

**阿美：** 给你。

**图书员：** 对不起，报纸和周刊是不外借的。

**阿美：** 好的，那如果是我要看怎么办呢？

**图书员：** 只能够在我们的阅览室阅读。

**阿美：** 好的。

**图书员：** 这些书都是你的吗？

**阿美：** 是的，这些都是我爸爸的。

**Librarian：**OK，that's done. Please check your record and deadline in the computer over there.

**May：**Thanks.

**图书员：**好了,办完了。请去那边的电脑查询你的记录和书到期的时间。

**阿美：**谢谢。

## 生词小结

**reference**　*n.* 参考
**periodical**　*n.* 期刊

**circulation**　*n.* 流通
**record**　*n.* 记录

## 语音小结 Pronunciation —— 同词异义的不同重读

有些单词重音位置不同,词性会不同。如有些单词重音在第一个音节上词性是名词,而在第二个音节上词性却是动词。同时随着重音位置的变化,一些词的元音字母的读音也会发生变化。以下总结了三类:

| 分类 | 例词 | 词性 | 音标 | 短语举例 |
|---|---|---|---|---|
| 第一类 | import | 名词 | /ˈimpɔːt/ | the import of oil 石油的进口 |
| | | 动词 | /imˈpɔːt/ | import oil from Middle East 从中东进口石油 |
| | upset | 名词 | /ˈʌpset/ | a great deal of upset 一片混乱 |
| | | 动词 | /ʌpˈset/ | upset one's cup 弄翻杯子 |
| | progress | 名词 | /ˈprəugres/ | the progress of civilization 文明的进步 |
| | | 动词 | /prəˈgres/ | the civilization is progressing 文明在进步 |
| | export | 名词 | /ˈekspɔːt/ | the export trade 出口贸易 |
| | | 动词 | /ikˈspɔːt/ | export cars to Asia 向亚洲出口汽车 |
| | record | 名词 | /ˈrekɔːd/ | records of birth 出生纪录 |
| | | 动词 | /riˈkɔːd/ | record the progress 记录发展情况 |
| 第二类 | content | 名词 | /ˈkɔntent/ | the content is excellent 内容好极了 |
| | | 形容词 | /kənˈtent/ | she was content with her salary 她对薪水很满意 |
| | minute | 名词 | /ˈminit/ | five minutes 五分钟 |
| | | 形容词 | /maiˈnjut/ | a minute examination 详细的检查 |
| | august | 名词 | /ˈɔːgəst/ | August 八月 |
| | | 形容词 | /ɔːˈgʌst/ | an august man 德高望重的人 |
| 第三类 | perfect | 形容词 | /ˈpɜːfikt/ | a perfect result 极好的结果 |
| | | 动词 | /pəˈfekt/ | perfect one's behavior 使行为完美 |
| | minute | 形容词 | /ˈprezənt/ | be present 到场 |
| | | 动词 | /priˈzent/ | present oneself 出席 |
| | frequent | 形容词 | /ˈfriːkwənt/ | frequent changes 经常的变化 |
| | | 动词 | /friˈkwənt/ | frequent the zoo 经常去动物园 |

Recitation 经典背诵

**May：** Dad and I go to the library sometimes. The problem is newspapers and periodicals are not for circulation. I can only read them in their reading room. It's not very convenient this way. But the good thing is that I can check my records and the book's deadlines on the computer near the counter.

# Topic 2 问询处
## Information

爸爸在查询台让图书员帮他查一本书,但是健忘的他却忘记了书的作者和书名。那么最后爸爸找到了他想要的书吗?

(Information desk)

Benjamin：Could you please help me to check out the book?

Librarian：Sure, what's the author's name, please.

Benjamin：I can't remember that clearly. It probably be Charles...

Librarian：Charles Dickens?

Benjamin：No, no, no. I'm not interested in literature.

Librarian：OK, do you know the title of the book?

Benjamin：Oh, sorry. I'm always absent-minded. I remember that I've put a note in my pocket.

Librarian：So, show me the note please.

Benjamin：I can't find it now.

Librarian：Oh, such bad luck, sir. Can you please name the category of the book?

Benjamin：Let me see. It's not fiction. It's biography.

Librarian：OK, I'll search it for you. A moment, please.

Benjamin：Thanks.

(信息查询台)

本杰明:你能帮我查一本书吗?

图书员:当然可以啊,请告诉我作者的名字。

本杰明:我记得不太清楚了。好像是查尔斯……

图书员:查尔斯·狄更斯吗?

本杰明:不不不,我对文学不是很感兴趣。

图书员:好,那你知道书名吗?

本杰明:对不起,我总是很健忘。我记得我放了个便条在我的口袋里。

图书员:那把便条给我看看。

本杰明:我现在找不到了。

图书员:那真是倒霉啊,先生。那你知道书是哪一类的吗?

本杰明:让我想想啊,不是科幻小说。是自传。

图书员:好的,我帮你搜索一下。请等一会儿。

本杰明:谢谢。

---

**生词小结**

| | |
|---|---|
| **probably** *adv.* 可能地 | **note** *n.* 便条 |
| **literature** *n.* 文学 | **category** *n.* 类别 |
| **title** *n.* 标题 | **biography** *n.* 自传 |
| **pocket** *n.* 口袋 | **search** *vt.* 搜寻 |

## 单词扩展 Vocabulary Builder

图书种类词汇

| 基础词汇 | 提高词汇 |
| --- | --- |
| science fiction 科幻小说 | Gothic fiction 哥特式小说 |
| fantasy 奇幻小说 | horror fiction 恐怖小说 |
| novel 小说 | literature 文学 |
| cartoon 动画片 | military 军事 |
| science 科学 | preference 参考书 |
| geography 地理 | thriller 惊险故事 |
| history 历史 | adventure 冒险 |
| biography 自传 | biology 生物 |

## Do it together 家庭总动员

两人一组,一方随机大声读出上面基础词汇的英文和中文,另一方用该词汇填入下面的句子,大声朗读出来,并用中文给出一个理由。

**I'm not interested in** (                    ).

【例】家长读 horror fiction 恐怖小说

孩子读 I'm not interesting in horror fiction. 因为太恐怖了。

**Recitation** 经典背诵

**Librarian**: I am a librarian in our city library. My job calls for great patience because there are so many people with a poor memory.

They would always ask you to check out a book without telling you the author's name or even the title of the book. Anyway, I still like my job.

# Topic3 好书推荐
## Recommended Books

阿美借完书，坐在旁边的椅子上等爸爸，突然看见旁边有个人一边看书一边笑，那个人到底在看什么书呢？往下看就知道了。

May: Excuse me, can you tell me the name of the book you read?

Woman: Harry Potter.

May: Harry Potter? Is that book funny?

Woman: Actually, the language itself is not so funny, but you can imagine the scene, that's funny.

May: Got it.

Woman: Have you ever read this book before?

May: No, but my little brother likes it very much.

Women: It's really a good book. You will like it too.

May: I'll try to read it. Actually, I like literature very much.

Woman: Wow, that sounds like a scholar. By the way, who's your favorite writer?

May: Jane Austen.

Woman: Me too. *Pride and Prejudice* is my favorite.

May: I like it too. But *Sense and Sensibility* is my favorite.

阿美: 不好意思，打扰一下，你能告诉我你看的是什么书吗？

女士: 哈利波特。

阿美: 哈利波特。书很有趣吗？

女士: 事实上，文字本身不是很有趣，但是你可以想象那个场景，那非常的有趣。

阿美: 原来是这样啊。

女士: 你看过这本书吗？

阿美: 没有，但是我弟弟特别喜欢看。

女士: 确实是本好书，你会喜欢的。

阿美: 我试着去读一下。事实上，我非常喜欢文学。

女士: 是吗！听起来你像个学者。那你最喜欢的文学作者是谁呢？

阿美: 简·奥斯丁。

女士: 我也是。《傲慢与偏见》是我的最爱。

阿美: 我也非常喜欢那本书，但是《理智与情感》才是我的最爱。

### 生词小结

read *vt.* 阅读
language *n.* 语言
scene *n.* 场景

pride *n.* 傲慢
prejudice *n.* 偏见
sensibility *n.* 敏感

## S 情景练习
### Scene practice —— 感情句型练习

**仔细阅读下面五个场景,两人一组,使用感情句型(见 138 页),用一用,练一练。**

(1) If you were May, Gucci says to you that she's going on a trip to Tibet. What would you say?

(2) If you were Daniel, your family are going out for picnic this weekend, what would you say?

(3) If you were Shirley, you know that May has won the speech competition, how would you express your pleasure?

(4) If you were Benjamin, you have just been given the promotion. Express your pleasure.

(5) If you are Daniel, you get high marks in your examination, how would you express your pleasure?

*Recitation* 经典背诵

**May**: Harry Potter is really the best-seller all over the world. You can see people read it everywhere. My younger brother is a big fan of it, though I don't really have any special interest in it. But maybe I should read it some time. Just to catch up with the trend.

## Topic 4 还书
### Returning Books

阿美去还书,而且还想续借英文版的《理智与情感》。爸爸借的自传超过了借书期限,这下该怎么办呢?

**May:** This is my admission card, and these are the books.

阿美:这是我的借书卡,这些是书。

**Librarian:** OK, a moment, please.

图书员:好的,请等一下。

**May:** By the way, can I renew the borrowing?

阿美:顺便问一下,我能续借吗?

**Librarian:** For which one?

图书员:借哪一本呢?

**May:** *Sense and Sensibility*, English version.

阿美:《理智与情感》,英文版的。

**Librarian:** Yes, of course.

图书员:可以,当然可以。

**May:** Can I just do it here?

阿美:那我就在这儿续借可以吗?

**Librarian:** Sorry. No. You should go to the other counter.

图书员:对不起,不行。你要到那边的那个柜台去。

**May:** OK, thanks.

阿美:好的,谢谢。

**Librarian:** Sorry, this biography is over the deadline. You should pay extra for it.

图书员:不好意思,这本自传已经超过了期限。你得付超期的钱。

**May:** I was thinking of buying this from the bookstore when my father got this from the library... anyway, how much should I pay?

阿美:我爸爸从图书馆借回来的时候我就觉得他还不如去买一本……不管怎么样,我该付多少钱?

**Librarian:** 3 Yuan, please.

图书员:3 块钱。

**May:** Here you are. Thanks.

阿美:给你。谢谢。

**Librarian:** You are welcome. See you next time.

图书员:不用谢。下次见。

**May:** See you!

阿美:再见!

---

### 生词小结

**admission**  *n.* 许可,承认
**renew**  *vt.* 重新
**version**  *n.* 版本

**counter**  *n.* 柜台
**deadline**  *n.* 最后期限
**extra**  *adj.* 额外的

## G语法小结 Grammer —— 过去进行时

过去进行时表示过去某一时刻或某段时间正在进行的动作,由"was/ were + 动词-ing"构成。

(1) 表示过去某一时刻正在进行的动作

*What were you doing when I phoned you last night?* 昨晚我给你打电话时,你正在干什么?

*I was drawing a horse when the teacher came in.* 当老师进来时,我正在画一匹马。

(2) 表示过去某段时间正在进行的动作

*We were building a bridge last winter.* 去年冬天我们在建一个桥。

*I was living in my uncle's house when I was 14.* 我 14 岁时,住我叔叔家里。

(3) 描写故事发生的背景

*It was a dark night. The wind was blowing hard.* 一个漆黑的夜晚,狂风大作。

## D家庭总动员 Do it together

**两人一组,一方朗诵下面的中文句子,另一方挑选出合适的翻译。**

1. 昨天下午这个时候丹尼尔正在图书馆看书。

2. 老师进来时阿美正在和同学说话。

3. 去年这个月我们在做一个很大的项目。

4. 昨天晚上她正在看哈利伯特。

5. 昨天爸爸给我书的时候我在看电视。

1. When my father gave me the book yesterday, I was watching TV yesterday.

2. She was reading Harry Potter last night.

3. We were doing a big project this month last year.

4. When teacher came into the classroom, May was talking with her classmate.

5. Daniel was reading in the library at this time yesterday.

May: I have a problem with borrowed books from a library. I always can't finish the books before the deadline comes. So as it happens, I'd pay extra for the delay. Though it's not much I still don't like it. You know it's so embarrassing.

# Act 4

# 餐饮和零售业场景
# Catering Industry and Retail Trade

## SCENE 19

# 餐厅 Restaurant

## Goals

**在这个场景中，我们将学到：**

1. 元音字母语音规则（一）
2. 表示菜肴名称的词汇
3. 建议劝告句型
4. 被动语态（一）

## Topic 1 点菜 Order

### 玩转语音

1. A tutor who tooted a flute tried to tutor two tooters to toot. Said the two to their tutor, "Is it harder to toot or to tutor two tooters to toot?"

2. Amidst the mists and coldest frosts, with stoutest wrists and loudest boasts, he thrusts his fist against the posts and still insists he sees the ghosts.

及格时间：20 秒
你的纪录：——秒
及格时间：20 秒
你的纪录：——秒

丹尼尔和汤姆中午放学后到餐馆吃午餐，两个小家伙要吃虾球，好像又碰上了好玩的事情，究竟是怎么回事呢？

**Daniel:** Tom, we are in the restaurant now!

**Waiter:** May I take your order?

**Daniel:** I'd like to see the menu, please.

**Waiter:** OK, here you are.

**Daniel:** Thanks. I am starving. Tom, what are you getting?

**Tom:** I have no idea. First time here.

**Daniel:** Let me see…What's this, shrimp rolls?

**Waiter:** Oh, it's rice rolls with fried shrimp inside.

**Tom:** Twenty five yuan is a little expensive.

**Waiter:** There are twenty rolls in a bowl. You can get another bowl for free if there aren't enough rolls.

**丹尼尔:** 汤姆，我们到了饭馆了。

**服务员:** 可以点菜了吗？

**丹尼尔:** 我想看看菜单。

**服务员:** 好的，给你菜单。

**丹尼尔:** 谢谢。我快饿死了。汤姆，你吃点什么？

**汤姆:** 不知道，我是第一次来这儿。

**丹尼尔:** 让我看看……这是什么，虾球？

**服务员:** 哦，就是面卷里包着炸虾。

**汤姆:** 25块钱有点贵了吧.

**服务员:** 一碗里有二十个。如果面卷不够的话，还可以免费再点一些。

**Daniel：** Sounds nice. We will take this, two bowls of shrimp rolls.

**Waiter：** OK, shrimp rolls. Do you want anything else?

**Daniel：** We will have this one first and order something else later.

**Waiter：** OK, wait a moment please.

**丹尼尔：** 听上去不错。我们就要这个，两碗虾球。

**服务员：** 好的，虾球。还要点别的什么吗？

**丹尼尔：** 我们先要这个，一会儿再点别的。

**服务员：** 好的，请等一下。

### 生词小结

| | | |
|---|---|---|
| **restaurant** | n. 餐馆 | **idea** n. 主意 |
| **menu** | n. 菜单 | **roll** n. 卷 |
| **starve** | vi. 饿死 | **shrimp** n. 虾 |

## 语音小结 —— 元音字母语音规则（一）
### Pronunciation

a e i o u y

开音节:(1)以发音的元音字母结尾的音节,如 he /hiː/。

(2)以辅音字母(r 除外)加不发音的 e 结尾的音节,如 cake/keik/。

闭音节:以一个或几个辅音字母结尾(r 除外),而中间只有一个元音字母的音节,如 sit /sit/。

除了单音节词外,在双音节和多音节词中,如果某个音节符合以上规则且重读则为重读开音节或重读闭音节。

**元音在重读开音节和闭音节中的语音规则（6 个字母）**

a 一般在开音节中发 /ei/ take  late  date  table

一般在闭音节中发 / æ/ thanks  am  have  can

或 /ɔ / what  want

对比练习  make and map  lake and tap  save and ball  date and want

e 一般在开音节中发 /iː/ me  he  meet  we

一般在闭音节中发 /e/ menu  let  twenty  get

对比练习  she and pen  see and get  be and let  free and set

i 一般在开音节中发 /ai/ rice  five  nice  like

一般在闭音节中发 /i/ with  shrimp  in  it

对比练习  five and fill  fine and city  rice and in  like and will

o 一般在开音节中发 /əu / OK  no  moment  open

一般在闭音节中发 /ɔ/ clock  dog  hot  not

对比练习  home and hot  no and sock  dote and clock  role and soft

u 一般在开音节中发 /juː/ menu  mute  cube  use

一般在闭音节中发 /ʌ/ cut  but  bus  duck

对比练习  menu and but  June and cup  use and but  Susan and sun

y 一般在开音节中发 /ai/ try  by  my  spy

一般在闭音节中发 /i/ twenty  lynch  gym  olympic

对比练习  try and cloudy  cry and speedy  spy and rainy

### Recitation 经典背诵

**Daniel：** My friend Tom and I like eating at the restaurant together. He is not good at ordering things, so most of the time I'm the one that orders the dishes. The only problem is that he always complains about the prices and I think that is not a cool thing to do.

# Topic 2 用餐
## Dining

听 学 读 看

　　服务员把他们要的虾球端上来.爱吃油炸食品的丹尼尔觉得虾球好吃极了,酥脆味美。但是汤姆却觉得有点淡,于是加了芥末,那么加了芥末之后的虾球汤姆会喜欢吗?

**Waiter:** Sorry to have kept you waiting. This is your order.

**服务员:** 对不起,让你们久等了。这是你们点的菜。

**Tom:** But we ordered two bowls. There is only one.

**汤姆:** 但我们点了两碗。这只有一碗。

**Waiter:** Oh, I am sorry. The other one is going to be ready in a minute.

**服务员:** 哦,对不起,另一碗一会儿就好。

**Tom:** It doesn't matter. Let's eat this one together.

**汤姆:** 没关系。这碗我们就一起吃吧。

**Daniel:** Hmm…It tastes delicious. The rice rolls are so crispy. Fried food is my favourite!

**丹尼尔:** 呣……真好吃。这面卷真脆。我最喜欢吃油炸食品了!

**Tom:** I think the shrimp is a little bland.

**汤姆:** 我觉得虾球有点淡耶。

**Daniel:** Put some mustard on it.

**丹尼尔:** 加点芥末。

(*Tom puts some mustard into the dish.*)

(汤姆往盘子里加了点芥末。)

**Daniel:** How does it taste now?

**丹尼尔:** 现在味道怎么样?

**Tom:** It's too hot!

**汤姆:** 太辣了!

**Daniel:** You put too much. Waiter, could you please give me a glass of water?

**丹尼尔:** 你放太多了。服务员,能给我一杯水吗?

**Waiter:** Here you are.

**服务员:** 水来了。

**Tom:** Thanks. Oh, I don't like spicy food.

**汤姆:** 谢谢。哎,我不喜欢辣的东西。

**Daniel:** I think mustard tastes strange, but not spicy. Anyway, I think the shrimp rolls are delicious!

**丹尼尔:** 我觉得芥末味道很奇怪,可是不辣。反正,我觉得虾球好吃极了!

---

### 生词小结

| | |
|---|---|
| **order** *n.* 订单,命令 | **crispy** *adj.* 脆的 |
| **minute** *n.* 分钟 | **mustard** *n.* 芥末 |
| **taste** *vi.* 尝,体会 | **spicy** *adj.* 辣的 |

## 单词扩展 Vocabulary Builder

### 表示菜肴名称的词汇

| 基础词汇 | 提高词汇 |
| --- | --- |
| ice cream 冰淇淋 | steak 牛排 |
| potato chips 薯条 | bacon 熏肉 |
| sandwich 三明治 | pasta 意大利面 |
| pizza 比萨 | sushi 寿司 |
| hotdog 热狗 | noodle 面条 |
| chocolate 巧克力 | salad 色拉 |
| cheese 奶酪 | pancake 煎饼 |

## D 家庭总动员
o it together

两人一组,一方随机大声读出上面词汇的英文和中文,另一方用该词汇填入下面的句子,大声朗读并表演出来,并用中文给出一个理由。

The(          ) tastes dilicious!

【例】家长读 noodles 面条
宝贝读 The noodles taste delicious! 因为那是妈妈做的!

**Recitation** 经典背诵

Daniel: I love shrimp rolls. Actually I think everything fried is good. I can eat up a whole bowl of shrimp rolls all by myself which is really surprising to my friends. It's a shame that "there ain't such a thing as free lunch". Maybe, I should work at a restaurant in the future.

## Topic3 健康饮食
### Healthy Diet

汤姆说吃油炸的虾不利于健康,丹尼尔却说他特爱吃油炸的。两个小家伙似乎又要策划什么特别活动了。一起来看看吧!

**Tom：** The fried shrimp is crunchy! But my mom will never cook shrimp this way. She always says that fried food is not healthy.

**Daniel：** How does she cook the shrimp?

**Tom：** She often cooks it in a large pan of boiling water.

**Daniel：** I don't like that. I like fried food, fried potatoes, fried chicken, fried sausage... I can't see why fried food is not healthy.

**Tom：** My mom says it has a lot of fat. I also suggest you do not eat so many fried things.

**Daniel：** It's all right! I often fry sausages when my mom is not at home.

**Tom：** Really? I really want to have a try!

**Daniel：** Come to my house this Sunday. My mom will not be at home then. We can cook some wonderful fried food by ourselves!

**Tom：** That sounds like a good idea! But I'm afraid my mom will be angry about it.

**Daniel：** If we don't tell her, nobody will know. Come on, If I were you, I would never miss a good chance like that.

**Tom：** That sounds good, but...

**Daniel：** Oh, come on...

**Tom：** Well, you win.

**汤姆：** 炸虾好脆耶! 可我妈妈从来不这么煮虾。她老是说吃油炸的东西不利于健康。

**丹尼尔：** 那她是怎么煮虾的?

**汤姆：** 她经常把虾放在一大盆沸水里煮。

**丹尼尔：** 我可不喜欢。我喜欢吃炸的东西,炸土豆,炸鸡,炸香肠什么的。我可不觉得那有什么不健康的。

**汤姆：** 我妈说它含有很多脂肪。我劝你也少吃点油炸食品。

**丹尼尔：** 没事! 我经常趁我妈妈不在的时候炸香肠吃。

**汤姆：** 真的? 我真想试一下耶!

**丹尼尔：** 那这个星期天来我家。我妈妈那时不在。我们可以自己炸点好吃的!

**汤姆：** 好主意! 但我怕我妈妈知道了会生气。

**丹尼尔：** 如果我们不告诉她,没人会知道。来吧,我要是你就决不会错过这种好机会。

**汤姆：** 好是好,可是……

**丹尼尔：** 哎,来吧……

**汤姆：** 好吧,你赢了。

## 生词小结

| | | | |
|---|---|---|---|
| **crunchy** | *adj.* 脆的，易碎的 | **boil** | *vt.* 沸腾，煮沸 |
| **healthy** | *adj.* 健康的 | **chance** | *n.* 机会 |
| **pan** | *n.* 平底锅 | **chicken** | *n.* 小鸡，鸡肉 |

# **F**unctional structure 功能性句型扩展 —— 建议劝告句型

**请朗读以下句型，家长和孩子交替进行**

1. 提出建议

I suggest that… 我建议……

I suggest you do not (do)… 我建议你不要……

Would you mind if I make a suggestion? 能给您提个建议吗？

I wouldn't suggest that… 我不建议那样做……

If I were you, I would… 如果我是你，我会……

2. 接受建议

That sounds like a good idea. 好主意！

That sounds great/wonderful! 听上去很好！

That's certainly good! 那当然好啦！

3. 拒绝建议

I'd rather not. 我可不要。

That's a good idea, but I'd rather not. 好是好，不过我可不要。

Thank you, but I'm afraid I can't do that. 谢谢，但是恐怕我不能那么做。

I don't think it's a good idea. 我觉得这主意不好。

I'd like to, but I'm afraid… 我是想，但是恐怕……

**R**ecitation 经典背诵

Tom：My mom believes in healthy diet. She often cooks food in a large pan of boiling water, and never allows me to eat any fried foods, saying that they have a lot of fat which is bad for my health. But I would try some in the future, just for a change.

Topic 4 买单
**Payment**

另一碗虾球端上来了。丹尼尔和汤姆竟然数起了碗里虾球的数目,如果要是少一个就叫餐馆再赔一碗。结果怎么样呢! 这真能如他们所愿吗?

**Daniel:** Here comes the other bowl.

**Waiter:** It is seasoned with more salt, as you required.

**Daniel:** Great! Oh, I can eat up all of them!

**Tom:** No way.

**Daniel:** How many rolls are there?

**Tom:** Let me count, if there are less than twenty, we could have another bowl.

**Daniel:** For free!

**Tom:** Daniel, no luck. There are twenty-one.

**Daniel:** There goes the free lunch. Well, let's finish this and get the check.

**Tom:** But there is one more. That's not bad.

(*Daniel and Tom finish their meal.*)

**Daniel:** Waiter, the check please.

**Waiter:** Fifty *yuan*, please. There is a ten percent discount for students. That makes the total of forty-five yuan.

**Daniel:** Here you are.

**Waiter:** Thanks. Have a nice day!

**丹尼尔:**另一碗上来了。

**服务员:**按你的要求,这碗多加了些盐。

**丹尼尔:**太好了! 噢,我能把它们全吃光!

**汤姆:**没门。

**丹尼尔:**一共有几个啊?

**汤姆:**我数数,要是没有二十个,我们就叫他们再给一碗。

**丹尼尔:**免费!

**汤姆:**丹尼尔,我们不走运耶。里面有二十一个。

**丹尼尔:**免费餐泡汤了。我们还是乖乖吃完了付账吧。

**汤姆:**但还多了一个嘛,不赖啊。

(丹和汤姆吃完了饭。)

**丹尼尔:**服务员,请结账。

**服务员:**五十块。学生有百分之十的折扣。一共是四十五块。

**丹尼尔:**给你钱。

**服务员:**谢谢。祝你们愉快!

---

**生词小结**

| season | *vt.* 调味 | require | *vt.* 要求 |
| salt | *n.* 盐 | lucky | *adj.* 幸运的 |
| check | *n.* 账单 | lunch | *n.* 午餐 |

# G语法小结 rammer —— 被动语态(一)

我们已经学习了英语中的五种时态,现在来看语态。英语中有两种语态,主动语态和被动语态。现在我们来看一下各种时态的被动语态。

1. 一般现在时的被动语态 am, is, are + 过去分词

   *The boy is called Daniel.* 那个男孩叫丹尼尔。

   *You are invited to give us a talk.* 邀请您给我们做个讲座。

2. 一般过去时的被动语态 was, were + 过去分词

   *I was given a present.* 我收到了礼物。

   *Trees were planted every spring by us.* 我们每年春天都种树。

3. 一般将来时的被动语态 will / shall be + 过去分词

   *The job will be finished by him.* 他很快就会完成工作了。

   *A new railway will be built in this city next year.* 明年市里将建新铁路。

4. 现在进行时的被动语态 am, is, are + being + 过去分词

   *A new cinema is being built here.* 新的电影院正在修建。

   *Money is being collected for the project.* 我们正为工程集资。

5. 过去进行时的被动语态 was, were + being + 过去分词

   *A meeting was being held when I was there.* 会议举行时我在那里。

   *The pen was being used by May yesterday.* 昨天阿美在用这支笔。

# D家庭总动员 o it together

**两人一组,一方朗诵下面的中文句子,另一方挑选出合适的翻译。**

1. 巧克力不能炸。
2. 新的餐馆将被修建。
3. 正在准备晚饭。
4. 正在清点行李。
5. 蛋糕被丹尼尔吃了。

1. The cake was eaten by Daniel.
2. The supper is being prepared.
3. The luggage is being counted.
4. The chocolate can't be fried.
5. A new restaurant will be built soon.

# R ecitation 经典背诵

**Tom:** My friend Daniel loves shrimp rolls. Everytime we go out eating, he would order them. He keeps on saying that fried food is his favourite, but I don't really like it, especially if it's spicy. Other than that, anything will do for me.

# 旅馆 Hotel

## Goals

**在这个场景中,我们将学到:**

1. 元音字母语音规则(二)
2. 表示房间种类设施的词汇
3. 建议劝告句型练习
4. 被动语态(二)主动形式表示被动意义的用法

## Topic 1 预定 Reservation

及格时间: 10 秒
你的纪录:——秒
及格时间: 15 秒
你的纪录:——秒

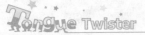
### Tongue Twister 玩转语音

1. Betty beat a bit of butter to make a better batter.
2. Knife and a fork, bottle and a cork, that is the way you spell New York.

听 学 看

一位美国教授托德要来本杰明的研究所参加为期一周的学术交流会。他妻子也随他来到了中国旅游。托德是本杰明的老朋友,于是本杰明就打电话到酒店帮他预订房间。

**Waitress:** Good morning. Morre Hotel. At your service.

**Benjamin:** Good morning! I'd like to make a reservation, please. Do you have any rooms available for the next week.

**Waitress:** All right. Single-room or double-room?

**Benjamin:** Double-room, please. It's for an American couple.

**Waitress:** Hold on, please. Let me check the bookings.
Yes, we have double-rooms available. What kind of room would you like, sir?

**Benjamin:** I'd like a room with a nice view, please.

**Waitress:** We have a nice garden-view room.

**Benjamin:** Good. I'll take that one. Is there a

**服务生:** 早上好。这里是摩尔酒店,竭诚为您服务。

**本杰明:** 早上好。我想要预定一个房间。你们有下周的空房吗?

**服务生:** 有的。请问要单人间还是双人间。

**本杰明:** 双人间。我是为一对美国夫妇预定的。

**服务生:** 请稍等。让我查一下房间的预定情况。
是的,我们有剩余的双人间。请问您要什么样的房间?

**本杰明:** 我想要一个带漂亮风景的房间。

**服务生:** 我们有一个带漂亮花园风景的房间。

**本杰明:** 好的。我就要那一间了。酒店

bar in your hotel?

**Waitress**：Yes, sir. And there is also a party going on each Saturday night in the bar till next morning.

**Benjamin**：Party all night? *Hotel California*? No kidding. Anyway, what's the room charge?

**Waitress**：888 yuan per night. With breakfast. "Northern star" buffet！

What's their arriving time?

**Benjamin**：They turn up around 4p. m. next Monday, and they check out on next Sunday.

**Waitress**：I see. May I have your name and phone number?

**Benjamin**：Yes. 67101213. Benjamin.

里有酒吧吗?

**服务生**：有的。每周六晚上酒吧里都会有晚会,而且会一直持续到第二天早上。

**本杰明**：整晚的晚会。《加州旅馆》吗? 别开玩笑了。不管怎样,房间收费标准是怎么样的?

**服务生**：每晚 888 元。带早餐。早餐叫"北极星"自助餐。

他们什么时候到?

**本杰明**：他们下周一下午 4 点左右入住,下周日离开。

**服务生**：知道了。可以留一下您的名字和电话号码吗?

**本杰明**：好的。67101213。本杰明。

---

### 生词小结

**hotel** *n.* 旅馆
**service** *n.* 服务
**reservation** *n.* 预定
**double** *adj.* 双的
**single** *adj.* 单一的
**view** *n.* 风景

### 注释

**Hotel California** 《加州旅馆》,美国著名摇滚乐队"老鹰乐队"( The Eagles ) 的经典歌曲

---

## P语音小结
**ronunciation** —— 元音字母语音规则(二)

元音字母在 r 音节中的读音(在美语中 r 要发音,而在英音中 r 不发音)

"元音字母＋r"的重读音节为 r 音节。在 r 音节中元音字母的读音规则为:

1. ar/ɑ:/ :**party  bar  charge  star**
   朗读练习:car  far  jar  bark

2. er/ir/ur /ə:/:**her  service  girl  turn**
   朗读练习:serve  birth  bird  burn

3. or/ɔ:/ :**morning  Northern  story  horn**
   朗读练习:fork  north

**Recitation** 经典背诵

**Receptionist**：I'm a receptionist in a hotel. We get a lot of calls for reservations each day. Many customers call us to reserve rooms ahead of time in order to have nice view rooms. Some just want to know if there is a bar in the hotel. You know people like different things. I like my job.

## 入住
### Check-in

托德和本杰明在酒店门口见面。本杰明带托德夫妇到前台登记入住。来看一下具体情况吧。

**Benjamin**: Hi, Todd. Long time no see.

**Todd**: Hi. Nice to see you here. Oh, this is my wife Lena. Lena, this is Benjamin.

**Lena**: Nice to see you.

**Benjamin**: Nice to see you too. I've made a reservation for you guys. Wanna go and have a look?

**Todd**: Sure, you are the boss.

**Waitress**: Good afternoon. Can I help you, sir?

**Benjamin**: Well, I made a reservation last week for this American couple by the name of Benjamin. Here they are.

**Waitress**: A minute, please. Benjamin... Oh, yes, here it is. One double-room for a whole week, Here is the registration card. Will you please fill this form out, sir?

**Todd**: Love to.
Done. Here you are.

**Waitress**: Thank you. Now everything is in order. Your room number is 8715.

**Todd**: Is it on the 87th floor? Wow?

**Waitress**: No, sir. In China, 8 is only a lucky number. It's on the 7th floor.

**Todd**: Thank you. By the way, is there a dressing table in the room?

**Waitress**: Yes. A traditional wooden one.

**本杰明**：嗨,托德,好久不见了。

**托德**：嗨。见到你真高兴。哦,对了,这是我妻子蕾娜。蕾娜,这是本杰明。

**蕾娜**：我也很高兴见到你。

**本杰明**：我已经为你们预订好一个房间了。现在想去看一下吗?

**托德**：当然可以,听你的。

**服务生**：下午好。有什么能为您效劳的吗?

**本杰明**：上周我用本杰明这个名字为这对美国夫妇预订了一个房间。现在他们来了。

**服务生**：请稍等。本杰明…… 哦,是的,这儿呢。一个双人间预订一周。这是登记卡。能麻烦您填一下吗?

**托德**：非常乐意。
填完了。给你。

**服务生**：谢谢。全都处理好了。你们的房间号是8715。

**托德**：房间在87层吗? 哇噻!

**服务生**：不,先生。在中国8只是一个幸运数字。房间在第七层。

**托德**：谢谢你。顺便问一下,房间里有梳妆台吗?

**服务生**：有的。是一个传统的木质梳妆台。

## 生词小结

couple　*n.* 一对夫妻

whole　*adj.* 整个的

registration　*n.* 登记

skip　*vt.* 跳过

dressing table　梳妆台

traditional　*adj.* 传统的

## 注释

1. wanna＝want to 口语的常见表达方式，意思是"想要做……"

2. lucky number 幸运数字，中外的幸运数字有很大不同，在中国 6 和 8 是幸运数字，4 是不吉的数字，在国外很多国家 13 被视为是不吉利的数字，而且有很多人不喜欢星期三。

# 单词扩展 Vocabulary Builder

## 表示房间种类设施的词汇

| 基础词汇 | 提高词汇 |
| --- | --- |
| bed 床 | bookshelf 书架 |
| door 门 | fireplace 壁炉 |
| chair 椅子 | cupboard 壁橱 |
| mirror 镜子 | armchair 扶手椅 |
| table 桌子 | cabinet 橱柜 |
| drawer 抽屉 | folding chair 折(叠)椅 |
| window 窗户 | fitment 家具 |
| couch 长沙发 | |

# Do it together 家庭总动员

两人一组，一方随机大声读出上面词汇的英文和中文，另一方用该词汇填入下面的句子，大声朗读并表演出来，并用中文给出一个理由。

There is a (　　　　　　) in the room?

【例】家长读 bed 床

宝贝读 There is a bed in the room. 妈妈买的。

**Recitation** 经典背诵

Todd：I'm an American scientist. Sometimes I travel to China for work. I have a good Chinese friend named Benjamin. He always helps me a lot when I'm in China. So I can always enjoy the time there. It's interesting that I always get a room on the 8th floor. A waitress once told me that 8 was the lucky number in China. It made me happy.

因为房间的隔音设备很差，建筑噪音使教授夫妻不能睡好觉。蕾娜在入住的第二天早上来到前台要求换房。那么她能成功吗？请往下看。

**Waitress**: Good morning, Ma'm. Can I help you?

**Lena**: Yes. I'm in room 8715. The room's insulation is too bad. My husband and I couldn't get any real sleep last night.

There was a construction going on all night outside. It's just a nightmare for us!

**Waitress**: I'm terribly sorry.

**Lena**: Anyway, I'd like to change a room. Do you have a quiet double-room available now?

**Waitress**: A minute, please. Let me check on the computer to see if there is any room available.

What about this one? It's on the sunny side with a big balcony. And it's a pretty quiet room.

**Lena**: Sounds good. Can I have a look at it first?

**Waitress**: Sure. It's 8736. Come with me.

**Waitress**: Here it is. Come on in, Ma'am.

**Lena**: Nice! I'll take this one. I think I can have a good sleep.

**Waitress**: That's for sure, Ma'am. Everything is taken care of.

**Lena**: Thank you very much.

**Waitress**: I think you may need a porter with your belongings, Ma'am.

**Lena**: I'll appreciate that. Thank you.

服务生：早上好，女士。有什么能为您效劳的吗？

蕾娜：我住在8715房间。房间的隔音设备太差了。我和我先生昨晚都没睡好觉。

外面整晚都在施工。那对于我们来讲简直是噩梦。

服务生：真的很抱歉。

蕾娜：不管怎样，我要求换一个房间。你们现在还有安静的双人间吗？

服务生：请稍等。让我在电脑上查一下看看有没有空余的房间。

这间怎么样？朝阳，带一个大阳台，而且非常安静。

蕾娜：听起来不错。我可以先看一下吗？

服务生：当然。房间号是8736。请跟我来。

服务生：就是这一间。请进来，女士。

蕾娜：很不错。我就要这间吧？我想今晚我能睡个好觉了。

服务生：那是当然的，女士。一切都会安排妥当的。

蕾娜：非常感谢。

服务生：我觉得您会需要一位服务生帮您搬东西（到这个新房间）。

蕾娜：我很感激。谢谢。

**生词小结**

| | | | |
|---|---|---|---|
| insulation | *n.* 隔离 | sunny | *adj.* 阳光充足的 |
| husband | *n.* 丈夫 | balcony | *n.* 阳台 |
| terribly | *adv.* 可怕地 | appreciate | *vt.* 感激 |
| nightmare | *n.* 噩梦 | | |

**S情景练习**
**Scene practice** —— 建议劝告句型练习

仔细阅读下面五个场景,两人一组,使用建议劝告句型(见 155 页),用一用,练一练。

(1) If your were Benjamin, Todd wants to go to a good restaurant in Beijing. Give your advice to him where to go?

(2) If you were Shirley, Lena asks you for advice about somewhere to go in Beijing to buy Chinese silk. What would you say?

(3) It's Daniel's birthday next week. May doesn't know what to get for him, if you were Gucci, what would you suggest?

(4) Todd advises Benjamin to go to the lecture tonight, but he can't go there, if you were Benjamin, what would you say to Todd?

(5) Shirley suggests going to Hunan restaurant for a meal, but Lena doesn't like hot food very much. If you were Lena, what would you say?

**Lena:** I'm Lena. Todd is my husband. It's my first time in China. We stay in a nice hotel. Though we've changed our room for some reasons, we still enjoy our time. The service has been really good and I think I will come to China again in the future. I love this place!

## 餐饮和零售业场景 · Catering Industry and Retail Trade

## 退房
### Check-out

听 学
读 看

美国教授在前台退房付款,对酒店的环境和服务赞赏有加,并请酒店工作人员把他的行李预先送到机场,酒店会提供这项服务吗。往下看就知道了。

**Todd**：I'm checking out now. Can I have my bill, please?

**Waiter**：Sure. What's your room number, sir?

**Todd**：It's 8736. Here is my key card.

**Waiter**：A minute, please. It's 6212 yuan all together. Tax included.

**Todd**：Can I pay with traveler's check?

**Waiter**：Sure. Can I have your passport, please?

**Todd**：Here you are.

**Waiter**：Thanks. Are you satisfied with your stay here with us, sir?

**Todd**：Very much. The room is cozy and the service is jolly good. By the way, could you deliver my luggage to the airport in advance?

**Waiter**：Sure. It will be taken care of, sir. Which flight do you take?

**Todd**：Flight 17. And my luggage should be delivered there by 4 o'clock.

**Waiter**：Got it, sir. It'd be great to see you again, sir.

**Todd**：Thank you.

**托德**：我现在想结账。请给我账单,好吗?

**服务生**：好的,先生。您的房间号是多少?

**托德**：8736. 这是我的门卡。

**服务生**：请稍等。一共是 6212 元。含税。

**托德**：我可以用旅行支票支付吗?

**服务生**：当然可以,我可以看一下您的护照吗?

**托德**：给你。

**服务生**：谢谢。先生,您在这里住得满意吗?

**托德**：非常满意。房间很舒适,服务很周到。顺便问一下,你们可以提前把我的行李送到机场吗?

**服务生**：当然可以。我们会办好的。您乘坐的是哪趟班机?

**托德**：第 17 号班机。我的行李需要在 4 点之前送到。

**服务生**：没问题,先生。希望能再次见到您。

**托德**：谢谢。

### 生词小结

| | |
|---|---|
| **check out** 结账 | **passport** *n.* 护照 |
| **bill** *n.* 账单 | **satisfy** *vt.* 使满足 |
| **include** *vt.* 包括 | **cozy** *adj.* 舒适的 |
| **traveller's check** 旅行支票 | **fascinating** *adj.* 迷人的 |

## G 语法小结 —— 被动语态(二)

英语的被动意义除了用及物动词的被动语态形式表示外,还可以用其他方法来表示,就像在汉语中并非一定要用"被"字来表示被动意义一样。以下的四种情况即为主动形式表示被动。

1. wash、clean、cook、look、cut、sell、read、wear、feel、draw、write、sell、drive 可用主动形式表示被动

 *The book sells well.* 这本书销路好。

 *This knife cuts easily.* 这刀子很好用。

2. blame、remain、keep、rent、build 可用主动形式表示被动

 *Much work remains.* 还有很多工作没做。

3. need、require、want、worth (形容词) 后的动名词用主动形式

 *The door needs repairing.* 相当于 *The door needs to be repaired.* 门需要修了。

 *This room needs cleaning.* 这房间应该打扫一下。

 *This book is worth reading.* 这本书值得一读。

4. 特殊结构中用主动表示被动

 *make sb. heard / understood* (使别人能听见/理解自己)

 *have sth. done* (要某人做某事)

## D 家庭总动员 Do it together

两人一组,一方朗诵下面的中文句子,另一方挑选出合适的翻译。

1. 阿美的头发要洗了。
2. 这支笔好用。
3. 这鞋穿着很舒服。
4. 这部电影值得再看一遍。
5. 还有一点作业没做。

1. A little work remains.
2. This pair of shoes wears well.
3. May's hair need washing.
4. This film is worthing seeing.
5. The pen writes well.

### Recitation 经典背诵

**Porter:** I'm a porter in a big hotel. My job is to help the customers carry their luggage in and out of their hotel rooms. Sometimes, I even carry them to the airport which takes a bit more time and makes me tired. But still I think it's fun to carry things around. Do you think so?

## SCENE 21

# 停车场 Parking Lot

### Goals

在这个场景中,我们将学到:

1. 元音字母组合发音(一)
2. 汽车种类的词汇
3. 表达抱怨的句型
4. 反意疑问句

 停错车位
**Wrong Parking**

 玩转语音

1. Say this sharply, say this sweetly, say this shortly, say this softly. Say this sixteen times in succession.
2. I saw Esau kissing Kate. I saw Esau, he saw me, and she saw I saw Esau.

及格时间: 20 秒
你的纪录: —— 秒
及格时间: 15 秒
你的纪录: —— 秒

本杰明把车停在自家的车位上,可是保安却说本杰明停错了地方,究竟是谁错了呢?

(*Benjamin is parking his car when a security guard comes by.*)

**Security guard**：Excuse me, sir, I'm afraid you can't park your car here.

**Benjamin**：Why not? It's my parking space.

**Security guard**：I'm afraid not, sir.

**Benjamin**：Oh? That's a surprise. Let me see… D 0411 Our dog's birthday.
Yes, I'm sure this is my parking space!

**Security guard**：But I saw a red car always parking here before.

**Benjamin**：Oh, we've just repainted our car. It was red.

(本杰明正在停车,这时一个保安走了过来。)

**保安**：对不起,先生,恐怕您不能把您的车停在这儿。

**本杰明**：为什么不能? 这是我的停车位。

**保安**：恐怕不是的,先生。

**本杰明**：是吗? 真叫人吃惊。我看看……D0411 我们家狗的生日。是的,我肯定这就是我的停车位!

**保安**：但我以前都是看到一辆红色的车停在这儿来着。

**本杰明**：哦,我们昨天刚刚给它重新上过漆,它以前是红色的。

Security guard：Maybe. But the car of this space has a broken rearview mirror on the left.

Benjamin：Yeah. It used to. We got that fixed yesterday too.

Security guard：Could you wait for a minute, sir? I'd like to have a check.

Benjamin：Sure, go ahead.

Security guard：Sorry, sir, my mistake. This is your parking space.

Benjamin：That's all right. It's not your fault.

保安：也许吧。但这个车位的车的左后视镜是坏的。

本杰明：是啊。它以前是。我们昨天也已经把它修好了。

保安：您能等一会儿吗，先生？我得核实一下。

本杰明：可以，你核实吧。

保安：对不起，先生，我弄错了。这是您的停车位。

本杰明：没关系。这不能怪你。

---

### 生词小结

| | | | |
|---|---|---|---|
| **afraid** | *adj.* 害怕的，担心的 | **maybe** | *adv.* 也许 |
| **birthday** | *n.* 生日 | **fix** | *vt.* 修理 |
| **paint** | *n.* 油漆 | | |

---

## P语音小结
ronunciation —— 元音字母组合发音（一）

ai/ay    au/aw

1. ai/ay 组合在一起经常发 / ei /
   （1）ai 组合 /ei/ afraid  paint  wait  gain
      朗读练习：pain  train  obtain  remain
   （2）ay 组合 /ei/ yesterday  birthday  play  day
      朗读练习：may  say  delay  display

2. au/aw 组合在一起经常发 /ɔː/
   （1）au 组合 /ɔː/ fault  caught  taught  default
      朗读练习：because  autumn  daughter  audio
   （2）aw 组合/ɔː/ saw  awful  raw  law
      朗读练习：draw  dawn  drawer  lawyer

---

**Recitation**
经典背诵

Benjamin：I never like cars. Parking a car is especially a big trouble for me. The security guard would always come up and check if I've parked in right space. I wonder whether he does the same thing to the others. Anyway he is just doing his job.

## 停车与收费
### Parking Fee

停车场经常有很多空着的车位,于是有人想做车位出租的买卖,可是价格是怎么定的呢? 一起来看看吧!

| | |
|---|---|
| **Benjamin**: How big is this parking lot in our community? | **本杰明**: 我们社区的停车场有多大? |
| **Security guard**: It has fifty parking spaces. | **保安**: 这儿有 50 个停车位。 |
| **Benjamin**: So you guys should be always busy. | **本杰明**: 那你们一定会很忙吧。 |
| **Security guard**: Why? | **保安**: 为什么呢? |
| **Benjamin**: I bet it is always full of cars. | **本杰明**: 我猜它一直车满为患。 |
| **Security guard**: Quite the contrary, sir. Plenty of the spaces here are free when people drive their cars out to work. | **保安**: 恰恰相反,先生。人们把车开出去上班时,这儿很多车位都空了。 |
| **Benjamin**: Ah... I see. | **本杰明**: 呵……我知道了。 |
| **Security guard**: We plan to rent some of them out at the hourly rates. | **保安**: 我们打算把一部分车位按小时收费租出去。 |
| **Benjamin**: What is the hourly rate for a car like this? | **本杰明**: 那每小时停车收费是多少呢? |
| **Security guard**: I am not sure. But it'll be at least ten yuan an hour. | **保安**: 我不敢肯定。不过不会少于 10 块钱。 |
| **Benjamin**: How much would it cost if someone parks here for one hour and ten minutes? | **本杰明**: 如果有人在这里停了 1 小时零 10 分钟呢? |
| **Security guard**: That would be twenty yuan, sir. We charge only by the number of hours, no split of each hour. | **保安**: 那就是 20 块钱了,先生。我们只按小时整点收费,不按部分收费。 |
| **Benjamin**: That's expensive. | **本杰明**: 真贵。 |

---

**生词小结**

| | |
|---|---|
| **community** *n.* 社区 | **rate** *n.* 比率 |
| **bet** *vi.* 打赌 | **cost** *vt.* 花费 |
| **contrary** *n.* 反面,相反 | **split** *n.* 部分,裂片 |
| **rent** *vt.* 出租 | |

## 单词扩展 Vocabulary Builder

### 汽车种类的词汇

| 基础词汇 | 提高词汇 |
| --- | --- |
| jeep 吉普车 | sports car 跑车 |
| truck 卡车 | ambulance 救护车 |
| bus 巴士 | racing car 赛车 |
| taxi 出租车 | minibus 面包车 |
| mail car 邮车 | saloon 轿车 |
| police car 警车 | station wagon 旅行车 |
| van 面包车 | wrecker 清障车 |
| trailer 拖车 | convertible 敞篷车 |

## 家庭总动员
Do it together

两人一组，一方随机大声读出上面词汇的英文和中文，另一方用该词汇填入下面的句子，大声朗读并表演出来，并用中文给出一个理由。

**You can't park your (                    ) here.**

【例】家长读 jeep 吉普车
孩子读 You can't park your jeep here. 因为这儿是救护车专用车位！

### Recitation 经典背诵

**Security guard：** There are fifty parking spaces in our community's parking lot. But it's almost empty during the day time because people drive their cars out to work. So I suppose it's a good idea to rent some of the parking spaces out at hourly rates. That would be a good way to make some money.

## 事故
### Accidents

本杰明今天好像很不顺。刚才停车遇到麻烦,现在车是停好了,可新麻烦又来了,那么究竟发生什么事了呢?

| | |
|---|---|
| **Benjamin**：Hey, look out! | **本杰明**：嘿,当心点! |
| **Mr Li**：What happened? | **李先生**：出什么事了? |
| **Benjamin**：You've just scratched my car. Oh, God, a paint was scratched off. | **本杰明**：你刚刚刮到我的车了。哦,天哪,有一块漆刮掉了! |
| **Mr Li**：Where? my car? | **李先生**：哪儿? 我的车? |
| **Benjamin**：No, mine! | **本杰明**：不,我的! |
| **Mr Li**：Thank goodness! | **李先生**：谢天谢地! |
| **Benjamin**：I've just had it repainted. | **本杰明**：我才上的漆。 |
| **Mr Li**：That's terrible. | **李先生**：太可怕了。 |
| **Benjamin**：I am sorry to say this, sir, but you should've been more careful. | **本杰明**：我很抱歉说这些,先生,但你应该更小心点的。 |
| **Mr Li**：I apologize for that. But the space is too small. | **李先生**：我为此而抱歉。但这儿地方太小了。 |
| **Benjamin**：What about the damage to my car? What are you gonna do about that? | **本杰明**：那么我的车的损失呢? 你打算怎么办? |
| **Mr Li**：Can we solve this later? I am calling the insurance company. | **李先生**：我们可以等会儿再解决吗? 我正在打电话叫保险公司。 |
| **Benjamin**：OK. I gotta call mine too. | **本杰明**：好吧,那我也叫我的。 |

---

**生词小结**

**look out** 当心,注意
**scratch** *vt.* 划,刮
**careful** *adj.* 小心的
**apologize** *vi.* 道歉

**damage** *n.* 损坏
**solve** *vt.* 解决
**insurance** *n.* 保险

---

# F 功能性句型扩展
unctional structure —— 表达抱怨的句型

**请朗读以下句型，家长和孩子交替进行。**

1. 表示抱怨

I'm sorry to have to say this, but... 我很抱歉说这些，可……

Sorry, I am afraid... 对不起，我恐怕……

I'm sorry, but... 对不起，可是……

I'm sorry to trouble you, but... 对不起麻烦您，可……

2. 接受抱怨

Sorry, my mistake. 对不起，是我的错。

I apologize for... 我为……而道歉。

I can't tell you how sorry I am. 我真不知有多么抱歉。

I'm so sorry, but I'll do what I can. 对不起，但我会尽力的。

Forgive me for... 请原谅我……

Sorry, I will make it up for you. 对不起，我会帮您解决的。

3. 拒绝和延迟抱怨

Well, I'm afraid there is nothing we can do about it. 恐怕我们也无能为力。

Leave it with us, and we'll see what we can do. 让我们来吧，看看我们能做点什么。

I'm afraid...is not in at the moment. 恐怕这时候不在。

Can we solve this later? 我们能一会儿再解决吗？

I'm afraid I can't help it. 恐怕我也没办法。

R*ecitation*
经典背诵

**Benjamin：**There are more and more cars in Beijing. The parking space is too small to hold so many cars. And my parking space is getting smaller. Sometimes my car gets scratched when I park it. That's really a big problem. We have to solve it as soon as possible.

# Topic 4 交通问题
**Traffic**

听 学 看

停车场的故事还真不少，这不，好像以前也发生了一些小事故，还真是无巧不成书！

**Mr Li：** I am sorry for damaging your car, sir.

**Benjamin：** Don't worry about it. Just leave it to the insurance companies.

**Mr Li：** The car park in this community is over crowded, isn't it?

**Benjamin：** Yeah, more and more cars. People should try to take public transportation.

**Mr Li：** There aren't enough buses in this city, are there?

**Benjamin：** Yeah, sometimes I really feel like writing a letter to the mayor.

**Mr Li：** That's too much of hassel. We just want a little bigger parking space.

**Benjamin：** Have you taken this to the property management, yet?

**Mr Li：** No. but I'm gonna. You know, several months ago, I backed into a red Honda when parking.

**Benjamin：** Where? On the road?

**Mr Li：** No, right here in the parking lot. It was parked right here in your space. The left rearview mirror was smashed.

**Benjamin：** Is the car owner a lady with deafening voice?

**Mr Li：** Yes! How do you know that?

**Benjamin：** That's my wife!

**Mr Li：** You mean…

**李先生：** 真抱歉弄坏了你的车，先生。

**本杰明：** 别担心。让保险公司来处理吧。

**李先生：** 我们小区的停车场太拥挤了，不是吗？

**本杰明：** 是啊，私家车越来越多了。人们应该试着使用公共交通。

**李先生：** 我们市里没有那么多公交车，不是吗？

**本杰明：** 是啊，有时我真想给市长写信。

**李先生：** 那倒不至于。我们只要有一个大点的停车场就好了。

**本杰明：** 你跟小区管理处反映过这事儿了吗？

**李先生：** 没有。但我正有此打算。几个月前，我停车时，倒车倒到一辆红色丰田车上去了。

**本杰明：** 在哪儿？路上吗？

**李先生：** 不，就在这个停车场。那辆车就停在你现在的地方。我把它的左后视镜给撞碎了。

**本杰明：** 那辆车的车主是不是一个嗓门很大的女人？

**李先生：** 是啊！你怎么知道的？

**本杰明：** 那是我太太！

**李先生：** 你是说……

### 生词小结

| | | | |
|---|---|---|---|
| **crowded** | *adj.* 拥挤的 | **mayor** | *n.* 市长 |
| **private** | *adj.* 私人的 | **property** | *n.* 财产,物业 |
| **transportation** | *n.* 交通 | **rearview mirror** | 后视镜 |

# G语法小结
## rammer —— 反意疑问句

反意疑问句由两部分组成,前面是陈述句,后面是简短的问句,如果前面是肯定,后面一般为否定,如果前面是否定,则后面多为肯定。

1. 句中有 I am,反意疑问应该是 aren't I,而不是 am not I 或 amn't I

*I am right, aren't I?* 我是对的,不是吗?

2. everything 和 nothing 作为陈述句的主语是单数,因此反意疑问句的主语要用 it,值得大家注意的是,nothing 做主语时,反意疑问句中的动词要用肯定形式

*Nothing is wrong, is it?* 没有什么错误,是吗?

3. 主语为 everyone,everybody,anyone,nobody 或 no one 时,反意疑问句中的主语用 they,要注意 nobody 和 no one 是否定词,因此反意疑问句同样应该用肯定的形式

*Nobody knows it, do they?* 没人知道这个,是吗?

4. 如果陈述句部分有 no,never,hardly,scarcely,rarely,seldom 等,那么,陈述句本身就是否定的,所以要接一个肯定的反意疑问句

*She has never been there, has she?* 她从来没去过那里,是吗?

5. 如果陈述句的动词是 wish,那么反意疑问句中要用 may

*I wish to go there with you, may I?* 我想和你一起去,行吗?

6. 包括听话人在内时,let's 的反意疑问句要用 shall we。反之,反意疑问句要用 will you

*let's go, shall we?* 我们走吧,好吗?

*Let us go, will you?* 大家走吧,好吗?

# D家庭总动员
## o it together

两人一组,一方朗诵下面的中文句子,另一方挑选出合适的翻译。

| | |
|---|---|
| 1. 等我一下,行吗? | 1. I wish to park my car here, may I? |
| 2. 市里没有足够的公交车,是吗? | 2. Everybody knows it, do they? |
| 3. 爸爸的车被损坏了,对吗? | 3. Wait for me, will you? |
| 4. 我希望把车停在这儿,行吗? | 4. Dad's car is destroyed, isn't it? |
| 5. 每个人都知道,是吗? | 5. There aren't enough buses in this city, are there? |

**Recitation** 经典背诵

Benjamin:We need a little bigger parking space in our community. My car was damaged twice because of the narrow parking space last year. First the rearview mirror, and then the new paint. Things are getting worse these days because there are more and more cars. I think we just need more buses.

# 冰吧 Ice Bar

## Goals

**在这个场景中,我们将学到:**

1. 元音字母组合发音(二)
2. 甜点的词汇
3. 抱怨句型练习
4. 祈使句

# Topic 1 酷暑
## The Heat

   **玩转语音**

1. Sheep shouldn't sleep in a shack. Sheep should sleep in a shed.
2. She sells seashells by the sea shore. The shells she sells are surely seashells. So if she sells shells on the seashore, I'm sure she sells seashore shells.

及格时间: 6 秒
你的纪录:—— 秒
及格时间: 18 秒
你的纪录:—— 秒

听 学 看

夏天的一个中午,阿美和好朋友古奇在街上闲逛,天气特别炎热,两个人不停地抱怨,她们都在抱怨些什么呢? 来看看吧!

**Gucci:** May, we are fools to hang out at noon. It's dying hot today. My skin is too weak to be exposed under the summer sun.

**May:** Do you have any sunscreen lotion?

**Gucci:** You know, honey, I used it all on the way over.

**May:** I think I'm getting a heartstroke.

**Gucci:** The heat is driving crazy and I hate my new hat.

**May:** Why? It's brand new, and it's perfect on you.

**Gucci:** But I bought it to get rid of the heat.

**古奇:** 阿美,我们选择中午出来逛街,真是不明智,今天太热了。我的皮肤很敏感,不能暴露在夏天烈日下。

**阿美:** 你有防晒霜吗?

**古奇:** 亲爱的,你该知道,我一路上都在用啊。

**阿美:** 我的心脏都快受不了了。

**古奇:** 酷热要把我逼疯了,而且我讨厌我的新帽子。

**阿美:** 为什么? 它是全新的,而且你戴着很漂亮。

**古奇:** 但是我买它是为了防晒的,现在除

Now it does nothing but burning my head.

May：Beauty costs，honey.

Gucci：Laugh all you want，whatever. We need to get out of the heat.

May：Walking under the sun is certainly not the way.

Gucci：Give me a break. It's not funny.

May：Right. Sorry. Anyway, the radio said that it'll rain later today.

Gucci：Hope so! Good thing is that autumn is just around the corner.

了让我的头感觉像火烧之外,它什么也没做。

**阿美**:亲爱的,美丽是要付出代价的。

**古奇**:只管笑吧! 不过我们真的要避避暑。

**阿美**:在太阳下走肯定不是个办法。

**古奇**:饶了我吧。一点都不好玩。

**阿美**:好的。对不起啦。不管怎么说,广播说今天晚一点会下雨的。

**古奇**:希望如此! 还好秋天就快要来了。

## 生词小结

**hang out**　　闲荡(俚语)

**skin**　　*n.* 皮肤

**weak**　　*adj.* 虚弱的

**expose**　　*vt.* 使暴露

**sunscreen lotion**　　防晒霜

**crazy**　　*adj.* 疯狂的

**anyway**　　*adv.* 不管怎样

**corner**　　*n.* 角落

## 注释

1. **It's dying hot today.** 这里的 dying 并不是"死"的意思,而是作为副词来修饰后面的形容词 hot,表示程度很大,中文中也有相似的表达:"我饿死了。"(当然其实谁也不会死。)

2. **Beauty costs.** 这里是阿美开古奇玩笑时的幽默表达,因为前文中提到古奇新买的帽子,看着漂亮,其实却特别热。中文中我们也常说的相似表达有:"要风度不要温度"。

## 语音小结 **P**ronunciation —— 元音字母组合发音(二)

1. 元音字母 ee 组合在一起经常发 /iː/ :sunscreen need sleep deep

2. 元音字母 ei 组合在一起经常发 /ei/ /ai/ /iː/ :eight height either seize

3. 元音字母 ea 组合在一起经常发 /iː/ /ei/ :weak heat break great

朗读练习:sweetheart 亲爱的

My thoughts are deep into you. 我深深地想念着你。

From the moment that I wake up, and to the whole day through. 从我每天早上起来的那一刻起,每一分每一秒直到一天结束。

Happy Valentine's Day! 情人节快乐!

Gucci：I'm Gucci. I don't like summer because it's always too hot. And my skin is also too delicate to be exposed under the summer sun. I use sunscreen lotion for protection. But it takes a lot of time to put it on all over. And this is not so fun.

## 巧克力火锅
### Chocolate Hot Pot

下午3点,阿美和古奇都感到有些饿,古奇是个很时尚很西化的女孩,又爱吃巧克力,于是就建议阿美两人去吃巧克力火锅。巧克力火锅? 感觉很诱人哦!

**Gucci**: Hey, I'm starving. I can eat a horse.

**May**: May it be a chocolate horse.

**Waitress**: Can I take your order now, girls?

**May**: What do you recommend?

**Waitress**: The chocolate hot pot is really popular with young girls. The chocolate hot pot. You know, the hot pot with chocolate in it and you can throw in cookies or whatever.

**Gucci**: Wow. That should be perfect for me!

**May**: Okay, that's it.

**Waitress**: Anything else?

**Gucci**: No, be quick, please!

(*After a short while, the chocolate hot pot is dished up. It's time to enjoy it!*)

**May**: Oh, they look so cute! So delicate and colorful!

**Gucci**: No girls can resist this!

**May**: It's true that one piece of chocolate can just cheer you up!

**Gucci**: That's for sure. Chocolate is something to die for!

**May**: How about us coming here every weekend?

**Gucci**: No, that's a suicide. You know, calories!

**May**: Forget about it. Just wait till we turn thirty.

**古奇**: 嗨,我饿死了。我能吃下一匹马。

**阿美**: 希望它是一匹巧克力马。

**服务生**: 女孩们,现在点餐吗?

**阿美**: 你有什么可以推荐的吗?

**服务生**: 最近巧克力火锅特别受年轻女孩子欢迎。巧克力火锅,就是火锅里面放有巧克力,你可以往里放甜点或者别的任何东西。

**古奇**: 哇噻,对我来说那太诱人了。

**阿美**: 好的,我们就点它吧。

**服务生**: 还要别的吗?

**古奇**: 不要了,请快一点。

(没过多久,巧克力火锅就上来了,该开吃了!)

**阿美**: 哦,它们看起来好可爱啊,那么精美,还五颜六色的。

**古奇**: 没有哪个女孩能抵挡它。

**阿美**: 一块巧克力就能使人高兴起来,说得真没错啊。

**古奇**: 那当然。为巧克力死都愿意呢!

**阿美**: 那我们每周都来这里怎么样?

**古奇**: 不行,那是自杀。你知道,卡路里!

**阿美**: 算了。等我们30岁时再说吧。

## 生词小结

**hot pot** 火锅
**throw** *vt.* 扔
**delicate** *adj.* 精美的
**colorful** *adj.* 色彩丰富的
**resist** *vt.* 抵挡
**suicide** *n.* 自杀

## 注释

**1. I can eat an horse.** 我能吃下一匹马。能吃下一匹马，可见饿的程度之大，很容易想到这是表示"太饿了"。中文中也有相似的表达："我饿得能吃下一头牛。"有趣的是，中国人饿了选择吃牛，外国人选择吃马。

**2. chocolate hot pot** 巧克力火锅，与中国火锅的不同在于，它的汤底一般是液态的巧克力和奶酪等，而各式菜品则代之为各式甜点。巧克力火锅受年轻情侣喜欢，不过由于卡路里太高，令很多女孩子望而止步。

**3. Chocolate is something to die for!** 意思是我愿意为巧克力而死。这是夸张的表达方式，表示了对巧克力的极大喜欢，口语中很常见。如果一个男孩喜欢女孩，他可以说："She is to die for."意思为：她值得我为她而死。

## 单词扩展 Vocabulary Builder

### 甜点的词汇

| 基础词汇 | 提高词汇 |
| --- | --- |
| cake 蛋糕 | sundae 圣代 |
| apple pie 苹果馅饼 | mousse 奶油冻 |
| cheese 奶酪 | croissant 牛角包 |
| biscuits 甜饼干 | custard tart 蛋塔 |
| ice cream 冰淇淋 | banana split 香蕉船 |
| jelly 果冻 | crackers 咸饼干 |
| cookie 曲奇饼 | muffin 脆皮松饼 |
| pudding 布丁 | onion rings 洋葱圈 |

## 家庭总动员 Do it together

两人一组，一方随机大声读出上面词汇的英文和中文，另一方用该词汇填入下面的句子，大声朗读并表演出来，并用中文给出一个理由。

**The (          ) is very popular with the girls.**

【例】家长读 cake 蛋糕

孩子读 The cake is very popular with the girls. 因为它们看起来很精致。

**Recitation** 经典背诵

**Waitress**：I'm a waitress in a special restaurant. We serve "chocolate hot pot" which is becoming popular among young girls. They love it so much. They always believe that one piece of chocolate can cheer them up. But they also think it's suicidal to eat too much chocolate. You know, calories!

# Topic3 自助餐饮
## Buffet

刚吃了巧克力火锅，古奇和阿美怎么算都觉得太贵。恰好楼上有意大利自助餐，于是就决定去试试看。还真是别出心裁，收费竟然按体重，究竟怎么回事呢？请往下看。

**Gucci:** It's too expensive. Ten cookies cost a bundle.

**May:** I noticed that they have Italian buffet upstairs. Maybe we should have chosen that?

**Gucci:** Let's do it, now.

**May:** What is the charge of buffet for each person?

**Waitress:** It depends on your weight. Come on to the scale, please!

**Gucci:** Interesting! Look, I'm 45kg.

**May:** Me, 46kg.

**Waitress:** 50 yuan for each.

**Gucci:** I love it. Look, they've got everything.

**May:** Wow, coffee and cheese puddings. Love it.

**Gucci:** It's the only neat decision we made today!

**May:** It is. And it's not all bad now.

**Gucci:** No more for me. I'll all set.

**May:** Me either. That's the problem about buffet. Always over eating.

**Gucci:** You can't get everything.

**古奇：**这也太贵了。10 块小甜饼就要那么多钱。

**阿美：**我发现楼上有意大利自助餐。也许我们本该去那里的。

**古奇：**那我们现在去吧。

**阿美：**自助餐每个人的收费是多少？

**服务生：**收费是按体重来算的。上这个秤看看吧！

**古奇：**真有趣。看，我是 45 公斤。

**阿美：**我是 46 公斤。

**服务生：**每人 50 元。

**古奇：**我很喜欢这个地方，这里什么都有。

**阿美：**哇噻，咖啡、奶酪布丁，我最喜欢了。

**古奇：**这是我们今天做的唯一正确的决定。

**阿美：**是啊，看来今天也不是什么都差劲。

**古奇：**吃不下了，我搞定了。

**阿美：**我也吃不下了。这就是自助餐的问题啊，总是吃太多。

**古奇：**总是不能十全十美嘛！

**生词小结**

bundle   *n.* 堆, 捆
notice   *vt.* 注意
buffet   *n.* 自助餐
cheese   *n.* 奶酪
pudding   *n.* 布丁

**注释**

**1. Ten cookies cost a bundle.** Bundle 本意为 "一大堆", 这里指的是 "一大堆钱", 中文口语中也有相似的表达方法, 例: "好贵啊, 花了我一大堆钱。"
**2. You can't get everything.** get 在这里的意思是 "得到", 直译为你不能得到每一件东西。(可见总有遗憾。) 所以也较容易想到意译应为: 做不到十全十美。

# 情景练习
## Scene practice —— 抱怨句型练习

仔细阅读下面五个场景, 两人一组, 使用抱怨句型(见 171 页), 用一用, 练一练。

1. May bought a CD in a shop, but it was not the right CD inside, if you were May, what would you complain to the manager?
2. May and Gucci are having lunch in a restaurant, but the soup tastes horrible. If you were Gucci, what would you complain to the waitress?
3. Benjamin's neighbor has two young children, they are very noisy. They scream and shout even at midnight. His neighbor doesn't seem to care about their screaming. Benjamin has just had a sleepless night as a result, if you were Benjamin, what would you complain to the neighbor?
4. Shirley bought some shoes to wear in the rain but they leak. She takes them back to change them. If you were Shirley, what would you say to the shop assistant?
5. If you were Daniel, your mother complains about your laziness, what would you say to your mother?

**Recitation** 经典背诵

**May:** I love buffet. Better yet if it's an Italian buffet. There is one such place, downtown. It's interesting that the customers there would be charged by their weight. The only problem about it is overeating. People just don't know when to stop. Anyway you can't have everything.

## Topic 4 情人节
### Valentine's Day

听 学 读 看     吃完自助餐,古奇和阿美决定好好休息一下,两人聊起了"中国情人节",这下有人要有麻烦了,究竟怎么回事呢?看了就明白了。

**Gucci:** What's so special today?

**May:** Why?

**Gucci:** Didn't you notice all the roses?

**May:** It's July 7th. Chinese Valentine's Day!

**Gucci:** Oh, God. I just forgot it.

**May:** I thought you had trouble with Clive!

**Gucci:** No. But now he will be in bigger trouble! What's a boyfriend for? Forget about Valentine's Day?

**May:** Poor guy! It's not fair. You forgot it too.

*(Gucci's telephone rings. Is it the person who will be in trouble?)*

**Gucci:** Oh, it's Clive.

**May:** Wow! Good timing.

**Gucci:** Excuse me for a while.

*(After calling, Gucci comes back with a big smile on her face.)*

**Gucci:** Clive asked me out to a movie! Do you want to join us?

**May:** Come on. Two is company.

**Gucci:** So what?

**May:** It's Valentine's Day. Come on. Just go.

**古奇:** 今天有什么特别的吗?

**阿美:** 为什么(这么问)?

**古奇:** 你没有注意到到处都是玫瑰花吗?

**阿美:** 今天是七月初七啊,中国情人节。

**古奇:** 哦,天啊,我竟然忘记了。

**阿美:** 我还以为你和克莱夫吵架了。

**古奇:** 没有啦。但是他现在可有大麻烦了!男朋友是干吗的?(竟然)忘记情人节?

**阿美:** 可怜的家伙。这不公平。你不也忘了。

(古奇的电话响了,会是那个要有麻烦的人吗?)

**古奇:** 哦,是克莱夫。

**阿美:** 哇。时间可真巧。

**古奇:** 对不起,等一下(我要出去接个电话)。

(古奇接完电话回来,脸上带着微笑。)

**古奇:** 克莱夫叫我去看电影,你想和我们一起去吗?

**阿美:** 拜托。两个才叫伴。

**古奇:** 那(你)怎么办呢?

**阿美:** 今天是情人节嘛。拜托。你就去吧。

## 生词小结

| | | |
|---|---|---|
| while | *n.* | 一会儿 |
| special | *adj.* | 特殊的 |
| trouble | *n.* | 麻烦 |
| boyfriend | *n.* | 男朋友 |
| poor | *adj.* | 可怜的 |
| movie | *n.* | 电影 |

## 注释

**1. Chinese Valentine's Day:** 中国情人节,指的是农历七月初七,是传说中牛郎织女相会的日子。相当于西方公历 2 月 14 日的情人节(Valentine's Day)。

**2. What're friends for!** 这里是阿美表示自己会站在古奇一边的表达,意思为:我肯定站在你这一边,要不怎么说是朋友呢! 在日常生活中,经常是一方表示感谢,另一方会用这种表达方式来表示不用客气,意思为:朋友是用来干吗的呀,这是做朋友该做的。

**3. Two is company.** 完整的表达应是:Two's company, three's none. 意思为:两人成伴,三人不欢。

## 语法小结 Grammer —— 祈使句

与中文中的定义一样,英语中的祈使句也是表示提出命令、劝告、警告、禁止和请求等的句子,以动词原形开头,句末用感叹号或句号,一般用降调。祈使句的主语通常都是第二人称,所以通常都省略。

1. 祈使句的肯定形式

(1)动词原形开头

*Look at the blackboard, please.* 请看黑板。

*Pass the paper to me, please!* 请把纸传给我。

(2)在开头的动词前加 *do* 可加强语气

*Do come to school on time tomorrow.* 明天务必准时到校。

*Do keep your bedroom clean and tidy.* 务必保持你的卧室干净、整洁。

(3)用祈使句也可以表达客气的语气,在句首或句尾加 *please*。在句尾加 *please* 时,要在 *please* 前加逗号

*Keep quiet, please.* 请保持安静。

*May, come earlier next time, please.* 阿美,下次请早点儿来。

2. 祈使句的否定形式 *Don't* + 动词原形

*Don't look out of the window.* 别朝窗外看。

*Don't be angry with me.* 不要生我气了。

## 家庭总动员 Do it together

两人一组,一方朗诵下面的中文句子,另一方挑选出合适的翻译。

1. 请买单。
2. 记住今天是中国情人节!
3. 不要吃太多巧克力火锅。
4. 下次请务必要听老师的。
5. 不要在中午逛街!

1. Don't eat too much the chocolate hot pot!
2. Don't hang out at noon.
3. Do listen to the teacher next time.
4. Remember today is Chinese Valentine's Day.
5. Please take the bill.

## Recitation 经典背诵

**Clive:** I'm Clive. Gucci is my girlfriend. I'm a bit careless which always gets me in trouble. One time I almost forgot the Chinese Valentine's Day. You know, it's okay for a girl to forget these "big days". But for a guy, to do that it would definitely be a big trouble. You may think it's unfair. But I'd rather call it reality or the pride to be a guy.

# Act 4

餐饮和零售业场景 · Catering Industry and Retail Trade

# 服装市场 Clothing Market

## Goals

**在这个场景中,我们将学到:**

1. 元音字母组合发音(三)
2. 服装的词汇
3. 表达讨价还价的句型
4. 感叹句

## 选择服饰
### Choosing Cloth

 玩转语音

1. If Stu chews shoes, should Stu choose the shoes he chews?
2. A tidy tiger tied a tie tighter to tidy her tiny tail.
3. You know New York. You need New York. You know you need unique New York.

及格时间: 10 秒
你的纪录: ——秒
及格时间: 10 秒
你的纪录: ——秒
及格时间: 10 秒
你的纪录: ——秒

阿美和古奇去逛时装店。店里的衣服很时尚但非常贵,阿美觉得不划算,可是当看到自己喜欢的衣服时,似乎立场就没有那么坚定了!

**Salesclerk:** Good morning, can I help you?

**Gucci:** No, thanks. We are just looking around.

**Salesclerk:** Take your time. Please let me know if you need any help.

**Gucci:** OK, thanks. We will.

**May:** Oh, Gucci, the clothes here are expensive! No wonder there are only a few people in here.

**Gucci:** Beauty costs, friend. Oh, look at this pink skirt, how cute!

**May:** Believe it or not, they look cute, but not very practical.

**Gucci:** Come on, May, don't talk like my Mom.

**售货员:** 早上好,我能为您做点什么?

**古奇:** 不,谢谢。我们只是看看。

**售货员:** 请随便看。如果您需要帮助的话请告诉我。

**古奇:** 好的,谢谢。一定。

**阿美:** 哦,古奇,这儿的衣服真贵! 难怪这儿没什么人。

**古奇:** 美丽的代价啊,朋友。噢,看看这条粉红色的裙子,好可爱啊!

**阿美:** 不管你信不信,它们看起来漂亮,可是不怎么实用。

**古奇:** 行啦,阿美,别说话像我妈一样。

May：When you buy clothes, you must consider the material, quality and price.

Gucci：But fashion changes!

May：Make sure the clothes can be worn for various occasions.

Gucci：All right, May. Hey, look, I'm sure this is the same skirt that Spice Girls wear.

May：Definitely! Oh, I love Spice Girls! I gotta get this skirt!

阿美：买衣服时,你得考虑它们的材料、质量和价格。

古奇：但流行都在变啊!

阿美：确定衣服可以适合于多种不同场合。

古奇：好吧,阿美。嘿,看,我肯定这是辣妹中的一人穿过的。

阿美：真的耶! 哦,我爱死辣妹了! 我一定要把这裙子买下来!

### 生词小结

**salesclerk**　　*n.* 售货员
**around**　　*prep.* 在……周围
**wonder**　　*n.* 惊奇
**pink**　　*n.* 粉红色
**practical**　　*adj.* 实用的
**quality**　　*n.* 质量

### 注释

**Spice Girls**：辣妹,英国流行演唱组合

## 语音小结 Pronunciation —— 元音字母组合发音(三)

**1.** 元音字母 ey 组合在一起经常发 /ei/ they
　　　　　　　　　　　　　　　　　/ai/ eye
　　　　　　　　　　　　　　　　　/iː/ key
　　　　　　　　　　　　　　　　　/ i/ monkey

　　朗读练习：obey　grey　eyelash　key　valley　money

**2.** 元音字母 ew 组合在一起经常发 /juː/ few

**3.** 元音字母 ie 组合在一起经常发 /e/ friend
　　　　　　　　　　　　　　　　　/iː/ believe
　　　　　　　　　　　　　　　　　/ai/ die

　　朗读练习：dew　new　friendly　satisfied　wield

Recitation 经典背诵

　　May：Fashion changes quickly today. The fashionable clothes are really expensive. I have my own considerations about clothes. I will consider their material, quality and price. However, my friend Gucci just cares about their cute lookings. That's why we can't agree with each other while shopping.

**餐饮和零售业场景 · Catering Industry and Retail Trade**

# 试穿
**Try-on**

买衣服的学问还真不少，颜色搭配好像就很不简单，这下阿美和古奇要好好"研究"一下了。

**May：** I'd like to try this on, please. Where is the fitting room?

**Salesclerk：** This way, please.

**May：** How do I look in this skirt, Gucci? Am I Spice Girl, or what?

**Gucci：** No, you look ridiculous. I suggest you try some other colors.

**May：** OK, I will try on that green one. …Now, how do I look?

**Gucci：** You look like a Christmas tree. Why not try on the red one?

**May：** But red doesn't go with my green sweater.

**Gucci：** It surely does. Trust me, red is the global fashion now.

**May：** All right, I will try on the red one. … Now, what do you think?

**Gucci：** Terrific!

**May：** But I feel I look like a pepper in green and red.

**Gucci：** That makes you a Spice Girl.

**May：** Don't be kidding! Anyway I will take this one.

**Salesclerk：** Thank you. I will wrap it up for you. You can pay at the front counter. It's 500 yuan.

**阿美：** 我想试试这件。试衣间在哪儿？

**售货员：** 请这边走。

**阿美：** 我看起来怎么样，古奇？像不像辣妹啊？

**古奇：** 不像，你看上去真滑稽。我建议你试一试别的颜色。

**阿美：** 好吧，我试试那件绿的。我现在看起来呢？

**古奇：** 你看上去像棵圣诞树。干嘛不试试那件红色的？

**阿美：** 但是红色跟我的绿毛衣不配啊。

**古奇：** 当然配啦。相信我吧，红色是现在全球流行的颜色。

**阿美：** 好吧，我就试试那件红色的。现在你觉得呢？

**古奇：** 棒极了！

**阿美：** 但我感觉穿得又红又绿像个辣椒。

**古奇：** 那样你才是辣妹啊。

**阿美：** 别开玩笑了！不过，这件我买了。

**售货员：** 谢谢。我帮您包好。您可以到前台去付款。一共500块。

184

## 生词小结

| | | | |
|---|---|---|---|
| **size** | *n.*号码 | **Chrismas tree** | *n.* 圣诞树 |
| **fitting room** | *n.* 试衣间 | **global** | *adj.* 全球的 |
| **ridiculous** | *adj.* 荒谬的 | **terrific** | *adj.* 棒极了的 |

## 单词扩展 Vocabulary Builder

### 服装的词汇

| 基础词汇 | 提高词汇 |
|---|---|
| suit 西装 | overalls 工装裤 |
| coat 女大衣 | evening dress 晚礼服 |
| jacket 夹克 | dress 女服 |
| shirt 衬衫 | raincoat 雨衣 |
| jeans 牛仔裤 | uniform 制服 |
| skirt 裙子 | tails 燕尾服 |
| trousers 裤子 | sweater 运动衫 |
| pants 短裤 | vest 汗衫 |

## D 家庭总动员
### o it together

两人一组, 一方随机大声读出上面词汇的英文和中文, 另一方用该词汇填入下面的句子, 大声朗读并表演出来, 并用中文给出一个理由。

**I'd like to try on (                    ).**

【例】家长读 suit 西装
孩子读 I'd like to try on the suit. 因为爸爸穿西装很帅!

### Recitation 经典背诵

May: I like trying on new clothes in the stores. I hope I could be a star, like the Spice Girls, that way I will have many chances to try on fashionable clothes. Sometimes they are just too expensive. So I just try them on without buying any of them. It's fun!

## Topic3 折扣
### Discount

听学看

阿美总算是挑中了一件自己喜欢的衣服,但衣服的价格可不便宜,最后阿美买了吗? 一起来看看吧!

**May:** This skirt is overpriced.

**Salesclerk:** We never overcharge. It is a fair price to pay.

**May:** Is it on sale?

**Salesclerk:** In this season? No. But if you come two months later, maybe it will be on sale.

**May:** Will it still be here then?

**Salesclerk:** Maybe. I can't guarantee.

**Gucci:** Could you give us a discount anyway?

**Salesclerk:** Sorry, we can't. This is the lowest price.

**Gucci:** Come on! You are ripping us off.

**May:** Give us a better price, and we're definitely gonna take this one.

**Salesclerk:** Sorry, lady. We can't do that.

**May:** What do I do, Gucci? I can't afford a skirt at that price.

**Gucci:** I think it is worth, May.

**May:** OK, I will take it then.

**阿美:**这条裙子太贵了。

**售货员:**我们从来不乱出价。这是公道价钱。

**阿美:**这条裙子有打折吗?

**售货员:**在这个季节? 没有。但您如果两个月以后来的话,也许会打折。

**阿美:**到那时它还会在吗?

**售货员:**也许吧。我不能保证。

**古奇:**那能不能给我们一点折扣啊?

**售货员:**对不起,我们不能。这已经是最低价了。

**古奇:**哎呀,你这是在骗我们。

**阿美:**给我们一个合理的价格,我们一定会把它买下来。

**售货员:**对不起,小姐。我们不能那么做。

**阿美:**我该怎么办啊,古奇? 我可付不起那个价钱。

**古奇:**我觉得值耶,阿美。

**阿美:**好吧,那我就买下来吧。

---

### 生词小结

| | | | |
|---|---|---|---|
| **overprice** | *vt.* 要价过高 | **rip off** | 诓,骗 |
| **overcharge** | *vt.* 要价过高 | **afford** | *vt.* 付得起,供得起 |
| **guarantee** | *vt.* 保证 | **worth** | *adj.* 值的 |
| **discount** | *n.* 折扣 | | |

# **F**unctional structure
功能性句型扩展 —— 表达讨价还价的句型

**请朗读以下句型,家长和孩子交替进行。**

## 1. 表达价高

The goods are priced too high. 这个商品太贵了。

The price is unreasonable! 这个价格不太合理!

Your price is unacceptable. 这个价格不太能让人接受。

It's a little overpriced. 这有点太贵了。

That's too expensive. 那太贵了。

## 2. 直接还价

Can you give me this for cheaper price? 这个能便宜点吗?

Can you give me a little deal on this? 能给我便宜点吗?

Give me a discount. 给我打点折吧。

If you don't give me a better price, I won't buy this. 你不给我一个合理的价格,我就不买了。

Come on, give me a break on this. 算了,就给我便宜点吧。

How much do you want for this? 你想要卖多少钱?

## 3. 委婉还价

What's the lowest you're willing to go? 你最低卖多少钱?

I can get this cheaper at other places. 我在其他地方买还便宜些。

I'd buy this if it were cheaper. 便宜点我就买了。

Lower the price, and I'll consider it. 便宜点,我就考虑一下。

I like everything about it except the price. 其他的都好,就是价格高了一点。

I've seen this cheaper (in) other places. 其他地方比你这还便宜。

**R**ecitation
经典背诵

**May:** There are often clothes on sale, because they are out of season. It is a good chance to buy clothes. You may probably get a big discount, then. But if you are good at bargaining, you can get a good price anytime! Gucci is very good at bargaining!

## Topic 4 售后服务
### After-Sale Services

阿美的衣服刚穿了一周就发现线头松了。她拿到店里要求退货,但是事情似乎并没有预想的那么顺利。问题究竟是怎么解决的呢? 往下看吧!

| | |
|---|---|
| **Salesclerk**: Can I help you? | **售货员**:有什么需要帮忙的吗? |
| **May**: Yes, I have a complaint to make. | **阿美**:恩,我有点意见。 |
| **Salesclerk**: What's the problem? | **售货员**:有什么问题吗? |
| **May**: I bought this skirt in your store last week. What a famous brand is that! The stitches are coming off. | **阿美**:上周我在你们店里买了这条裙子。这是什么名牌啊!线头都松了! |
| Anyway, I'd like to ask for a refund for this skirt. | 不管怎么说,我想要退货。 |
| **Salesclerk**: I'm sorry. They are not refundable. But we can exchange it for you, OK? | **售货员**:对不起,它们是不能退的。但我们可以给您换一条,行吗? |
| **May**: OK. | **阿美**:好吧。 |
| **Salesclerk**: Wait for a moment. I think we have another one... Here you go. | **售货员**:稍等一下。我想我们还有一件……这就是。 |
| **May**: But this one is blue. Mine is red. | **阿美**:但这条是蓝色的。我的是红色的。 |
| **Salesclerk**: Sorry, lady. This is the only one we've got now. How about we fix it up for you? | **售货员**:对不起,小姐。我们现在只剩这件了。我们帮您补一下怎么样? |
| **May**: That's certainly good. When will it be ready? | **阿美**:那好啊。什么时候能补好? |
| **Salesclerk**: It will be ready tomorrow. | **售货员**:明天就能补好。 |
| **May**: That's quick. | **阿美**:那挺快的。 |
| **Salesclerk**: Come along then and bring this receipt with you. And I am afraid we're gonna have to charge you 20 for that. | **售货员**:那到时候来吧,把这张发票带上。恐怕补一次我们得收您 20 块钱。 |
| **May**: What! | **阿美**:什么! |

生词小结

| | | | |
|---|---|---|---|
| **complaint** | *n.* 抱怨 | **refund** | *n.* 退款 |
| **brand** | *n.* 品牌 | **fix up** | 修好,补好 |
| **stitch** | *n.* 线头 | **receipt** | *n.* 发票 |

# G语法小结
## rammer —— 感叹句

感叹句一般是用来表示说话时的喜悦、惊讶等情感。英语感叹句常用"what"和"how"引导,句子其他部分用陈述句语序。

1. "what"引导的感叹句 what + ( a/an ) + *adj.* + *n.* + 主语 + 谓语 + ( it is ).

   "what"意为"多么",用来修饰名词(被强调部分),单数可数名词前要加 a/an,例如:

   *What a clever girl May is*! 多么聪明的阿美呀!

   *What a funny story it is*! 多么有趣的故事呀!

   *What good children they are*! 他们是多么好的孩子呀!

2. "how"引导的感叹句 How + *adj.* ( *adv.* ) + 主语 + 谓语 + ( it is ).

   "how"意为"多么",修饰形容词或副词(被强调部分)。如果修饰形容词,则句中的谓语动词用系动词;如果修饰副词,则句中的谓语动词用行为动词,例如:

   *How cold it is today*! 今天多么冷呀!

   *How well May writes*! 阿美写得多好呀!

   *How hard they are working now*! 他们现在干得多么起劲呀!

3. 在表示同一意义时,既可用"what"引导,也可用"how"引导

   (1) *What a hot day it is*! *How hot a day is*! 多么热的天气呀!

   (2) *What beautiful sunshine it is*! *How beautiful the sunshine is*! 多么明亮的阳光呀!

4. 感叹句在表示激动强烈的感情时,口语中常常省略后面的主语和谓语

   *What red apples*! 多么红的苹果呀!

   *How cool*! 好凉快呀!

   *How wonderful*! 精彩极了!

# D家庭总动员
## o it together

两人一组,一方朗诵下面的中文句子,另一方挑选出合适的翻译。

1. 多么好的售货员啊!
2. 多漂亮的裙子啊!
3. 好伤心啊!
4. 你穿上这件衣服真棒!
5. 好荒唐呀!

1. What the nice salesman he is!
2. How terrific when you wear this skirt!
3. What the beautiful skirt it is!
4. How depressed!
5. How ridiculous it is!

**Recitation** 经典背诵

**May**:Don't believe in brands. People have so many complaints about them. There was one time I bought a really expensive skirt with a well-known brand, but the stitches came off within a week. When I returned to the shop, the salesperson told me that it was not refundable. Poor service!

**SCENE 24**

# 家电超市
# Household Appliances Supermarket

## Goals

**在这个场景中,我们将学到:**

1. 元音字母组合发音(四)
2. 电器的词汇
3. 打折句型练习
4. There be 存在句型

# Topic 1 电器促销
## Household Appliances on Sale

 **玩转语音**

1. A noise annoys an oyster, but a noisy noise annoys an oyster more!
2. Mr. Cook said to a cook: "Look at this cookbook. It's very good. " So the cook took the advice of Mr. Cook and bought the book.

及格时间: 7 秒
你的纪录:——秒
及格时间: 13 秒
你的纪录:——秒

家电商场在进行电器促销,看看雪莉这回又看上什么了。

**Sales person:** May I be of any assistance?

**Shirley:** I want to have a look at the microwave ovens.

**Sales person:** You can have a broad choice here. Are you interested in a particular brand?

**Shirley:** Not really. What are these toys over there?

**Sales person:** Ma'am, these are complimentary with each purchase. How about that one below the toys? This is the best seller. They are of the latest model that can be found in town.

**Shirley:** I don't like its color. A bit too bright. Do you have a grey one?

**Sales person:** Yes, we do. What a great taste you

**销售员:** 有什么能为您效劳的?

**雪莉:** 我想看一下微波炉。

**售货员:** 这里有很多的(微波炉)供您选择。您有喜欢的品牌吗?

**雪莉:** 没有。那边的玩具是什么?

**服务生:** 女士,那是赠品。对了,您看玩具下面的那款"微波炉"怎么样? 那款很畅销。它们是现在市面上能找到的最新的款式。

**雪莉:** 我不喜欢它的颜色。有点太亮了。(这款)你们有灰色的吗?

**售货员:** 是的,我们有。您真有品位! 但

have! But we only have one left in stock.

**Shirley**：Really? How so?

**Sales person**：You know a good product will always sell! Would you mind waiting for a while, we'll get it right away.

**Shirley**：Okay.

(*The salesperson brings a beautiful grey microwave oven.*)

**Sales person**：Here it is. It's very elegant, I think you will like it.

**Shirley**：How about its quality?

**Sales person**：Its durability will be a big surprise to you.

**Shirley**：What about the price?

**Sales person**：500 yuan. And if you buy it today, there will be a 15% discount for you.

是我们只有一件,还放在仓库里。

**雪莉**:真的? 为什么?

**售货员**:好东西总是买得快啊。麻烦您能稍等一下吗? 我现在马上去给您取来。

**雪莉**:好的。

(销售人员拿来一款漂亮的灰色微波炉。)

**售货员**:就是这个了。很漂亮,我想您会喜欢的。

**雪莉**:它的质量怎么样?

**售货员**:它的耐用性会使您吃惊的。

**雪莉**:价格怎么样呢?

**售货员**:500 元。如果您今天买,你还可以享受 8.5 折的折扣。

---

**生词小结**

**assistance**    *n.* 援助

**microwave oven**    微波炉

**particular**    *adj.* 特殊的

**complimentary**    *adj.* 赠送的

**purchase**    *n.* 购置

**stock**    *n.* 库存

**durability**    *n.* 耐用性

**注释**

**A good product will always sell.**    好东西总是卖得快。

---

**P语音小结**
**Pronunciation** —— 元音字母组合(四)

1. 元音字母 **oa** 组合在一起经常发/əu/: **coat boat goat**
   朗读练习:boat    boat and goat

2. 元音字母 **oi/oy** 组合在一起经常发/ɔi/: **choice toy coin boy**
   朗读练习:join and point    joy and toy

3. 元音字母 **oo** 组合在一起经常发/u:/ /u/: **too boot good look**
   朗读练习:foot and good    hood and wood

4. 元音字母 **ow** 组合在一起经常发/au/, /əu/: **how town below know**
   朗读练习:allow and wow    snow and blow

**Recitation**
经典背诵

**Sales person**：I'm a salesperson in a big supermarket. Sometimes we put on sales promotion to attract more customers. Though good products sell themselves, it's surely right to believe in advertising. We all know that people love discounts. Believe it or not, price does matter most of the time!

# Act 4

餐饮和零售业场景 · Catering Industry and Retail Trade

## Topic 2 买电器
### Purchasing Household Appliances

听 学 看

本杰明接到雪莉的电话,匆匆赶来家电商场,最终雪莉买了那款她钟情的微波炉了吗?

| | |
|---|---|
| **Benjamin**: A microwave oven? | **本杰明**:(你要买)一个微波炉? |
| **Shirley**: Yes, it's really two-pence colored. | **雪莉**:是的,那款真的是物美价廉。 |
| **Benjamin**: Okay, honey, we already have two. There is no more space for a third one! | **本杰明**:亲爱的,我们已经有两个了,实在没有地方放第三个了! |
| **Shirley**: But it's so elegant. | **雪莉**:但是这款真的很棒。 |
| **Benjamin**: Honey, maybe something else, just no more microwave oven, okay? | **本杰明**:亲爱的,要不我们买点别的,只是别买微波炉了,好吗? |
| **Shirley**: All right. Then what about a MD player? For May to learn English with. | **雪莉**:好吧,要不我们买个 MD 播放机,让阿美用来学英语。 |
| **Benjamin**: Better. | **本杰明**:(买这个比买微波炉)好多了。 |
| **Shirley**: Do you have any MD players? | **雪莉**:请问你们有 MD 播放机吗? |
| **Sales person**: Yes, various. Here are the samples. What about this one? | **售货员**:是的,有很多款式。这里有样品。这款怎么样? |
| **Shirley**: What are its features? | **雪莉**:它有什么特点? |
| **Sales person**: Well, it has a lithium battery which lasts for 20 hours. With MP3 mode, you can download about 9 hours of music or English audio texts. It's especially popular with students for their English study! | **销售员**:它有能持续使用 20 小时的锂电池。用 MP3 模式,可以下载 9 个小时的音乐或英语听力材料,现在特别流行于学生的英语学习。 |
| **Shirley**: What else? | **雪莉**:还有其他的(优点)吗? |
| **Sales person**: Maybe you should just have it operated then you would know how well it works. | **销售员**:你可以现在就操作一些,然后你就知道它的性能有多好了! |
| **Shirley**: Oh, "*My heart will go on*", I love the song. | **雪莉**:哦,《我心永恒》,我喜欢这首歌。 |
| **Benjamin**: Nothing can stop her from buying it now, I suppose. | **本杰明**:我想,现在没有什么能阻止她买这个了。 |
| **Sales person**: Just think about the advantage you are going to get. | **售货员**:想想你买它所得到的好处吧! |

# Scene 24

家电超市·Household Appliances Supermarket

## 生词小结

penny    *n.* 便士
player   *n.* 唱机
sample   *n.* 样品
feature  *n.* 特色
lithium battery   锂电池
download  *vt.* 下载
advantage  *n.* 优点

## 注释

1. **It's really two-pence colored.** pence 是 penny 的复数形式，color 的意思是染色，文中的意思为，它真的是物美价廉。

2. **My heart will go on:** 经典电影"*Titanic*"（《泰坦尼克号》）的主题曲，中文名字是《我心永恒》。

## 单词扩展 Vocabulary Builder

### 电器的词汇

| 基础词汇 | 提高词汇 |
| --- | --- |
| radio 收音机 | electric fan 电风扇 |
| television 电视机 | electric vacuum cleaner 电吸尘器 |
| bulb 电灯泡 | electric iron 电熨斗 |
| refrigerator 电冰箱 | electric shaver 电动剃须刀 |
| flashlight 手电筒 | dictating machine 录音机 |
| computer 电脑 | electric calculator 电子计算机 |
| microphone 麦克风 | electric cooker 电炉 |
| air conditioning 空调 | electric heater 电暖器 |

## 家庭总动员 Do it together

两人一组，一方随机大声读出上面词汇的英文和中文，另一方用该词汇填入下面的句子，大声朗读并表演出来，并用中文给出一个理由。

**Do you have any (　　　　　　　　)?**

【例】家长读 radio 收音机
孩子读 Do you have any radios? 我想买一个。

## Recitation 经典背诵

**Benjamin：**Women are shopping animals. At least, my wife really is. She would always say something is two-pence colored. She would just keep on buying stuff without thinking whether we need it or not. Things are gonna to be worse if there were a discount. So I don't like discount stores very much.

# Topic 3 家电维修
## Maintenance

雪莉听得正陶醉,突然之间,播放器的音乐没了,雪莉想:难道是质量问题?

**Shirley**: Oh, what's wrong? How it comes that the music stopped all in a sudden!

**Salesperson**: Really? Let me have a look.

**Shirley**: Poor quality!

**Salesperson**: No, Ma'am. It's just out of battery.

**Shirley**: Oh, sorry.

**Benjamin**: What if it doesn't work well, I mean in case?

**Salesperson**: The guarantee provides for free service and parts. But judging from my experience, I'd say you'll never have to use that.

**Benjamin**: How long is it guaranteed for?

**Salesperson**: Three years. And you can exchange it provided there is no damage to the product.

**Benjamin**: What about the price?

**Salesperson**: 1000 yuan.

**Benjamin**: Wow. That's a lot of money. Is there any discount?

**Salesperson**: Yes, if you get it today, there will be a 10% off for you.

**Benjamin**: Honey, what do you think?

**Shirley**: We'd better stick with what we like. Money comes and goes anyway.

**Benjamin**: Okay, we'll take it.

**雪莉:** 哦,怎么了? 为什么音乐突然停了?

**售货员:** 真的吗? 让我看一下。

**雪莉:** 质量真差啊!

**销售员:** 不是的,女士。只是没有电了。

**雪莉:** 哦,对不起。

**本杰明:** 要是坏了怎么办啊,我是说万一。

**售货员:** 保修期内提供免费的维修服务。根据经验,您永远都不需要使用这个(指维修)。

**本杰明:** 保修期有多长。

**售货员:** 三年。只要没有受到损伤,你可以随时拿来调换。

**本杰明:** 价格呢?

**售货员:** 1000 元。

**本杰明:** 哇,好贵啊。可以打折吗?

**售货员:** 是的,如果今天买,可以享受9折的优惠。

**本杰明:** 亲爱的,你觉得怎样?

**雪莉:** 我们还是坚持我们所喜欢的吧。钱用了还会来的。

**本杰明:** 好吧,那我们就买这个了。

## 生词小结

| | | |
|---|---|---|
| sudden | *adj.* | 突然的 |
| in case | | 免得 |
| exchange | *vt.* | 更换 |
| damage | *n.* | 损害 |
| discount | *n.* | 折扣 |
| stick | *vi.* | 坚持 |

## 注释

**Money comes and goes anyway.** 钱总是来来去去，对应的中文意思是"钱财乃是身外之物"。

## 情景练习
Scene practice —— 打折句型练习

**仔细阅读下面五个场景，两人一组，使用讨价还价的句型（见187页），用一用，练一练。**

1. May likes the skirt very much, but she thinks that is too expensive. If you were May, what would you say to the shop keeper?

2. Shirley likes the shoes very much, but she wants to know whether there is a discount or not. If you were Shirley, what would you say?

3. If you were Daniel, you want to buy the basketball in the store. How would you bargain with the shop keeper?

4. If you were Benjamin, you think the suit in the store is so expensive that you can't believe it, what would you say?

5. May wants to buy a bag, but that is too expensive, if you were May, how would you bargain with the shop keeper directly?

**Salesperson：** My job is to introduce the features of a product to the customers in a market place. Judging from my experience, I find quality is the thing that really matters. It's funny that customers want the merchandise to be guaranteed for a longer time period. But at the same time, they also hope there would be no chance to use that.

## 信用卡
### Credit Cards

好不容易决定买了，可是好像付款的时候又出问题了，究竟是怎么一回事呢？请往下看。

| | |
|---|---|
| **Salesperson**：What else, Ma'am? | **售货员**：还要别的吗，女士？ |
| **Shirley**：No, thanks. My husband said："We'd like to pay now." | **雪莉**：不用了，谢谢。我丈夫说："我们现在要去付款。" |
| **Salesperson**：Let me show you to the cashier's. | **售货员**：我带你们去收银台。 |
| **Salesperson**：It's 905 yuan in total. | **售货员**：一共是905元。 |
| **Shirley**：What? Where does that five come from? | **雪莉**：那5元是怎么来的？ |
| **Salesperson**：Oh, it's a service charge. | **售货员**：哦，那是服务费。 |
| **Shirley**：But I only have 900 in cash here. Can you let it go for 900 yuan? | **雪莉**：但是我只有900元现金，就900元可以吗？ |
| **Salesperson**：Sorry, but we can't do that. It's store's rule. | **售货员**：对不起，但是不可以，这是商场的规定。 |
| **Shirley**：My husband said he had a credit card. Do you accept credit card? | **雪莉**：我丈夫说他有信用卡，你们受理信用卡吗？ |
| **Salesperson**：Yes. | **售货员**：是的。 |
| **Shirley**：Great. Here it is. | **雪莉**：太好了。给你。 |
| **Salesperson**：Here is the receipt. Wanna to have it wrapped, Ma'am? | **售货员**：这是发票。您需要包装吗？ |
| **Shirley**：Yes, please. Thank you very much. | **雪莉**：是的。非常感谢。 |
| **Salesperson**：It'll be great to have you again. | **售货员**：欢迎下次光临。 |
| **Shirley**：Thank you very much. | **雪莉**：谢谢。 |

### 生词小结

**cashier** *n.* 收银员

**in total** 总共

**rule** *n.* 规则

**credit card** 信用卡

**wrap** *vt.* 包装

### 注释

**1. Can you let it go for 900 yuan?** 直译：你可以让900元走吗？意思为：我可以花900元买它吗？这里是要求收银员把零头抹去的表达方法。

**2. It'll be great to have you again.** 这是欢迎下次光临的正确表达方法，而不可以说成是"Welcome back again"。

## G rammer 语法小结 —— There be 存在句型

there be 句型就是我们说的"某地有某物",表示存在,它常用于一般现在时、一般过去时和一般将来时。

1. 基本结构是 there be + 主语 + 地点,如果要表示"某地没有某物",直接加入否定词就可以了,there be not(any, much) + 主语 + 地点

   *There are some chairs in your room.* 在你房间里有些椅子。
   *There aren't any chairs in your room.* 你房间里没有椅子。

2. there be 与 have 的区别

   *There are six chairs in my room.*（强调某地有某物）在我的房间里有6把椅子。
   *I have six chairs.*（强调某人拥有某物）我有6把椅子。

3. be 动词与后面所接的名词的单、复数保持一致

   *There is a girl over there.* 那边有一个女孩。
   *There are five girls over there.* 那边有5个女孩。

4. 就近原则,即当 be 动词后面不止一个名词时,要和紧跟其后的名词单、复数保持一致

   *There is a boy and two girls in the room.* 房间里有一个男孩和两个女孩。
   *There are two girls and a boy in the room.* 房间里有两个女孩和一个男孩。

5. there be 时态变化

   *There was an apple on the table yesterday.* 昨天在桌子上有一个苹果。
   *There is a pear on the table today.* 今天桌子上有一个梨。
   *There is going to be a meeting this afternoon.* 今天下午要开会。

## D o it together 家庭总动员

两人一组,一方朗诵下面的中文句子,另一方挑选出合适的翻译。

1. 我家有一台微波炉和两个 MP3 播放器。
2. 昨天这里还有一个椅子的。

3. 这有自动取款机。
4. 那儿有很多玩具。
5. 今天下午将会有打折。

1. There are a lot of toys there.
2. There is a microwave oven and two MP3 players in my family.

3. There was a chair right here yesterday.
4. There will be a discount this afternoon.
5. There is ATM here.

 **Recitation 经典背诵**

**Shirley：**I love shopping. It makes me feel happy. My husband doesn't agree with me on this. He always tries to stop me from buying the things I like. He says having a credit card gets me out of control. Well, maybe he is right, for I always can't tell where does the money go.

SCENE 25

# 超市 Supermarket

## Goals

在这个场景中，我们将学到：

1. 元音字母组合发音（五）
2. 商品类别的词汇
3. 表达义务和需求的句型
4. 基数词和序数词

 寄存 **Depositing**

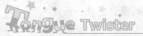 玩转语音

1. Bill's big brother is building a beautiful building between two big brick blocks.
2. I cannot bear to see a bear bear down upon a hare. When bare of hair he strips the hare, right there I cry, "Forbear!"

及格时间：20秒
你的纪录：——秒
及格时间：25秒
你的纪录：——秒

周末，爸爸、妈妈、阿美和丹尼尔全家四口人一起到超市购物。超市的自动存包柜已经满箱，服务台也不能存包，这下该怎么办呢？一起看看吧！

**Shirley**：Be quick. Put our bags in the deposit box.

**Benjamin**：We got a problem. The deposit boxes are all full. We should have come earlier.

**Shirley**：I told you to hurry up a thousand times. You just put a deaf ear to it.

**Benjamin**：Did you? I didn't hear you. It was too noisy.

**Shirley**：I surely did! Ask the customer service counter if we can deposit our stuff there.

(*Benjamin goes and returns*)

**Benjamin**：They say we can't. They don't look after customers' stuff.

**Shirley**：It's all your fault! Now we can't get in

**雪莉**：快一点儿，把我们的包放在存包柜里。

**本杰明**：我们遇到麻烦了，存包柜已经全满了。我们应该早一点儿来的。

**雪莉**：我告诉你多少遍了，叫你快一点儿。你就是不听。

**本杰明**：你叫了吗？太吵了，我没听见。

**雪莉**：我当然叫啦！问问服务台我们能不能把包存在他们那儿。

(本杰明去了又回来了)

**本杰明**：他们说不行。他们不为顾客看包。

**雪莉**：都怪你！我们现在不能进去买东

shopping.

Benjamin：OK, it's my fault. I'll stay here and look after our stuff. You can get in, shopping with Daniel and May.

Shirley：That sounds like a good idea!

Benjamin：Hey, don't forget to buy a suit for me.

Shirley：What color do you want?

Benjamin：Black, of course.

西了。

**本杰明**：好吧,是我的错。我留下来看东西。你和阿美、丹尼尔一起进去买东西吧。

**雪莉**：这是个好主意!

**本杰明**：嘿,别忘了给我买件西装。

**雪莉**：你要什么颜色的?

**本杰明**：当然要黑色的。

### 生词小结

| | | | |
|---|---|---|---|
| **deposit** | *vt.* 存放 | **customer** | *n.* 顾客 |
| **loud** | *adj.* 大声的 | **stuff** | *n.* 东西 |
| **thousand** | *num.* 千 | | |

## 语音小结 —— 元音字母组合发音(五)
Pronunciation

1. 元音字母 ou 组合在一起经常发 /ʌ/ trouble couple

/ɔ/ cough ought

/uː/ group coup

/au/ thousand loud sound trout

/əu/ shoulder

朗读练习：would wood though although about cloud

2. 元音字母 ui 组合在一起经常发 /juː/ suit tuition

/uː/ bruise cruise

/i/ build quick biscuit

朗读练习：quick biscuit cruise bruise build guilt

3. 元音字母 ear 组合在一起经常发 /əː/ early heard learn earn

/iə/ hear clear smear

/ɛə/ wear

朗读练习：learn earn ear hear fear tear

**Recitation** 经典背诵

Benjamin：Shirley loves going to the supermarket. But for me it's a big pain. Almost every time we're down there, there are no free lockers for our stuff. Then I would be the one that stays outside looking after our stuff. And that is not so fun especial when it keeps me waiting for long at times.

## 购物
### Shopping

妈妈、阿美和丹尼尔在超市里逛,四个人各有所好。阿美想到音像区去看看,丹尼尔想到体育用品专区,妈妈想在服装区里逛,看来只好分头行动了。

**Mom**:Stay with me, kids. Don't get lost.

**Daniel**:I am not Dad. I never get lost in the supermarket.

**May**:I am not a kid anymore, Mom.

**Mom**:Anyway, stay with me. I want to check out some daily necessities.

**May**:No, Mom. I want to go to the video products section. The new album of *Westlife* just comes out.

**Daniel**:I want to buy some sports supplies.

**Mom**:OK, kids. You can go. We'll meet by lunch time.

**May**:How about Dad? He is outside with our stuff.

**Daniel**:We can call him then.

**Mom**:All right, kids. Remember, 12 o'clock, at the 2nd cash counter.

(*Mom's phone rings, and she answers the phone*)

**May**:Who is that?

**Mom**:It's Dad. He got a free deposit box.

**May**:Finally, he is released.

**Mom**:He called to tell us that he was in the book section.

妈妈:跟着我,孩子们。别丢了。

丹尼尔:我才不是老爸呢。我在超市里从来不走丢。

阿美:我不是小孩子啦,妈妈。

妈妈:不管怎么说,跟着我。我想去买点日用品。

阿美:不,妈妈,我要去音像区看看。西城男孩刚刚出了本新专辑。

丹尼尔:我想去买点体育用品。

妈妈:好吧,那你们去吧。我们大约在午饭时间见。

阿美:那爸爸呢?他在外面看东西呢。

丹尼尔:我们到时候可以给他打电话。

妈妈:好吧,孩子们。记着,12点,在第二个收银台。

(妈妈的电话响了,她接起了电话)

阿美:是谁?

妈妈:是爸爸。他找到一个空的存包柜。

阿美:他终于解放了。

妈妈:他打电话说他在书籍区。

## 生词小结

**daily** *adj.* 每天的
**necessity** *n.* 必需品
**video** *n.* 音像
**deposit box** 存物柜
**cash counter** *n.* 收银台
**section** *n.* 部门

## 注释

**Westlife** 西城男孩。英国演唱组合。

## 单词扩展 Vocabulary Builder

### 商品类别的词汇

| 基础词汇 | 提高词汇 |
| --- | --- |
| fruit 水果 | pet food 宠物食品 |
| vegetable 蔬菜 | poultry 家禽类 |
| sports goods 体育用品 | household supply 家用电器 |
| sugar 糖 | cosmetics 化妆品 |
| condiment 调味品 | stationery 文具 |
| flour 面粉 | confectionery 糖果糕点 |
| snacks 零食 | pickles 腌菜 |
| cereal 谷物 | |

## 家庭总动员 Do it together

两人一组，一方随机大声读出上面词汇的英文和中文，另一方用该词汇填入下面的句子，大声朗读并表演出来，并用中文给出一个理由。

**I want to check out some** (        ).

【例】家长读 sports goods 体育用品
孩子读 I want to check out some sports goods. 因为星期天我要去爬山。

## Recitation 经典背诵

**Shirley：** I go to the supermarket everyday. And my children love going with me. But sometimes they are also trouble, because they always want to go to different sections. Shopping separately is the only way to solve the problem but I don't think it's safe. Even my husband gets lost in there.

## Topic3 预防偷盗
### Preventing Shoplifting

听 学 读 看 外国人泰瑞付完账出去时，超市门口的报警器突然叫了起来。结果发现问题出在泰瑞的太阳镜上。泰瑞的太阳镜里到底有什么问题呢？

| | |
|---|---|
| **Casher**：Thank you, 175 *yuan*. | **收银员**：谢谢您，175 块。 |
| **Terry**：Here you go. | **泰瑞**：给你钱。 |
| **Casher**：Here is your change and your receipt. | **收银员**：这是您的找零和发票。 |
| (*Just as he leaves, the infrared alarm burps.*) | （正当他离开时，红外线报警器响了。） |
| **Casher**：Do you have goods unpaid on you, sir? | **收银员**：您身上带着什么还没付款的东西吗，先生？ |
| **Terry**：No, I don't think so. | **泰瑞**：不，我想没有。 |
| **Casher**：I'm sorry I need to call the security to have a look. | **收银员**：对不起，我得叫保安来看看。 |
| **Terry**：There must be a mistake. | **泰瑞**：肯定是什么地方出错了。 |
| **Casher**：Sorry, sir, it's my job to make sure the goods are paid. | **收银员**：对不起，先生，我的职责是保证商品的货款付清。 |
| **Terry**：Wait, can you check these sunglasses? I bought it in the second floor. I think they forgot to demagnetize it. | **泰瑞**：等一下，您能看看这副太阳镜吗？我在二楼买的。我想他们忘了给它消磁了。 |
| **Casher**：Sure. Ah…That's the problem. Have you paid for it? | **收银员**：好的。啊……问题就在这儿。您付款了吗？ |
| **Terry**：Of course I did. Here is the receipt. | **泰瑞**：当然了，这是发票。 |
| **Casher**：Let me see … Oh, I am awfully sorry sir. | **收银员**：让我看看……哦，真是太对不起了，先生。 |
| **Terry**：That's all right. | **泰瑞**：没关系。 |

### 生词小结

| | | | |
|---|---|---|---|
| **infrared** | *n.* 红外线 | **security** | *n.* 保安 |
| **alarm** | *n.* 警报 | **mistake** | *n.* 错误 |
| **burp** | *vi.* 响 | **sunglass** | *n.* 太阳镜 |
| **unpaid** | *adj.* 未付款的 | **demagnetize** | *vt.* 消磁 |

# **F**unctional structure
功能性句型扩展 —— 表达义务和需求的句型

**请朗读以下句型,家长和孩子交替进行。**

1. 需要

   I need... 我需要……

   I am in need of... 我需要……

   I want... 我想要……

2. 不需要

   You don't need to... 你不需要……

   There's no need to... 没有必要……

   It's not necessary. 这没必要。

   That's not required. 这没有要求。

3. 义务

   I am in charge of... 我负责……

   It's my duty to... ……是我的职责。

   That's my responsibility. 这是我的责任。

   I am responsible for... 我对……负责。

   It's my obligation. 这是我的责任。

   I should/shall/must... 我必须……

   I'm bound to... 我必须……

**R**ecitation
经典背诵

**Terry**：Hello, I'm Terry, from Australia. I like travelling in China. The Nation's capital Beijing is a nice place. But one time I had a trouble with the cashier in a supermarket. It turned out to be a mistake but it reminded me that you could never be too careful.

# Topic 4 城市变迁
## Changes

这些年北京的变化特别大，这不，10 年前曾经来过北京的泰瑞，现在故地重游，却找不到原来的烤鸭店！一起来看看吧。

**Terry:** Excuse me. Where is Q-Duck? I remember it was around the second intersection of this street.

**Benjamin:** Q-Duck? Do you mean the famous roast-duck store?

**Terry:** Yes, definitely.

**Benjamin:** They have moved to some other places long time ago.

**Terry:** Wow, this place is quite different from ten years ago when I first came to China.

**Benjamin:** Yeah, a lot of changes have happened here.

**Terry:** This street used to have few stores. But now, you can see supermarkets, shopping malls and department stores everywhere.

**Benjamin:** Yeah, they are my wife's heaven, but not mine. I always get lost in the supermarket.

**Terry:** Me too! I was lost three times ten years ago. There were no English directions then.

**Benjamin:** Is that better now?

**Terry:** Yeah, there are many English signs, and wrong spellings as many as them.

**Benjamin:** Maybe you should help deal with this problem.

**Terry:** Sure, if there is a good pay. Just kidding.

**泰瑞:** 对不起,请问 Q-DUCK 在哪儿? 我记得它就在这条街第二个十字路口。

**本杰明:** Q-DUCK? 你指那家著名的烤鸭店吗?

**泰瑞:** 是啊,就是那家。

**本杰明:** 他们很早以前就搬到别的地方去了。

**泰瑞:** 哦,这地方跟我 10 年前来中国时可大不一样了。

**本杰明:** 是啊,这儿变化很大。

**泰瑞:** 以前这儿几乎没有什么店铺。但是现在,你到处都能看到超市、购物广场和百货商店。

**本杰明:** 是啊,它们是我太太的天堂,可是不是我的。我总在超市里走丢。

**泰瑞:** 我也是耶! 我 10 年前来时丢了三次。那时可没有英语指路牌。

**本杰明:** 现在应该好点了吧?

**泰瑞:** 是啊,很多英语标识,还有几乎差不多的拼写错误。

**本杰明:** 或许你可以帮忙解决这个问题。

**泰瑞:** 如果报酬合理的话,我当然愿意啊。只是开玩笑而已。

### 生词小结

| | | |
|---|---|---|
| **roast** *adj.* 烘烤的 | **store** *n.* 商店 |
| **duck** *n.* 鸭 | **heaven** *n.* 天堂 |
| **definite** *adj.* 确定的 | **spelling** *n.* 拼写 |

## **G**rammer 语法小结 —— 序数词

1. 序数词

(1) 第一、第二、第三

*first*（1*st*）第一　　*second*（2*nd*）第二　　*third*（3*rd*）第三

(2) 第四——第十九

*fourth*（4*th*）第四　　*fifth*（5*th*）第五　*sixth*（6*th*）第六　*seventh*（7*th*）第七

*eighth*（8*th*）第八　*ninth*（9*th*）第九　*tenth*（10*th*）第十　*eleventh*（11*th*）第十一

*twelfth*（12*th*）第十二　*thirteenth*（13*th*）第十三　*fourteenth*（14*th*）第十四

*fifteenth*（15*th*）第十五　*sixteenth*（16*th*）第十六　*seventeenth*（17*th*）第十七

*eighteenth*（18*th*）第十八　*nineteenth*（19*th*）第十九

这 16 个序数词均在相应的基数词后面加上后缀 – th 构成。要注意其中 fifth、eighth、ninth、twelfth 四个词的拼法。

(3) 十的整数倍序数词

*twentieth*（20*th*）第二十　*thirtieth*（30*th*）第三十　*fortieth*（40*th*）第四十　*fiftieth*（50*th*）第五十

*sixtieth*（60*th*）第六十　*seventieth*（70*th*）第七十　*eightieth*（80*th*）第八十　*ninetieth*（90*th*）第九十

这一组序数词先将相应的十位整数的基数词词尾 – ty 中的 y 改成 i，然后再加上后缀-eth。

(4) 表示"第几十几"的序数词

*thirty-first*（31*th*）　第三十一　　*sixty-second*（62*nd*）　第六十二

*eighty-seventh*（87*th*）　第八十七　　*ninety-eighth*（98*th*）　第九十八

这类表示"第几十几"的序数词，跟表示"几十几"的基数词一样在构成方法上均由基数词"几十几"变化而来，十位数不变，仅把个位上的基数词变成序数词就行了。

## **D**o it together 家庭总动员

两人一组，一方写出下面的基数词/序数词，另一方写出其对应的英语序数词/基数词。

第三十九　　　　_____　　　　_____

第六十三　　　　_____　　　　_____

第二十　　　　　_____　　　　_____

第九十八　　　　_____　　　　_____

第六十　　　　　_____　　　　_____

第六　　　　　　_____　　　　_____

第二　　　　　　_____　　　　_____

第十一　　　　　_____　　　　_____

**R**ecitation 经典背诵

Terry：Beijing has changed a lot. It is quite different from what it was ten years ago. There are supermarkets, shopping malls and department stores everywhere. The public transportation is also better than before. Beijing is becoming more and more beautiful!

# Act 5

# 运动场景
## Sports

# 操场 Playground

## Goals

**在这个场景中,我们将学到:**

1. 辅音字母发音
2. 团体体育项目的词汇
3. 义务和需求句型练习
4. 直接引语和间接引语

比赛
**Competitions**

 玩转语音

1. Sarah saw a shot-silk sash shop full of shot-silk sashes as the sunshine shone on the side of the shot-silk sash shop.

2. Moses supposes his toes are roses, but moses supposes erroneously. For moses, he knows his toes aren't roses as moses supposes his toes to be!

及格时间:12 秒
你的纪录:——秒

及格时间:15 秒
你的纪录:——秒

阿美在古奇的鼓动下,逃课来看篮球比赛,比赛精彩吗? 一起来看看吧。

**May:** Wow, this is drop-dead gorgeous.

**Gucci:** So no more regret now?

**May:** Don't remind me of that. This would be the last time I cut any classes for a basketball game.

**Gucci:** Come on. Don't be so hard on yourself. Enjoy your life.

**May:** I just can't help it. Oh, look at Clive, he is really a big hit. They are definitely gonna win.

**Gucci:** It's only seven minutes into the game, too early to cheer up.

**May:** Come on, 18 points already, they are never gonna catch up.

**Gucci:** Who knows! It's a long game. Look! That was a really nice shot!

**May:** They are coming back to narrow the gap.

**阿美:** 哇噻,(比赛)真是太精彩了!

**古奇:** 那么现在不再后悔了吧?

**阿美:** 别提醒我这个。这会是我最后一次为篮球比赛而逃课。

**古奇:** 拜托。别这么为难自己。要享受人生啊!

**阿美:** 我就是忍不住嘛。哦,看克莱夫,他真是耀眼啊! 他们一定会赢的。

**古奇:** 才刚刚开场 7 分钟,要高兴现在还太早。

**阿美:** 拜托,已经领先 18 分了,对方不可能赶超了啊。

**古奇:** 谁知道呢? 比赛还长着呢。看,刚才的进球真漂亮!

**阿美:** 对方在拉进比分。

运动场景·Sports

**Gucci:** Wait, that guy, I know him. He is just a bench warmer.

**May:** A secret weapon. They'd better set up the defense now.

**Gucci:** Clive is ready to explode. Keep your eyes open.

**May:** Oh, man! I can't believe it. A slam dunk!

**Gucci:** Good that he resembled his old, quick self.

**古奇:** 等等,那个男生,我认得他。他只是一个"板凳"。

**阿美:** 一个秘密武器哦。(克莱夫)他们现在最好加强防守了。

**古奇:** 克莱夫要爆发了。把你的眼睛睁大了。

**阿美:** 哦,好家伙。我真难以相信。灌篮了。

**古奇:** 真好,他总算恢复动作飞快的他了。

---

**生词小结**

| | | | |
|---|---|---|---|
| drop-dead | *adv.* 非常 | bench warmer | 候补球员 |
| gorgeous | *adj.* 极好的 | defense | *n.* 防守 |
| explode | *vi.* 爆发 | slam dunk | 灌篮 |
| doubt | *n.* 怀疑 | resemble | *vt.* 恢复 |
| cheer up | 高兴起来 | | |

**注释**

bench warmer: bench 是长凳的意思,warmer 的意思是取暖器,打球的时候有一部分技术比较弱的球员得不到上场的机会而要坐在场外长凳上,所以候补球员被称为 bench warmer。

---

## P ronunciation 语音小结 —— 辅音字母发音

1. 多数发字母本身音

   d /d/: dead would hard definitely

   m /m/: more remind minute warmer

   r /r/: regret really already secret

   v /v/: seven never have very

   **朗读练习:** dead and would    hard and definitely

            more and remind    minute and warmer

            regret and really    already and secret

            seven and never    have and very

2. 少数辅音字母不只是一个读音

   c 在单词中经常发/k/ /s/: cut class nice cell

   g 在单词中经常发/g/ /dʒ/: game gap cage strange

   n 在单词中经常发/n/: no now remind enjoy

   x 在单词中经常发/ks/ /g/: box explode example exact

   **朗读练习:** cut and class    nice and cell

            game and gap    cage and strange

            no and now    remind and enjoy

            box and explode    example and exact

3. 双写辅音字母在单词中,常常只读一个音节的音如,bb /b/ rabbit   pp/p/ apple dd /d/ daddy   ll /l/ ball 但是 gg 组合在一起发 /g/ egg 和 /dʒ/ suggest

   **朗读练习:** ball and really    allow and allege

            class and miss    glass and dress

            happy and slipper    shipper and happen

            egg and bigger    logger and beggar

            better and letter    battery and battle

---

**Recitation** 经典背诵

**May:** I'm a good girl in people's eyes. But my best friend Gucci always reminds me to give myself a break, saying "Don't be too hard on yourself." She just trys to show me the right way to enjoy a better life. Once we cut classes for a basketball game. I didn't regret about what I did because it was really a terrific game.

# Topic 2 体育明星
## Sports Stars

克莱夫显然成了众人眼中的篮球明星,这不,这边的两个女生珍妮和苏珊聊得那么起劲,她们在聊什么呢?我们一起来听听吧。

**Jenny**: Who is that guy?

**Susan**: It's Clive of course. Where did you come from? Every girl knows Clive!

**Jenny**: Really? He is my type.

**Susan**: He is everybody's type.

**Jenny**: What position does he play?

**Susan**: Shooting guard. The same as Michael Jordan!

**Jenny**: Oh, I love Michael Jordan. He fills people's lives with great excitement.

**Susan**: Used to. But now he is too old to play in a fierce game like this. But Kobe is the upcoming superstar now.

**Jenny**: Kobe is a good player but I heard he is a womanizer.

**Susan**: That is not true. They are just jealous of him!

**Jenny**: Jordan is a legend, anyway. An idol that no one can replace. I think Clive can make a good professional basketball player. He is not just about muscles he also plays smart.

**Susan**: You know what, he is also an outstanding football player. He is surely to be a star of tomorrow.

**Jenny**: By the way, do you know if he has a girl friend?

**Susan**: You are so not here! His girlfriend is

珍妮:那个人是谁?

苏珊:他当然是克莱夫。你是从哪里来的啊?每个女孩都知道克莱夫啊!

珍妮:是吗?他是我喜欢的类型。

苏珊:他是每个人都喜欢的类型。

珍妮:他打什么位置啊?

苏珊:得分后卫。和迈克尔·乔丹是一样的位置。

珍妮:哦,我喜欢迈克尔·乔丹。他给人们的生活带来了那么多激动的时刻。

苏珊:曾经是。但他现在太老打不了像这样激烈的比赛了。但是科比却是新起的超级明星。

珍妮:科比打球打得好,但是我听说他很花心。

苏珊:那不是真的。(说的人)他们是嫉妒科比罢了。

珍妮:不管怎样,乔丹是个传奇。一个没有谁能取代的偶像。我觉得克莱夫会成为一名出色的专业篮球选手。他不只是靠肌肉,他打得很聪明。

苏珊:知道吗,他足球也踢得很好哦。他将来一定会成为一个(体育)明星的。

珍妮:顺便问一下,你知道他有女朋友吗?

苏珊:你是新来的吧!他的女朋友是啦

one of the cheer leaders

Jenny：Oh. My chance is slim then.

啦队队长啊。

珍妮：哦，看来我（要做他女朋友）没有希望了。

**生词小结**

| | |
|---|---|
| **shooting guard** | 得分后卫 |
| **fierce** adj. | 剧烈的 |
| **upcoming** adj. | 即将来临的 |
| **womanizer** n. | 花心的男人 |
| **jealous** adj. | 妒忌的 |
| **legend** n. | 传奇 |
| **slim** adj. | 微小的 |

**注释**

**You are so not here!** 与上文中的 Where did you come from? 是一样的用法，珍妮当然在这里，苏珊说她不在这里，同样是表示惊讶，因为大家都知道克莱夫的女朋友就是拉拉队队长。

## 单词扩展 Vocabulary Builder

### 团体体育项目的词汇

| 基础词汇 | 提高词汇 |
|---|---|
| baseball 棒球 | rugby 橄榄球 |
| football 足球 | shuttlecock kicking 踢毽子 |
| basketball 篮球 | softball 垒球 |
| badminton 羽毛球 | hockey 曲棍球 |
| wrestling 摔跤 | roller skating 滑旱冰 |
| golf 高尔夫 | tug of war 拔河 |
| boxing 拳击 | rowing 划船 |
| tennis 网球 | boat race 赛艇 |

## D 家庭总动员
### Do it together

两人一组，一方随机大声读出上面词汇的英文和中文，另一方用该词汇填入下面的句子，大声朗读并表演出来，并用中文给出一个理由。

**He is an outstanding (                ) player.**

【例】家长读 baseball 棒球

孩子读 He is an outstanding baseball player. 因为他每天都坚持训练。

**Recitation** 经典背诵

Jenny：People always ask me where I'm from because I always don't know much about what's going on around me. And there is a guy named Clive who is really cool. He plays basketball really well. People in my school believe that he will be a star of tomorrow. He is my type. But unluckily, my chance is slim since he has got a girlfriend already.

# Topic3 拉拉队队长
## Cheerleader

听 学 读 看

没有想到,丹尼尔也逃课来看比赛,小家伙不仅看篮球看得开心,而且还"喜欢"上了姐姐的好朋友,原来她是拉拉队的,这下阿美真要哭笑不得了。

May：Daniel, what are you doing here? Aren't you supposed to be at school now?

阿美：丹尼尔,你在这里做什么,你不是应该在上课吗?

Daniel：The same question to you.

丹尼尔：我也想问你同样的问题。

May：Well, we shall make it a secret between us.

阿美：好吧,我们就把它当成我们两个之间的秘密吧。

Daniel：Deal. Where is Gucci?

丹尼尔：行。古奇在哪里?

May：She is the cheer-leader. They are required to put on a performance. Look! Here they come.

阿美：她是拉拉队队长。她们等下要表演。看! 她们来了。

Daniel：Oh, look at her. She looks like one of the basketball babies in NBA.

丹尼尔：哦,你看她,她看起来就像是NBA 里的篮球宝贝。

May：(*Mumble*) I want to be like her.

阿美：(喃喃自语)我想像她一样。

Daniel：Get real. Don't be so pathetic.

丹尼尔：现实点吧。别那么可悲。

May：Hey, young man! I'm your sis. Don't talk to me like that.

阿美：嗨,年轻人,我是你姐姐哎,别这么和我说话。

Daniel：Oh, man, look at her, go! She is amazing! She should be my sis.

丹尼尔：哦,看她,那里。她真棒! 她要是我姐姐就好了。

May：Boy, you've got such a crush on her, haven't you?

阿美：小家伙,你已经迷上她了,是吗?

Daniel：Yes, I want to be her boyfriend. Just like in the movie.

丹尼尔：是啊,我要做她的男朋友,就像电影里一样。

May：Are you out of your mind?

阿美：你疯了吗?

Daniel：She told me she liked my new haircut. She thought it was cool.

丹尼尔：她说她喜欢我的新发型,她觉得我很酷。

May：Go ahead, have a try and be a joke.

阿美：那尽管去吧,试试看,(你可以)成为一个笑话。

Daniel：We'll see.

丹尼尔：走着瞧。

## Act 5

运动场景 · Sports

生词小结

| | | |
|---|---|---|
| **suppose** | *vt.* | 应该 |
| **secret** | *n.* | 秘密 |
| **cheer-leader** | *n.* | 拉拉队长 |
| **basketball baby** | | 篮球宝贝 |
| **pathetic** | *adj.* | 可悲的 |
| **amazing** | *adj.* | 令人惊异的 |
| **crush** | *n.* | 迷恋 |
| **joke** | *n.* | 笑话 |

注释

**basketball babies** 美国的 NBA（美国职业篮球联赛）比赛中，会在中场休息的时候有拉拉队的表演，表演非常出色，受到很多人的喜欢，被大家称为 basketball babies（篮球宝贝）。

## S情景练习
Scene practice —— 义务和需求句型练习

仔细阅读下面五个场景，两人一组，使用表达义务和需求的句型（见 **203** 页），用一用，练一练。

1. Daniel is the leader of their football team, if you were Daniel, what would you say to your team members before an important competition?

2. If you were Benjamin, you have to maintain the whole family, what would you say if you want to tell your good friend your responsibility in your family?

3. Shirley is an accountant of a factory, she is asked to tell her detail work, if you were Shirley, what would you say?

4. May wants to be a volunteer of the Olympic Games, if you were May, how would you state the responsibility of the volunteer?

5. May is the monitor of her class, if you were May, you are asked to tell your responsibility, what would you say?

**Recitation** 经典背诵

Daniel: I like Gucci. She is my older sister's best friend. She is an amazing cheerleader. She thinks I'm cool, and I want to be her boyfriend though May always laughs at me, saying that I would be nothing but a joke. But I don't care about what she says. We'll see someday.

# Topic4 后勤服务
## Rear Services

听 学 看

比赛结束了,大家还意犹未尽地谈论着比赛,不过后勤小组的女生珍妮和苏珊还有最后一件事情要做,猜猜是什么?

**Jenny：** Have we handed out all the water?

**Susan：** Yes. So what else to do now?

**Jenny：** Nothing. The teacher said the only thing left was to get back all the disposable cups later.

**Susan：** I see. How do you like the game?

**Jenny：** Terrific. There is one girl said："It is the best game I've ever watched."

**Susan：** Who do you think do better?

**Jenny：** Clive was really outstanding. Not only he put on a big show himself, but also he inspired the whole team.

**Susan：** Exactly. He is unbelievable.

**Jenny：** On the other hand, I think the other team won everyone's respect. The leader said they could have crumpled at the beginning, but they just carried on and never lost their cool.

**Susan：** They were really tough.

**Jenny：** The thing I like most about them is that they did not play with a heavy heart even though at that time the odds seemed to be against them.

**Susan：** I can't agree more. Okay, time is up. Let's do "the last thing".

**珍妮：** 我们发完所有的水了吗?

**苏珊：** 是的。那我们现在还有别的事要做吗?

**珍妮：** 没有了。老师说唯一要做的就是等一下把所有的一次性纸杯收回来。

**苏珊：** 知道了。你觉得比赛怎么样?

**珍妮：** 很精彩啊。我听到一个女孩子说："这是我看过的最精彩的比赛。"

**苏珊：** 你认为谁得得更精彩?

**珍妮：** 克莱夫真的很出众。他不仅自己表现突出,他还鼓舞了整支队伍。

**苏珊：** 真是这样的。他真让人难以置信。

**珍妮：** 另外,我觉得另一队赢得了每个人的尊敬。他们的队长说他们本可能在开场的时候就溃败的,但是他们坚持住了,而且一直都没有丢掉信心。

**苏珊：** 他们确实很顽强。

**珍妮：** 他们最让我喜欢的一点是他们没有打得很沉重尽管成功似乎在跟他们作对。

**苏珊：** 我完全同意,好了,时间差不多了,让我们把最后的事做完吧。

### 生词小结

| | | | |
|---|---|---|---|
| **hand out** | 分发 | **respect** | *n.* 尊敬 |
| **disposable** | *adj.* 用后即丢弃的 | **crumple** | *vi.* 崩溃 |
| **outstanding** | *adj.* 出众的 | **tough** | *adj.* 顽强的 |
| **inspire** | *vt.* 鼓舞 | **odds** | *n.* 成功的希望 |
| **unbelievable** | *adj.* 难以置信的 | **against** | *prep.* 对着 |

## Grammer 语法小结 —— 直接引语和间接引语

直接引语就是直接引用别人的话,话语放在引号内;间接引语就是用自己的话转述别人的话,不加引号。直接引语变成间接引语时,间接引语通常以宾语从句的形式出现,要注意人称、时态、指示代词、时间及地点状语的变化。

#### 1. 直接引语和间接引语

(1)直接引语

*He said, "I get on well with children here."* 他说:"我在这里和小朋友们相处得很好。"

(2)间接引语

*He said that he got on well with children there.* 他说他在那里和小朋友们相处得很好。

#### 2. 直接引语变为间接引语

(1) 如果直接引语是陈述句,在变为间接引语时,由连词 that 引导(that 可省略)。主句中如果有 say to somebody(对某人说),通常变为 tell somebody(告诉某人)

*She said to me, "You speak English better than me."* 她对我说:"你的英语说得比我好。"

*She told me that I spoke English better than her.* 她对我说我的英语说得比她好。

(2)直接引语如果是一般疑问句,变为间接引语时,要用连词 whether 或 if 引导,同时把原来的疑问句语序变为陈述句语序。主句中的谓语动词是 said 时,要改为 asked

*She asks, "Do you like the city?"* 她问:"你喜欢这个城市吗?"

*She asked whether/ if I liked the city.* 她问我是否喜欢这个城市。

(3)直接引语如果是特殊疑问句(即 what, which, who, whom, whose, how, why, when, where, how many, how long 等引导的疑问句),变为间接引语时,仍用原来的疑问词引导,但要把原来的疑问句语序改为陈述句语序

*He asks, "who lives next door?"* 他问:"谁住在隔壁?"

*He asked who lived next door.* 他问谁住在隔壁。

## Do it together 家庭总动员

两人一组,一方朗诵下面的中文句子,另一方挑选出合适的翻译。

1. 他告诉我,这会是他最后一次因为篮球比赛逃课。
2. 她告诉我她喜欢我的新发型。
3. 他告诉我刚才的进球很漂亮。
4. 老师问,"这是谁做的?"
5. 妈妈生气了,"把电视关掉!"

1. Mom was angry, "turn off the television!"
2. He told me that this would be the last time he cut any classes for a basketball game.
3. The teacher asks, "who did these?"
4. He told me that it was a really nice shot.
5. She told me that she liked my new haircut.

Susan: I like serving for the basketball players. It makes me happy to hand water to them especially after a fierce game. What I like most about them is that they always carry on to the last minute no matter what. There is no one single loser among them.

# 慢跑 Jogging

## Goals

**在这个场景中,我们将学到:**

1. 辅音字母组合发音
2. 上班族运动种类的词汇
3. 自我介绍的句型
4. 直接宾语和间接宾语

 白领运动
**Sports for White-collar Workers**

 玩转语音

1. A pleasant peasant keeps a pleasant pheasant and both the peasant and the pheasant are having a pleasant time together.

2. A writer named Wright was instructing his little son how to write Wright right. He said: "It is not right to write Wright as 'rite'—try to write Wright aright!"

及格时间: 30秒
你的纪录:——秒
及格时间: 30秒
你的纪录:——秒

雪莉的一个同事在办公时间看《健康顾问》,被雪莉逮了个正着。一起来看看雪莉是怎么处理的,是公事公办吗?

( *Shirley sees her colleague reading a magazine* )

**Shirley**: What are you reading?

**Maria**: Gee! You scared me!

**Shirley**: Aha, *Fitness Consultant*. Very good, Don't you know about the rules in this office?

**Maria**: Yes, Ma'am. No magazines during the office hours. I'm sorry.

**Shirley**: Well, don't do this again next time. What is it about, anyway?

**Maria**: It is about sports for white-collar workers, people like you and me.

(雪莉看到她的一个同事正在看杂志)

雪莉:你在看什么?

玛丽亚:哎呀!你吓我一大跳!

雪莉:啊哈,《健康顾问》。好极了,难道你不知道办公室里的规矩吗?

玛丽亚:当然知道了。工作时间不准看杂志。对不起。

雪莉:下次可别再这么做。嘿,这是本什么杂志啊?

玛丽亚:是关于上班族的运动的书,就是像你我这样的。

215

Shirley：What kind of sports?

Maria：Aerobic sports, for example, jogging, yoga, skating…

Shirley：Interesting. What were you reading just now?

Maria：Stretching exercise after sitting a long time.

Shirley：Really? That sounds interesting!

Maria：Can I have my magazine back now?

Shirley：No. It's confiscated for now. And I will return it to you after I finish reading it.

雪莉:什么样的运动啊?

玛丽亚:有氧运动,比如,慢跑、瑜珈,滑雪……

雪莉:有意思。你刚刚在读的是什么啊?

玛丽亚:长期久坐后的伸展运动。

雪莉:真的吗? 有意思!

玛丽亚:我现在能拿回我的杂志了吗?

雪莉:不行。现在它被没收了。我读完了以后再还给你。

---

**生词小结**

| | | | |
|---|---|---|---|
| colleague | n. 同事 | white-collar | n. 白领 |
| fitness | n. 健美,健康 | yoga | n. 瑜珈 |
| consultant | n. 顾问 | stretch | vi. 伸展 |
| rule | n. 规定 | magazine | n. 杂志 |

---

## 语音小结 Pronunciation —— 辅音字母组合发音

1. 一些常见的辅音字母组合在一起,常见的发音

   ck /k/ sick back　　　　　　　　le /l/ little people example

   gh /f/ tough 和 /g/ ghost　　　　ph /f/ photo

   wh /w/ what white　　　　　　　ch /tʃ/ teach 和 /k/ technic

   sh /ʃ/ shine　　　　　　　　　　qu /kw/ quick

   朗读练习:pick and peck　sing and thing　when and win　phone and photo

   　　　　　　sheep and sheet　cheap and chip

2. 在单词读音中,有些单词的辅音字母不发音

   h hour/'auə /　b comb/kəum/　k knee /niː/　w write /rait /　g sign/sain/　gh daughter /'dɔːtə /

   朗读练习:tough and laugh　climb and lamb　wrong and write

---

**Recitation** 经典背诵

Maria：I'm Maria, I'm Shirley's colleague. I like reading magazines. It's just part of my life. There is a rule in my working place which says no magazines during office hours. But sometimes I just can't help it. There was one time I was caught reading *Fitness Consultant*, so it was confiscated. Stupid rules!

# Topic2 慢跑
## Jogging

一天清晨,雪莉和本杰明去慢跑。雪莉想减肥,便拼命地快跑。可本杰明却说那不是减肥之道,那怎样才是呢? 来听听本杰明的高见吧!

| | |
|---|---|
| (*Shirley and Benjamin are jogging*) | (雪莉和本杰明在慢跑) |

**Shirley**：Come on, you are left behind!

**Benjamin**：Wow, I can't catch my breath. You are running too fast, honey.

**Shirley**：You just need more exercise.

**Benjamin**：Yes, but you need to slow down. This is jogging, not racing!

**Shirley**：I don't care. I want to burn up my fat.

**Benjamin**：But running so fast is not good for people over forties.

**Shirley**：Why?

**Benjamin**：We are not as athletic as we were when young. Mild exercise is more suitable for us.

**Shirley**：But I want to burn up more calories!

**Benjamin**：In fact, in order to burn up your fat, you must take it slowly for a longer time.

**Shirley**：Really? I will slow down then.

**Benjamin**：That's right, honey. Oh, you don't need to be as slow as a tortoise.

**Shirley**：I don't care.

---

雪莉:加油啊,你落后了!

本杰明:哇哦,我快喘不过气来了。你跑得太快了,亲爱的。

雪莉:你得多运动了。

本杰明:是啊,但是你也得跑慢点啊。这是慢跑,不是赛跑!

雪莉:我不管,我要减掉我的脂肪。

本杰明:但跑这么快不适合过 40 的人啊!

雪莉:为什么?

本杰明:我们没有像年轻时候那样有活力了。中等强度的运动更适合我们。

雪莉:但我想燃烧掉更多的卡路里!

本杰明:事实上,要减肥,你就得慢慢地跑很长一段时间。

雪莉:真的吗? 那我就慢点跑。

本杰明:对啦,亲爱的。喔,你也不必慢得跟乌龟一样。

雪莉:我不管。

---

### 生词小结

**jog** *vi.* 慢跑

**catch my breath** 喘过气来

**athletic** *adj.* 运动的

**mild** *adj.* 中度的,温和的

**calory** *n.* 卡路里

**tortoise** *n.* 乌龟

运动场景·Sports

## 单词扩展 Vocabulary Builder

### 上班族运动种类的词汇

| 基础词汇 | 提高词汇 |
| --- | --- |
| table tennis 乒乓球 | badminton 羽毛球 |
| tennis 网球 | golf 高尔夫球 |
| hill climbing 登山 | yoga 瑜珈 |
| jogging 慢跑 | taekwondo 跆拳道 |
| cycling 自行车 | aerobics 健美操 |
| skating 滑冰 | skiing 滑雪 |
| bowling 保龄球 | roller skating 滑旱冰 |
| hiking 远足 | |

## 家庭总动员
### Do it together

两人一组，一方随机大声读出上面词汇的英文和中文，另一方用该词汇填入下面的句子，大声朗读并表演出来，并用中文给出一个理由。

(                    ) is more suitable for us.

【例】家长读 table tennis 乒乓球

孩子读 Table tennis is more suitable for us. 因为乒乓球有利于锻炼灵活性。

### Recitation 经典背诵

Benjamin：Shirley and I are in our forties. So in order to keep fit, we've started to do some morning exercises these days. I've heard mild exercise is suitable for us so we've chosen jogging. Shirley ran very fast at first. But I told her that was not jogging. Then she started to slow down.

# Topic3 运动交友
## Workout Buddies

本杰明和雪莉在路上碰到了雪莉的同事。于是三人大谈健身,不过好像还有事情没有解决哦,来看看是什么吧!

**Maria**：Hi, Shirley, it's a surprise to see you here!

**Shirley**：Hi, nice to see you!

**Maria**：What are you doing here?

**Shirley**：Jogging. Maria, I want you to meet my husband, Ben. Ben, this is my colleague, Maria.

**Maria**：I am Maria, glad to meet you.

**Benjamin**：Nice meeting you, Maria. I am Benjamin. Call me Ben.

**Maria**：Do you exercise in the morning regularly?

**Shirley**：No, this is our first time doing morning exercises. God, my bones are sore!

**Maria**：As beginners, you need to start slowly, or you'll get tired soon.

**Shirley**：Thank you, Maria. Thank you for your advice.

**Maria**：Oh, one more thing.

**Shirley**：Yeah? Any more suggestions?

**Maria**：Can I have my magazine back now?

玛丽亚：你好啊,雪莉,真没想到在这儿遇见你!

雪莉：你好,见到你真高兴!

玛丽亚：你在这儿做什么?

雪莉：慢跑。玛丽亚。向你介绍我的丈夫,本。本,这是我的同事,玛丽亚。

玛丽亚：我是玛丽亚,很高兴见到你。

本杰明：很高兴见到你,玛丽亚。我是本杰明。叫我本好了。

玛丽亚：你经常在早上锻炼吗?

雪莉：不,这是我们第一次晨练。天哪,我的骨头又酸又痛!

玛丽亚：刚开始,你得慢慢来,不然你很容易就会疲劳的。

雪莉：谢谢你,玛丽亚。谢谢你的建议的。

玛丽亚：哦,还有件事。

雪莉：什么? 还有什么别的建议吗?

玛丽亚：我现在能要回我的杂志了吗?

---

### 生词小结

| | | | |
|---|---|---|---|
| **regularly** | *adv.* 经常地 | **tired** | *adj.* 累的 |
| **bone** | *n.* 骨头 | **advice** | *n.* 建议 |
| **sore** | *adj.* 酸痛的 | **suggestion** | *n.* 建议 |

## F 功能性句型扩展 —— 自我介绍的句型
unctional structure

**请朗读以下句型,家长和孩子交替进行。**

1. 介绍别人

   I want you to meet... 我想让你认识……

   May I introduce...to you? 我能否向你介绍……?

   It's a great pleasure for me to introduce... 我很高兴能向你介绍……

2. 回应介绍

   Hello! 你好!

   Hi. Nice to meet you! 你好,很高兴见到你!

   How do you do. 你好。

   I'm very pleased to meet you. 我很高兴见到你。

   It's a great pleasure to meet you. 很高兴认识你。

3. 介绍自己

   My name is... 我叫……

   I'm... 我是……

   May I introduce myself? I'm... 能让我介绍一下自己吗? 我是……

   Allow me to introduce myself. My name is... 请允许我介绍一下自己。我叫……

**Recitation** 经典背诵

**Shirley:** Morning exercises are very good for your health. What's more, it's also a good way to make friends. I just started to do exercises this morning. As a beginner, I should start slowly, or I would soon get tired. That is a very good advice from my colleague Maria.

# Topic 4 运动受伤
## Sports Injuries

听 学
读 看

雪莉穿皮鞋跑步,把脚踝扭伤了。本杰明用冷敷的方法,把冰放在雪莉受伤的脚踝上。到底有没有效果呢?

| | |
|---|---|
| Shirley：Honey, wait! I've sprained my ankle. | 雪莉：亲爱的,等等! 我把脚踝给扭了。 |
| Benjamin：Oh, my god, are you OK? | 本杰明：哦,天哪! 你还好吗? |
| Shirley：Of course not! | 雪莉：当然不好啦! |
| Benjamin：Come on, sit down, and let me have a look. | 本杰明：来吧,坐下,让我看一看。 |
| Shirley：The pain is killing me. | 雪莉：疼死我了。 |
| Benjamin：I told you to wear running shoes. But you don't listen. | 本杰明：我叫你穿跑鞋。可你就是不听。 |
| Shirley：I thought leather shoes will do just as well. | 雪莉：我以为穿皮鞋也可以跑嘛。 |
| Benjamin：Hold on, don't move, I will take care of that. | 本杰明：等一下,别动,我来处理。 |
| Shirley：What are you going to do? | 雪莉：你打算怎么办? |
| Benjamin：I will get some ice, and put it on your ankle. | 本杰明：我打算拿些冰来,敷在你的脚踝上。 |
| (*Benjamin gets some ice and put it on Shirley's ankle.*) | (本杰明拿来了点冰,放在雪莉的脚踝上。) |
| Benjamin：How does that feel? | 本杰明：感觉怎么样? |
| Shirley：God! It's freezing! | 雪莉：天哪! 冷极了! |
| Benjamin：Be brave. Don't worry. You will be able to walk soon. | 本杰明：勇敢点。别担心。你一会儿就能走路了。 |

### 生词小结

| | |
|---|---|
| **sprain** *vt.* 扭伤 | **leather** *n.* 皮革 |
| **ankle** *n.* 脚踝 | **freezing** *adj.* 冷的,冻的 |
| **pain** *n.* 疼痛 | **brave** *adj.* 勇敢的 |

## G 语法小结 —— 直接宾语和间接宾语
### rammer

1. 什么是宾语

宾语是动作的承受者,一般置于及物动词之后,例如:

*Our team beat them.* 我们的球队击败了他们。(宾语:*them*)

*You can leave your luggage here.* 你可以把你的行李放在这儿。(宾语:*your luggage*)

*We like English.* 我们喜欢英语。(宾语:*English*)

2. 直接宾语和间接宾语

有些及物动词可以带两个宾语,往往一个是人,一个是物,指人的叫间接宾语,指物的叫直接宾语。直接宾语是谓语动词的承受者,间接宾语表示谓语动作的方向(对谁做)或动作的目标(为谁做)。

*My mother teaches me English.* 我妈妈教我英语。(直接宾语:*English* 间接宾语:*me*)

*Please show me your passport.* 请把护照给我看一下。(直接宾语:*your passport* 间接宾语:*me*)

*I will fetch you a cup of milk.* 我给你拿杯牛奶。(直接宾语:*a cup of milk* 间接宾语:*you*)

## D 家庭总动员
### o it together

两人一组,一方朗诵下面的中文句子,另一方挑选出合适的翻译。

1. 本杰明拿来了点冰给雪莉。
2. 丹尼尔给了阿美一些建议。
3. 售货员向我介绍这本书。
4. 妈妈让丹尼尔弹钢琴。
5. 请给我你的信用卡。

1. Mom let Daniel play piano.
2. The salesman introduces this book to me.
3. Please show me your credit card.
4. Benjamin takes some ice to Shirley.
5. Daniel gives May some suggestions.

**Recitation** 经典背诵

Benjamin:There are things to remember when doing exercises. First, you must wear running shoes, because they are soft. It's easy to sprain your ankles if you wear leather shoes. If that happens, don't worry, just get some ice and put it on your ankle. Then you will be fine soon.

# 健身房 Gymnasium

## Goals

**在这个场景中,我们将学到:**

1. 名词词形变化的读音
2. 健身房器械的词汇
3. 自我介绍句型练习
4. 动词不定式作主语、宾语

Topic 1 办理健身卡
Membership Cards

### 玩转语音

1. Bake big batches of bitter brown bread.
2. Luke's duck likes lakes. Luke Luck licks lakes. Luke's duck licks lakes. Duck takes licks in lakes Luke Luck likes. Luke Luck takes licks in lakes duck likes.

及格时间: 9 秒
你的纪录: —— 秒
及格时间: 30 秒
你的纪录: —— 秒

听 学 看

雪莉有点中年发福,于是想去健身房做点运动,该怎么办理健身卡呢,你知道吗? 雪莉是怎么做的呢? 一起往下看。

**Clerk**: Good afternoon, madam. How can I help you?

**Shirley**: Well, I am a bit out of shape. I'm thinking about getting some exercises to keep fit.

**Clerk**: Oh, that's good news for us.

**Shirley**: So what do you provide?

**Clerk**: First of all, we'll design a custom-made work-out plan according to your habits.

**Shirley**: How can you get that done?

**Clerk**: Well, we give each of our customers a personal trainer who is qualified. And he will give you a fitness assessment and then come up with the work-out plan for your needs.

**Shirley**: What else?

**Clerk**: Since everyone is different, your personal trainer will find you a suitable type of

**职员**: 下午好,女士。有什么能为您效劳的吗?

**雪莉**: 那个,我身体有点走形了,我在考虑做点运动来保持体型。

**职员**: 哦,这对我们是好消息啊。

**雪莉**: 你们能提供什么(服务)?

**职员**: 首先,我们会根据顾客的兴趣为顾客定做一个健身计划。

**雪莉**: 你们会怎么做呢?

**职员**: 哦,我们会为每一个顾客安排一名专业的私人健身教练。他会给你做一份健康评估,然后根据需求制定出相应的健身计划。

**雪莉**: 还有别的吗?

**职员**: 因为每个人的情况不同,所以私人教练会帮你找一个合适的运动器材

exercise equipment and teach you all the techniques to help you achieve your fitness level and goal.

**Shirley**：Sounds pretty good. What about the charge?

**Clerk**：That depends. We offer membership for one month, half a year and one year.

**Shirley**：Maybe one month. Just have a try first. Not too tough at the beginning.

**Clerk**：Wise decision. You'll find it's totally worth it.

**Shirley**：What's your business hours?

**Clerk**：We are open all day long from 6:00am till 12:00pm. And you are welcome anytime.

**Shirley**：Thank you.

和具体使用方法以帮你达到健身的目标。

**雪莉**：听起来很不错。怎么收费呢?

**职员**：看情况的。我们提供一个月,半年和一年的会员卡。

**雪莉**：我要一个月的。先试一下。开始先别太多了。

**职员**：很聪明的决定。你会发现它很超值的。

**雪莉**：你们的营业时间是什么?

**职员**：我们从早上6点一直开到晚上12点。随时欢迎您的光临。

**雪莉**：谢谢。

---

### 生词小结

| | |
|---|---|
| **out of shape**　体型不好 | **assessment**　*n.* 评估 |
| **design**　*vt.* 设计 | **come up with**　想出 |
| **habit**　*n.* 习惯 | **equipment**　*n.* 设备 |
| **personal trainer**　私人教练 | **technique**　*n.* 技术 |
| **qualified**　*adj.* 有资格的 | **achieve**　*vt.* 达到 |

---

## P语音小结
### Pronunciation —— 名词词形变化的读音

一般情况下名词的复数发音现象有以下几种,但是由于英语当中有些名词的复数形式属于不规则变化,这些词的发音在以后的学习当中还要慢慢摸索。

**1.** 在词尾加-s

①-s 在清辅音后面发/s/音：caps cats sheets ships

②-s 在浊辅音后发/z/音：cabs lambs games arms

③-s 在元音后都发/z/音：seas peas bees fleas

**朗读练习**：hats sheets ships lambs cows arms hands peas bees faces

**2.** 在以/s//z//ʃ//tʃ//dʒ/等音结尾的名词后面加 es;当词尾为不发音的-e 时,只加-s;末尾的-(e)s 自成一个音节,读成/iz/ glasses classes gates cates

**朗读练习**：glasses classes roses faces

**3.** 当词尾-f 或-fe 变为-ves 时,-ves 读/vz/：life-lives　knife-knives

**朗读练习**：life and lives　knife and knives

**4.** 词尾为辅音字母加-y,则将-y 改为-i,再加-es;-ies 读/iz/：babies　lobbies

**朗读练习**：babies lobbies ladies countries

词尾是辅音字母 o 结尾的,加上-es;读/z/：heroes potatoes tamatoes

**朗读练习**：potatoes and tomatoes　heroes and negroes

**特别提示**：动词一般现在时,第三人称单数的词尾读音与名词复数的读音规则相同。

---

**Recitation** 经典背诵

**Shirley**：I'm a bit out of shape these days. In order to be healthy I go to a gym to do some exercise. I have a personal trainer who gives me a custom-made work-out plan which is really effective. Though it costs me a lot of money, I think it's worth it. Anyway health comes first.

## Topic2 健身器械
### Fitness Equipment

我们的小捣蛋丹尼尔偷偷来到了妈妈的健身房，说是要到健身房做点运动，长大了要当李小龙，结果怎么样呢？

**Clerk**：Welcome, young man. No offence, but I haven't seen you here before.

**Daniel**：Of course, this is my first time here. My Mom has a membership here. Here is the card.

**Clerk**：Okay then. You are the youngest customer here ever.

**Daniel**：It's not so wise that you do not explore the children's market.

**Clerk**：It's the marketing's fault, I suppose. What do you want to do?

**Daniel**：Well, I want to become just like Bruce Lee. What should I do?

**Clerk**：That's a long way to go, I'm afraid. First of all, you gotta grow up.

**Daniel**：I am still young. And I'm growing every minute.

**Clerk**：Sure. Then what about trying the treadmill or the skipping rope.

**Daniel**：I love running. Anything else?

**Clerk**：Please change your clothes first!

**Daniel**：I'm perfect with my clothes. And I do not have anything else with me.

**Clerk**：Sorry, but no jeans here.

**Daniel**：Oh, that's the only place where jeans are not popular. I'd better just go home.

**职员**：欢迎光临，年轻人。没有冒犯的意思，但是我好像以前没有见过你。

**丹尼尔**：当然了，这是我第一次来。我妈妈是这里的会员。这是她的会员卡。

**职员**：那好吧。你是我们最年轻的顾客。

**丹尼尔**：你们不开发儿童市场，这样做非常不明智。

**职员**：我想这应该是市场部的错误。你想做点什么（运动）呢？

**丹尼尔**：嗯，我想成为李小龙，我该怎么做呢？

**职员**：恐怕那有一段很长的路哦！首先，你得先长大。

**丹尼尔**：我还年轻。而且我每一分钟都在长啊！

**职员**：当然。那么要不要试试跑步机或者是跳绳？

**丹尼尔**：我喜欢跑步。还有别的吗？

**职员**：请先换衣服吧！

**丹尼尔**：我穿这个就可以了。而且我身边也没有带别的衣服。

**职员**：对不起，但是这里不允许穿牛仔裤（运动）。

**丹尼尔**：哦，这是唯一一个不流行牛仔裤的地方！我最好还是回家算了。

225

## 生词小结

**membership** *n.* 会员资格
**explore** *vt.* 开发
**marketing** *n.* 行销
**treadmill** *n.* 踏车
**skipping-rope** 跳绳
**jeans** *n.* 牛仔裤

## 注释

**Bruce Lee:** 李小龙。已故的著名武打动作明星。

## 单词扩展 Vocabulary Builder

### 健身房器械的词汇

| 基础词汇 | 提高词汇 |
|---|---|
| barbell 杠铃 | Vertical knee raise 单杠提膝器 |
| Running Machine 跑步机 | Flat bench 哑铃平椅 |
| treadmill 踏车 | Chest Press 胸部推举机 |
| Stepper 台阶器 | Back machine 背部训练机 |
| Step 负重踏步机 | Abdominal 腹部前屈机 |
| Cycling machine 健身车 | Dip station 双杠练习器 |
| Upper back 背肌训练机 | Recumbent cycle 卧式健身车 |
| Seated calf machine 小腿训练机 | |

## D 家庭总动员
Do it together

两人一组，一方随机大声读出上面词汇的英文和中文，另一方用该词汇填入下面的句子，大声朗读并表演出来，并用中文给出一个描述。

**What about trying the (　　　　)?**

【例】家长读 treadmill 踏车
　　　孩子读 What about trying the treadmill? 它比较适合你的需要。

## Recitation 经典背诵

**Daniel:** I like sports because I want to be just like Bruce Lee when I grow up. My Mom has a membership in a gym. So sometimes I use her membership card to work out there. The thing I don't like is that I can't wear jeans there. Maybe it's the only place where jeans are not popular.

# Topic3 健康与节食
## Health and Diet

听 学 看 自从妈妈开始健身之后,精神变得特别好,不过胃口似乎也跟着长,这么一来减肥是没希望了,看看阿美给妈妈出了什么好主意?

**May:** Mom, this is your third bowl of rice!

**Shirley:** I know but I have no choice. My stomach just keeps crying for more and more.

**May:** Why? I never saw you eat so much before.

**Shirley:** I've been going to the gym these days. The exercise makes me hungry all the time.

**May:** So your stomach is the one that actually gets a lot of work-out.

**Shirley:** Don't pull my leg.

**May:** This way you'll probably put on more weight. Will you give up?

**Shirley:** Surely not. I can feel the results. I'm starting to feel different now.

**May:** Then how are you gonna deal with the problem of getting extra weight?

**Shirley:** I'm planning to meet my personal trainer to have the work-out plan fixed.

**May:** Oh, I've got an idea. Why don't you ask Dad to go with you? He badly needs some exercise.

**Shirley:** Your father is a bit too timid. He even doesn't know how to introduce himself.

**May:** He can just say: "I'm Benjamin. I'm new and shy."

**Shirley:** Girl, don't make fun of your Daddy. But I can introduce him to my personal

阿美:妈妈,这是你的第三碗米饭了!

雪莉:我知道,但是我没办法,我的胃总是想要吃更多。

阿美:为什么?以前我从没见你吃这么多啊。

雪莉:我最近去健身房。锻炼时我总是觉得很饿。

阿美:你的胃一定做了很多的运动喽!

雪莉:别拿我开心了。

阿美:这样你可能会增肥的。你会放弃吗?

雪莉:当然不了。我觉得非常有效果。现在,我开始感觉到(身体的)变化了。

阿美:那你要怎么处理变胖的问题呢?

雪莉:我在考虑见一下我的私人健身教练,改一下健身计划。

阿美:哦,我有一个主意。干吗不叫爸爸和你一起去呢? 他很需要运动。

雪莉:你爸爸太胆小了。(我想)他连怎么介绍自己都不知道。

阿美:他只要说:"我是本杰明,我是新来的,我很害羞。"

雪莉:嗨,别拿你爸爸开玩笑。不过,我可以把你爸爸介绍给我的健身教

trainer. Maybe one day he will be a fitness freak instead of a couch potato.

**May**: Who knows!

练,也许有一天,你爸爸会变成一个健身狂而不是现在的电视精。

**阿美**: 谁知道呢!

---

**生词小结**

**stomachache** *n.* 胃痛
**badly** *adv.* 极度地
**timid** *adj.* 胆怯的
**introduce** *vt.* 介绍
**shy** *adj.* 害羞的
**freak** *n.* 怪人

**注释**

1. fitness freak: fitness 的意思是健康, freak 的意思是怪物, 有的人疯狂迷恋健身, 所以被称为 fitness freak(健身狂)。
2. couch potato: couch potato 长沙发, 土豆, 当然这里既没有沙发也没有土豆, 这是幽默的手法, 因为有的人老看电视, 什么都不做, 像种在沙发中的土豆一样, 意思是"电视精"。

---

**S情景练习** —— 自我介绍句型
**cene practice**

仔细阅读下面五个场景, 两人一组, 使用自我介绍的句型(见 220 页), 用一用, 练一练。

1. A new neighbor has just moved into the flat next to Shirley. If you were Shirley, how will you introduce yourself?

2. If you were Benjamin, you meet an important person for the first time. What do you say?

3. If you were May, you are introduced to Gucci's boyfriend, he shakes your hands and greets you. How would you reply?

4. If you were Jane, you are at a party and you see someone you don't know. How do you introduce yourself?

5. If you were Benjamin, someone new arrives at your place of work. How will you introduce yourself?

**R**ecitation
经典背诵

**May**: My mom goes to a gym these days. She says she can feel the difference now. But I think her stomach is the one that actually gets a lot of work-out because she is eating more than before. This way she puts on even more weight. To solve this problem she decides to ask her personal trainer to fix her work-out plan.

# Topic4 瑜伽
### Yoga

为了降低锻炼强度,私人教练建议雪莉练强度较小的瑜伽,一堂课下来,雪莉有什么感受呢?

**Trainer**: You look great!

**Shirley**: Thanks to you. I'm totally pumped up.

**Trainer**: So you are happy that you made the decision to join us.

**Shirley**: I surely am. But still there is one single problem.

**Trainer**: What's that?

**Shirley**: I eat more and more these days. And it puts even more weight on me.

**Trainer**: It's not good to start with too much work-out at the beginning. What about trying something else?

**Shirley**: I'd love to do that. What do you recommend?

**Trainer**: More and more people are warm up to Yoga these days. Do you want to have a try?

**Shirley**: Do you think it's a good option for health and relaxation?

**Trainer**: Absolutely. But it takes great perseverance to master.

**Shirley**: I can do that.

**Trainer**: Here is a free class going on right over there. Go and join them.

(*After having the Yoga lesson, Shirley comes back to the trainer.*)

**Trainer**: How did it go?

**Shirley**: Everything was okay when it started, but the music made me drowsy. So I think I may have dozed off for a minute over there.

**教练**:你看起来真棒!

**雪莉**:多亏了你。我感觉很精神。

**教练**:所以你应该高兴做了加入我们的决定。

**雪莉**:当然了。但是,还有一个问题。

**教练**:是什么呢?

**雪莉**:我最近吃得越来越多。我甚至比以前更胖了。

**教练**:开始的时候运动量过大是不好的。要不要试点别的?

**雪莉**:很乐意。你有什么推荐的吗?

**教练**:越来越多的人热衷于瑜伽。你想试试看吗?

**雪莉**:你觉得那是健康和放松的好选择吗?

**教练**:当然了。但是想要掌握的话需要很大的毅力。

**雪莉**:我可以的。

**教练**:那边正在上一堂免费的瑜伽课,过去加入他们吧!

(雪莉练完瑜伽回来找教练。)

**教练**:怎么样?

**雪莉**:开始的时候一切都很好。但是音乐让我感觉昏昏欲睡。后来有好几分钟我都在打瞌睡。

Act **5**

运动场景 · Sports

### 生词小结

| | | | | |
|---|---|---|---|---|
| **pump** | *vi.* 激发 | **master** | *vt.* 掌握 |
| **option** | *n.* 选择 | **join** | *vt.* 加入 |
| **relaxation** | *n.* 放松 | **drowsy** | *adj.* 昏昏欲睡的 |
| **perseverance** | *n.* 毅力 | **doze off** | 打瞌睡 |

## G语法小结
### rammer —— 动词不定式作主语、宾语

动词不定式一般由"*to* + 动词原形"构成。"*to*"仅为符号，无实义，个别情况下可省略。

1. 动词不定式作主语

(1)动词不定式作主语,看作单数第三人称,它的谓语应用单数第三人称

*To do more exercise is good for health.* 多做运动对身体有益。

*To see is to believe.* 眼见为实。

(2)"疑问词 + 动词不定式"作主语

*How to use computer is a question.* 如何使用电脑是个问题。

*What to do in holiday is a question.* 在假期做什么是个问题。

2. 作宾语

(1)带 *to* 的不定式直接作动词的宾语

*They failed to meet each other.* 他们没看见对方。

*I want to be an English teacher.* 我想当个英语老师。

(2)不定式和疑问词一起作宾语( what、where、when、who、whom、which、whether、how 等)

*I don't know how to get there.* 我不知道怎么去那里。

*She asked what to do next.* 她问接下来做什么。

## D家庭总动员
### o it together

**两人一组,一方朗诵下面的中文句子,另一方挑选出合适的翻译。**

1. 如何才能见到我的私人教练是个问题。
2. 开始运动量过大不适合身体健康。
3. 他不知道怎样介绍自己。
4. 想出这种办法不容易。
5. 雪莉不知道怎样保持好的身材。

1. How to meet my personal trainer is a problem.
2. To come up with these thoughts is not easy.
3. He doesn't know how to introduce himself.
4. Shirley doesn't know how to keep a nice figure.
5. To start with too much work-out is bad for health.

**R**ecitation  经典背诵

**Trainer**：I'm a personal trainer in a gym. My job is to help people achieve their fitness levels and goals. Everything would be exciting at the beginning when it starts but it calls for great perseverance to hold on to it. But they can do it if they try. And the biggest reward for me is to see my customers look good.

# 奥运体育馆 Olympic Stadium

## Goals

**在这个场景中，我们将学到：**

1. 动词过去式变化的读音
2. 竞技类体育项目的词汇
3. 询问和给予信息的句型
4. 动词不定式作定语、状语、表语

**Topic 1** 奥运场馆
Olympic Stadium

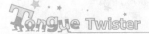 **玩转语音**

1. Round and round the rugged rock the ragged rascal ran.
2. Peter Piper picked a peck of pickled peppers. A peck of pickled peppers Peter Piper picked.
3. If Peter Piper picked a peck of pickled peppers, where's the peck of pickled peppers Peter Piper picked?

及格时间：10 秒
你的纪录：——秒

及格时间：20 秒
你的纪录：——秒

及格时间：20 秒
你的纪录：——秒

导游带领阿美在参观奥运公园。奥运公园大极了，非常壮观！一起来看看吧！

**May：** This Olympic park is so big!

**Guide：** Yes. Now we are in the Olympic stadium, the center of this park.

**May：** Splendid! When is it gonna be finished?

**Guide：** The whole stadium is to be finished this June.

**May：** How many seats are there in the stand?

**Guide：** Oh, there are 5000 seats in total.

**May：** I didn't know it would be so big!

**Guide：** It is! Look there, those are the tracks. And the jumping pit is over there.

**May：** Ah … I see. Hey, look the sign here：

**阿美：**这个奥运公园可真大啊！

**导游：**是啊，我们现在在奥运体育场，公园的中心。

**阿美：**真壮观！它什么时候能完工？

**导游：**整个体育场将在这个 6 月完成。

**阿美：**看台上有多少个座位？

**导游：**哦，一共有 5000 个。

**阿美：**我以前不知道它竟有这么大！

**导游：**是很大！看那儿，那是跑道，远一点那边是沙坑。

**阿美：**啊……我看到了。嘿，看这块标

"No climbing".

**Guide**：We put many signs with English translations for foreign visitors.

**May**：Does it mean not to climb over the railings?

**Guide**：Yes. But my little daughter once got across it without climbing.

**May**：Oh? How did she do that?

**Guide**：She crawled under it.

识："禁止攀爬"。

**导游**：我们为外国观光者设置了很多带有英语翻译的标识。

**阿美**：它是不是说禁止攀爬栏杆呢?

**导游**：是啊。但是我的小女儿有一次没有攀爬就过去了。

**阿美**：哦? 她怎么办到的呢?

**导游**：她是从下面爬过去的。

---

**生词小结**

**stadium**　*n.* 体育场
**center**　*n.* 中心
**stand**　*n.* 看台
**pit**　*n.* 坑

**translation**　*n.* 翻译
**crawl**　*vi.* 爬
**across**　*prep.* 横越,穿过

---

# P語音小结
ronunciation —— 动词过去式变化的读音

规则动词过去式的读音规则-(e)d

**1.** 在清辅音后面,读/t/ finished　jumped　watched　knocked

**2.** 在元音或浊辅音后面,读/d/ crawled　saved　spoiled　played

**3.** 在/t/和/d/后面,读/id/ seated　holded　fainted　repeated

　　不规则动词过去式的变化与动词原型区别挺大,读音变化也大,具体单词还得具体查找读音。

**朗读练习**：hoped　hopped　mixed　missed　finished　banished　played　layed　loved　moved　tried　flied

# R ecitation
经典背诵

**May**：The Olympic park is to be completed this June. The Olympic Stadium is the center of the park. It is so big. It holds about 5000 seats in the stand in total. For foreign visitors, they put up many signs with English translations. Everything is getting ready for the 2008 Olympics!

# 奥运项目
## Olympic Sports

阿美在导游的指引下，一一参观了跳高、跳远、撑竿跳、铁饼等项目的比赛场地。她还看到了一幢设计很特别的建筑物。那到底是什么建筑呢？

**Guide:** Look there, the long jump is going to be held there.

**May:** Ah…I see. What other sport events are held there?

**Guide:** Oh, many. The high jump, the long jump, the pole vault, the discus competition, etc.

**May:** Is the soccer game held in this stadium?

**Guide:** I'm not sure. I'll just have to find it out.

**May:** That building's design is quite special. Hey, what's that?

**Guide:** Oh, That's the indoor gymnasium. Basketball games, badminton games, table tennis…are going to be held there.

**May:** How about gymnastics? Is it held there too?

**Guide:** Hmm let me think for a moment.

**May:** Gymnatstics is my favourite. I love watching gymnastics!

**Guide:** Sorry, I don't really know. Probably it is not held in this stadium.

**May:** Anyway, thanks.

**Guide:** Maybe you can find it out later on line.

**May:** Good idea.

**导游：** 看那边，跳远要在那边举行。

**阿美：** 阿……我看到了。还有什么其他的项目要在那边举行？

**导游：** 哦，很多。跳高、跳远、撑竿跳、铁饼，等等。

**阿美：** 足球赛也是在这个体育场举行的吗？

**导游：** 我不太清楚。我得查一下。

**阿美：** 那个建筑的设计很特别。嘿，那是什么？

**导游：** 哦，那是室内体育馆。篮球、羽毛球、乒乓球……都要在那里举行。

**阿美：** 那体操呢？也在那里举行吗？

**导游：** 恩，我想想。

**阿美：** 我最喜欢体操了。我最爱看体操比赛。

**导游：** 对不起，我真的不知道。也许它不在这儿举行。

**阿美：** 不管怎么样，都谢谢你。

**导游：** 或许你可以在网上找到答案。

**阿美：** 好主意。

運動場景 · Sports

| | | | |
|---|---|---|---|
| pole vault | 撑竿跳 | gymnasium | *n.* 体育馆 |
| discus | *n.* 铁饼 | gymnastics | *n.* 体操 |
| design | *n.* 设计 | | |

## 单词扩展 Vocabulary Builder

### 竞技类体育项目的词汇

| 基础词汇 | 提高词汇 |
|---|---|
| swimming 游泳 | shooting 射击 |
| diving 跳水 | fencing 击剑 |
| volleyball 排球 | sailing 帆船 |
| track 径赛 | weight lifting 举重 |
| triple jump 三级跳 | wrestling 摔跤 |
| discus 铁饼 | freestyle 自由泳 |
| walk 竞走 | gymnastics 体操 |
| hockey 曲棍球 | team events 团体赛 |

## D 家庭总动员
### o it together

两人一组，一方随机大声读出上面词汇的英文和中文，另一方用该词汇填入下面的句子，大声朗读并表演出来，并用中文给出一个理由。

I love watching (　　　　　　　　　　　).

【例】家长读 gymnastics 体操
孩子读 I love watching gymnastics. 因为我最喜欢霍尔金娜！

### Recitation 经典背诵

Guide：There are many sport events to be held in this Olympic stadium. The high jump, the long jump, the pole vault, the discus competition, etc. In the indoor gymnasium, basketball games, badminton games, table tennis…are going to be held. For gymnastics? Though, it's my favorite, I don't know where it's gonna be held.

# Topic 3 指引外宾
## Guiding Foreigners

阿美和导游碰到了正在参观奥运体育场的泰瑞。他们便一起往室内体育馆走去。
泰瑞惊讶于体育馆之大,我们一起来看看具体的情况吧!

**Terry**：Excuse me. Could you tell me where the swimming pool is?

**Guide**：It's in the indoor gymnasium. We are on the way there too. You can come along with us.

**Terry**：Thanks. This Olympic stadium is gorgeous!

**Guide**：It is not finished yet.

**Terry**：Could you tell me how big it is?

**Guide**：Sorry, I don't really know.

**Terry**：I suppose it can hold three air-buses.

**Guide**：Three buses? No, far more than that.

**Terry**：Air-bus jets! Not bus!

**Guide**：Oh, gotcha!

**Terry**：Hey, your English is amazing!

**Guide**：I'm a guide. I'll probably lose my job if my English is poor.

**Terry**：I see. Nice job!

**泰瑞**：对不起,能不能告诉我游泳池在哪里?

**导游**：在室内体育馆。我们正要去那儿,你可以跟我们一起。

**泰瑞**：谢谢。这个奥运体育场真是太壮观了!

**导游**：它还没完工呢。

**泰瑞**：你能告诉我它有多大吗?

**导游**：对不起,我不知道。

**泰瑞**：我猜它能容纳下三辆空中客车。

**导游**：三辆客车? 不,远不止那些。

**泰瑞**：空中客车飞机,不是巴士!

**导游**：哦,知道了!

**泰瑞**：你的英语很不错!

**导游**：我是导游,所以如果我英语不好的话就有可能失去我的工作。

**泰瑞**：我明白了。你很棒!

---

**生词小结**

**pool** *n.* 池子

**gorgeous** *adj.* 壮观的,雄伟的

**jet** *n.* 飞机

# F功能性句型扩展 —— 询问和给予信息的句型
unctional structure

**请朗读以下句型，家长和孩子交替进行**

## 1. 询问信息

Excuse me, could you tell me... 对不起，能不能告诉我……

Would you mind telling me... 您能不能告诉我……

Could you give me some information about... 您能不能提供点关于……的信息？

Excuse me, I'd like to know... 对不起，我想知道……

I wonder if you could tell me... 您能否告诉我……

## 2. 给予信息

Yes, of course. 是的，当然啦。

I'm sorry, I don't know. 对不起，我不知道。

I'm afraid I don't really know. 恐怕我不是很清楚。

I'm not sure, I'll just have to find out... 我不敢肯定，我得查一下。

Umm, let me think for a moment... 恩，让我想想。

## 3. 没听清

Pardon? 什么？

I beg your pardon? 请您再说一遍？

Could you say that again? 您能再说一遍吗？

Sorry, I didn't catch you. 对不起，我没听清。

What was that again? 您刚刚说什么？

**Recitation** 经典背诵

**Terry**: The Olympic stadium is gorgeous! I suppose it's big enough for three air-bus jets. The swimming pool is in the indoor gymnasium. There are three swimming pools in total. But they are not completed yet. How big is the swimming pool? I don't really know.

# Topic4 奥运文化
## Olympic Culture

听 学 看

泰瑞碰巧是 2000 年悉尼奥运会的志愿者。阿美和他立刻找到了共同语言。来看看两个人都在聊些什么吧！

**Terry**: Olympics again! Been four years.

**May**: Yes. But there are also winter Olympics, two years after the summer Olympics.

**Terry**: I was a volunteer for 2000 Sydney Olympic Games. I came here just for the sentiment of it.

**May**: Oh? You are from Australia?

**Terry**: Yes. I am from Sydney.

**May**: The next Olympics is to be held in England. Are you gonna go there too?

**Terry**: Of course, I have plans to participate in the Marathon.

**May**: That's great! In fact, I want to be a volunteer for the Beijing Olympic Games, too.

**Terry**: Really? Great! Do you know where the Olympics is originated from?

**May**: Of course! It's from Greece.

**Terry**: You are clever! When I was a volunteer, I didn't know that.

**May**: What did you say if people asked you that?

**Terry**: Just told them the truth.

**May**: Truth?

**Terry**: The truth is that I didn't know.

泰瑞：奥运会又来了啊！4 年了。

阿美：是啊。但是还有冬奥会啊，在夏季奥运会两年后。

泰瑞：我是 2000 年悉尼奥运会的志愿者。我到这儿来是为了重温当年。

阿美：哦？你是从澳大利亚来的？

泰瑞：是啊。我来自悉尼。

阿美：下届奥运会在英国举行。你也去吗？

泰瑞：当然啦，我还打算参加马拉松呢！

阿美：太棒了！事实上，我也打算在北京奥运会做一名志愿者。

泰瑞：真的吗？太好了！你知道奥运会的发源地在哪儿吗？

阿美：当然啦！它起源于希腊。

泰瑞：你真聪明。我是志愿者时，我还不知道呢。

阿美：那人们问你时你怎么说呢？

泰瑞：就告诉他们事实。

阿美：事实？

泰瑞：事实就是我不知道。

生词小结

**Sydney** *n.* 悉尼
**sentiment** *n.* 感情
**Australia** *n.* 澳大利亚
**participate** *vi.* 参加

**Marathon** *n.* 马拉松
**originate** *vi.* 起源
**Greece** *n.* 希腊

## 运动场景 · Sports

### Grammer 语法小结 —— 动词不定式作定语、状语、表语

1. 动词不定式作定语。不定式常可用于修饰人，也可以用来修饰物，或跟在不定式后作定语

   *May is the first student to arrive.* 阿美是第一个到的学生。

   *I have a lot of things to do today.* 今天我有很多事情要做。

   *Would you like something to drink?* 你想喝点什么？

   *It's time to go to bed.* 该睡觉了。

2. 动词不定式作状语。不定式作状语的情况很多，主要有 be + 形容词 + 不定式

   *She was eager to see her friends.* 她急于见她的朋友们。

   *I am afraid to tell her.* 我很怕告诉她。

   *I am not ready to go back.* 我还不准备回去。

3. 动词不定式作表语，不定式位于系动词如 be 之后用来说明主语的身份、特征、属性或状态

   *Her ambition was to be a star.* 她的志向是当明星。

   *My task is to take care of my little brother.* 我的任务是照顾弟弟。

### Do it together 家庭总动员

两人一组，一方朗诵下面的中文句子，另一方挑选出合适的翻译。

1. 阿美总是第一个到奥运体育场的学生。
2. 为了 2008 年奥运会，我们还有很多事情要做。
3. 阿美的梦想是做一名志愿者。
4. 该到体育馆看体操了。
5. 我怕输掉这场比赛。

1. May's dream is to be a volunteer.
2. I am afraid to lose the competition.
3. It's time to go to the gymnasium to watch gymnastics.
4. May is always the first student to arrive at the Olympic Stadium.
5. We have a lot of things to do for Beijing 2008 Olympic Games.

### Recitation 经典背诵

**May：**Olympics is held every four years. But winter Olympics is two years after each summer Olympics. The Olympics is originated in Greece. Marathon is originated in Greece too. I want to be a volunteer for the Beijing Olympic Games. So exciting!

# Act 6

# 公共服务场所
# Public Service

# Act 6

公共服务场所 · Public Service

**SCENE 30**

# 居委会 Neighborhood Committee

## Goals

**在这个场景中，我们将学到：**

1. 连读（一）
2. 民俗活动的词汇
3. 询问信息练习
4. 现在分词做定语、表语

## Topic 1 遛鸟 Pet Bird

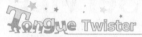

### 玩转语音 (Tongue Twister)

1. And they scuffled and huffled and muffled and puffled and muffled and buffled duffled and fuffled and guffled and bruffled.
2. Sounding by sound is a sound method of sounding sounds.

及格时间：13 秒
你的纪录：—— 秒

及格时间：6 秒
你的纪录：—— 秒

社区里的老爷爷克劳斯早上出来遛鸟，碰到了在晨读的阿美，又会有什么好玩的事情发生呢？一起来看吧！

**Klas：** Good morning, May. Good girl, you are reading English books again.

**May：** Good morning. There is no reason to miss so beautiful a morning.
Is that a new bird?

**Klas：** Oh, yes, my daughter bought it yesterday. We call her Lulu.

**May：** It looks so cute. Is it a parrot?

**Klas：** Yes. Just look at her colorful feathers. What else can it be?

**May：** I see. It's interesting that there is also a parrot in my English book. His name is Polly.

**克劳斯：** 阿美，早上好。真是好孩子，又在读英语了！

**阿美：** 早上好。没有理由错过这么美丽的早晨。
那是只新鸟吗？

**克劳斯：** 哦，是的，我女儿昨天给我买的。我们叫它鲁鲁。

**阿美：** 它看起来真可爱。它是只鹦鹉吗？

**克劳斯：** 是的。你看它多彩的羽毛，还能是别的什么鸟吗？

**阿美：** 知道了。真有趣，我的英语书里也有一只鹦鹉。它的名字是波利。

**Klas**：Really? A foreign parrot!

**May**：He can speak English, too.

**Klas**：Maybe you can teach Lulu some English words.

**May**：Lulu. Lulu. Say "hello". "hello". Oh, she is so smart. Good bird.

**Klas**：You are a good teacher. Okay, I am gonna play some chess now. Just go back to your book.

**Lulu**：Hello. Hello. Hello.

**Klas**：Haha. After all, she is just a bird.

**克劳斯**：真的吗？一只外国鹦鹉！

**阿美**：它也会说英语哦。

**克劳斯**：也许你可以教鲁鲁几个英语单词啊。

**阿美**：鲁鲁,鲁鲁,说"哈喽""哈喽"。哦,它真聪明。真是只好鸟。

**克劳斯**：你是个好老师。好了,我要去下象棋了。你继续读书吧。

**鲁鲁**："哈喽""哈喽""哈喽"。

**克劳斯**：哈哈,它毕竟只是一只鸟啊。

---

### 生词小结

| | | | | |
|---|---|---|---|---|
| **reason** | *n.* 理由 | | **after all** | 毕竟 |
| **parrot** | *n.* 鹦鹉 | | **chess** | *n.* 象棋 |
| **feather** | *n.* 羽毛 | | | |

---

## **P**ronunciation 语音小结 ——连读（一）

**1.** 辅音 + 元音连读

前一个字以辅音结尾,后一词以元音开头：bought it; look at; put it off; speak English

**朗读练习**：put it off and take it off; not at all and good afternoon

**2.** r 音节的连读

如果单词 r 或 re 结尾,r 一般不发音,但当后面又一个元音开头的单词时,r 要发音,并与后面的单词元音连读：after all; answer it; cheer up; for ever

**朗读练习**：after all and answer it; cheer up and for ever

　　—Can I take your order?

　　—Yes, a bottle of beer please!

　　—You have a good taste! The beer is good.

　　—Thanks, please be quick as soon as possible.

　　—OK, wait a minute!

**R**ecitation 经典背诵

**Klas**：I like birds especially the parrot which is really cute and smart. My daughter just got me a parrot days ago. We call her Lulu. Lulu is so smart that she can even say some English words. The only problem is that Lulu can't find the right time to say these words, but it also brings us a lot of fun.

## 扭秧歌
### Yangge Dance

为了参加政府举办的风俗文化节,雪莉和好朋友简商量着社区该出个什么样的传统表演节目,一起来看看吧!

**Jane:** The government is going to organize a folk-custom activity at the end of the month. And our community is supposed to put on a performance.

**Shirley:** What kind of performance? A lion dance?

**Jane:** Stuff like that but I think the lion dance is a bit too difficult and dangerous.

**Shirley:** Sure, you'll be dancing with lions. What do you expect? Then what about Yangge Dance which we did before.

**Jane:** Good idea. Shall we get everyone in the community?

**Shirley:** Maybe not. I think we should just focus on the retired people.

**Jane:** I know that they already have a Yangge Dance team and then what we need is just to do some rehearsals.

**Shirley:** What about the costumes?

**Jane:** We can raise money in the community. You know each family 10 yuan maybe.

**Shirley:** Try something new. We can find a supporting agency.

**Jane:** Great idea. There is a travel agency nearby who would love to be our sponsor. It's a perfect chance for them to promote ethnic tourism.

**Shirley:** Let's go for it.

**Jane:** Maybe we should take part in the Yangge

简:政府要在这个月底举办民俗活动,要求我们社区出一个表演节目。

雪莉:什么样的表演? 舞狮行吗?

简:像(舞狮)那样的,但是我觉得舞狮有点难而且也很危险。

雪莉:当然,你要和狮子一起跳舞,能期待什么啊? 那么扭秧歌怎样,我们以前跳过的。

简:好主意。我们要动员社区每个人参加吗?

雪莉:可能不行。我觉得我们应该把对象设定为退休人员。

简:我知道他们已经有一支秧歌队了,那我们只要做一些彩排就可以了。

雪莉:服装怎么办?

简:我们可以在社区里集资啊。每家集资10元。

雪莉:我们用点新办法吧。我们可以找一个赞助商。

简:好主意。这附近有一个旅行社,他们一定会乐意赞助我们的。对他们而言,这是推销民俗旅游的好机会。

雪莉:让我们放手去做吧。

简:也许我们也可以参加扭秧歌。这是

Dance too. Good exercise to lose weight.

Shirley：Oh, my work-out card is about to expire.

Jane：Good timing.

很好的减肥运动。

**雪莉**：是哦,我的健身卡也快到期了。

**简**：真凑巧啊。

| 生词小结 | |
| --- | --- |

**government** *n.* 政府

**organize** *vt.* 组织

**focus** *vi.* 集中

**retire** *vi.* 退休

**rehearsal** *n.* 彩排

**supporting agency** 赞助单位

**ethnic tourism** 民俗旅游

**expire** *vi.* 期满

| 注释 | |
| --- | --- |

**Sure, you'll be dancing with lions. What do you expect?** 雪莉当然知道舞狮其实并没有真正的狮子,她是故意开玩笑说:要和狮子跳舞,你能指望什么啊? 意思其实是同意简说的舞狮跳起来难度比较大,有受伤的危险。

## 单词扩展 Vocabulary Builder

### 民俗活动的词汇

| 基础词汇 | 提高词汇 |
| --- | --- |
| paper cut 剪纸 | acrobatics 杂技 |
| cross-talk 相声 | puppet show 木偶戏 |
| cock-fighting 斗鸡 | clay sculpture 泥塑 |
| couplet 对联 | riddle solving 猜灯谜 |
| kite flying 放风筝 | dragon boat rowing 赛龙舟 |
| shadow shoe 皮影戏 | embroidery 刺绣 |
| firework display 放烟火 | pay New Year call 拜年 |
| monkey tricks 耍猴戏 | cricket fighting 斗蟋蟀 |

## D 家庭总动员
o it together

两人一组,一方随机大声读出上面词汇的英文和中文,另一方用该词汇填入下面的句子,大声朗读并表演出来,并用中文给出一个理由

### What about ( )?

【例】家长读 paper cut 剪纸

孩子读 What about paper cut? 我觉得很好玩。

**Recitation**
经典背诵

Jane：I like Yangge Dance. We have a Yangge Dance team in our community. Most of us are retired. We have put on many performances in some folk activities. Now a travel agency's agreed to be our sponsor. So I think it won't be long before we have beautiful costumes. How exciting!

 照顾老人
## Caring for the Old

丹尼尔今天放学回家特别早,看到妈妈正在做饭,觉得奇怪,因为平时妈妈做饭可没有那么早。这到底是怎么回事呢?

**Daniel**: Mom, I'm starving.

**Shirley**: Here are some biscuits. Why are you back so early today?

**Daniel**: My teacher had a sudden stomachache, so the class was cut short. You?

**Shirley**: Me what?

**Daniel**: You are cooking at least two hours earlier than the usual.

**Shirley**: It's not for us.

**Daniel**: Then it's for Dad, isn't it? It's so unfair!

**Shirley**: Don't be a smarty-pants. It's for Grandma Wang.

**Daniel**: What was that again?

**Shirley**: It's for Grandma Wang. She is sick and her only daughter went abroad weeks ago. So she needs our help.

**Daniel**: I'm sorry, I didn't know that. But I wanna help.

**Shirley**: Umm, let me think for a moment. We can meet her together after I finish cooking.

**Daniel**: I'll get knee to knee with her.

**Shirley**: Good boy. I can only imagine how happy she will be to see you.

丹尼尔:妈妈,我饿死了。

雪莉:这有些饼干。你今天怎么回来这么早?

丹尼尔:老师突然胃疼,所以课提前结束了。你呢?

雪莉:我什么?

丹尼尔:你做饭至少比平时早两个小时。

雪莉:不是给我们的。

丹尼尔:你是给爸爸做的吧? 不公平!

雪莉:别自作聪明了。是给王奶奶准备的。

丹尼尔:你再说一遍是什么?(我刚才没有听清楚)

雪莉:这是给王奶奶准备的。她病了,她女儿又在几周前出国了,她需要我们的帮助。

丹尼尔:对不起,我不知道。我也要帮忙。

雪莉:嗯,我想一下(看你要怎么做)。等我做完饭我们可以一起去看望她。

丹尼尔:我要和她好好地坐一起(聊天)。

雪莉:好孩子。我可以想象她见到你一定特别高兴。

## 生词小结

**starving**   *adj.* 饥饿的
**biscuit**   *n.* 饼干
**sudden**   *adj.* 突然的
**stomachache**   *n.* 胃疼
**cut short**   缩短
**at least**   至少
**abroad**   *adv.* 到国外
**together**   *adv.* 一起
**knee**   *n.* 膝盖

## 注释

**Don't be a smarty-pants** 不要当一条自作聪明的裤子。意思是不要自以为是，是英文中的拟人手法。

**I'll get knee to knee with her.** 我要和她膝盖对着膝盖，意思其实是我要和她坐在一起亲密无间地聊天，中文中也有相应的表示，即"促膝长谈"。

## 情景练习
### Scene practice —— 询问信息练习

仔细阅读下面五个场景，两人一组，使用询问和给予信息的句型(见 236 页)，用一用，练一练。

1. Tom can't follow his English teacher very well, he wants the teacher to repeat the language point again, if you were Tom, what would you say to your teacher?
2. May wants to know more details about the book, if you were May, what will you say to the librarian?
3. Shirley asked May to buy some food, but May didn't catch her mother, if you were May, what would you say to your mother?
4. If you were Daniel, you don't understand you father, what will you say to him?
5. Mom told a story about an ancient hero which was really exciting. Daniel wants to listen to the story again. If you were Daniel, what would you say to your mom?

### Recitation 经典背诵

Daniel：I am starving each time I come back home after school. My Mom would always give me some bland biscuits to deal with it. I think if it was Daddy she would probably cook for him which is really unfair. So maybe I'd better learn how to cook for myself, or get a wife.

# Topic 4 二手房
## Second-hand Houses

雷弗是雪莉的侄子,快大学毕业了,已经决定留京工作,他打算买一个二手的套房,这不,他找精明的雪莉商量来了。

**Leif:** Aunt Shirley, it's being years since we last met. How were you doing in the passing years?

**Shirley:** Pretty well. What about you?

**Leif:** Fine. Where are the other guys?

**Shirley:** It's a bit disappointing that they are all out for a movie.

**Leif:** Bad timing. I want to see them so much. How are they?

**Shirley:** Not bad. I heard you are going to graduate this coming summer, right?

**Leif:** Yes, that's why I'm here. I'm thinking about buying a second-hand apartment.

**Shirley:** Did you go to a real estate agent?

**Leif:** No, that will be too expensive.

**Shirley:** That's true. By the way, what kind of apartment are you looking for?

**Leif:** My first job's salary will be a bit low. So the cheaper the better. Just one I can afford.

**Shirley:** Sure. I'll try my best to find a satisfying one for you.

**Leif:** I'll appreciate it so much.

**雷弗:** 雪莉阿姨,好多年没有见了。这些年您怎么样?

**雪莉:** 挺好的。你呢?

**雷弗:** 还可以。其他人呢?

**雪莉:** 真可惜他们都出去看电影去了。

**雷弗:** 真不巧。我真想见他们。他们都好吗?

**雪莉:** 都不错。我听说这个夏天你就要毕业了,是吗?

**雷弗:** 是的,这就是我为什么今天来这儿的原因。我在考虑买一个二手套间。

**雪莉:** 你有去找过房产中介吗?

**雷弗:** 没有,那样会很贵。

**雪莉:** 这倒是。顺便问一下,你想要什么样的套间呢?

**雷弗:** 我的第一份工作的薪水会有点低,所以越便宜越好。要一个我能负担得起的。

**雪莉:** 那是。我会尽量帮你找一套让你满意的。

**雷弗:** 那太感激了。

---

**生词小结**

**passing** *adj.* 经过的,越过的
**disappointing** *adj.* 令人失望的
**timing** *n.* 时间的掌握
**graduate** *vi.* 毕业
**coming** *adj.* 即将到来的

**second-hand** *adj.* 二手的
**apartment** *n.* 公寓房间
**salary** *n.* 薪水
**satisfying** *adj.* 令人满意的

## **G**rammer 语法小结 —— 现在分词作定语、表语

1. 现在分词作定语

（1）现在分词作定语时表示该动作正在进行，单个现在分词作定语通常放在被修饰词的前面

*The rising sun looks very beautiful.* 冉冉升起的太阳看着很美。

*This is an exciting news.* 这是个激动人心的消息。

（2）若被修饰词与现在分词是被动关系时，须用现在分词的被动式（being done）作定语

*The song being broadcast is very popular with the young.* 正在播放的歌曲深受年轻人的欢迎。

2. 现在分词作表语

（1）现在分词做表语常是一些表示情绪、心理的词，如 excite，interest 等，他们的现在分词形式可以表示"令人激动的"，"令人感兴趣的"等。若表示人对……感兴趣，就是 somebody is interested in…，若人或物本身有趣时，就是说 sb./sth. is interesting

*interesting* 使人感到高兴

*exciting* 令人激动的

*delighting* 令人高兴的

*disappointing* 令人失望的

*encouraging* 令人鼓舞的

*pleasing* 令人愉快的

*satisfying* 令人满意的

*surprising* 令人惊异的

*worrying* 令人担心的

（2）现在分词做表语表示主语的性质、特征，这时通常可以看作形容词，可以用 very，so 或 much 等修饰

*The news that your team had been beaten in the match was very surprising.*

你们队在比赛中被打败的消息让人感到很意外。

*The sound I heard last night was so frightening.* 我昨晚听到的声音令人恐怖。

*If the book is very interesting, I will buy it.* 如果这本书真的很有趣，我会买它。

## **D**o it together 家庭总动员

两人一组，一方朗诵下面的中文句子，另一方挑选出合适的翻译。

1. 我可以帮你找一套令人满意的房子。

2. 他告诉了大家一个令人激动的消息。

3. 这本书很有趣，你不能错过它。

4. 他是个很有意思的人，每个人都喜欢他。

5. 很遗憾你不能参加秧歌队。

1. He is a very interesting person, and everybody likes him.

2. The book is very interesting, and you can't miss it.

3. It's so disappointing that you can not join Yangge Dance.

4. He tells us an exciting news.

5. I can help you to find a satisfying apartment.

**Leif**：I'm a senior college student in Beijing. It's expensive to live in this city. My graduation is coming soon so it would cost me even more for accommodations and also I plan to buy a second-hand apartment here. But luckily, my aunt Shirley said she would help me to look for a satisfying one for me. I really appreciate it.

# 医院 Hospital

## Goals

在这个场景中,我们将学到:

1. 连读(二)
2. 医院各个部门的词汇
3. 表达确定与否的句型
4. 现在分词做状语

**Topic 1** 咨询 **Consultation**

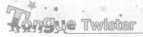 **Tongue Twister** 玩转语音

1. Near an ear, a nearer ear, a nearly eerie ear. Each Easter Eddie eats eighty Easter eggs.
2. One black beetle bled only black blood, the other black beetle bled blue.
3. A skunk sat on a stump and thunk the stump stunk, but the stump thunk the skunk stunk.

| 及格时间: 20秒 |
| 你的纪录: ——秒 |
| 及格时间: 15秒 |
| 你的纪录: ——秒 |
| 及格时间: 20秒 |
| 你的纪录: ——秒 |

听 学 看

丹尼尔身体不舒服,第一次自己去看医生。却不知道要先挂号,还居然跑到妇产科去了,结果怎么样呢,一起往下看吧!

**Daniel:** Excuse me, doc. I am not feeling well. Can you help me?

**Doctor 1:** Yes, but not here. Have you got registered yet?

**Daniel:** No, I haven't. Where do I go for that?

**Doctor 1:** The registration office. Did you bring your records with you?

**Daniel:** Yes.

**Doctor 1:** Is anybody here with you? Parents, or siblings?

**Daniel:** No, I'm here all by myself.

**Doctor 1:** You are a brave kid. Go ahead to the

**丹尼尔:** 对不起,医生。我有点不舒服。您能帮我吗?

**医生1:** 可以啊,但不是在这儿。你挂号了吗?

**丹尼尔:** 不,还没。我在哪儿挂号?

**医生1:** 在挂号处。你带了你的病历吗?

**丹尼尔:** 带了。

**医生1:** 有谁陪你一起来吗? 爸妈,还是兄弟姐妹?

**丹尼尔:** 没有,我一个人来的。

**医生1:** 你是个勇敢的孩子。先到挂号

registration office first, then to the doctors.

Daniel：But I don't know where the registration office is.

Doctor 1：It's in the hall on the first floor.

Daniel：Do I have to come back here after getting registered?

Doctor 1：No, kid. This is the gynecology department.

Daniel：Gynecology?

Doctor 1：Yeah, It's only for girls.

处,再到医生那儿。

丹尼尔:但我不知道挂号处在哪儿啊。

医生1:在一楼大厅。

丹尼尔:我挂完了号来您这儿吗?

医生1:不,孩子。这儿是妇科。

丹尼尔:妇科?

医生1:是啊,女孩子来的地方。

---

**生词小结**

| | | | |
|---|---|---|---|
| **register** | *vi.* 注册,挂号 | **gynecology** | *adj.* 妇科的 |
| **sibling** | *n.* 兄弟姐妹 | **department** | *n.* 部门 |

---

# **P**ronunciation 语音小结 —— 连读(二)

**1.** 元音 + 元音连读

为了说话流畅,词末尾元音与词首元音连读,不停顿,如:

three hours    the end    the accident    go on    hurry up

**2.** 辅音 + 辅音连读

当两个词首尾有两个或两个以上的辅音时,为使说话流畅,可以将这些辅音连在一起读,而不停顿。如:

help yourself    a good cheese    you look sad    I'm sorry to hear the bad news.

读下面的短文,注意连读的地方:

Mary is a beautiful girl. But she seems quite shy. She lives in a two-bedroom flat with her parents. She hopes to find a good job after graduation. And at the end of this semester, she got the first place in her class, and her parents couldn't help smiling.

**R**ecitation 经典背诵    .    Daniel：When I'm sick I go to see the doctor all by myself because my parents are busy. And also I think that's the thing that a big boy like me should do. The problem is sometimes I can't find the registration office. Luckily, there is always someone to tell me where to go.

# Topic 2 挂号
### Registration

丹尼尔找到了挂号处,却不知道要挂哪一科的号。说了自己的一大堆症状,又头疼,又喉咙痛,来看看医生说该挂哪一科吧!

**Daniel:** Is this the registration office?

**Doctor 2:** Yes, it is. Which department for?

**Daniel:** I don't know exactly.

**Doctor 2:** What's your problem then?

**Daniel:** I've got a sore throat, a runny nose, and a headache.

**Doctor 2:** OK, I will register you with medical department.

**Daniel:** Medical department? Are you sure?

**Doctor 2:** Yes. Just go there!

**Daniel:** Where is it?

**Doctor 2:** It's on the second floor. Have you got your records?

**Daniel:** Yes. Here you are.

**Doctor 2:** OK, here is your registration card.

**Daniel:** Thank you.

**丹尼尔:** 这儿是挂号处吗?

**医生2:** 是啊,你要看哪一科?

**丹尼尔:** 我其实也不知道。

**医生2:** 你哪儿不舒服?

**丹尼尔:** 我喉咙痛,流鼻涕,头疼。

**医生2:** 好的,我帮你挂内科。

**丹尼尔:** 内科? 你确定吗?

**医生2:** 是的。你去就可以了。

**丹尼尔:** 它在哪儿呢?

**医生2:** 在二楼。你带了你的病历了吗?

**丹尼尔:** 带了。这就是。

**医生2:** 好的,这是你的就诊单。

**丹尼尔:** 谢谢。

---

### 生词小结

**exactly** *adv.* 精确地
**throat** *n.* 喉咙
**nose** *n.* 鼻子

**running nose** 流鼻涕不止
**ear** *n.* 耳朵
**headache** *n.* 头疼

## 单词扩展 Vocabulary Builder

医院各个部门的词汇

| 基础词汇 | 提高词汇 |
| --- | --- |
| dental department 牙科 | medical department 内科 |
| registration office 挂号处 | surgical department 外科 |
| waiting room 候诊室 | general surgery 普通外科 |
| clinic 诊疗所 | orthopedics department 骨科,整形外科 |
| emergency room 急诊室 | consulting room 诊室 |
| X-ray department 放射科 | neurology department 神经科 |
| ward 病房 | |

## D家庭总动员
o it together

两人一组,一方随机大声读出上面词汇的英文和中文,另一方用该词汇填入下面的句子,大声朗读并表演出来,并用中文给出一个理由。

**I will go to the (**                         **).**

【例】家长读 dental department 牙科

孩子读 I will go to the dental department. 因为我牙疼得厉害!

**Recitation**
经典背诵

Daniel:I don't like the registration office. Because the doctors always ask you which department it's for. I always wonder how I should know that? They are the doctors, not me. And also I don't like to show them my records. Can there be a simpler way in the future?

# Topic 3 就诊
## Seeing a Doctor

听 学 读看

　　丹尼尔看医生时，医生说他患了流感，要打针。小孩好像都很怕打针，我们的丹尼尔呢，他也怕吗？往下看就知道了。

**Doctor 3**：What seems to be the problem, kid?

**Daniel**：I've got a sore throat, a runny nose and a headache.

**Doctor 3**：Ah... How long have you been like this?

**Daniel**：I am not very sure. Maybe for three days.

**Doctor 3**：Do you have any stomachache?

**Daniel**：I guess so. It comes and goes.

**Doctor 3**：Open your mouth and say "ah..." God, you are suffering from the swelling of tonsils.

**Daniel**：Is that serious, doctor?

**Doctor 3**：Yes, I am sure that you got the flu. You need a shot.

**Daniel**：Oh, doctor. Do I have to? I am afraid of needles!

**Doctor 3**：Yes, that's for sure. But it is not that bad. It's gonna be all right.

**Daniel**：Oh, doctor, please...

**Doctor 3**：Be brave, young man. Only girls cry when given an injection.

**Daniel**：You are right. I won't cry anymore.

**医生3**：你有什么事吗，孩子？

**丹尼尔**：我喉咙痛，流鼻涕，头疼。

**医生3**：啊……你这个样子多久了？

**丹尼尔**：我不敢肯定。也许三天了吧。

**医生3**：你肚子痛吗？

**丹尼尔**：我猜是的。时有时无。

**医生3**：张开嘴，说"啊……"天哪，扁桃体肿大。

**丹尼尔**：严重吗，医生？

**医生3**：是的。我肯定你是得了流感。你得打一针。

**丹尼尔**：哦，医生。真的要打针吗？我害怕打针！

**医生3**：是啊，肯定的。但是没那么糟糕。就会好起来的。

**丹尼尔**：哦，医生，求您了……

**医生3**：勇敢点，小家伙。只有女孩子打针才会哭。

**丹尼尔**：你说得对，我不会哭了。

生词小结

| | |
|---|---|
| **mouth** *n.* 嘴 | **shot** *n.* 打针 |
| **tonsil** *n.* 扁桃体 | **be scared of** 害怕 |
| **swell** *vi.* 肿大 | **needle** *n.* 针 |
| **flu** *n.* 流感 | **injection** *n.* 注射 |

# F 功能性句型扩展
## unctional structure —— 表达确定和不确定的句型

**请朗读以下句型，家长和孩子交替进行**

1. 确定

    I'm sure that... 我肯定……

    I firmly believe that... 我确信……

    Definitely. 毫无疑问。

    Absolutely. 绝对是。

    There is no doubt about it. 没什么可怀疑的。

2. 不确定

    I doubt it. 我怀疑。

    I am not very sure. 我不是很肯定。

    Maybe... 也许……

    I guess so. 我猜是的。

    Probably. 也许是。

    That's possible. 那有可能。

    It may/can/could be true. 那也许是真的。

**Daniel：**Like all the children, I hate injections. Well, the needles scare me easily. I don't understand why the doctors give patients injections so often. They would always say it's not that bad. Not that bad? Not for them, of course!

## Topic 4 探望
### Paying a Visit

在病房里,汤姆来看丹尼尔。丹尼尔好像病得不轻。汤姆却很羡慕,生病也羡慕?这究竟是怎么回事呢? 一起来看看吧。

**Tom:** How are you feeling?

**Daniel:** Bad. My nose keeps running. And my forehead is burning.

**Tom:** You said you never went to hospital.

**Daniel:** I will get better soon.

**Tom:** The good thing is you don't need to go to school.

**Daniel:** Yeah, I love that, no class, no homework, and no exams.

**Tom:** And your Mom and Dad will buy you anything you ask for.

**Daniel:** Haha, I just got the Ultraman costume. My Dad bought it.

**Tom:** I really envy you, Danny.

**Daniel:** Come on, I got numerous shots for that. You have no idea what I've been through with the needles.

**Tom:** Your sister said you fainted three times during the injection.

**Daniel:** May told you? Oh, May, she's such a tattletale.

**Tom:** No matter what, you are still my hero, Daniel.

**Daniel:** Tom, promise me to keep this a secret, will you?

**Tom:** OK, I promise. You promise you will be well soon?

**Daniel:** Deal.

汤姆:你觉得怎样?

丹尼尔:糟透了。我一直在流鼻涕。我一直在发烧。

汤姆:你说你从来不上医院的。

丹尼尔:我很快就会好的。

汤姆:还好,你不用去上学。

丹尼尔:是啊,我喜欢这点,不用上课,不用写作业,也不用去考试。

汤姆:还有你要什么你爸妈就会给你买什么。

丹尼尔:哈哈,我刚刚得到一件奥特曼的制服。我爸爸给我买的。

汤姆:我真羡慕你,丹丹。

丹尼尔:得了吧,我为这个挨了无数针呢。你都无法想象我怎么熬过来的?

汤姆:听你姐姐说你打针时晕倒了三次。

丹尼尔:阿美告诉你的? 哦,阿美,她真是个多嘴婆。

汤姆:不管怎样,丹尼尔,你仍然是我的英雄。

丹尼尔:汤姆,你发誓替我保守这秘密,行吗?

汤姆:好的,我保证。你保证你快点儿好起来哦?

丹尼尔:行啊!

### 生词小结

| | | | |
|---|---|---|---|
| **forehead** | *n.* 前额 | **faint** | *vi.* 晕倒,昏厥 |
| **exam** | *n.* 考试 | **tattletale** | *n.* 闲谈者 |
| **costume** | *n.* 服装 | **hero** | *n.* 英雄 |

## G 语法小结 —— 现在分词作状语

现在分词作状语非常常用,我们从分词在句子中的位置来看现在分词作何种状语。

**1. 现在分词作时间状语**

一些动词如 *hear*, *see*, *arrive*, *return*, *get to*, *look*, *open*, *close*, *leave*, *turn around*, *walk* 等表示一个极短暂动作的词的现在分词可以表示此动作一发生,谓语动作就紧跟着发生,相当于"一(刚)……就……"。

*Hearing their teacher's voice, the pupils stopped talking at once.*

相当于 *On hearing their teacher's voice, the pupils stopped talking at once.*

相当于 *When they heard their teacher's voice, the pupils stopped talking at once.*

一听到老师的声音,学生们立即停止讲话。

*Looking at the photo, I couldn't help missing my school days.*

一看这些照片,我就情不自禁地想起我的学生时代。

*Hearing the news, they all jumped with joy.* 听到这消息,他们高兴得跳起来了。

**2. 现在分词作原因状语**

*Being a student, she is naturally busy studying.* 因为她是学生,她自然要忙于学习。

*Not knowing her phone number, I couldn't get in touch with her.*

因为不知道她的号码,我没法跟她联系。

**3. 现在分词作伴随状语**

分词短语表示伴随情况是比较常见的,它用来说明动作发生的背景或情况。一般情况下,现在分词所表示的动作与谓语所表示的动作同时发生。

*She was lying in bed crying.* 她躺在床上哭。

*The girls are busy dressing up.* 姑娘们忙着打扮。

*The children ran out of the room, laughing and talking.* 孩子们跑出房间,笑着,说着。

## D 家庭总动员 Do it together

两人一组,一方朗诵下面的中文句子,另一方挑选出合适的翻译。

1. 一听说丹尼尔不舒服,妈妈就着急了。
2. 因为我是医生,我自然要关心病人。
3. 丹尼尔病了在家躺着。
4. 孩子们说着,笑着,走进了教室。
5. 一看到妈妈回来,阿美就关了电视机。

1. Seeing Mom was back, May turned off the television.
2. The children walked into the classroom, laughing and talking.
3. Hearing the news that Daniel was not feeling good, Mom was worried.
4. Daniel was ill lying in bed at home.
5. Being a doctor, I should take care of my patients.

**Recitation** 经典背诵

Daniel: I often go to the hospital, for this or that problem. Now I am in the ward lying on the bed. I've got a runny nose, and my forehead is burning. I fainted three times during the injection. I've been through some terrible experience with the needles. Oh, God, no more injections, please!

## 药店 Pharmacy

### Goals

在这个场景中，我们将学到：

1. 清辅音浊化规律
2. 常见疾病的词汇
3. 确定与否句型练习
4. 过去分词做定语

**Topic 1** 家庭药箱
Medicine-kit

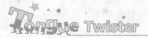 玩转语音

及格时间：7 秒
你的纪录：——秒
及格时间：20秒
你的纪录：——秒

1. The batter with the butter is the batter that is better!
2. Betty bought some butter, but the butter Betty bought was bitter, so Betty bought some better butter, and the better butter Betty bought was better than the bitter butter Betty bought before!

听 学 看

丹尼尔生病了，偏偏爸爸妈妈又加班不能回家，只有阿美帮着照顾，阿美照顾得怎么样呢？我们一起往下看吧！

**May**：Poor Danny. You are so enfeebled!

**Daniel**：Don't worry. No big deal. Just a common cold.

**May**：Mom called just now saying that she and Dad will be back later. Do you want to speak to them on phone?

**Daniel**：No. You can never count on the grown-ups when there is something.

**May**：Whatever. Have a drink of water.

**Daniel**：Come on, sister. This is the seventh glass already.

**May**：Maybe later. I think we have a medicine-kit.

**Daniel**：Do we? Where is it?

**阿美**：可怜的丹丹。你那么虚弱！

**丹尼尔**：别担心。没什么大不了的。只是普通的着凉。

**阿美**：妈妈打电话来说她和爸爸会晚一点回来，你想跟他们打电话吗？

**丹尼尔**：不用了。有事发生的时候你别指望依靠大人。

**阿美**：不管怎样。喝杯水吧。

**丹尼尔**：拜托，姐姐。这已经是第七杯水了。

**阿美**：那晚点（再喝）吧。我想我们有一个药箱。

**丹尼尔**：我们有吗？在哪里？

May：Probably on the top of the cabinet. I'll go and get it.

Daniel：Be careful. Now I have no one but you to depend on.

May：Oh, here it is. Patulin. Oh, no!

Daniel：What's the new strike?

May：Keep lying down. The matter is that all the medicine here is past expiration.

Daniel：Poor me!

阿美：很可能在橱柜上面。我去拿来。

丹尼尔：小心点。我现在只能依靠你了。

阿美：哦，在这里。感冒药。天啊，不会吧？

丹尼尔：又有什么新的灾难？

阿美：躺着，别动。问题是这里所有的药都过期了。

丹尼尔：可怜的我啊！

### 生词小结

| | | | |
|---|---|---|---|
| enfeebled | *adj.* 虚弱的 | Patulin | *n.* 一种感冒药 |
| count on | 指望 | strike | *n.* 打击 |
| medicine-kit | *n.* 药箱 | lie down | 躺下 |
| depend on | 依赖 | expiration | *n.* 期满(尤指合同等的有效期) |

## 语音小结 Pronunciation —— 清辅音浊化规律

清辅音浊化就是清辅音在单词中的发音被浊化。它只是一种现象,而不是一种规律。要想掌握好这一发音现象,只有平时多注意模仿。以下我们着重挑选了几个比较有代表性的发音点。

**1.** s后面的清辅音浊化现象：s + 清辅音 + 元音的结构无论是在单词的最前面还是中间,只要是在重读音节或次重读音节里,一般都读成对应浊辅音。

朗读练习：speak  strike  stay  sky  school

**2.** 在大多数情况下,在美式英语的读音中,t 在词中发 /d/ 的音是一个很明显的发音特征：

朗读练习：later and matter  whatever and sister  better and letter

I guess I better just come out and say it.

You better go to school in time from now on.

You better keep your mouth shut.

I better keep it to myself.

We better follow the advice of the doctor.

☆ **特别提示**：在英语口语中,"I'd better",常会说成"I better",即把原来"had"的"d"省略,同理,"we'd better"简化为"we better"；"you'd better"简化为"you better"

**Recitation** 经典背诵

Daniel：I catch a cold from time to time. And I find that you can never count on the grown-ups when there is some emergency. Instead I choose to depend on my sister May, though sometimes she can't even find our medicine-kit. So maybe it's wise to stay put, then everything would be just fine.

公共服务场所 · Public Service

买药
Buying Medicine

听 学 看

　　家里的药都过期了,没办法阿美只好到药店买药,她买了什么药呢,我们接着往下看!

Doctor：What can I do for you?

May：I need some medicine.

Doctor：For whom?

May：My younger brother. He suffers from a bad cold.

Doctor：What symptoms does he have?

May：Fever and a bad cough.

Doctor：I got it. Don't worry, just a common cold.

May：What kind of medicine does he need?

Doctor：Patulin will do.

May：How many pills for each time?

Doctor：Six per day, and two after each meal.

May：Thank you very much.

Doctor：My pleasure.

医生:有什么需要的吗?

阿美:我需要一些药。

医生:给谁的。

阿美:我弟弟。他着凉了,很难受。

医生:他有什么症状?

阿美:发烧,咳嗽也很厉害。

医生:知道了,别担心,只是普通感冒。

阿美:他需要什么样的药品呢?

医生:感冒药就可以了。

阿美:每次要吃多少粒啊?

医生:一天六粒,每顿饭后两粒。

阿美:非常感谢。

医生:乐意效劳。

生词小结

**suffer** *vi.* 遭受

**symptom** *n.* 症状

**fever** *n.* 发烧

**cough** *n.* 咳嗽

**medicine** *n.* 医药

**pill** *n.* 药丸

**per** *prep.* 每一

**pleasure** *n.* 愉快

## 单词扩展 Vocabulary Builder

### 常见疾病的词汇

| 基础词汇 | 提高词汇 |
|---|---|
| fever 发烧 | diabetes 糖尿病 |
| headache 头疼 | rabies 狂犬病 |
| stomachache 胃疼 | influenza 流感 |
| cancer 癌症 | chronic 慢性病 |
| heart disease 心脏病 | mad cow disease 疯牛病 |
| lung cancer 肺癌 | acute gastritis 急性胃炎 |
| tumor 肿瘤 | cataract 白内障 |
| stroke 中风 | leukemia 白血病 |

## D 家庭总动员
o it together

两人一组，一方随机大声读出上面词汇的英文和中文，另一方用该词汇填入下面的句子，大声朗读并表演出来，并用中文给出一个理由。

**He suffers from (          ).**

【例】家长读 fever 发烧

孩子读 He suffers from fever. 因为他淋雨了。

Recitation
经典背诵

**Doctor:** I'm a doctor, working in a drug store. My job is to give people the right medicine according to the symptoms they have and tell them the right way how to take the medicine. It makes me feel that I'm important, think about it I may possibly save someone's life. So I feel satisfied with my job.

## Topic3 中药
### Chinese Medicine

最近感冒好像很流行,阿美想着买点药预防。但是由于过度担心,阿美竟然把药落在了药店,只好回来拿。

| | |
|---|---|
| **Doctor**：Here you are. You left the medicine here. | 医生:你回来了。你把药落在这里了。 |
| **May**：Sorry. I was too worried. | 阿美:对不起。我刚才太担心了。 |
| **Doctor**：I firmly believe that you love your brother very much. | 医生:我相信你一定很爱你的弟弟。 |
| **May**：Absolutely. By the way, do you sell any traditional Chinese medicine? | 阿美:当然了。顺便问一下,你们卖中药吗? |
| **Doctor**：Yes, we have some Chinese medicine for common cold. | 医生:是的,我们有治疗普通感冒的中药。 |
| **May**：I heard Chinese medicine has a better lasting effect in cure. | 阿美:我听说中药的治疗效果更持久。 |
| **Doctor**：It depends. It's true that you can take some for prevention. | 医生:要看情况。不过你可以买一些做预防(感冒)。 |
| **May**：Sure. Prevention is better than cure. | 阿美:好的。预防总比治疗强。 |
| **Doctor**：There is no doubt about it. | 医生:那是毫无疑问的。 |
| **May**：What do you recommend? | 阿美:你有什么推荐的吗? |
| **Doctor**：What about this one? It's very effective in preventing the flu. | 医生:这种怎么样? 它对预防感冒很有效。 |
| **May**：Okay, I'll take this one. | 阿美:好的,我就买这种吧。 |

### 生词小结

| | |
|---|---|
| **firmly** *adv.* 牢牢地 | **cure** *n.* 治疗 |
| **lasting** *adj.* 持久的 | **effective** *adj.* 有效的 |
| **prevention** *n.* 预防 | |

## S情景练习
### cene practice —— 确定与否句型练习

仔细阅读下面五个场景,两人一组,使用确定与不确定的句型(见 253 页),用一用,练一练。

1. If you were Daniel, you promise that you will finish your homework in one single day, what would you say to your mother?

2. Daniel promises that he won't watch Ultraman until he finishes his homework, if you were Daniel, what would you say to your father?

3. If you were May, you are not sure about the final result of your examination, what would you say to your mother?

4. If you were May, you don't know whether you can see the film with Gucci or not, what would you say to her?

5. If you were Benjamin, Daniel asks you about the time for picnic, but you are not sure with that, what would you say to Daniel?

### Recitation
经典背诵

**May:** I think Chinese traditional medicine is more effective than Western medicine. The doctors say it depends. But I do firmly believe that Chinese traditional medicine is really good as a prevention method. And you know prevention is better than cure. There is no doubt about it.

# Topic 4 处方 Prescriptions

听 学 看

回来的路上,阿美竟然碰到了妈妈和弟弟,原来在阿美买药的时候,妈妈已经带弟弟去了一趟医院。妈妈要阿美再去一趟药店,阿美只好第三次去药店,那么这次又是去干什么呢?

**May:** Here you are. How is Danny?

**Shirley:** Better now. We are just back from the hospital. We were lucky to meet a well-known doctor.

**May:** What did the doctor say?

**Shirley:** He said that he had a really bad cold.

**May:** Shall we go back home now?

**Shirley:** The dispensary closed. Here is the given prescription.

**May:** I bought some advanced medicine. Is there anything you need?

**Shirley:** Probably not. Some medicine we need is ethical drug which you can't buy without a prescription.

**May:** Now what?

**Shirley:** I'll go back home with Danny. You go to the pharmacy again.

**May:** Okay, this is the third time.

**Shirley:** What? How come? The third time?

**May:** You don't have to know. Bye for now.

**Shirley:** Be careful.

**阿美:** 你们在这里啊。丹丹怎么样了?

**雪莉:** 现在好多了。我们刚刚从医院回来。很幸运我们碰到了一位很好的大夫。

**阿美:** 大夫怎么说?

**雪莉:** 他说丹尼尔的感冒很严重。

**阿美:** 我们现在回家吗?

**雪莉:** (医院的)药房关了。这是(医生)给的处方。

**阿美:** 我买了一些高级的药。看它们有你要的吗?

**雪莉:** 很可能没有。我们需要的一些药是处方药,没有处方你是买不到的。

**阿美:** 那现在怎么办?

**雪莉:** 我带丹丹先回家,你再去趟药店。

**阿美:** 好的,这是第三次了。

**雪莉:** 什么?怎么会是第三次?

**阿美:** 你不需要知道了。那再见了。

**雪莉:** 小心点。

---

**生词小结**

| | | | | |
|---|---|---|---|---|
| **well-known** | *adj.* 著名的 | | **advanced** | *adj.* 高级的 |
| **dispensary** | *n.* 药房 | | **ethical drug** | 处方药 |
| **given** | *adj.* 给定的 | | **without** | *prep.* 没有 |
| **prescription** | *n.* 处方 | | **pharmacy** | *n.* 药店 |

## 语法小结 Grammer —— 过去分词作定语

单个的过去分词作定语,通常放在被修饰的名词之前,称为前置定语,可以表示被动意义和完成意义。

1. 过去分词作前置定语

被动意义:

*an honored teacher* 一位受尊敬的老师

*the injured workers* 受伤的工人

完成意义:

*She is a retired teacher.* 她是个退休教师。

*They are cleaning the fallen leaves in the yard.* 他们正在打扫院子里的落叶。

2. 过去分词作后置定语

*They decided to change the material used.* 他们决定更换使用的材料。

3. 过去分词短语作定语

通常放在被修饰的名词之后,它的作用相当于一个定语从句,例如:

*This will be the best novel ever written.* 这将是小说中写得最好的。

相当于 *This will be the best novel that has ever been written.*

4. 其他情况

如果被修饰的词是由 every, some, any, no + thing/body/one 所构成的复合代词或指示代词 those 等时,分词要放在被修饰词的后面

*Is there anything unsolved?* 还有没解决的问题吗?

*There is nothing changed here since I left.* 自从我离开以来,几乎没有什么变化。

## 家庭总动员 Do it together

**两人一组,一方朗诵下面的中文句子,另一方挑选出合适的翻译。**

1. 我需要的是一些高级的药。
2. 这是一位受人尊敬的医生。
3. 这是指定的处方。
4. 他们决定扔掉用过的药。
5. 丹尼尔看见一个受伤的工人。

1. They decide to throw away the medicine used.
2. Daniel saw an injured worker.
3. All I need is some advanced medicine.
4. This is a prescription given.
5. This is an honored doctor.

**Recitation 经典背诵**

**Shirley:** My husband and I are always too busy to take care of our children. So we are not always available when they get sick. The good thing is that there is a pharmacy near my home where they sell many kinds of medicine. The problem is we may need some ethical drug at times but we just can't buy them without a prescription.

# 派出所 Police Station

## Goals

在这个场景中，我们将学到：

1. 系/助动词与 not 连读
2. 各种职业的单词
3. 表达希望的句型
4. 过去分词做状语、表语

## Topic 1 · 110 报案
### Reporting a Case

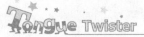 玩转语音

1. Fuzzy Wuzzy was a bear, Fuzzy Wuzzy had no hair, Fuzzy Wuzzy wasn't very fuzzy, was he?
2. If you understand, say "understand".
   If you don't understand, say "don't understand".
   But if you understand and say "don't understand".
   how do I understand that you understand. Understand!?

及格时间：20秒
你的纪录：——秒
及格时间：40秒
你的纪录：——秒

本杰明中午下班后回到家，发现锁被人砸坏了，于是他就猜是有小偷入室盗窃，这可怎么办呢？一起来看看吧！

Benjamin：Hello, police office?

Policeman：Yes, May I help you?

Benjamin：Yes, I'd like to report a case. Somebody broke into my house.

Policeman：When did that happen?

Benjamin：It happened in the morning. I just came home from work and found the lock broken.

Policeman：Is anything lost?

Benjamin：I don't know. I called the police as soon as I found the lock broken.

本杰明：你好，派出所吗？

警察：是的，我能帮你什么吗？

本杰明：是啊，我要报案，有人闯进我的家了。

警察：什么时候发生的？

本杰明：早上发生的。我刚刚下班回到家就发现锁被砸坏了。

警察：丢了什么东西吗？

本杰明：不知道。我一发现锁被砸坏了就报警了。

Policeman：OK, we will send some men as soon as possible.

Benjamin：Please be quick.

Policeman：OK, we will. What's your name and address?

Benjamin：My name is Benjamin, and I live in Broad-Gate Street 2101#.

Policeman：OK, got it. Please don't worry sir. We will be there soon.

Benjamin：Thank you very much.

警察：好的,我们会尽快派人去。

本杰明：请快一点。

警察：好的,我们会的。您的姓名和地址是什么?

本杰明：我叫本杰明,我住在广门街2101号。

警察：好的,记下了。别担心,先生。我们马上就会到。

本杰明：谢谢。

---

### 生词小结

| | |
|---|---|
| **police office** 派出所 | **possible** *adj.* 可能的 |
| **case** *n.* 情况,案例 | **address** *n.* 地址 |
| **lock** *n.* 锁 | |

---

## P语音小结
### Pronunciation —— 系/助动词与 not 连读

系动词和助动词与 not 的缩写和读音

is not→isn't  are not→aren't  was not→wasn't  were not→weren't

do not→don't  does not→doesn't  did not→didn't

完成并朗诵下面的句子

—Is your community safe?

—No, it _____. Many neighbours have lost their valuables last week.

—Do the polices arrive there?

—No, they _____, maybe there is a traffic jam.

—Did you get the ID card?

—No, I _____. The police I should meet was on vacation.

---

Benjamin：I'd like to report a case to the police office. Somebody broke into our house in the morning. I just came home from work and found the lock broken. I called the police immediately. I hope they will be here as soon as possible.

民警出警
On the Case

警方赶到了本杰明家。发现他家的锁被砸坏了,屋内被翻得一片狼藉。这真的是小偷干的吗?来看看吧。

Policeman：What's the matter here?

Benjamin：Somebody broke into my house in the morning.

Policeman：When did you find out?

Benjamin：About 12 o'clock, when I came home from work.

Policeman：Apparently forced entry. The lock is battered to pieces.

Benjamin：I wonder how the burglar did it.

Policeman：He is so unskillful. I have never seen such an awkward burglar.

Benjamin：That's because we have a strong lock.

Policeman：Probably. Let's check the inside then.

Benjamin：Did you find anything?

Policeman：Yes, the house was in a terrible mess. It was almost turned upside down by the burglar.

Benjamin：Oh, er ... sorry that's because we didn't have time to clean it.

Policeman：You mean it is not created by the burglar?

Benjamin：Definitely not, sir.

警察：这儿出什么事了?

本杰明：今天早上有人闯进我家了。

警察：你什么时候发现的?

本杰明：大约12点,当我下班回家的时候。

警察：很明显是强行入室。锁被砸烂了。

本杰明：真不明白小偷怎么干的。

警察：他技术太烂了。我从没见过技术这么烂的小偷。

本杰明：那是因为我们有一把结实的锁。

警察：也许吧。我们看看室内吧。

本杰明：你发现什么了吗?

警察：是的,这房里乱透了。它几乎被小偷翻了个底朝天。

本杰明：哦,嗯……不好意思那是因为我们没时间打扫。

警察：你的意思是这不是小偷干的?

本杰明：确实不是,警官。

### 生词小结

| | | | |
|---|---|---|---|
| **find out** | 找出 | **burglar** | *n.* 窃贼 |
| **apparently** | *adv.* 明显地 | **unskillful** | *adj.* 技术差的 |
| **forced** | *adj.* 强行的 | **awkward** | *adj.* 笨拙的 |
| **batter** | *vt.* 打坏 | **upside down** | 底朝天 |

## 单词扩展 Vocabulary Builder

### 各种职业的单词

| 基础词汇 | 提高词汇 |
| --- | --- |
| teacher 教师 | Editor 编辑 |
| lawyer 律师 | journalist 记者 |
| driver 司机 | designer 设计师 |
| worker 工人 | professor 教授 |
| engineer 工程师 | manager 经理 |
| doctor 医生 | accountant 会计 |
| cook 厨师 | translator 翻译 |
| writer 作家 | secretary 秘书 |

## D 家庭总动员
## o it together

两人一组，一方随机大声读出上面词汇的英文和中文，另一方用该词汇填入下面的句子，大声朗读并表演出来，并用中文给出一个理由。

**I want to be a (　　　　　) in the future.**

【例】家长读 teacher 教师

孩子读 I want to be a teacher in the future. 因为当老师能教书育人。

## Recitation 经典背诵

Benjamin：Somebody broke into my house in the morning. It was apparently a forced entry. The lock was battered to pieces. The burglar seemed to be unskillful. Our house was in a terrible mess. But it was not created by the burglar. It was because we had no time to clean it.

## Topic 3 社区安全
### Community Security

听 学 看

当警方在检查时,雪莉回来了。本杰明告诉她,他们家的锁被砸了,家里被盗了。可是雪莉却很镇定。这是为什么呢?

**Shirley:** What's happening here?

**Benjamin:** Our lock was broken, honey. Somebody broke into our house.

**Shirley:** Oh, that was me.

**Benjamin:** You? What? What the hell are you talking about?

**Shirley:** I left my keys inside so I called the superintendent to break the lock.

**Policeman:** Hey, what are you guys doing here?

**Shirley:** Sorry, sir. There's been a mistake.

**Benjamin:** But you can't leave with an opening door!

**Shirley:** I got to buy a new lock! Plus, the superprintendent won't let any stranger in...

**Benjamin:** Oh, you are always a trouble maker.

**Policeman:** It seems that there is not my job here. This seems that it's been a false alarm.

**Benjamin:** Er... look, here, sir, I am terribly sorry.

**Policeman:** Well, don't call the police unless there is a real case. I hope this won't happen again.

**Shirley:** Oh, "I hope this won't happen again" I hate hearing this.

**Policeman:** Is there anything wrong, Ma'am?

**Shirley:** The superintendent said the same thing to me today a thousand times!

雪莉:这儿出了什么事?

本杰明:我们的锁被砸了,亲爱的。有人闯进我们家了。

雪莉:哦,是我。

本杰明:你?什么?你在说什么啊?

雪莉:我把锁落在里面了,所以我叫了物业来把锁砸开。

警察:嘿,你们这些人在做什么啊?

雪莉:对不起,警官。恐怕这里面有点误会。

本杰明:但你不能让门开着就离开啊!

雪莉:我得去买把新的锁!再说,物业不会让陌生人进来的……

本杰明:哦,你总是惹麻烦。

警察:看起来这儿没我的事了。好像有人报错了警。

本杰明:嗯……您看,警官,真是非常抱歉。

警察:下次没有真情况可不要报警。我希望下次不要发生这种事。

雪莉:哦,"我希望下次不要发生这种事"我讨厌听到这个。

警察:怎么拉,太太?

雪莉:这话物业今天已经跟我说过一千遍了!

## 生词小结

| | |
|---|---|
| **superintendent** *n.* 物业管理员 | **false alarm** 虚假警报 |
| **plus** *conj.* 并且 | **unless** *conj.* 除非 |

## F 功能性句型扩展
unctional structure —— 表达希望的句型

**请朗读以下句型，家长和孩子交替进行**

1. 表达希望

I'd like to... 我想要……

I want to... 我想要……

I wish to... 我希望……

I hope so. 我希望如此。

I hope that... 我希望……

I'm eager to... 我急切地想要……

I'm looking forward to... 我期待着……

I feel like... 我想要……

I expect to... 我期望……

2. 表达不希望

I hope not. 我不希望这样。

I don't wish to... 我不想……

I'd like not to... 我不想要……

I don't want to... 我不想要……

I don't feel like... 我不想要……

I don't expect to... 我不期望……

**Shirley：** I always forget to take my keys, and I get myself locked out. Then I would just call the superintendent to break the lock for me. He is not so willing to do that. It's because he thinks that I should be more careful. Maybe, he is right.

# Topic 4 办理身份证
## Applying for I. D. Card

本杰明来到派出所。他的身份证丢了，得重新办一张新的。先登记，然后照相，最后一星期后来拿新身份证，一切就这么简单。

**Police officer**：Good morning, sir. May I help you?

**Benjamin**：Good morning. I need a new identification card.

**Police officer**：Why?

**Benjamin**：My ID card is lost.

**Police officer**：OK, did you bring your household register or residence booklet?

**Benjamin**：I only have my household register.

**Police officer**：It doesn't matter, they are the same thing.

**Benjamin**：Here you are, sir. What do I do next?

**Police officer**：OK, I will register you in our database system. What's your name, please?

**Benjamin**：Benjamin.

**Police officer**：Please get a mug shot in the next room.

**Benjamin**：I've brought with me some of my old ones.

**Police officer**：But we need them taken with digital cameras.

**Benjamin**：OK, what's next then?

**Police officer**：That's all. Come here a week later and get your ID card.

**警察**：早上好，先生。我能帮您点什么吗？

**本杰明**：早上好。我想办一张新的身份证。

**警察**：怎么拉？

**本杰明**：我的身份证丢了。

**警察**：好的，您带户口簿或是户口本了吗？

**本杰明**：我只带了户口簿。

**警察**：没关系，它们是一回事。

**本杰明**：这就是，警官。我下面做什么？

**警察**：好的，我把您登记在我们的数据库系统。您的名字叫什么？

**本杰明**：本杰明。

**警察**：请在隔壁房间照一张脸部照片。

**本杰明**：我带来了几张我的旧照片。

**警察**：但我们需要几张用数码相机照的。

**本杰明**：好的，然后呢？

**警察**：就这些了。一星期后来拿你的身份证。

---

### 生词小结

| | | | |
|---|---|---|---|
| identification card | 身份证 | database | n. 数据库 |
| household register | 户口簿 | mug shot | 面部照片 |
| residence booklet | 户口本 | | |

## G 语法小结
## rammer —— 过去分词作状语和表语

1. 过去分词作状语

过去分词作状语表示动作是被动和完成的,例如:

*Written in a hurry, your article was not so good!* 因为写得匆忙,你的文章写得不是很好。

*Seated in the sofa, she didn't know what to do next.* 她坐在沙发上,不知道接下来该做什么。

*Lost in deep thought, I didn't hear the phone.* 沉溺在深思中,我没听到电话声。

*Given another hour, I can finish it.* 再给我一个小时,我能完成它。

2. 过去分词作表语

过去分词作表语用时,总是在连系动词如:*be, appear, feel, remain, seem, look* 等之后,构成系表结构。

*She is beautifully dressed.* 她衣着美丽。

*She seemed terribly shocked.* 她似乎极度震惊。

*The children looked puzzled.* 孩子们都像是迷惑不解。

## D 家庭总动员
## o it together

**两人一组,一方朗诵下面的中文句子,另一方挑选出合适的翻译。**

1. 房间的锁坏了。
2. 本杰明看起来很迷惑。
3. 本杰明不知道身份证丢了。
4. 回答完警察的话,雪莉不知道下面该怎么办了。
5. 大雨使桥身受损,这座桥已经不安全了。

1. Benjamin doesn't know his ID card is lost.
2. The lock of the house is broken.
3. Ruined by the rain, this bridge is not safe.
4. Benjamin looks puzzled.
5. Having answered the questions of the police, Shirley doesn't know what to do next.

## Recitation
经典背诵

Benjamin:To get a new ID card is not a very complicated thing. You can just go to the police office and take a mug shot on digital camera, then just wait till it's done. The only thing to care about is that don't forget to bring the household register with you, without which they can't get it done.

# 理发店 Barbershop

## Goals

在这个场景中，我们将学到：

1. 情态动词与 not 的连读
2. 五官和体型的词汇
3. 表达希望的句型练习
4. 动名词做主语、表语

 洗发
**Washing Hair**

 玩转语音

1. I would if I could! But I can't, so I won't!
2. The cat catchers can't catch caught cats.
3. Will you, William? Will you, William? Will you, William?
4. Can't you, don't you, won't you, William?

| | |
|---|---|
| 及格时间：6 秒 | |
| 你的纪录：——秒 | |
| 及格时间：5 秒 | |
| 你的纪录：——秒 | |
| 及格时间：6 秒 | |
| 你的纪录 ——秒 | |
| 及格时间：5 秒 | |
| 你的纪录 ——秒 | |

妈妈带着丹尼尔到到理发店理发，坐着无聊，于是就想洗个头发，这洗头发最近也有新花样，究竟有什么不同呢？我们往下看吧！

**Hairdresser:** Would you please take a seat over there? There are some interesting magazines on the coffee-table.

**Shirley:** Thank you. How long does it take to get my son's hair cut?

**Hairdresser:** It shouldn't be long. Thirty minutes, tops. Are you in a hurry?

**Shirley:** No. I'm thinking that maybe I can get my hair shampooed.

**Hairdresser:** Good idea. Do you want a wash or a massage? Massage is especially good when you are tired.

**Shirley:** How come?

**理发师:** 您先在那边坐一下好吗？咖啡桌上有一些有趣的杂志。

**雪莉:** 谢谢。我儿子理发需要多长时间啊？

**理发师:** 不会很长的。最多 30 分钟，你有急事吗？

**雪莉:** 没有。我在考虑也许应该洗个头发。

**理发师:** 好主意。你希望只洗头发还是想要按摩？当你疲劳的时候，按摩是特别好的。

**雪莉:** 为什么呢？

**Hairdresser**：Because it helps you speed up your circulation.

**Shirley**：Then I won't say no to that.

(*The massage is finished.*)

**Hairdresser**：How do you like it?

**Shirley**：I feel totally refreshed.

**Hairdresser**：We have discount coupons. 100 yuan for ten times. Would you like to have one?

**Shirley**：This time included?

**Hairdresser**：Of course.

**Shirley**：Then yes.

理发师：因为它能帮助你加快血液循环。

雪莉：那好吧。

(按摩完了。)

理发师：感觉怎么样?

雪莉：我感觉焕然一新。

理发师：我们有优惠券。100 元 10 次。
您想办理一张吗?

雪莉：可以包含这一次吗?

理发师：当然可以。

雪莉：那好吧(我办一张)。

---

### 生词小结

| | | | | |
|---|---|---|---|---|
| **coffee-table** | *n.* 咖啡桌 | | **especially** | *adv.* 尤其 |
| **in a hurry** | 匆忙 | | **circulation** | *n.* 循环 |
| **shampoo** | *vt.* 洗发 | | **coupon** | *n.* 礼券 |
| **massage** | *n.* 按摩 | | | |

---

## G语法小结 rammer —— 情态动词与 not 的连读

情态动词与 not 的缩写和读音

should not→shouldn't  will not→won't  have not→haven't  has not→hasn't  can not→can't

could not→couldn't  would not→wouldn't  must not→mustn't

朗读练习：shouldn't  won't  haven't  hasn't  can't  couldn't  wouldn't  mustn't

---

### Recitation 经典背诵

**Hairdresser**：I'm a Hairdresser working in a barbershop. More and more people want massages after they get their hair shampooed. The massage is especially good when you are tired because it helps speed up your circulations. To attract more customers we offer people discount coupons which seems to be a good strategy.

# Topic 2 理发
## Haircut

听 学 读 看 　我们的小淘气丹尼尔剪头发也有新花招,不过这次他可把自己给害苦了,究竟怎么回事呢?

**Hairdresser:** How do you want your hair cut?

**Daniel:** I want it the way Beckham wears it.

**Hairdresser:** Who is Beckham?

**Daniel:** Are you kidding me? Even the girls know Beckham. Whatever, I have a picture of him here.

**Hairdresser:** You are a big fan of him! He has strong legs.

**Daniel:** Sure, he is a soccer star.

(*After cutting Daniel's hair, the hairdresser finds Daniel sleeping.*)

**Hairdresser:** Hey, wake up. It's done. How do you like it?

**Daniel:** Oh, my God. It's a disaster. It makes my head look like a soccer ball.

**Hairdresser:** But it's the same hairstyle.

**Daniel:** It looks like the hairstyle of Kahn who stands beside him in the picture.

**Hairdresser:** Oh. I made a mistake. I thought the guy on the right was Beckham.

**Daniel:** He plays outside right but it doesn't mean he has to stand on the right.

**Hairdresser:** Sorry, but do not worry. I think I can fix it. Just cut a little more off the temple.

**Daniel:** Do it, please.

理发师:你想要理什么样的发型?

丹尼尔:我想要贝克汉姆的发型。

理发师:贝克汉姆是谁?

丹尼尔:你跟我开玩笑吗? 连女生都知道贝克汉姆。不管了,我这里有他的照片。

理发师:看来你很迷他了。他的腿很强壮哦。

丹尼尔:当然,他是足球明星嘛。

(头发理玩了,理发师发现丹尼尔竟然睡着了。)

理发师:嗨,醒醒。头发理好了。你看怎么样?

丹尼尔:哦,天啊。这是场灾难。我的头看起来像个足球。

理发师:但是你们的头型看起来是一样的啊。

丹尼尔:它看起来像站在他(贝克汉姆)身边的卡恩的发型。

理发师:哦,我搞错了。我以为右边的那个是贝克汉姆。

丹尼尔:他踢右边锋,但这并不表示他非要站在右边啊。

理发师:真对不起,不过别担心。我想修剪一下就可以了。只要修剪一下鬓角就好了。

丹尼尔:就照你说的剪吧。

## 生词小结

wear　*vt.* 蓄，留
kid　*vt.* 开玩笑
picture　*n.* 图片
fan　*n.* 狂热者
soccer　*n.* 足球
disaster　*n.* 灾难
hairstyle　*n.* 发型
beside　*prep.* 在…旁边
outside right　右边锋
temple　*n.* 鬓角

## 注释

**1. Even the girls know Beckham.** （即使女孩子们也知道贝克汉姆。）因为丹尼尔认为会有更多的男孩子喜欢足球，所以作为一个男理发师当然更应该知道，这里丹尼尔用的是讽刺的说法。

**2. He plays outside right but it doesn't mean he has to stand on the right.** （他打右边锋并不意味着他一定要站在右边。）贝克汉姆踢的位置是右边锋，而在丹尼尔的照片中他站在左边，理发师把站在右边的卡恩当成了贝克汉姆，所以丹尼尔这样讽刺他。

## 单词扩展 Vocabulary Builder

### 五官和体型的词汇

| 基础词汇 | 提高词汇 |
| --- | --- |
| hand 手 | waist 腰 |
| leg 腿 | neck 脖子 |
| eye 眼睛 | thumb 拇指 |
| mouth 嘴巴 | ring finger 无名指 |
| teeth 牙齿 | wisdom tooth 智齿 |
| arm 手臂 | wrist 腕 |
| nose 鼻子 | fingernail 指甲 |
| foot 脚 | eyebrow 眉毛 |

## D 家庭总动员
## o it together

　　两人一组，一方随机大声读出上面词汇的英文和中文，另一方用该词汇填入下面的句子，大声朗读并表演出来，并用中文给出一个理由。

**How do you like my (　　　　　　　)?**

【例】家长读 hand 手
　　　孩子读 How do you like my (　　)? 我觉得它是我全身最成功的地方。

**Recitation**
经典背诵

　　Daniel：I'm a big fan of Beckham, the great football player. I wear my hair the same way he does. He plays outside right and he is really cool. He is so famous that even the girls know him. I hope I can meet him in the future.

# Topic 3 美发
## Hairdressing

雪莉看到杂志里的一款烫发特别心动,于是决定要做,又烫发又染发,折腾了三个多小时,这下该轮到丹尼尔等妈妈了。

**Shirley**：I feel like to wear my hair in this way.

**Hairdresser**：Oh，it's really popular these days.

**Shirley**：Do you think it's suitable for me?

**Hairdresser**：Honestly speaking, I think the one next to it suits you better.

**Shirley**：Even though I really like it，it's just too modern for me.

**Hairdresser**：That's not true. Look over there! That lady chose the same one and she is surely older than you.

**Shirley**：Okay then. And I also want to have my hair colored.

**Hairdresser**：Which color do you like?

**Shirley**：Claret-red.

**Hairdresser**：Nice choice.

**Shirley**：How long will it take? I hope it won't be too long.

**Hairdresser**：I hope not but it will take at least three hours.

**Shirley**：Now it's my son's turn to wait.

**雪莉**：我想要这样的发型。

**理发师**：哦,这发型最近很流行。

**雪莉**：你觉得它合适我吗?

**理发师**：说实话,我觉得旁边的那款更适合你。

**雪莉**：尽管我很喜欢,但是对我而言它有点太时髦了。

**理发师**：不会的。你看那边。那位女士也选了这款,她看起来总比你年纪大吧。

**雪莉**：那好吧。另外我也想把头发染个颜色。

**理发师**：你喜欢什么颜色。

**雪莉**：酒红色。

**理发师**：不错的选择。

**雪莉**：(做这个)要多长时间? 希望别太久。

**理发师**：我也希望不长,但是那至少要三个小时。

**雪莉**：现在轮到我儿子等我了。

---

**生词小结**

sutiable  *adj.* 合适的
honestly  *adv.* 真诚地
suit  *vt.* 适合
modern  *adj.* 时髦的

surely  *adv.* 的确
claret-red  *adj.* 酒红色的
turn  *n.* 顺序

---

## S情景练习
### cene practice —— 表达希望的句型练习

仔细阅读下面五个场景，两人一组，使用表示希望的句型（见 269 页），用一用，练一练。

1. If you were Benjamin, you are too tired to climb the mountain with your family, what would you say to them?

2. Gucci and May are going for a live show of a pop star. Unluckily that they get stuck in a traffic jam. If you were in such a situation, what would you say?

3. Clive got hurt in a basketball game days ago. An important basketball game is coming but he can do nothing but lie on bed now. If you were Clive, what would you say to your team members?

4. Shirley and Jane has been waiting for the bus for more than 20 minutes. They are going to a discount store. If you were Shirley, what would you say?

5. It's has been raining for days. Daniel wants to fly kites tomorrow with his father. What would you say if you were Daniel?

### Recitation
经典背诵

**Shirley**: I like changing my hairstyle from time to time. Sometimes I would choose some popular hairstyles which are a bit too modern for me. But I think it's okay as long as I like them. The only thing that bothers me is that it always takes too much time to have it done. But we all know beauty costs.

## 公共服务场所 · Public Service

# Topic 4 形象设计
### Designing

听学 读看

总算弄完了,付钱回家吧! 哎,还没有完,又有事情发生了,会是什么好事呢? 看看就知道了。

**Shirley:** Can I have my check, please.

**Clerk:** Here it is. 350 yuan all together.

**Shirley:** My son adores my new hairstyle so I suppose it is worth it.

**Clerk:** Hearing you say that is a big reward for us. And here is the receipt.

**Shirley:** Thank you.

**Clerk:** Wait! Congratulations! You are the lucky customer of our anniversary celebration.

**Shirley:** Wow, it's surprising. So what do I get?

**Clerk:** You can have a free facial and then make up free for you. Do you want it now?

**Shirley:** Probably not. Doing that will probably take another three hours which I can't afford now.

**Clerk:** Here is our number. Call us when you are ready to come.

**Shirley:** You mean I should make an appointment ahead of time?

**Clerk:** Yes.

**Shirley:** Got it. Bye for now.

雪莉:我可以要我的账单吗?

店员:给您。一共是350元。

雪莉:我儿子喜欢我的新发型,所以我想它值这个价。

店员:你这么说是给我们最好的回报。这是收据。

雪莉:谢谢。

店员:稍等。祝贺你,你被选中为我们周年庆的幸运顾客。

雪莉:哇,真是惊喜啊。那我能得到什么呢?

店员:你可以得到一次免费的美容和免费的化妆。你想现在就做吗?

雪莉:不了。做这个很有可能又要三个小时,我没有时间了。

店员:这是我们的联系电话。等你想做的时候请给我们打个电话。

雪莉:你是说我需要提前预约吗?

店员:是的。

雪莉:知道了。再见。

### 生词小结

**adore** *vt.* 喜爱
**reward** *n.* 报答
**anniversary** *n.* 周年纪念日

**celebration** *n.* 庆祝
**facial** *n.* 美容
**make up** 化妆

# **G**rammer 语法小结 —— 动名词作主语、表语

**1. 动名词作主语**

*Listening to music gives me pleasure.* 听音乐给我带来快乐。

*Running is a good exercise.* 跑步是一项不错的运动。

*Walking to school is a good idea.* 走路去学校是个好主意。

有时可以用 *it* 作主语，把动名词主语放到句子后面，例如：

*It's nice to seeing you again.* 再次见到你真好。

**2. 动名词作表语**

（1）动名词作表语说明主语的内容

*One of the best exercises is swimming.* 游泳是最好的运动项目之一。

*What pleases him most is sleeping in the bed.* 最使他高兴的事是在床上睡觉。

（2）动名词作表语，表语和主语几乎处于同等地位，可以互换位置，其句意不变

*Our work is serving the people.* 我们的工作是为人民服务。

相当于 *Serving the people is our work.*

# **D**o it together 家庭总动员

**两人一组，一方朗诵下面的中文句子，另一方挑选出合适的翻译。**

1. 做按摩可以加快你的血液循环。
2. 雪莉在等着剪头。
3. 读这种书是浪费时间。
4. 提前预约是完成这件任务的第一步。
5. 住在这里很有意思！

1. Reading such kind of books is just wasting time.
2. Making an appointment ahead of time is the first step to finish the task.
3. Living here is very interesting!
4. Doing a massage can speed up your blood circulation.
5. Shirley is waiting for hair cut.

# **R**ecitation 经典背诵

**Clerk**：People are willing to pay to be beautiful. They would think if others adore their new hairstyle then it's worth whatever it costs. Nowadays facials are becoming more and more popular among girls so sometimes you have to call to make an appointment for that.

# 旅行社 Travel Agency

## Goals
在这个场景中,我们将学到:

1. 连读加音(3 组)
2. 国家名称的单词
3. 表达邀请的句型
4. 动名词做宾语

 假期安排
**Holiday Plans**

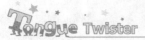 玩转语音

1. Sally is a sheet slitter, she slits sheets.
2. Rory the warrior and Roger the worrier were reared wrongly in a rural brewery.

及格时间: 5 秒
你的纪录:——秒
及格时间: 8 秒
你的纪录:——秒

听学看

阿美参加了摄影俱乐部,为了参加展览,她让爸爸周末带她去京郊摄影,爸爸会同意吗? 还有谁会一起去呢?

**May**: Daddy, shall we go out this weekend?

**Benjamin**: We can do it, if you want. But why this weekend? We planned to enjoy some drama and music.

**May**: I attended a photography club. Each member is asked to hand in some photos for the coming exhibition. You will see it!

**Benjamin**: Okay then. Do you have a theme?

**May**: Yes. I want to take some photos about folk customs.

**Benjamin**: Sounds interesting. Why do you pick this theme?

**May**: Olympics is close. As a volunteer, I want to show our folk customs to the people from all over the world.

**Benjamin**: Good. Where do you want to go?

**May**: I think the suburbs of Beijing will do.

阿美:爸爸,我们这个周末出去玩吧?

本杰明:可以啊,如果你想。但是为什么是这个周末呢? 我们不是打算看看戏曲听听音乐吗?

阿美:我参加了摄影俱乐部。每个会员要为即将举行的展览拍些照片。你到时能看展览哦!

本杰明:那好吧。你有主题吗?

阿美:是的。我想拍一些关于风俗的照片。

本杰明:听起来很有趣。为什么选这个主题?

阿美:奥运会就快到了。作为一个志愿者,我想向来自世界各地的人们展示我们的民族文化。

本杰明:真不错。你想去哪里呢?

阿美:我想北京的郊区就可以了。漂亮

Beautiful sceneries, fresh air, a rustic cottage, and a country retreat.

**Benjamin:** What about we asking Daniel to go with us?

**May:** Sure. I've got some idea about him.

**Benjamin:** What did you mean?

**May:** I want him to be my model. Pose for my photos.

**Benjamin:** He will be really excited about it.

的风景,新鲜的空气,乡村小屋,还有乡间的静处。

**本杰明:** 要不要叫丹尼尔和我们一起去吗?

**阿美:** 当然。对于他,我有个好主意。

**本杰明:** 你是指什么?

**阿美:** 我想他做我的模特。为我的照片摆姿势。

**本杰明:** 听到这个他一定会很兴奋。

---

**生词小结**

| | |
|---|---|
| **weekend** *n.* 周末 | **folk custom** 风俗 |
| **photography club** 摄影俱乐部 | **rustic** *adj.* 乡村的 |
| **exhibition** *n.* 展览 | **cottage** *n.* 村舍 |
| **theme** *n.* 主题 | **retreat** *n.* 休息寓所 |

---

# 语音小结 Pronunciation —— 连读加音

在一些元音跟元音的快速连读中,会产生一些微弱的加音,这主要有三种情况:

(1) 加音/j/ 当两词相连,前一个词发音以/i/或/i:/结尾,后一个词发音以/i/或/i:/起首,在朗读时,前一词后加一个轻微的/j/音,并与后一个词的词首连读。

【例】You can see it. /si:(j)it/

朗读练习:Say it again.

Enjoy it, please!

Please copy it!

Absolutely impossible!

(2) 加音/w/ 两个元音连读,如果前一个元音发/u/或/u:/时,产生一个轻微的加音/w/,并与后一个词的词首的元音连读。

【例】We can do it! /du:(w)it/

朗读练习:It's too easy!

The kite flew in the sky.

(3) 加音/r/ 两词相连,前一个词以/ə/结尾,后一个以/ə/起首时,前一个音加上/r/音,并与后面的元音/ə/连读。

【例】I've got an idea of it. /ai'diə(r)əv/

朗读练习:This bottle is made of china and glass.

· Mary likes drama and music.

---

**Recitation 经典背诵**

**May:** I'm interested in photographing so I attend a photographer's club. My father thinks it's a good thing so he is willing to take me to the suburbs for photo shooting. Most of the time we would ask my younger brother to go with us. And he makes a really good model, and he enjoys posing for me.

丹尼尔晕车,阿美问导游小姐要来了几片晕车药,没想到吃了药之后,丹尼尔一直
睡觉,到了目的地还没有醒,这究竟怎么回事呢?

**May:** Excuse me? Do you have anything for a carsickness?

**Guide:** Yes, but you look fine.

**May:** Oh, it's for my brother. The little boy over there. He is getting a carsickness.

**Guide:** Poor boy! But don't worry. Here are two pills made in Germany. It's really effective. He will be just fine.

**May:** Thank you so much.

**Guide:** Take some with you next time, just in case.

(*Arriving at the destination, May comes to see the guide again.*)

**May:** Sorry to interrupt, but my brother is still sleeping.

**Guide:** You mean the boy who felt carsick just now?

**May:** Yes. It's so strange that he slept all the time after taking the pills.

**Guide:** Oh, sorry, maybe I gave you the wrong medicine.

**May:** What?

**Guide:** It's just sleeping pills made in America which is also very good. But don't worry. It has no undesirable side-effects.

**May:** I see.

阿美:打扰了。你有晕车药吗?

导游:是的,有,但是你看起来很好(不像晕车)。

阿美:哦,是给我弟弟的。那边的那个小男孩,他有点晕车。

导游:可怜的小男孩。但是别担心。这里有两片德国制造的药片,它很有效,他会没事的。

阿美:非常感谢。

导游:下次身边带一点(晕车药),以防万一。

(到达目的地,阿美又跑来找导游。)

阿美:不好意思打扰了,但是我弟弟还在睡觉。

导游:你是说刚才晕车的小男孩吗?

阿美:是的。很奇怪他吃了药片之后一直睡到现在。

导游:哦,对不起,我可能拿错药了。

阿美:什么?

导游:那是些美国制造的效果很好的安眠药。但是别担心。它没有任何副作用。

阿美:知道了。

## 生词小结

| | | | |
|---|---|---|---|
| carsick | *adj.* 晕车的 | sleeping pills | 安眠药 |
| just now | 刚才 | undesirable | *adj.* 不良的 |
| strange | *adj.* 奇怪的 | side-effect | *n.* 副作用 |

## 单词扩展 Vocabulary Builder

### 国家名称的单词

| 基础词汇 | 提高词汇 |
|---|---|
| China 中国 | Sweden 瑞典 |
| England 英国 | Brazil 巴西 |
| Canada 加拿大 | India 印度 |
| America 美国 | Russia 俄国 |
| France 法国 | Finland 芬兰 |
| Germany 德国 | Korea 韩国 |
| Japan 日本 | Australia 澳大利亚 |
| Italy 意大利 | Norway 挪威 |

## Do it together 家庭总动员

两人一组，一方随机大声读出上面词汇的英文和中文，另一方用该词汇填入下面的句子，大声朗读并表演出来，并用中文给出一个理由。

**This pills are made in (　　　　　　　　　　　).**

【例】家长读 England 英国

孩子读 This pills are made in England. 效果很好哦!

**Recitation** 经典背诵

**Guide**：I'm a guide for bus trips. Each time I would take some pills with me in case that some of my customers may get carsick on the way. There was one time that I gave the wrong medicine to a young boy which is really embarrassing. Lucky that I just gave him some sleeping pills which didn't have any undesirable side-effects. But I've been more careful ever since then.

# Topic 3 民俗旅游
## Folk – custom Tourism

丹尼尔和阿美来到了一个美丽的民俗村,时间过得很快,转眼就快天黑了,晚上会有什么好玩的吗? 一定会很特别! 一起来领略一下民俗文化吧!

**Daniel:** I like this beautiful Folk Culture Village. It's a shame that it's getting dark now.

**May:** That'll be more fun. There will be more folk activities going on then.

**Daniel:** Really? Look! It's a fire. Anything wrong?

**May:** No. It must be the bonfire party. People would gather round the fire and sing songs. Would you like to go and join them?

**Daniel:** Sure.

(*They come to the bonfire party.*)

**Daniel:** Oh, the clothes they wear are so strange. It's wired to see men in skirts.

**May:** Come on. It's their traditional costumes. They put them on to show their hospitality.

**Daniel:** That's very interesting. Oh, what is the smell? Where does the delicious smell come from?

**May:** It must be the roasted leg of lamb, which is very delicious.

**Daniel:** Oh, I'll love it. Let's go.

**May:** No. It won't be done until later. Let's watch the traditional performance first.

**Daniel:** Sure. Sis, their songs are strange too. I've never heard anything like this before, either on TV or on the radio.

**May:** They are traditional folk songs. I suppose only the local old people can sing them. We are so lucky to hear them. So just enjoy them.

**丹尼尔:** 我喜欢这个美丽的民俗文化村。只可惜现在天快黑了。

**阿美:** 那会更好玩的。到时候会举行更多的民俗活动。

**丹尼尔:** 真的吗? 看! 着火了。出什么事了?

**阿美:** 不是的。那一定是篝火晚会。人们会聚集在一起围坐在火堆旁唱歌。想去加入他们吗?

**丹尼尔:** 当然。

(他们来到了篝火晚会上。)

**丹尼尔:** 哦,他们穿的衣服真奇怪。男人穿裙子好古怪。

**阿美:** 拜托。这是他们的传统服饰。他们这样穿是为了表示他们的好客。

**丹尼尔:** 那倒挺有趣的。哦,是什么气味? 这香味是从哪里来的啊?

**阿美:** 那一定是烤羊腿,很好吃的。

**丹尼尔:** 哦,我爱吃那个。我们去吃吧。

**阿美:** 先别。等一下才能做好呢。我们先去看传统表演吧!

**丹尼尔:** 好的。姐姐,他们的歌也很奇怪。我以前从来没听过,电视和广播上都没有。

**阿美:** 这是传统的民歌。我想只有当地的老人才会唱了。我们能听到它们真是幸运。所以就好好听吧。

## 生词小结

| | | | |
|---|---|---|---|
| **Folk Culture Village** | 民俗文化村 | **skirt** *n.* 裙子 | |
| **bonfire** *n.* 篝火 | | **hospitality** *n.* 好客 | |
| **gather** *vi.* 聚集 | | **lamb** *n.* 羊羔 | |

# F功能性句型扩展
## unctional structure —— 表达邀请的句型

请朗读以下句型。

### 1. 发出邀请

Would you like to...? 你想要……吗？

Are you free to...? 你有空……吗？

Why don't you... 为什么不……？

I was just wondering... 我刚在想……

Do you feel like doing... 你想要……吗？

### 2. 接受邀请

That sounds very nice. 听上去很好。

I will, if I can. 如果我能，我会的。

What a nice idea! 好主意！

That's very kind of you. 你太好了！

### 3. 拒绝邀请

I'd like to, but I'm afraid... 我想去，但我恐怕……

Thank you for your invitation, but I'm afraid I can't. 谢谢你的邀请，但我恐怕我不能接受。

I'd love to, but I'm afraid I can't. 我想去，但是恐怕不行。

Thank you for asking me, but I can't. 谢谢你的邀请，但是我不能去。

**Recitation** 经典背诵

Daniel：May and I went to a really beautiful Folk Culture Village. In the evening there were a lot of folk activities going on, even more than throughout the day. There was a bonfire, and the people gathered around it and had a party, singing songs and enjoying themselves. I was able to eat some really delicious roasted lamb there. Moreover, some old people sang some really old folk songs. Everything was so fun.

## Topic 4 背包客 Back-packers

旅店的老板带着爸爸和阿美去外面摄影了,丹尼尔一个人留在了住的地方,来了一个外国的"背包客",看他们都谈了些什么。

**Foreign back-packer:** Excuse me. Is there anybody here?

**Daniel:** Yes.

**Foreign back-packer:** I've finished up all my water. I would kill for a sip of water.

**Daniel:** Sure, come on in.

**Foreign back-packer:** Thank you very much. Are you here alone?

**Daniel:** My father and sister are out to do photographing. What about you?

**Foreign back-packer:** I'm a back-packer from America.

**Daniel:** What is a back-packer?

**Foreign back-packer:** It means a hiker who loves travelling around the world.

**Daniel:** Cool. You must have been to a lot of places.

**Foreign back-packer:** Yes, actually almost half of all the countries over the world. I love travelling places.

**Daniel:** So cool. I want to be a back-packer when I grow up.

**Foreign back-packer:** You can do it. But do work hard on your English to make it easier.

**Daniel:** I'll try my best.

**外国背包客:**打扰了。这里有人吗?

**丹尼尔:**有啊。

**外国背包客:**我把水喝光了。只要给我一口水,我什么事情都可以做。

**丹尼尔:**当然可以,进来吧。

**外国背包客:**非常感谢。你一个人吗?

**丹尼尔:**我爸爸和姐姐出去拍照片了。你呢?

**外国背包客:**我是一个来自美国的背包客。

**丹尼尔:**什么是背包客?

**外国背包客:**就是喜欢在全世界旅游的徒步旅行者啊!

**丹尼尔:**太酷了。那你一定到过很多地方了。

**外国背包客:**是的,实际上我几乎到过全世界一半的国家。我喜欢到处旅游。

**丹尼尔:**真的很酷。等我长大了我也想做一名背包客。

**外国背包客:**你可以做的,不过你要先学好英语,这样会容易一些。

**丹尼尔:**我一定会努力的。

### 生词小结

| | | | |
|---|---|---|---|
| **sip** | *n.* 啜吸 | **hiker** | *n.* 徒步旅行者 |
| **alone** | *adj.* 单独的 | **grow up** | 长大 |
| **photographing** | *n.* 摄影 | **try my best** | 竭尽所能 |
| **back-packer** | *n.* 背包客 | | |

## G rammer 语法小结 —— 动名词作宾语

在英语中,下面这些动词后面直接接动名词,也就是说,动名词在句子中充当宾语。

| | | | |
|---|---|---|---|
| admit 承认 | appreciate 感激,赞赏 | avoid 避免 | complete 完成 |
| consider 认为 | delay 耽误 | deny 否认 | endure 忍受 |
| enjoy 喜欢 | escape 逃脱 | prevent 阻止 | fancy 想象 |
| finish 完成 | imagine 想象 | mind 介意 | miss 想念 |
| practise 训练 | recall 回忆 | resent 讨厌 | resist 抵抗 |
| resume 继续 | risk 冒险 | suggest 建议 | face 面对 |
| include 包括 | stand 忍受 | understand 理解 | forgive 宽恕 |

*Would you mind turning down your radio, please?* 可以把收音机声音调小点吗?

*After hearing the funny story, all of us couldn't help laughing.* 听过这个有趣的故事后,所有人都忍不住笑了。

*Do you enjoy teaching?* 你喜欢教书吗?

*I finished reading the story book yesterday.* 我昨天看完了这本故事书。

## D o it together 家庭总动员

两人一组,一方朗诵下面的中文句子,另一方挑选出合适的翻译。

1. 你建议在这儿照相吗?
2. 我建议你带一些晕车药。
3. 那个外国背包客喜欢周游世界。
4. 你的意思是你要先学好英语?
5. 阿美无法忍受晕车带来的痛苦。

1. The foreign back-packer loves travelling the world.
2. May can't stand suffering from the carsickness.
3. Do you mean learning English well first?
4. Do you mind taking a photos here?
5. I suggest you take some medicine for the carsickness.

## R ecitation 经典背诵

**Foreigner**: I'm a back-packer from America. I love travelling around the world. I'm young but I've been to many places, actually almost half of all the countries in the world. I love meeting people from different places and making friends with them. I enjoy every single day of my life!

# 邮局 Post Office

## Goals

在这个场景中,我们将学到:

1. 陈述句、感叹句语调
2. 杂志期刊种类的词汇
3. 表达邀请的句型练习
4. 情态动词 must 和 have to

 寄包裹
Send a Parcel

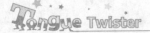 玩转语音

及格时间:40秒
你的纪录:——秒
及格时间:30秒
你的纪录:——秒

1. At noon I took a good book. And sat by the pool in the wood. I soon took off my boot. And put my foot in the pool. Oh! How cool, how cool!

2. This fish has a thin fin. That fish has a fat fin; This fish is a fish that has a thinner fin than that fish.

听 学 读 看

本杰明想寄一个包裹到上海去。他来到了邮局,那么究竟寄包裹需要什么程序呢?一起来看看吧!

Postal clerk 1:Hello, may I help you?

Benjamin:Yes, I'd like to have this parcel delivered to Shanghai.

Postal clerk 1:Oh, we only take care of mail. For parcels, you can go to the next window.

Benjamin:Thanks! … Hello, I have a parcel to deliver.

Postal clerk 2:Where do you need it to be delivered to?

Benjamin:I want to post it to Shanghai.

Postal clerk 2:OK, please fill out this form.

Benjamin:Sure, what's the postcode of Shanghai?

Postal clerk 2:Wait a moment, let me check it out for you. It's 200085.

邮局职员1:您好,请问有什么可以帮助您?

本杰明:是的,我想把这个包裹寄到上海去。

邮局职员1:哦,我们只负责信件。寄包裹,您得到隔壁窗口去。

本杰明:谢谢! ……您好,我想寄一个包裹。

邮局职员2:您想要寄到哪儿?

本杰明:我想寄到上海去。

邮局职员2:好的,请填一下这张单子。

本杰明:好的,上海的邮编是多少?

邮局职员2:等一下,我帮您查一下。是 200085。

**Benjamin**：Thanks, here you go. What's the postage, please?

**Postal clerk 2**：Hold on, let me put it on the scale. It weighs up to 10 kg and that will be 30 yuan, please.

**Benjamin**：Ten kg! Dear Shirley must have put a lead ball in it!

**本杰明**：谢谢，填好了。请问邮资是多少？

**邮局职员2**：等一等，让我称称看。它有10千克，一共30元钱。

**本杰明**：10千克！亲爱的雪莉大概放了个铅球在里面！

---

### 生词小结

**post** *vt.* 邮寄
**parcel** *n.* 包裹
**fill out** 填写
**postcode** *n.* 邮编

**postage** *n.* 邮资
**weigh** *vt.* 称
**lead ball** 铅球

---

## 语音小结
### Pronunciation —— 陈述句、感叹句语调

1. 陈述句
   陈述句表示陈述一件事时用降调,例如:
   It's difficult. ↓
   It's very difficult to understand. ↓

2. 感叹句
   (1) 感叹句表示强烈感叹时用降调,例如:
   What a beautiful girl! ↓
   Good heavens! ↓
   (2) 表示惊奇时用升降调,例如:
   —Petter got the first! ↓
   —Yes, how clever he is! ↓ I can't believe it! ↓
   —But there is only two students in his class. ↓
   请朗读下列句子,注意语调。
   —I just bought a garment for 800 RMB. ↓
   — 800 RMB? ↑ I don't think I had misheard you! ↓
   —But look, how charming I am when I put it on! ↓
   —Yeah, like a peacock! ↓

**Benjamin**：It's simple to have a parcel delivered through the post office. First the clerks would ask you to fill out a form and then they would put your parcel on a scale and tell you how much you should pay. That's all. So convenient!

## Topic 2 订阅 Subscribing

寄完了包裹,本杰明帮他太太订《健康顾问》,结果吓了一跳,究竟是什么吓到了本杰明呢,一起来看看吧。

**Benjamin**：Hello, I'd like to subscribe to a magazine.

**Postal clerk**：What magazine do you want to subscribe for?

**Benjamin**：*Fitness Consultant*.

**Postal clerk**：OK, *Fitness Consultant*. How many subscriptions do you want?

**Benjamin**：Only one, please.

**Postal clerk**：How long do you want the subscription for?

**Benjamin**：For six months, please.

**Postal clerk**：Your name, please?

**Benjamin**：Shirley, that's my wife's name. I subscribe to this magazine for her.

**Postal clerk**：I see. Please put your address here then.

**Benjamin**：OK. How much is the subscription?

**Postal clerk**：650 yuan.

**Benjamin**：650 yuan! You must be kidding! I can subscribe for evening newspapers for ten years with that much!

**本杰明**：你好,我想订本杂志。

**邮局职员**：你想订什么杂志?

**本杰明**：《健康顾问》。

**邮局职员**：好的,健康顾问。你想要订几份?

**本杰明**：就一份。

**邮局职员**：你需要订多久?

**本杰明**：请给我订六个月。

**邮局职员**：请问您的姓名?

**本杰明**：雪莉,这是我太太的名字。我帮她订的。

**邮局职员**：知道了。请在这儿填上您的地址。

**本杰明**：好的。订阅费是多少?

**邮局职员**：650 元。

**本杰明**：650 元! 你在开玩笑吧! 650 元够我订 10 年晚报了。

### 生词小结

**subscribe** *vi.* 订阅
**subscription** *n.* 订阅,订金

## 单词扩展 Vocabulary Builder

### 杂志期刊种类的词汇

| 基础词汇 | 提高词汇 |
| --- | --- |
| China daily 中国日报 | daily newspaper 日报 |
| Personal computer week 电脑周报 | morning paper 早报 |
| 21st century 21 世纪报 | evening paper 晚报 |
| People's daily 人民日报 | digest 文摘 |
| China youth daily 中国青年报 | weekly 周报 |
| The economic observer 经济观察报 | journal 期刊 |
| Shanghai weekly 上海壹周 | bound volume 合订本 |
| IT time IT 时代周刊 | quarterly 季刊 |

## D家庭总动员
o it together

　　两人一组，一方随机大声读出上面词汇的英文和中文，另一方用该词汇填入下面的句子，大声朗读并表演出来，并用中文给出一个理由。

**I want to subscribe to a(　　　　　).**

【例】家长读 daily newspaper 日报

　　孩子读 I want to subscribe to a daily newspaper. 因为报纸上有很多新闻.

Recitation
经典背诵

　　Benjamin：I'd like to subscribe to a evening newspaper. The name is *Beijing Evening Newspaper*. I have read the evening newspaper for ten years! I'd like to subscribe for another ten years! The subscription is only 600 yuan. That's wonderful!

# Topic 3 集邮 Stamp Collection

本杰明在邮局碰到了泰瑞。泰瑞来买一套最新发行的邮票。本杰明和泰瑞都是集邮迷。本杰明会买这套邮票吗？往下看就知道了。

(*Terry meets Benjamin in the post office.*)

Terry: Hi! Ben! Nice meeting you here!

Benjamin: Hi, Terry! Nice meeting you here.

Terry: What are you doing here? *Fitness Consultant*?

Benjamin: Subscribe to the magazine for my wife.

Terry: I see. I thought you had switched your hobby of stamp collection to fitness.

Benjamin: No, I love collecting stamps. Hey, what are you doing here?

Terry: I want to buy the newly issued stamps.

Benjamin: I have spent all my money on that magazine, otherwise I will buy some myself too.

Terry: Hey, do you have time this Sunday? I want you to come to my house.

Benjamin: Sure. Why?

Terry: I want to swap some stamps with you.

Benjamin: No problem. I will come by then.

Terry: See you.

Benjamin: See you.

（泰瑞在邮局碰到了本杰明。）

泰瑞：嗨！本！真高兴在这儿见到你！

本杰明：嗨！泰瑞！在这儿碰到你真好。

泰瑞：你在这儿做什么？《健康顾问》？

本杰明：我帮我太太订的。

泰瑞：知道了。我还以为你的兴趣由集邮转到健身去了呢。

本杰明：没有，我喜欢集邮。嘿，你在这儿做什么？

泰瑞：我想买一套最新发行的邮票。

本杰明：我的钱全订了那本杂志了。不然我也想买一套。

泰瑞：嘿，这个星期天有空吗？我想要你来我家。

本杰明：好的。为什么？

泰瑞：我想跟你换一些邮票。

本杰明：没问题。我到时去。

泰瑞：再见。

本杰明：再见。

## 生词小结

| | |
|---|---|
| **switch** *vt.* 转变 | **issue** *vt.* 发行 |
| **hobby** *n.* 兴趣,爱好 | **otherwise** *adv.* 否则 |
| **stamp** *n.* 邮票 | **swap** *vt.* 交换 |
| **collection** *n.* 收集 | |

## 情景练习 Scene practice —— 表达邀请的句型练习

**仔细阅读下面五个场景,两人一组,使用邀请的句型(见285页),用一用,练一练。**

1. Gucci asks May to go to the Happy Valley. But May has some other plans. If you were May, what would you say?

2. One of Shirley's colleague invites her for dinner on Saturday evening, but she is busy that night, if you were Shirley, how would you refuse your colleague politely?

3. Jenny invites Clive to go out for a picnic on the coming weekend. Clive decides to receive her invitation. What would he say to Jenny?

4. Benjamin asks Todd to a concert next Saturday. Todd accepts his invitation. If you were Todd, what would you say to Benjamin?

5. Jane asks Shirley to go for a sale tomorrow. But Shirley has to go to the gym then. So how will she refuse Jane politely?

**R**ecitation 经典背诵

**Terry:** Benjamin is a good friend of mine from China. We both love collecting stamps very much. To get more stamps, I often go to the post office to buy the newly issued ones. My biggest hobby is to swap some stamps with friends. It's really fun.

## Topic 4 汇款
### Remittance

听学看 寄完包裹,订完杂志,本杰明还想给马诺丽亚公司汇一千元钱。填邮政汇款的汇款单是一件比较麻烦的事,来看看都有哪些手续吧!

**Postal clerk**：Good morning, may I help you?

**Benjamin**：Hello, I want to remit one thousand yuan to Magnolia Company.

**Postal clerk**：Please fill out this form, please.

**Benjamin**：OK… Do I put on Magnolia Company for the receiver?

**Postal clerk**：Yes. You must put on its name and full address.

**Benjamin**：OK, I see. Here you are. Is that OK now?

**Postal clerk**：Let me check. Yes. Your one thousand remittance, please.

**Benjamin**：Here you are. What is the rate?

**Postal clerk**：This rate is one percent. That will be 10 yuan.

**Benjamin**：OK, when will this remittance arrive?

**Postal clerk**：Generally it will arrive within a week.

**Benjamin**：That's good. Is there anything else?

**Postal clerk**：No. That's all. You have to take good care of this copy of this transfer order.

**Benjamin**：Thanks, I will.

**邮局职员:**早上好,请问有什么可以帮您?

**本杰明:**你好,我想给马诺丽亚公司汇一千元钱。

**邮局职员:**请您填一下这张表格。

**本杰明:**好的……在收款人一项写马诺丽亚公司吗?

**邮局职员:**是的。您必须填写它的名称和完整地址。

**本杰明:**好的,知道了。给你。这样行吗?

**邮局职员:**我看看,可以了。请给我您的一千元汇款。

**本杰明:**这就是。请问手续费率是多少?

**邮局职员:**是百分之一。就是十元。

**本杰明:**好的。这些汇款什么时候能到?

**邮局职员:**一般来说,一周之内就会到。

**本杰明:**好的。还有别的什么事情吗?

**邮局职员:**不,没有了。您得保管好这张汇款单。

**本杰明:**谢谢,我会的。

---

### 生词小结

**remit** *vt.* 汇款
**receiver** *n.* 收款人
**remittance** *n.* 汇款

**generally** *adv.* 一般来说
**transfer order** 汇款单

## G语法小结 rammer —— 情态动词 must 和 have to

（1）情态动词 must 和 have to 都有"必须"的意思，但 have to 表示客观的需要，而 must 表示说话人主观上的看法，认为有义务、有必要去做某事

*My little brother was very ill, so I had to call a doctor.*

我弟弟病得厉害，我只得请医生了。（客观需要做）

*She said that she must work hard to get a high mark.*

她说她必须得努力学习得高分。（主观需要做）

（2）have to 有人称、数、时态的变化，而 must 只有一种形式

*He has to do it.* 他必须得做。

*I had to look after my brother because of his illness.* 我得照顾我弟弟，因为他病了。

（3）have to 和 must 的否定

have to 需要有助动词 do / did / does 的帮助才能表示其否定式，其否定式为 doesn't didn't don't have to，表示"不必"；而 must 的否定式是 mustn't，表示"禁止"，例如：

*You don't have to tell her about it.* 你不一定要把此事告诉她。

*You mustn't tell her about it.* 你一定不要把这件事告诉她。

## D家庭总动员 o it together

**两人一组，一方朗诵下面的中文句子，另一方挑选出合适的翻译。**

1. 我必须寄一个包裹。

2. 为了英语学习，我不得不订阅一些杂志。

3. 我必须买一套新发行的邮票。

4. 我不得不给马诺丽亚公司汇一千元钱。

5. 我不得不保管好这张汇款单。

1. I have to take good care of this copy of this transfer order.

2. I must buy a set of newly issued stamps.

3. For learning English, I have to subscribe to some magazines.

4. I must deliver a parcel.

5. I had to remit one thousand yuan to Magnolia Company.

## Recitation 经典背诵

**Benjamin**：I want to remit one thousand yuan to Magnolia Company. In the transfer order, I put on Magnolia Company for the receiver and full address. This rate is one percent of the total amount of the remittance. It takes about a week to be done. That's fast!

# 银行 Bank

## Goals

在这个场景中,我们将学到:

1. 疑问句的语调(一般和特殊)
2. 各国货币名称的词汇
3. 表达数量的句型
4. 情态动词 can 和 be able to,may

## Topic 1 存款 Depositing

玩转语音

1. How many sheets could a sheet slitter slit if a sheet slitter could slit sheets?
2. How much dew would a dewdrop drop if a dewdrop could drop dew?

及格时间:20秒
你的纪录:——秒
及格时间:20秒
你的纪录:——秒

听 学 看

本杰明想去银行往自己的账户里存1000元钱。让我们来看看存折、存款单、利率这些存款时常用的词汇在英语里怎么说。

| | |
|---|---|
| **Bank clerk**:Good morning, sir. Can I help you? | **银行职员:**早上好,先生。我能帮您点什么吗? |
| **Benjamin**:Yes, I want to deposit 1000 yuan in my bank account. | **本杰明:**是的,我想在银行账户中存1000元钱。 |
| **Bank clerk**:Please fill out this deposit form, first. | **银行职员:**请先填一下这张存款单。 |
| **Benjamin**:OK... Here you are. Any problem on that? | **本杰明:**好的……填好了。有什么问题吗? |
| **Bank clerk**:No, that's fine. Do you bring your bankbook with you? | **银行职员:**没有问题,很好。您带存折了吗? |
| **Benjamin**:Yes, I do. Here it is, and the cash. | **本杰明:**带了。这是存折,还有现金。 |
| **Bank clerk**:Wait a moment, please. | **银行职员:**请等一等。 |
| **Benjamin**:Sure. | **本杰明:**好的。 |

**Band clerk**：Is there anything else I can do for you?

**Benjamin**：Yes. Can you tell me what the interest rate is now?

**Bank clerk**：The deposit rate is 0.8% every month.

**Benjamin**：Thanks.

**银行职员**：您还需要其他帮助吗？

**本杰明**：你能告诉我目前的存款利率吗？

**银行职员**：存款利率是每月0.8%。

**本杰明**：谢谢。

---

**生词小结**

**deposit**　*n.* 存款
**bankbook**　*n.* 存折

**interest rate**　利息率

---

## 语音小结
### Pronunciation —— 疑问句的语调

1. 一般疑问句：一般问句用升调，它的回答用降调
   —Do you like my new hair style? ↗
   —Yes, like a cock being fighting. ↘

2. 特殊疑问句：特殊问句一般用降调，句首的疑问词一般重读
   —What are you talking about? ↘
   —I said you are a good girl. ↘
   —Who is that girl walked with you last night? ↘
   —Oh, I see it's not you! ↘

   听录音，并朗诵下面对话
   —Are you going to the bank? ↗
   —Yes, I need to deposit some money. ↘
   —What's the rate of exchange right now? ↘
   —Actually, I don't know. But I know the guy working in the bank knows. ↘

---

**Recitation** 经典背诵

**Benjamin**：It's easy to deposit money in your bank account. But you'd better bring your bankbook with you. If you don't, they will give you a new one. You just need to fill out the deposit form and they will take care of the rest. The deposit is often low for current account.

# Topic 2 换钱
## Changing Money

泰瑞在中国旅行,想换一些人民币。他来到银行,发现当天澳元对人民币的汇率比昨天低。他手里拿着一千澳元,换还是不换呢?

**Bank clerk**: Good morning, sir. What can I do for you?

**Terry**: Yes, I'd like to change Australian dollars for RMB.

**Bank clerk**: How much do you want to change?

**Terry**: I am not sure. What's the rate today?

**Bank clerk**: It's 1 Australian dollar to 6. 1 yuan RMB.

**Terry**: What was the rate yesterday?

**Bank clerk**: The rate was 1 Australia dollar to 6. 5 yuan yesterday.

**Terry**: Oh, the rate goes down.

**Bank clerk**: It does, sir. Do you still want to have it changed now?

**Terry**: Let me think…Will the rate still go down tomorrow?

**Bank clerk**: I don't know, sir. But it won't change much.

**Terry**: Well, I want to change 1000 Australian dollars for RMB.

**Bank clerk**: Okay. Please sign here in this form.

**Terry**: OK.

**Bank clerk**: Here is the 6,100 RMB.

**Terry**: Thank you very much.

银行职员:早上好,先生。请问有什么可以帮助您?

泰瑞:是的,我想把澳元换成人民币。

银行职员:您想换多少?

泰瑞:我不敢肯定。今天的汇率是多少?

银行职员:1澳元兑6.1元人民币。

泰瑞:那昨天的汇率呢?

银行职员:是1澳元兑6.5元人民币。

泰瑞:哦,汇率跌了。

银行职员:是的,先生。您还想换吗?

泰瑞:我想想……汇率明天还会跌吗?

银行职员:我不知道,先生。但不会有太大变化。

泰瑞:嗯,我想换1000澳元。

银行职员:好的。请在这张表格上签个名。

泰瑞:好的。

银行职员:这是你的6100元人民币。

泰瑞:谢谢。

生词小结

| | | | |
|---|---|---|---|
| **Australia dollar** | *澳元* | **sign** *vt.* 签名 |
| **change** *vt.* 兑换 | | **form** *n.* 表格 |

## 单词扩展 Vocabulary Builder

### 各国货币名称的词汇

| 基础词汇 | 提高词汇 |
|---|---|
| US dollar（USD）美元 | krone 克朗 |
| Canadian dollar（CAD）加元 | rouble 卢布 |
| Australian dollar（AUD）澳元 | peso 比索 |
| pound（GBP）英镑 | won（KRW）韩元 |
| euro（EUR）欧元 | Swiss franc（CHF）瑞士法郎 |
| Hongkong dollar（HKD）港币 | yen（JPY）日元 |
| | New Zealand dollar（NZD）新西兰元 |

## Do it together 家庭总动员

两人一组，一方随机大声读出上面词汇的英文和中文，另一方用该词汇填入下面的句子，大声朗读并表演出来，并用中文给出一个汇率。

**I want to exchange some（ ）for RMB.**

【例】 家长读 US dollar（USD）美元

孩子读 I want to exchange some US dollar for RMB.

家长说 人民币对美元的汇率是 7.98 比 1。

**Recitation** 经典背诵

**Terry**：I travel in China a lot. When I'm in need for some cash, I'd just go to a bank to convert Australian dollars to RMB. The converting rate is 1 Australian dollar to 6.1yuan RMB. Sometimes it goes up, sometimes it goes down. But it rarely changes much.

# Topic3 兑现
## Cashing a Check

泰瑞换完了澳元,又想兑换一些旅行支票。他问清了兑换比率、服务费,复签完后,发现自己竟然忘了带护照,这下又该怎么办呢?

**Bank clerk**: May I help you?

**Terry**: Yes, can I cash my traveler's check here?

**Bank clerk**: Of course, we'd be happy to cash it for you.

**Terry**: What's the cashing rate?

**Bank clerk**: Well, it's listed on the electronic board on the left. We cash it at present traveler's check buying rate.

**Terry**: Oh, I see. How much is the service charge?

**Bank clerk**: The service charge is 1% of the total amount of the check.

**Terry**: Well, I'd like to cash these four checks for $100 each.

**Bank clerk**: Would you please countersign them here?

**Terry**: OK, there you are.

**Bank clerk**: And your passport please.

**Terry**: Oh, I forgot to bring it. It is in my hotel room.

**Bank clerk**: Sorry, sir. We can't cash the checks for you without your passport.

**Terry**: Well, thanks. I will come again this afternoon, then.

**银行职员:**请问有什么可以帮助您的?

**泰瑞:**是的,我能在这儿兑换我的旅行支票吗?

**银行职员:**当然啦,我们很高兴能为您兑换。

**泰瑞:**兑换的比率是多少?

**银行职员:**比率都列在左边的电子榜上。我们是以现在旅行支票的买入比率兑换。

**泰瑞:**哦,我知道了。那服务费是多少?

**银行职员:**服务费是支票总额的 1%。

**泰瑞:**好的,我想换四张 100 美元的旅行支票。

**银行职员:**您能在这儿复签一下吗?

**泰瑞:**好的,签好了。

**银行职员:**您的护照?

**泰瑞:**哦,我忘带了。它在我的旅馆房间里。

**银行职员:**对不起,先生。没有护照我们不能为您兑换。

**泰瑞:**谢谢,那我下午再来。

生词小结

**cash** *vt.* 兑现  **check** *n.* 支票
**electronic** *adj.* 电子的  **countersign** *vt.* 复签
**board** *n.* 榜

# F功能性句型扩展 —— 表达数量的句型
unctional structure

**请朗读以下句型，家长和孩子交替进行。**

1. 用于可数名词

How many... ……有多少
Which one... 哪一个……
There are a few... ……只有一点。
There are few... ……几乎没有。
There are a lot of... ……有很多。
There are lots of... ……有很多。

2. 用于不可数名词

How much... ……有多少
There is a little... ……只有一点。
There is little... ……几乎没有。

3. 序数词和频率

The first, the second, the third... 第一，第二，第三……
Once, twice... 一次，两次
Three times, four times, five times... 三次，四次，五次……

**Recitation**
经典背诵

**Terry**：I always need to cash some of my traveler's checks. I can cash them in the hotel. But the bank gives a better rate. The service charge is 1% of the total amount of the check. The only problem is that I often forget to bring my passport with me, and without it, they can't get it done.

理财
**Financing**

本杰明想要在银行开个存款账户。银行存款账户的利息率还不算低,据说还有别的好事,会是什么呢? 往下看吧。

Benjamin：Hello, I'd like to open an account.

Bank clerk：Which account would you like to open?

Benjamin：I'd like to open a savings account. What's the interest rate now?

Bank clerk：It is 3.2%. You may earn a little interest on money.

Benjamin：Is there any minimum deposit for the first time?

Bank clerk：Yes, the opening minimum deposit is 1,000 yuan.

Benjamin：What about the later deposits?

Bank clerk：For the later deposits, you can deposit any you want. Even one yuan is OK.

Benjamin：OK, that's good.

Bank clerk：Your ID, please.

Benjamin：Here you are, a thousand yuan and my ID.

Bank clerk：Wait a moment, please... Here is your bankbook. Keep it well please.

Benjamin：Thanks I will.

本杰明：你好,我想开个账户。

银行职员：您想开什么样的账户?

本杰明：我想开个存款账户。现在的利率是多少?

银行职员：是 3.2%。您可以赚一点利息。

本杰明：第一次存款有最低额度限制吗?

银行职员：是的,第一次存款的最低额度是1000 元。

本杰明：那以后的额度呢?

银行职员：然后您可以任意存。存一元也行。

本杰明：好的。

银行职员：把您的身份证给我。

本杰明：给你,1000 块钱和我的身份证。

银行职员：请等一等。……这是您的存折。请好好保存。

本杰明：谢谢,我会的。

**生词小结**

account    *n.* 账户
savings account    存款账户

earn    *vt.* 赚
minimum    *adj.* 最低的

**G**rammer 语法小结 —— 情态动词 can 和 be able to，may

1. 情态动词 can 和 be able to

can 和 be able to 都可以表示有某种能力，但 can 只能用于现在时和过去时（could），而 be able to 可以用于任何时态。

*I can do this job.* 我能做这个工作。

*I will be able to do this job soon.* 我很快就能做这个工作。

如果要表示"成功地做了某事"时，只能用 was/were able to，例如：

*He was able to flee the country before the war broke out.* 在战争爆发之前，他成功地逃离了这个国家。

2. 情态动词 may

may 表示允许或请求，和没有把握的推测。当 may 放在句首，表示祝愿。

*May God bless you!* 上帝保佑你！

*He might be at home.* 他可能在家里。

might 是 may 的过去时，但在表示推测时，不表示过去的时态，只是 might 表示的可能性比 may 小。

*Might I use your pen?* 我能用你的笔吗？

**D**o it together 家庭总动员

两人一组，一方朗诵下面的中文句子，另一方挑选出合适的翻译。

1. 你可以开一个存款账户。
2. 我将能在银行账户里存一千块钱。
3. 你可以在支票上签名。
4. 你能带上存折吗？
5. 希望你能成功。

1. You can sign your name in this check.
2. Can you bring your bankbook with you?
3. May you success.
4. You can open a savings account.
5. I will be able to deposit 1000 yuan in my bank account.

 **R**ecitation 经典背诵

**Benjamin：**It's a wise decision to open a savings account because the interest rate is higher now. You may earn a little interest. There is often an opening minimun deposit. But for the later deposits, you can deposit any amount that you want.

## 电信 Telecom

**Goals**

在这个场景中,我们将学到:
1. 选择疑问句的语调
2. 世界 500 强部分大公司名称的词汇
3. 表达数量的句型练习
4. had better 的用法

**Topic 1  互联网**
**The Internet**

  玩转语音

1. Are there auks in the Arctic or are not there auks in the Arctic?
2. Whether the weather be fine or whether the weather be not.
3. Whether the weather be cold or whether the weather be hot.
4. We'll weather the weather whether we like it or not.

及格时间: 8 秒
你的纪录: ——秒
及格时间: 6 秒
你的纪录: ——秒
及格时间: 6 秒
你的纪录: ——秒
及格时间: 5 秒
你的纪录: ——秒

阿美的生日快到了,爸爸妈妈忽然想到在网上买个手机给阿美当作生日礼物,在他们正在感叹网络给生活带来的巨大方便时,电脑却突然出问题了。

**Shirley:** May's birthday is coming. Shall we buy her a birthday present or let her choose one for herself?

**Benjamin:** I think a surprise party may be better. But I forget when her birthday is.

**Shirley:** You are such a good father. It's next Sunday.

**Benjamin:** Sorry. What shall we get for her?

**Shirley:** What about a cellphone? She is old enough to have one.

**Benjamin:** Good idea. Shall we search on line to

**雪莉:**阿美的生日就快到了。我们该给她买个礼物还是让她自己挑一个呢?

**本杰明:**我觉得惊喜聚会可能更好。但我忘记她的生日是什么时候了。

**雪莉:**你可真是好爸爸啊,(她生日)就是下周日啊。

**本杰明:**抱歉,我们该给她买点什么呢?

**职员:**给她买个手机怎么样?她可以有一个了。

**本杰明:**好主意,我们是去上网找一款合适

find anappropriate one or go to a phone store?

Shirley：Maybe we can try shopping on line.

Benjamin：Sure. Okay, here is the website.

Shirley：I'm sure that May would love the pink one.

Benjamin：Probably. People's consumptive habit is changing rapidly because of the internet.

Shirley：Totally. Computers bring with them convenience.

Shirley：Oh, what's wrong?

Benjamin：The computer went frozen.

Shirley：Oh, it's such a pain. We'd better go to a store later.

的手机,还是去手机店啊?

雪莉:也许我们可以直接在网上购物。

本杰明:当然可以。好的,这有个网站。

雪莉:我确定阿美一定会喜欢这款粉红色的。

本杰明:很可能。因为因特网人们的消费习惯正迅速的改变着。

雪莉:确实如此。电脑带来了方便。

雪莉:哦,,怎么了?

本杰明:电脑死机了。

雪莉:它(电脑)也是个大麻烦。我们最好还是去手机店吧。

## 生词小结

| | |
|---|---|
| **present** *n.* 礼物 | **website** *n.* 网站 |
| **surprise party** 惊喜聚会 | **consumptive** *adj.* 消费的 |
| **cellphone** *n.* 手机 | **rapidly** *adv.* 迅速地 |
| **appropriate** *adj.* 适当的 | **internet** *n.* 因特网 |
| **on line** 联机的 | **convenience** *n.* 方便 |

## 语音小结 Pronunciation —— 选择疑问句的语调

**1.** 在说话人所说的几种选择中,前面的项用升调,最后一项用降调,中间的连接词用平调。

Shall we take a bus ↗ or a taxi ↘?

Shall we arrange our plan on Saturday ↗, Sunday or Monday ↘?

**2.** 如果其他选择说话人没有说出来,说话人说的几项几乎都用升调。

Shall we take the bus ↗ or take a taxi ↗?

Would you like some coffee ↗ or tea ↗?

**朗读练习**:Is your phone red ↗, green ↗, or black ↘?

Which kind of phone do you want to buy, Nokia ↗, Motorola ↗, or Lenovo ↘?

Should we turn in the money after a week ↗ or a month ↗?

Who wants to take class in Joy Chain, Daniel ↗ or May ↘?

## Recitation 经典背诵

Benjamin：Computers are changing people's lives so quickly. People's habits for consumption are so different from before. Through the internet we can shop on line. No doubt that computers bring with them convenience. But it's not always good, for sometimes it would go frozen at some key moments. That's a real pain.

## Topic 2 买手机
### Purchasing a Cellphone

无奈之下,雪莉还是来到了一家手机店,各种品牌的手机真不少,服务员的服务态度也还不错,又送挂饰又包装的,看来店铺还是有存在的理由。

**Salesperson:** What can I do for you, Ma'am?

**售货员:** 女士,有什么能效劳的吗?

**Shirley:** I want to buy a cellphone for my daughter.

**雪莉:** 我想给我的女儿买一个手机。

**Salesperson:** How old is she?

**售货员:** 她多大了?

**Shirley:** She is 17. It's for her birthday.

**雪莉:** 她 17 岁了。这是为她的生日买的。

**Salesperson:** We have a new-fashioned cellphone especially designed for young girls. The brand name is Nokia.

**售货员:** 我们有一款专门为年轻女孩设计的新款手机,是诺基亚的。

**Shirley:** Thanks, but I want to have a look at the Motorola's products.

**雪莉:** 谢谢,但是我想看看摩托罗拉的产品。

**Salesperson:** Sure. This is the one I will not hesitate to recommend. Its color and style is so attractive and also the quality is really reliable.

**售货员:** 好的。这款是我毫不犹豫要推荐的。它的颜色、款式很吸引人而且质量也很可靠。

**Shirley:** Sounds perfect. I'll take the pink one. Can you pack it for me?

**雪莉:** 听起来很不错。我要一款粉红色的。你能为我包装一下吗?

**Salesperson:** Sure. By the way, here are some free adornments. Would you like one?

**销售员:** 当然可以。顺便说一下,这些是免费的挂件,您想选一个吗?

**Shirley:** Why not? The Sweetheart pendant matches the cellphone well. I'd take this one.

**雪莉:** 为什么不呢? 这个爱心挂件很配手机,我就要这个了。

**Salesperson:** Have a seat over there. I'll pack it up for you right away.

**售货员:** 请在那边坐一会儿。我马上为您包装。

**Shirley:** Thanks.

**雪莉:** 谢谢。

## 生词小结

| | | | |
|---|---|---|---|
| newfashioned | *adj.* 新型的 | pack | *vt.* 包装 |
| product | *n.* 产品 | adornment | *n.* 装饰品 |
| hesitate | *vi.* 犹豫 | sweetheart | *n.* 爱人，恋人 |
| attractive | *adj.* 有吸引力的 | pendant | *n.* 挂件 |
| reliable | *adj.* 可靠的 | | |

## 单词扩展 Vocabulary Builder

### 世界 500 强部分大公司名称的词汇

| 基础词汇 | 提高词汇 |
|---|---|
| Sony 索尼(日) | Carrefour 家乐福(法) |
| Siemens 西门子(德) | Volkswagen 大众(德) |
| Ford Motor 福特汽车(美) | Citigroup 花旗集团(美) |
| Coca-cola 可口可乐(美) | Nestle 雀巢(瑞士) |
| Microsoft 微软(美) | Wal-Mart Stores 沃尔玛商店(美) |
| Sangsung 三星(韩) | Unilever 联合利华(荷) |
| Dell computer 戴尔电脑(美) | Procter&Gamble 保洁(美) |
| General Motors 通用汽车(美) | Credit Suisse 瑞士信贷集团(瑞士) |

## D 家庭总动员
## o it together

两人一组，一方随机大声读出上面词汇的英文和中文，另一方用该词汇填入下面的句子，大声朗读并表演出来，并用中文给出一个理由

**I want to have a look at the (          ) / (          )'s product.**

【例】家长读 Sony 索尼(日)

孩子读 I want to have a look at the Sony's product. 因为很有名。

**Recitation** 经典背诵

**Salesperson**：I work in a cellphone store. Each day we sell many new models which are designed for different kinds of people. We also give the customers some free adornments which can always make them feel satisfied. We'll also pack them up if they want. I think it's good to be busy and happy!

# Topic 3 手机充值卡
## Pre-paid Phone Cards

听 学 读 看

　　买了手机，接着自然是买电话卡，充话费了，手机套餐种类还真不少，还有专门为学生设计的套餐呢，真不错！

| | |
|---|---|
| **Clerk**：Can I help you, Ma'am? | **职员**：女士，有什么能效劳吗？ |
| **Shirley**：I need a phone card for this new cell-phone. | **雪莉**：我要为这部新手机买一张手机卡。 |
| **Clerk**：Cool phone. What kind of phone card do you want? | **职员**：手机很靓。你想要什么样的手机卡？ |
| **Shirley**：It's for my daughter who is still a senior high school student. | **雪莉**：是给我的女儿的，她还是一个高中生。 |
| **Clerk**：Then the M-Zone will be suitable. | **职员**：那么动感地带的卡会比较合适她。 |
| **Shirley**：What's special with the service? | **雪莉**：它的服务有什么特点呢？ |
| **Clerk**：You know students use texted message service. And they provide favourable service for that. | **职员**：你知道学生喜欢发短信。这个卡在这方面有很好的服务。 |
| **Shirley**：That's nice. And I need a pre-paid phone card. | **雪莉**：那不错。我还要一张充值卡。 |
| **Clerk**：Oh, there is a sales promotion for it now. | **职员**：哦，正好现在有（充值卡）促销活动。 |
| **Shirley**：Oh, good. Then what is it? | **雪莉**：哦，真好。什么样的（促销）？ |
| **Clerk**：If you buy a pre-paid phone card worth 100 yuan today, you will get 50 yuan for free. | **职员**：如果您今天买一张面值100元的充值卡，您还将免费获得50元话费。 |
| **Shirley**：May I have two of them? | **雪莉**：我可以买两张吗？ |
| **Clerk**：Sure. As many as you want. | **职员**：当然。要多少张都可以。 |
| **Shirley**：Okay, then a third one for my husband too. | **雪莉**：好的，那再给我丈夫买一张好了。 |

## 生词小结

**phone card**　手机卡

**texted**　*adj.* 编写的

**message**　*n.* 信息

**favorable**　*adj.* 良好的

**pre-paid**　*adj.* 预先支付的

**sales promotion**　促销

## 注释

**M-Zone**：动感地带，是在学生中比较流行的一种手机卡，它提供比较优惠的短信套餐。

## 情景练习
### Scene practice —— 表达数量的句型练习

仔细阅读下面五个场景，两人一组，使用表达数量的句型（见 301 页），用一用，练一练。

1. Shirley wants to know the price of the shoes, what would she say to the salesman?

2. Benjamin wants to express there are countless people in the supermarket, if you were Benjamin, how would you express it to your wife?

3. If you were Daniel, you are asked how often do you play football, what would you say?

4. Jane wants to know the number of Shirley's family member, if you were Jane, how would you ask Shirley?

5. May wants to know which book is hers, if you were May, what would you say to Daniel?

## Recitation 经典背诵

**Clerk**：My job is to sell phone cards. More and more people start to use cellphones especially the senior high school students. And they always use text message services. So I will always recommend the "M-zone" phone card if it's for students. Even though it's tiring, I still love my job.

网络安全
**Internet Security**

本杰明请来了电脑维修人员,经检查发现电脑是由于受到了病毒感染而死机,原来本家的电脑没有装杀毒软件,不想当"电脑盲"的话,看来只好恶补电脑知识了。

**Repairman**: What can I do?

**Benjamin**: The system crashed when I was surfing on the internet.

**Repairman**: Did you go to any illegal website?

**Benjamin**: No. But does that matter?

**Repairman**: Yes, your computer can be easily infected by virus if you do that.

**Benjamin**: I see. I'd better never try.

**Repairman**: That's wise.

**Benjamin**: Do you know what's wrong with my PC?

**Repairman**: One minute. Oh, yes, it was infected by a virus, and you had no antivirus software.

**Benjamin**: Is anti-virus software necessary for a PC?

**Repairman**: Of course. You'd better learn something about it.

**Benjamin**: I'm afraid yes. But what about the data I stored in the computer?

**Repairman**: Don't worry, it should have been protected automatically. And I take an anti-virus software with me. Do you want me to install it now?

**Benjamin**: Yes, please. I'll really appreciate that.

维修员:我需要做什么?

本杰明:我正在上网,电脑却突然死机了。

维修员:你上过非法网站吗?

本杰明:没有。那有关系吗?

维修员:是的,如果那么做您的电脑很容易受到病毒感染。

本杰明:知道了。那最好不要尝试。

维修员:那是明智的。

本杰明:你知道我的电脑怎么了吗?

维修员:等一下。哦,是的,它感染病毒了,你没有装杀毒软件啊?

本杰明:对于电脑,杀毒软件是必需的吗?

维修员:当然了。你最好对它多一些了解。

本杰明:恐怕是要这样。不过我原来存在电脑里的数据会怎样?

维修员:别担心。应该已经被自动保存了。我带了杀毒软件,您希望我现在帮您安装吗?

本杰明:请装吧。很感谢你。

## 生词小结

| | | | |
|---|---|---|---|
| **surf** | *vi.* 冲浪 | **anti-virus software** | 防病毒软件 |
| **illegal** | *adj.* 非法的 | **data** | *n.* 资料 |
| **infect** | *vt.* 感染 | **automatically** | *adv.* 自动地 |
| **virus** | *n.* 病毒 | **install** | *vt.* 安装 |
| **wise** | *adj.* 英明的 | | |

## G语法小结 —— had better 的用法
Grammer

had better(常简略为 'd better)是固定词组,常表示"最好",用于表示对别人的劝告、建议或表示一种愿望,主语不论是第几人称,句子不论是什么时态,都要用 had better 的形式。其用法有以下几点:

1. had better 后面必须跟动词原形

   had better 后跟动词原形,即不带 to 的不定式,构成 had better do sth. 句型,例如:

   *You'd better go to hospital at once.* 你最好立即去医院看病。

2. had better 的否定式

   常用的否定形式是将 not 直接放在 had better 的后面,例如:

   *You had better not do that stupid thing.* 你最好不要做那样愚蠢的事。

   *You had better not leave her alone.* 你最好别不理她。

3. 在祈使句中,had 有时可以省略

   *Better not do it.* 最好别做那事。

   *Better not wait for them.* 最好不要等他们。

## D家庭总动员
Do it together

两人一组,一方朗诵下面的中文句子,另一方挑选出合适的翻译。

1. 你最好上网找一部合适的手机。
2. 你最好学一些关于电脑的知识。
3. 你最好给这部新的手机买一张卡。
4. 你最好记住阿美的生日。
5. 你最好保护好电脑里的数据。

1. You'd better protect the data in the computer.
2. You'd better remember the birthday of May.
3. You'd better learn something about the computer.
4. You'd better search on line to find an appropriate cellphone.
5. You'd better buy a phone card for this new cellphone.

## Recitation
经典背诵

**Repairman**：I repair computers everyday. Many people don't know the right way to use computers. Many of them wonder how to protect their computers from being infected by virus. Some of them keep on logging on the illegal websites where some virus may be lurking. I think people should learn something about the computer before using it.

# 博物馆 Museum

## Goals

在这个场景中，我们将学到：

1. 反意疑问句的语调
2. 各类博物馆的词汇
3. 表达感叹的句型
4. so...that 的用法

Topic 1 电影 Movies

Tongue Twister　玩转语音

1. Would if I could, and if I couldn't, how could I? You couldn't, unless you could, could you?
2. Mares eat oats and does eat oats, and little lambs eat ivy. A kid will eat ivy too, wouldn't you?

及格时间：10 秒
你的纪录：—— 秒
及格时间：10 秒
你的纪录：—— 秒

听 学 看

丹尼尔和阿美来到了电影博物馆，他们谈起了各自喜欢的电影，我们来看看他们都喜欢什么电影吧？

**Daniel:** Hey, May, look, Is that the the poster of the movie we saw yesterday?

**May:** Yes, that's right. That's the poster of the "The Witch".

**Daniel:** May, I really regret watching it with you last night.

**May:** Did it scare you?

**Daniel:** Of course not. I just thought the movie was…boring.

**May:** Boring? Come on, you clutched to my arm all the time.

**Daniel:** Well, I admit. The ghosts were scary.

**May:** I like scary movies.

**Daniel:** That's Gucci's influence. I love science

丹尼尔：嗨，阿美，你看，那是我们昨天看的那个电影的海报吗？

阿美：是的，那是《巫婆》的海报。

丹尼尔：阿美，我真后悔昨晚跟你一起看《巫婆》。

阿美：它吓到你了吗？

丹尼尔：当然不是啦。我只是觉得那电影……很无聊。

阿美：无聊？得了吧，你一直抓着我的胳膊呢。

丹尼尔：好吧，我承认。那些鬼很吓人。

阿美：我喜欢恐怖电影。

丹尼尔：那都是受了古奇的影响。我喜

fiction movies!

May: Of course you do. They are silly stories just for little kids like you.

Daniel: Don't call me kid. I am a grownup.

May: Do you dare watch scary movies with me tonight?

Daniel: Of course! I can watch them without you!

May: Oh, really?

欢看科幻电影!

阿美: 你当然喜欢啦。它们都是些适合像你这样的小孩的幼稚电影。

丹尼尔: 别叫我小孩。我是大人了。

阿美: 那你今晚敢跟我看恐怖电影吗?

丹尼尔: 当然啦! 我敢一个人看。

阿美: 哦,是吗?

## 生词小结

| poster | n. 海报 | scary | adj. 恐怖的 |
|---|---|---|---|
| witch | n. 巫婆 | influence | n. 影响 |
| clutch | vi. 紧抓着 | science fiction | 科幻 |
| ghost | n. 鬼 | tonight | n. 今晚 |

## P语音小结 —— 反意疑问句的语调
ronunciation

反意疑问句前一部分用降调,后一部分分为两种情况

(1)提问者对所提问题没有把握时,希望对方回答时用升调

—Mary will marry next month, won't she? ↗

—Yes, I know. But the bridegroom is not me.

(2)提问者对所提问题有很大把握,希望对方证实时,句末用降调

—You had a quarrel with your roommates last night, didn't you? ↓

—Yes, she really irritated me.

朗读下面句子:

It's silly, isn't it?

The child isn't telling the truth, is he?

We are going to visit the Military Museum, aren't we?

The Chinese Four Invention is very famous, isn't it?

**R**ecitation
经典背诵

Daniel: My sister May loves horror movies. But I hate them because I don't dare to watch them. I like science fiction movies which are far more interesting in my eye. But May always laughs at me saying they are just silly stories for little kids. And that's not right.

# Topic 2 历史博物馆
## Museum of History

听 学 看

丹尼尔和阿美来到历史博物馆。丹尼尔被木乃伊的模型吓坏了，拉着阿美要离开。结果怎么样呢？

**May:** Danny, see, this is the museum of history. We are in the Egypt Hall.

**Daniel:** What's that in the white cloth?

**May:** It's a model of Egyptian mummy.

**Daniel:** Egyptian mummy ... May, could we leave here?

**May:** Why, Danny? We just came in.

**Daniel:** It looks scaring. May, I am afraid of ghosts.

**May:** They are preserved dead bodies, not ghosts.

**Daniel:** Ghosts, or dead bodies, whatever, I don't want to see them anymore. Let's go, May.

**May:** Oh, God. I shouldn't have let you watch "*The Witch*".

**Daniel:** I have been having nightmares these days.

**May:** Danny, listen, there are no ghosts in this world, OK?

**Daniel:** OK. But May, where do people go after they die?

**May:** I don't know, Danny.

**阿美：**丹丹，看，这就是历史博物馆。我们在埃及馆。

**丹尼尔：**那个裹着白布的是什么？

**阿美：**那是埃及木乃伊的模型。

**丹尼尔：**埃及木乃伊……阿美，我们能离开这儿吗？

**阿美：**为什么，丹丹？我们刚进来呀。

**丹尼尔：**它看起来吓人。阿美，我怕鬼。

**阿美：**它们是经过防腐处理的尸体，不是鬼。

**丹尼尔：**不管是鬼还是尸体，我再也不想看见它们了。我们走吧，阿美。

**阿美：**哦，天哪。我真不该让你看《巫婆》。

**丹尼尔：**我这几天一直做噩梦。

**阿美：**丹丹，听着，这世界上没有鬼，知道吗？

**丹尼尔：**知道了。但是阿美，人们死后去了哪里呢？

**阿美：**我不知道，丹丹。

---

**生词小结**

| | |
|---|---|
| **museum** *n.* 博物馆 | **mummy** *n.* 木乃伊 |
| **cloth** *n.* 布 | **preserve** *vt.* 防腐保存 |
| **Egyptian** *adj.* 埃及的 | **whatever** *pron.* 无论什么 |

## 单词扩展 Vocabulary Builder

### 各类博物馆的词汇

| 基础词汇 | 提高词汇 |
| --- | --- |
| museum of history 历史博物馆 | museum of natural history 自然博物馆 |
| science museum 科学博物馆 | memorial 纪念馆 |
| military museum 军事博物馆 | planetarium 天文馆 |
| art museum 艺术博物馆 | the Louvre 卢浮宫 |
| the British Museum 大英博物馆 | aquarium 水族馆 |
| Eco-Museum 生态博物馆 | |

## D家庭总动员
o it together

两人一组，一方随机大声读出上面词汇的英文和中文，另一方用该词汇填入下面的句子，大声朗读并表演出来，并用中文给出一个理由。

**I want to go to** (                              ).

【例】家长读 history museum 历史博物馆
孩子读 I want to go to history museum. 因为我想看历史展览。

**R**ecitation
经典背诵

May：There are various museums in Beijing. Most of them are free. Danny and I always enjoy visiting them in our spare time. But he doesn't like history museums because there are Egyptian mummies in it. After all, he is just a kid, no matter how he denys it.

## Topic3 文物保护
### Conservation of Cultural Relics

听 学 看

丹尼尔对博物馆里所有的文物都被装在玻璃瓶里表示疑惑,阿美告诉他那是为了保护文物不被腐蚀。丹丹还差点以为一个四千年前的三脚杯毫无价值。

| | |
|---|---|
| **Daniel**: May, is this the Hall of Ancient China? | **丹尼尔**: 阿美,这是古代中国馆吗? |
| **May**: Yes. Look at these historical relics here, amazing! | **阿美**: 是啊。看这些历史遗址,真令人惊叹! |
| **Daniel**: Why are they all in glass boxes? | **丹尼尔**: 为什么它们都被装在玻璃瓶里呢? |
| **May**: For protection. Some relics will turn to dust if exposed to air. | **阿美**: 为了保护它们啊。一些文物放在空气中就会变成粉末。 |
| **Daniel**: So there isn't air in the glass boxes? | **丹尼尔**: 那么玻璃瓶中没有空气了? |
| **May**: No, there isn't. They are all vacuumed. | **阿美**: 没有。它们都是真空的。 |
| **Daniel**: I wonder how old these things are, thousands of years? | **丹尼尔**: 真不知这些东西有多古老,几千年? |
| **May**: Yeah, they all come from a very ancient time. | **阿美**: 是啊,它们都是来自古代。 |
| **Daniel**: Hey, look at the three-leg cup. I've seen it on TV. | **丹尼尔**: 嘿,看这个三只脚的杯子。我在电视上看到过。 |
| **May**: The bronze cup was made 4,000 years ago. It's priceless! | **阿美**: 四千年前的青铜杯子。这可是无价之物! |
| **Daniel**: Yeah, it has no value at all. Who will use this cup today? | **丹尼尔**: 是啊,没有一点价值。如今谁会用这种杯子啊? |
| **May**: Danny, priceless means so valuable that you can't put a price on it. | **阿美**: 丹丹,无价意味着价值大得无法计算。 |
| **Daniel**: Oh, it does? | **丹尼尔**: 哦,是吗? |

**生词小结**

| | |
|---|---|
| ancient *adj.* 古老的 | bronze *n.* 青铜 |
| historical *adj.* 历史的 | priceless *adj.* 无价的 |
| dust *n.* 粉末,灰尘 | valuable *adj.* 有价值的,贵重的 |
| vacuum *vt.* 抽成真空 | |

# F功能性句型扩展
## unctional structure —— 表示感叹的句型

**请朗读以下句型,家长和孩子交替进行**

1. 愤怒

My god! 天!

What a nuisance! 真讨厌!

I am extremely displeased about... 我很气愤……

2. 赞叹

How marvelous! 真神奇!

How wonderful! 真了不起!

That's fantastic! 棒极了!

It looks terrific! 看上去棒极了!

It's so splendid! 太棒了!

3. 高兴

I am pleased about... 我很开心……

I am excited about... 我太兴奋了……

I can't say how pleased I am to... 我简直说不出自己有多开心……

I am delighted to hear that...我很高兴地听到……

*Recitation* 经典背诵

Daniel：I like the Hall of Ancient China in a history museum. The historical relics there, are amazing! They all come from a very ancient time. That's so cool. They are all kept in glass boxes which are all vacuumed for protection. May says they are priceless!

# Topic 4 四大发明
## The Four Great Inventions

丹尼尔和阿美在观看中国古代的四大发明。丹丹觉得那些都是简单的东西,没有什么意义。其实他们的发明者都是一些很聪明的人。那最后丹丹的观点有没有改变呢?

**May:** There are so many people that the tickets are all sold out!

**Daniel:** Luckily we got the last two.

**May:** Look, Danny. The Four Great Inventions!

**Daniel:** Gunpowder, compass, the paper making, and the printing.

**May:** I really admire those who made such great inventions!

**Daniel:** May, I don't see why they are great. They are just simple things.

**May:** They look simple today. But they were milestones in their times.

**Daniel:** Milestones? May, you must be kidding.

**May:** Just think Bill Gates, those inventions are as important as the Windows system.

**Daniel:** Well, I suppose the ancient inventors made a lot of money out of them.

**May:** No, quite the contrary.

**Daniel:** Why? Didn't you say that they were milestones?

**May:** Yes, but they went to the public without any patent protection.

**Daniel:** Well, their inventors were not as clever as Bill Gates.

阿美:人太多了,票都卖完了。

丹尼尔:幸好我们买了最后两张。

阿美:看,丹丹,四大发明!

丹尼尔:火药、指南针、造纸术和印刷术。

阿美:我真崇拜这些伟大的发明者。

丹尼尔:阿美,我不明白有什么伟大的。它们只是些很简单的东西啊。

阿美:它们今天看起来很简单。但在它们那个时代却是里程碑。

丹尼尔:里程碑? 阿美,你在开玩笑吧。

阿美:想想比尔·盖茨,那些发明的重要性不亚于 Windows 操作系统。

丹尼尔:我想古代的发明家们肯定从它们身上赚了不少钱吧。

阿美:不,恰恰相反。

丹尼尔:为什么? 你不是说它们是里程碑吗?

阿美:是啊,但是它们没有任何专利保护就进入市场了。

丹尼尔:哦,它们的发明者可没有比尔·盖茨那么聪明啊。

### 生词小结

| | |
|---|---|
| **ticket** *n.* 票 | **milestone** *n.* 里程碑 |
| **gunpowder** *n.* 火药 | **inventor** *n.* 发明家 |
| **compass** *n.* 指南针 | **patent** *n.* 专利 |
| **printing** *n.* 印刷术 | **clever** *adj.* 聪明的 |
| **simple** *adj.* 简单的 | |

## 语法小结
### Grammar —— so...that 的用法

"so... that..."句型表示"如此/这么……以至于……",常引导结果状语从句。…so that…则表示"以便,为了"。

(1)so... that...句型中的 so 是副词,常用句型为:

①主语 + 谓语 + so + *adj. /adv.* + that 从句

②主语 + 谓语 + so + many/much/ (a) few/(a) little + 名词 + that 从句

*My brother is so young that he cann't look after himself.* 我弟弟太小了而不能照顾自己。

*My mother was so angry that she couldn't say a word.* 我妈妈如此生气,以至于一句话也说不出来。

*This rich man has so much money that he can buy everything.* 这个富人这么有钱,他可以买一切东西。

*I have so much work to do that I cann't spend this weekend with you.* 我有如此多的工作要做,不能和你一起过周末了。

(2)so 与 that 也可连起来写,即变成:…so that… (以便 / 为了……),引导目的状语从句

*I got up early so that I could catch the early bus.* 我起得很早为了能赶上早班车。

*We must go now so that we won't be late.* 我们现在必须要走了,以防迟到(为了不迟到)。

## 家庭总动员
### Do it together

两人一组,一方朗诵下面的中文句子,另一方挑选出合适的翻译。

1. 电影很无聊,丹尼尔不喜欢。

2. 丹尼尔看了埃及木乃伊,所以晚上睡不着。

3. 青铜杯如此珍贵,没法给它标价。

4. 四大发明如此重要,我们应该崇拜那些发明者。

5. 我们必须快点以防买不着票。

1. The Four Great Inventions are so important that we should admire the inventors.

2. The bronze cup is so valuable that we can't put a price on it.

3. We should hurry up so that we can get tickets.

4. The film is so boring that Daniel doesn't like it.

5. Daniel has seen the Egyptian mummy so that he can't sleep well.

### Recitation 经典背诵

Daniel:The Four Great Inventions of China are very famous in the world. They are gunpowder, compass, paper making, and printing. They were milestones in human history. But they went to the public without any patent protection. Well, their inventors lost a good chance of making a lot of money out of them.

## 报亭/公共电话 Newsstand/Call Box

### Goals

在这个场景中，我们将学到：

1. 祈使句的语调
2. 报纸版面的词汇
3. 表达感叹的句型练习
4. as…as 的用法

# Topic 1 卖报
## Selling Newspaper

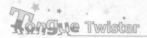 玩转语音

1. Don't spring on the inner - spring this spring or there will be an offspring next spring.
2. Don't pamper damp scamp tramps that camp under ramp lamps.

及格时间：9 秒
你的纪录：——秒
及格时间：6 秒
你的纪录：——秒

听学看

阿美陪着古奇到报亭买IC卡，结果却得到了一份兼职，好像很不错哦，一起来看看吧！

**Gucci：** What did the boss say?

**May：** He asked me if I'd like to be a newspaper salesperson?

**Gucci：** You are still student so I don't think you should have time for that.

**May：** Don't worry about that. He said I can do that at spare time. Anyway, it's just a part-time job.

**Gucci：** Okay, then. What kind of newspaper he wants you to sell?

**May：** It's a weekly newspaper named "*Olympic English*". So I need to be here only on Sunday.

**Gucci：** Sounds interesting. Especially that we are Olympic Volunteers.

**May：** That's exactly what I am thinking about.

古奇：老板说什么？

阿美：他问我愿不愿意做报纸促销员？

古奇：你还是学生怎么会有时间做这个。

阿美：这个倒不用担心。他说我可以用空余时间做。不管怎样，只是个兼职啊。

古奇：那挺好的。他想让你卖什么样的报纸呢？

阿美：是一份叫《奥运英语》的周刊。所以我只需要每个周日来这里就可以了。

古奇：听起来很有趣。尤其是我们还是奥运志愿者。

阿美：我也是这么想的。这也是增长社

And also it's a good way to get social experiences.

**Gucci:** And a good way to get some pocket money.

**May:** Let's do it together.

**Gucci:** I'll say yes. Wait a minute. I need an IC card.

**May:** For what? You have a telephone at home, don't you?

**Gucci:** Yes, but I don't want my Mom to tap my phone when I call Clive.

会经验的好方法。

**古奇:** 同时也是挣点零花钱的好方法。

**阿美:** 那让我们一起做吧。

**古奇:** 我同意啊。等一下,我要买一张 IC 卡。

**阿美:** 为什么? 你们家有电话机,不是吗?

**古奇:** 是的,但是我给克莱夫打电话的时候我不想让我妈妈偷听啊。

---

### 生词小结

| | | | |
|---|---|---|---|
| **spare** | *adj.* 多余的 | **social experience** | 社会经验 |
| **part-time job** | 兼职 | **pocket money** | 零用钱 |
| **weekly** | *n.* 周刊 | **tap** | *vt.* 窃听 |

---

## P语音小结 Pronunciation —— 祈使句的语调

1. 表示命令,语气强硬的祈使句,句末用降调

   Don't open the door. ↓不准开门。

   Don't be stupid. ↓不准犯傻。

2. 表示鼓励,态度亲切或客气的请求的祈使句,句末用升调。

   *Don't worry about that.* ↑别担心。

   *Let's do it together.* ↑让我们一起做吧。

3. 表示恳切地请求,或责备或表示关心的急切警告时用降升调,第一个重读音节用降调,句末用升调。

   *Don't ↓ open the door.* ↑别开门。(天会冷的)

   *Don't ↓ eat so much cheese.* ↑别吃这么奶酪。(太多奶酪对身体不好)

   **朗读训练:**

   Don't waste time.

   Have a good time.

   Do come tomorrow.

   Let me have a close look at you.

   Don't forget the changes after buying some newspaper.

---

### Recitation 经典背诵

**Gucci:** My mom taps my phone when I call my boyfriend which makes me upset. So I've decided to use the IC card. It's convenient, cheap and also safe. You can buy them everywhere, even at the newsstands. It's funny that I got a part-time job last time when I was buying an IC card.

# Topic 2 报亭轶事
## Anecdotes of the Newsstand

听 学 读 看

看报纸不用付钱,这样的事情没有见到过吧,可是这样的新鲜事在这里却发生了,究竟是什么特殊情况呢?

May: Come back. You haven't paid yet.

Boss: May, just let him go.

May: But he took some newspaper away without paying.

Boss: I know.

May: Why? You make me confused.

Boss: He lives nearby and he would just glance at the newspaper headlines, read the political sections and return them later.

May: Why does he have such a privilege?

Boss: He used to be a hero during the war time and everyone respect him.

May: I see. Does he live by himself?

Boss: Yes, he has no children and his wife passed away when he was in the battle.

May: He must be lonely?

Boss: I bet. But he is always busy telling the children stories.

May: How respectable!

阿美:请回来。你还没有付钱呢!

老板:阿美,让他走吧。

阿美:但是他没有付钱就把报纸拿走了。

老板:我知道。

阿美:为什么? 你把我弄糊涂了。

老板:他住在附近,他只是浏览一下报纸的大标题,看一下政治版,等一下就会把报纸还回来的。

阿美:为什么他有这种特权呢?

老板:战争时期他曾经是个英雄,这里的人都尊敬他。

阿美:知道了,他一个人住吗?

老板:是的,他没有孩子,他的妻子也在战争时期去世了。

阿美:他一定很孤独了?

老板:我猜是的。但是他总忙着给孩子们讲故事。

阿美:真是可敬!

生词小结

nearby    *adj.* 附近的
glance    *vi.* 瞥见
headline    *n.* 大标题
political    *adj.* 政治的

privilege    *n.* 特权
pass away    去世
respectable    *adj.* 值得尊敬的

## 单词扩展 Vocabulary Builder

### 报纸版面的词汇

| 基础词汇 | 提高词汇 |
| --- | --- |
| headline 大标题 | exclusive news 独家新闻 |
| column 专栏 | the top page 头版 |
| scoop 特讯 | criticism 评论 |
| feature 特写 | editorial 社论 |
| big news 头条新闻 | topicality 时事问题 |
| hot news 最新消息 | serial story 新闻小说 |
| book review 书评 | public notice 公告 |
| letters 读者投书栏 | city news 社会新闻 |

## 家庭总动员
Do it together

两人一组，一方随机大声读出上面词汇的英文和中文，另一方用该词汇填入下面的句子，大声朗读并表演出来，并用中文给出一个理由。

**He would just glance at the newspaper's (          ).**

【例】家长读 column 专栏

孩子读 He would just glance at the newspaper's column. 因为他只喜欢那个版块。

**Recitation** 经典背诵

**Boss**：I run a newsstand. I find that people love reading newspapers in different ways. Some of them never read the whole thing but just glance at the headlines to get the main information. Others do the opposite. Anyhow I don't really care about how people read their newspapers but I do want to know what their favorite newspapers are?

## Topic 3 免费赠品
### Free Gifts

卖什么都讲究策略,广告无处不在,看来阿美和古奇在卖报的过程中也学了不少的东西,果然做什么都不简单啊!

**Gucci:** Have we sold out all the newspapers for today?

**May:** Yes. What a good job we have done!

**Gucci:** Why are so many extra gifts left here?

**May:** Many customers didn't want them.

**Gucci:** How about giving them to that old man?

**May:** Good idea.

**Gucci:** By the way, do you think it's a good idea to give free gifts to attract customers?

**May:** I'm not sure, but still it did attract a large crowds today.

**Gucci:** I think it should be more useful to hand out some fliers which is also cheaper.

**May:** But people can just throw them into the trash can as they turn around.

**Gucci:** That's true.

**May:** Anyway, let's just finish our job and get back home.

**Gucci:** Okay. How tiring the job is!

古奇:我们把今天所有的报纸都卖完了吗?

阿美:是的。我们干得很不错哦!

古奇:为什么还剩下这么多的赠品呢?

阿美:很多顾客不想要。

古奇:把赠品送给那位老人怎么样?

阿美:好主意。

古奇:顺便问一下,你觉得用免费的赠品去吸引顾客是个好主意吗?

阿美:我不敢肯定,但是今天的确是吸引了一大批人。

古奇:我觉得分发一些宣传单张会更有效,而且那也会更便宜。

阿美:但是很有可能人们一转身就会把它们扔进垃圾桶。

古奇:倒也是。

阿美:不管怎样,我们赶快做完工作回家吧!

古奇:好的。这工作可真累人啊!

---

### 生词小结

**attract**  *vt.* 吸引
**flier**  *n.* 传单
**trash can**  垃圾桶

**turn around**  转身
**tiring**  *adj.* 引起疲劳的,累人的

---

## **S**情景练习 —— 表达感叹的句型练习
**cene practice**

仔细阅读下面五个场景,两人一组,使用表达感叹的句型(见317页),用一用,练一练。

1. Gucci and May are watching a fashionshow on TV. The models look amazing. If you were Gucci, what would you say?

2. One of Shirley's colleague has recently got married. What would Shirley say when she meets her?

3. If you are May, Gucci asks what you think of her new dress. What do you say?

4. Benjamin is watching the *American Idol*, but all of a sudden, there is a power failure. If you were Benjamin, what would you say?

5. May and her friends are going out on a picnic, but suddenly it begins to rain. If you were May, what do you say to your friends?

**R**ecitation
经典背诵

**Gucci**:Advertising is everywhere. The salespersons always try their best to attract more customers. Some of them would give complimentary to the customers. Others choose to hand out the fliers. Believe it or not, it does work. Even though we would just throw most of the fliers into the trash can as soon as we turn around.

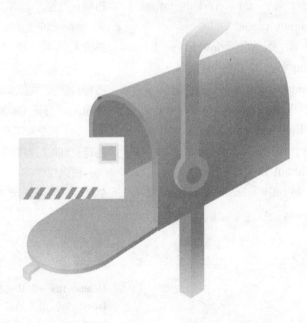

## Topic 4 买地图
### Buying a Map

迷路了怎么办？问路。不想问路怎么办？看地图。到哪里买地图？报亭。瞧,古奇还卖起了英文版本的地图,看来她会是一名很出色的奥运志愿者了。

**Foreigner**: Excuse me? Can you do me a favor, please?

**Gucci**: It's my pleasure, what can I do for you?

**Foreigner**: I'm from England and I'm trying to make a travel plan for today.

**Gucci**: What brings you here?

**Foreigner**: I'm a flight attendant and I'm here on vacation.

**Gucci**: Where are you staying?

**Foreigner**: I live in the Holiday Inn Lido Hotel.

**Gucci**: Oh, it's not very far. And as far as I know it is a fancy place.

**Foreigner**: Yes, it is. Do you know where I can get a town map?

**Gucci**: We sell them, right here.

**Foreigner**: Great, do you have any for foreigners? I mean English version?

**Gucci**: Sure. Yes, we have. As many as you want. What about this one?

**Foreigner**: That's exactly what I'm looking for. I'll take it.

**外国人**: 打扰了。你能帮我一个忙吗？

**古奇**: 很荣幸。我能帮什么忙？

**外国人**: 我是英国来的,我要为今天制定一个旅行计划。

**古奇**: 那你来这里做什么呢？

**外国人**: 我是机组乘务员。我是来这里度假的。

**古奇**: 你住哪里呢？

**外国人**: 我住在假日丽都饭店。

**古奇**: 哦,那不远啊。据我所知,那是个很不错的地方。

**外国人**: 是的。你知道我在哪里可以买一份城市地图吗？

**古奇**: 我们这里就卖啊。

**外国人**: 太好了,你们有给外国人看的地图吗？我是指英语版本(的地图)？

**古奇**: 当然了,我们有。要多少都有。这份怎样？

**外国人**: 这正是我在寻找的。我就买这个。

### 生词小结

| | | |
|---|---|---|
| **favor** | *n.* 支持 | **Holiday Inn** 假日酒店 |
| **flight** | *n.* 航班 | **fancy** *adj.* 精美的 |
| **attendant** | *n.* 服务员 | **town map** 城市地图 |

## Grammer 语法小结 —— as...as 的用法

1. as...as... 表示"和……一样……",在 as...as 之间加入形容词、副词原形

*My sister is as proud as a peacock.* 我姐姐非常高傲。

*She was as busy as before.* 她和从前一样忙。

2. as... as 的用法很多,并不是只能加形容词和副词的比较级

*There are as many books in our library as in your library.*

我们图书馆的书和你们图书馆的书一样多。(比较的是 *books*)

3. 在比较级的句型中,可以省略与前面重复的部分或者任何可以省略的部分

(1)否定句或疑问句中可用 so... as,中间是形容词或副词的原级

*He cannot do it so/as well as you.* 他不能和你做的一样好。

(2)as... as 中间有名词,"as + 形容词 + a /an + 单数名词",或"as + many/much + 名词复数"

*This is as good an example as the other is.* 这是一个和其他一样好的例子。

*I can carry as many books as you can.* 我能和你搬一样多的书。

(3)用表示倍数的做修饰语时,放在 as 的前面,结构是"倍数 + as + *adj.* + as"

*My room is twice as big as this one.* 我的房间是这个房间的两倍大。

*This bridge is three times as long as that one.* 这座桥是那座桥的三倍长。

## Do it together 家庭总动员

两人一组,一方朗诵下面的中文句子,另一方挑选出合适的翻译。

1. 你能和我卖一样的报纸。
2. 据我所知,你是空中服务员。
3. 我跟你一样快完成我的工作。
4. 这份地图跟你想象的一样有用。
5. 这位英雄的妻子跟他一样勇敢。

1. This map is as useful as you imagine.
2. I can finish my work as quickly as you can.
3. The hero's wife is as brave as him.
4. You can sell as many newspapers as I can.
5. As far as I know, you are a flight attendant.

**Recitation** 经典背诵

**Foreigner**：I am a flight attendant. I always come to China for vacations. I would stay at the Holiday Inn Lidu Hotel, which is really a fancy place. Chinese people are friendly and they are always willing to help when I'm in trouble. I always enjoy the time in China.

# 附录一：常用中英亲属称谓对应表

| 中文称谓 | 英文称谓 |
| --- | --- |
| 曾祖父/老爷爷 | Father's father's father; Great grandfather |
| 曾祖母/老奶奶 | Father's father's mother; Great grandmother |
| 表兄弟 | Mother's sister's sons; cousin |
| 表姊妹 | Mother's sister's daughters; cousin |
| 伯父/大爷 | Father's older brother; Elder uncle |
| 伯母/大娘 | Father's older brother's wife; Aunt |
| 长兄/哥哥 | Older Brother |
| 长姊/姐姐 | Older Sister |
| 大伯 | Husband's older brother |
| 大姑 | Husband's older sister |
| 弟妇/弟妹 | Younger brother's wife; sister-in-law |
| 儿子 | Son |
| 父亲/爸爸 | Father |
| 公公 | Husband's father |
| 姑夫 | Father's sister's husband; Husband of paternal aunt; uncle |
| 姑母 | Father's sister; Paternal aunt |
| 继父 | Step father |
| 继母 | Step mother |
| 舅父/舅舅 | Mother's brother; Maternal uncle |
| 舅母/妗子 | Mother's brother's wife; Maternal uncle's wife |
| 妹夫 | Younger sister's husband |
| 母亲/妈妈 | Mother |
| 内弟/小舅子 | Wife's younger brother |
| 内兄/大舅子 | Wife's older brother |
| 女儿 | Daughter |
| 女婿 | Daughter's husband; Son-in-law |
| 婆婆 | Husband's mother; mother-in-law |
| 妻子/老婆 | Wife |
| 嫂/嫂子 | Older brother's wife; sister-in-law |
| 婶母/婶子 | Father's younger brother's wife; Aunt |

| 中文称谓 | 英文称谓 |
| --- | --- |
| 叔父/叔叔 | Father's younger brother；Uncle |
| 孙女 | Son's daughter；Granddaughter |
| 孙女婿 | Son's daughter's husband；Granddaughter's husband |
| 孙媳妇 | Son's son's wife；Grandson's wife |
| 孙子 | Son's son；Grandson |
| 堂兄弟 | Father's brother's sons；Paternal male cousin |
| 堂姊妹 | Father's brother's daughters；Paternal female cousin |
| 同胞兄妹 | Sibling |
| 外甥 | Sister's son；nephew |
| 外甥女 | Sister's daughter；niece |
| 外孙 | Daughter's son；grandson |
| 外孙女 | Daughter's daughter；granddaughter |
| 外祖父/外公/老爷 | Mother's father；Maternal grandfather |
| 外祖母/外婆/姥姥 | Mother's mother；Maternal grandmother |
| 媳妇 | Son's wife；Daughter-in-law |
| 小姑 | Husband's younger sister；sister-in-law |
| 小叔 | Husband's younger brother；brother-in-law |
| 养父 | Foster，adopted father |
| 养母 | Foster，adopted mother |
| 姨夫 | Mother's sister's husband；Husband of mother's sister |
| 姨姐/大姨 | Wife's elder sister；sister-in-law |
| 姨妹/小姨 | Wife's younger sister；sister-in-law |
| 姨母/姨妈 | Mother's sister |
| 幼弟/弟弟 | Younger Brother |
| 幼妹/妹妹 | Younger Sister |
| 岳父 | Wife's father，Father-in-law |
| 岳母 | Wife's mother，Mother-in-law |
| 丈夫/老公 | Husband |
| 侄女 | Brother's daughter；niece |
| 侄子 | Brother's son；nephew |
| 祖父/爷爷 | Father's father；Paternal grandfather |
| 祖姑母/姑奶奶 | Father's father's sister； |
| 祖母/奶奶 | Father's mother；Paternal grandmother |
| 姊夫/姐夫 | Older sister's husband |
| 妯娌 | Brother's wife；sister-in-law |

# 附录二:常用中英量词一览表

## 1. 表示人的量词:

| | | | |
|---|---|---|---|
| 一个人 a man | 一个女孩 a girl | 一个画家 a painter | 一个工人 a worker |
| 一个农民 a farmer | 一位同学 a classmate | 一位老师 a teacher | 一位客人 a guest |
| 一位长官 an officer | 一位代表 a representative | 一条好汉 a bawcock | |

## 2. 表示动物的量词:

| | | | |
|---|---|---|---|
| 一只狗 a dog | 一只鸟 a bird | 一只猴子 a monkey | 一只鸡 a chick |
| 一只老鼠 a mouse | 一只蝴蝶 a butterfly | 一只虫 a worm | 一匹马 a horse |
| 一头牛 a cow | 一头羊 a sheep | 一头驴 a donkey | 一头豹子 a leopard |
| 一条蛇 a snake | 一条鱼 a fish | 一峰骆驼 a camel | |

## 3. 表示人和动物器官部位的量词:

| | | | |
|---|---|---|---|
| 一只眼睛 an eye | 一个鼻子 a nose | 一个耳朵 an ear | 一张嘴 a mouth |
| 一片嘴唇 a lip | 一颗牙齿 a tooth | 一条胳臂 an arm | 一只手 a hand |
| 一个手指头 a finger | 一个拳头 a fist | 一条腿 a leg | 一只脚 a foot |
| 一条尾巴 a tail | 一颗心 a heart | | |

## 4. 表示植物的量词:

| | | |
|---|---|---|
| 一棵树 a tree | 一棵松 a pine | 一株树 a tree |

## 5. 表示水果的量词:

| | | |
|---|---|---|
| 一个苹果 an apple | 一个橘子 an orange | 一个梨 a pear |
| 一串葡萄 a bunch of grapes | | 一根香蕉 a banana |

## 6. 表示植物部位的量词:

| | | |
|---|---|---|
| 一朵花 a flower | 一朵玫瑰 a rose | 一片叶子 a leaf |
| 颗种子 a grain of seed | 一簇花 a cluster of flowers | 一行树 a line of trees |

## 7. 表示食物的量词:

| | | |
|---|---|---|
| 一顿饭 a meal | 一顿早饭 a breakfast | 一份午餐 a lunch |
| 一份晚餐 a supper | 一个馒头 a steamed bread | 一根鸡腿 a drumstick |
| 一个鸡蛋 an egg | 一片肉 a piece of meet | 一块牛肉 a piece of beef |
| 一个三明治 a sandwich | 一道菜 a dish | 一片面包 a piece of bread |
| 一块蛋糕 a cake | 一篮鸡蛋 a basket of eggs | 一块巧克力 a bar of chocolate |
| 一根冰棒 an ice-lolly | 一片饼干 a biscuit | 一粒糖果 a candy |
| 一片西瓜 a piece of watermelon | 一满杯水 a cupful of water | |

**8. 表示餐具的量词：**

| | |
|---|---|
| 一双筷子 a pair of chopsticks | 一把叉子 a fork |
| 一把汤匙 a spoon | 一张餐纸 a piece of napkin |

**9. 表示家庭用品的量词，包括表示电器仪器的量词：**

| | | |
|---|---|---|
| 一张桌子 a desk | 一把椅子 a chair | 一张床 a bed |
| 一盏灯 a lamp | 一把牙刷 a toothbrush | 一块香皂 a perfumed soap |
| 一块桌布 a piece of tablecloth | 一块手表 a watch | 一面镜子 a mirror |
| 一个脸盆 a basin | 一把伞 an umbrella | 一条绳子 a string |
| 一部电话 a telephone | 一台电视机 a TV | 一个冰箱 a refrigerator |

**10. 表示穿戴用品和装饰品的量词：**

| | | |
|---|---|---|
| 一件上衣 a jacket | 一条裤子 a pair of trousers | 一个口袋 a pocket |
| 一顶帽子 a hat | 一条围巾 a shawl | 一副手套 a pair of gloves |
| 一双袜子 a pair of socks | 一副眼镜 a pair of glasses | |

**11. 表示建筑物的量词：**

| | | |
|---|---|---|
| 一座城 a city | 一座桥 a bridge | 一条路 a road |
| 一栋房子 a building | 一扇窗 a window | 一扇门 a door |
| 一面墙 a piece of wall | 一间房 a room | |

**12. 表示交通工具的量词：**

| | |
|---|---|
| 一辆车 a car | 一辆自行车 a bicycle |
| 一列火车 a train | 一架飞机 a plane |

**13. 表示工具的量词：**

| | |
|---|---|
| 一把锤子 a hammer | 一把锁 a lock |

**14. 表示文具的量词：**

| | | |
|---|---|---|
| 一支笔 a pen | 一张纸 a piece of paper | 一台电脑 a computer |

**15. 表示文艺作品的量词：**

| | | |
|---|---|---|
| 一封信 a letter | 一首诗 a poem | 一篇文章 an article |
| 一幅照片 a photo | 一幅画 a picture | 一首歌 a song |
| 一篇报告 a report | 一个字 a word | |

# 附录三:常用英美发音一览表

## 字母 a

字母 a 在一些常用的词语中,美式英语和英式英语的发音存在不同。在美音中字母 a 通常发 /æ/ 的音,而在英音中,字母 a 的发音通常是 /ɑ:/。

| 例词 音标 | 美音 /æ/ | 英音 /ɑ:/ |
|---|---|---|
| answer | /ˈænsə/ | /ˈɑ:nsə/ |
| can't | /kænt/ | /kɑ:nt/ |
| ask | /æsk/ | /ɑ:sk/ |
| chance | /tʃæns/ | /tʃɑ:ns/ |
| class | /klæs/ | /klɑ:s/ |

## 卷舌音 /r/

在英式英语中,字母 r 出现在元音前时才发音,在元音后时则不发音,但是在美式英语中,无论何种情况它都发 /r/ 的音,它相当于汉语的儿化音。

| 例词 音标 | 美音 /r/ | 英音 不发音 |
|---|---|---|
| arm | /ɑ:rm/ | /ɑ:m/ |
| her | /stɑ:r/ | /stɑ:/ |
| better | /dɑ:rk/ | /dɑ:k/ |
| letter | /ˈletər/ | /ˈletə/ |
| sir | /sə:r/ | /sə:/ |

## /ɔ:/  /ɔ/

在英式英语中,长短音比较明确,而美式英语里基本上不分长短音,短元音可以读成长元音。

| 例词 音标 | 美音 /ɔ:/ | 英音 /ɔ/ |
|---|---|---|
| sorry | /ˈsɔ:ri/ | /ˈsɔri/ |
| want | /wɔ:nt/ | /wɔnt/ |
| dog | /dɔ:g/ | /dɔg/ |

## /ɔ/  /ɑ/

在英式英语中,许多发 /ɔ/ 的音,在美式英语中却发作 /ɑ/。

| 例词 音标 | 美音 /ɑ/ | 英音 /ɔ/ |
|---|---|---|
| nod | /nɑd/ | /nɔd/ |
| hot | /hɑt/ | /hɔt/ |
| lot | /lɑt/ | /lɔt/ |
| doctor | /ˈdɑktə/ | /ˈdɔktə/ |
| rot | /rɑt/ | /rɔt/ |

## /u:/  /ju:/

在美式英语中,/ju:/ 在 /t//d//n/ 后面发 /u:/ 的音。

| 例词 音标 | 美音 /u:/ | 英音 /ju:/ |
|---|---|---|
| tune | /tu:n, tun/ | /tju:n/ |
| due | /du:, du/ | /dju:/ |
| dual | /ˈdu:əl/ | /ˈdju:əl/ |

# 附录四：中央人民广播电台"经济之声"全国各地收听频率表(FM、AM)

## 同名节目播出时间：(6:40—7:00)

### 调频(FM)全国区域覆盖情况

北京 96.6　　　上海 91.4　　　广州 106.6　　　武汉 97.8　　　西安 103.0

| 城市 | 调频 | 城市 | 调频 | 城市 | 调频 | 城市 | 调频 |
|------|------|------|------|------|------|------|------|
| 福州 | 100.4 | 拉萨 | 104.0 | 阜阳 | 103 | 南昌 | 96.9 |
| 南通 | 92.9 | 绵阳 | 100.6 | 天津 | 98 | 宁波 | 92.8 |
| 淄博 | 89 | 南宁 | 104 | 温州 | 94.9 | 泉州 | 98.3 |
| 太原 | 99 | 昆明 | 100 | 厦门 | 93.5 | 南平 | 99.8 |
| 沈阳 | 93.5 | 西宁 | 105.6 | 青岛 | 89.7 | 宜宾 | 98.9 |
| 杭州 | 97.9 | 银川 | 107.8 | 唐山 | 107.4 | 泸州 | 91.5 |
| 长沙 | 87.6 | 呼和浩特 | 104.5 | 大庆 | 96.7 | 乌鲁木齐 | 90.6 |
| 石家庄 | 97.2 | 宁波 | 92.8 | 汨罗 | 87.6 | 海口 | 87.8 |
| 保定 | 89.7 | 合肥 | 104.7 | 常德 | 102.9 | 涪陵 | 87.2 |
| 霍县 | 105.2 | 黄山 | 104.9 | 怀化 | 93.2 | 华蓥 | 107.1 |
| 长春 | 104.7 | 荥阳 | 96.7 | 衡山 | 100.3 | 贵阳 | 98.9 |
| 哈尔滨 | 88.1 | 开封 | 100.8 | 新会 | 92.0 | 重庆 | 102.9 |
| 齐齐哈尔 | 101.8 | 荆州 | 107.4 | 桂林 | 94.4 | 兰州 | 90.3 |

### 中波(AM)全国区域覆盖情况

| 地区/城市 | 频率(千赫) | 地区/城市 | 频率(千赫) |
|-----------|-----------|-----------|-----------|
| 东北地区 | 720 | 北京 | 720 |
| 华南地区 | 630 | 上海 | 855 |
| 青海地区 | 900 | 天津 | 720 |
| 西南地区 | 630 | 郑州 | 630 |
| 西北地区 | 1305/630 | 南昌 | 630 |
| 华北地区 | 720/630 | 昆明 | 855 |
| 皖北地区 | 801 | 福州 | 720 |
| 呼和浩特 | 114.3 | 厦门 | 720 |
| 全国覆盖 | 630/720/855 | 大连 | 720 |

# 80天攻克雅思系列

定价:25.00元

定价:58.00元

定价:93.00元

定价:48.00元

定价:48.00元

定价:19.00元　定价:13.00元

定价:45.00元

定价:38.00元

定价:48.00元

定价:43.00元

# 40天攻克四级710分新题型

定价:19.80元

定价:19.80元

定价:22.80元

定价:16.80元

定价:13.80元

定价:14.80元

# 超级蜘蛛网记单词系列

定价:25.80元

定价:39.80元

定价:28.00元

定价:29.80元

# "英语大赢家"卓成教育听说中心

"英语大赢家"卓成教育听说中心是卓成教育国际针对中国人练习英语听说专门推出的集教材、软件、培训、教学服务、人生规划于一体的大型教育培训实体。"英语大赢家"卓成教育听说中心，秉承卓成教育"一朝学子，全程服务"的教学服务理念，依托卓成国际教育集团优势，携现代信息、网络、语音识别技术，借助中央人民广播电台、北京电视台、湖南电视台、旅游卫视等全国性媒体优势，在同行业中率先实现了高科技语音测评训练、专家"处方式"学习规划、中外教面授、教学督导监督教学、全真语境实习、网上答疑等多元的"母语情景式"教学模式。

"英语大赢家"卓成教育听说中心以中央人民广播电台在全国150多所城市热播的"迎奥运全民讲英语"栏目教材《英语大赢家》为核心教材，采取国际先进的"选课制"的模式，结合中外教优势，面向普通市民及大学生提供"国际化"标准的"母语情景式"教学。是中国高端英语听说教学从"精英化"走向"大众化"的标志。为此，"英语大赢家"卓成教育听说中心被国内外多家媒体称为中国大众在学习英语的"普罗米修斯"。

## "英语大赢家"卓成教育听说中心教学体系优势：

一、 中央媒体指定教材——《英语大赢家》

《英语大赢家》为中央人民广播电台在2008年北京奥运来临之际强力推出的"迎奥运全民讲英语"栏目的指定教材。该套教材由中外教专家团共同编写审定，是专门适合中国人学习习惯的"英语母语"教材。

二、"高科技测评"入学

无论身处何处，学员入学即进行"全球标准"的高科技分项测试，全方位检测英语基础、语言学习能力及学习环境。由资深专家提供"处方式"学习规划。由教学督导监督指导教学，沟通解答疑难杂症，定期全国学习效果抽查，定期全国促学考试。

三、"母语情景式"教学

听说领先，读写跟进，模拟情景，表演式教学，真正条件反射式训练。唤起情景再现，真正口语脱口而出。中教促学，外教把关。

四、"选课制"授课

根据自己的时间，根据自己的爱好随心所欲选择课堂，一次培训，多名专家点拨。博采众家所长，练就英语真功夫。

五、"平民化"价格

平民大众均能承担得起的学费，奖学金制度帮助莘莘学子。

## "英语大赢家"卓成教育听说中心加盟优势：

一、统一店面及形象设计

店面外观，内部设计，内部家具摆设、各类宣传物资统一设计，免除装修设计及各类美术设计之忧。

二、核心老师总部派送，普通教员统一培训

外教及核心中教总部采取"派驻式"支持。所有教员均接受北京总部统一培训、考核，全国范围内统一持证上岗。

三、加盟支持

开业前后，总部在员工培训，市场活动，明星教师演讲，教学监督指导等多方面进行支持。

四、准入门槛低

准入门槛低，推出机制灵活，多重保障制度，适合中产阶级进行区域范围内创业。

**图书在版编目（CIP）数据**

英语大赢家：最新流行美语全情景话题320上册／江涛主编．
北京：石油工业出版社，2007.6
（江涛英语）
ISBN 978-7-5021-6023-4

Ⅰ．英…
Ⅱ．江…
Ⅲ．英语－口语－自学参考资料
Ⅳ．H319.9

中国版本图书馆 CIP 数据核字（2007）第 047130 号


**英语大赢家：最新流行美语全情景话题３２０（上册）**

主审　王丽君　主编　江涛　审订　[美]Alex G. Liu　[美]Devon Williams

---

出版发行：石油工业出版社
　　　　　（北京安定门外安华里2区1号　100011）
　　　　　网址：www.petropub.com.cn
　　　　　发行部：(010) 64523603　编辑部：(010) 64523646
经　　销：全国新华书店
印　　刷：北京晨旭印刷厂

---

2007 年 6 月第 1 版　　2007 年 6 月第 1 次印刷
787×1092毫米　开本：1/16　印张：22　插页：1
字数：518千字

---

定　　价：36.00元（超值附赠5小时 MP3 光盘1张）
（如出现印装质量问题，我社发行部负责调换）

# 读石油版书，获亲情馈赠

## 《英语大赢家》(上册)意见反馈卡

亲爱的读者朋友，首先感谢您阅读我社图书，请您在阅读完本书后填写以下信息。我社将长期开展"读石油版书，获亲情馈赠"活动，凡是关注我社图书并认真填写读者信息反馈卡的朋友都有机会获得亲情馈赠，我们将定期从信息反馈卡中评选出有价值的意见和建议，并为填写这些信息的朋友**免费**赠送一本好书。

1. 您购买本书的动因：书名、封面吸引人□ 内容吸引人□ 版式设计吸引人□

2. 您认为本书的内容：很好□ 较好□ 一般□ 较差□

3. 您认为本书在哪些方面存在缺陷：内容□ 封面□ 装帧设计□

4. 您认为本书的定价：较高□ 适中□ 偏低□

5. 您认为本书最好应附送：MP3□ CD□ 磁带□ 其他 _____

6. 您还读过哪些英语课外书？ _____
   _____

7. 您对本书有哪些不满意之处？ _____
   _____

8. 您还需要哪些英语课外读物？ _____
   _____

9. 您对本书的综合评价： _____
   _____

10. 您在何处哪个书店购买的本书？ _____
   _____

您的联系方式：

姓名 _____

单位 _____ 邮政编码 _____

地址 _____ 电话 _____

手机 _____ E-mail _____

回信请寄：北京安定门外安华里二区一号楼　　　石油工业出版社

　　　　　社会图书出版中心　　　　朱世元(收)

邮政编码：100011

电子信箱：shiyuanzhu@263.net　　　　(复印有效)